GAME
TIME

Book two of
Girls of Summer

by Kate Christie

SECOND GROWTH

Second Growth Books
Seattle, WA

Printed in the United States of America on acid-free paper
First published 2016

Cover Design: Kate Christie

ISBN: 0-9853677-5-X
ISBN-13: 978-0-9853677-5-6

DEDICATION

To KAM. You & me, babe—co-captains on team M-VW for life.

ACKNOWLEDGMENTS

Thank you, Erin Saluta, for your valuable insight and advice regarding Emma and Jamie's story. The Girls of Summer series wouldn't be the same without you!

CHAPTER ONE
~ NOVEMBER 2013 ~

Emma strolled the aisles of Fremont's natural foods co-op, basket slung over one arm, reusable bag and purse on the other. She was still getting over the cold she'd managed to pick up during a photo shoot in LA, and it had taken nearly all of her energy just to get ready to leave her condo. When the two teenage girls who had been trailing her since the ice cream section finally worked up the nerve to tap her shoulder, she was tempted to ignore them. But then she remembered how the last two American professional women's soccer leagues had folded due to lack of support, and she turned to face them, smile pinned to her face.

"You're Emma Blakeley, aren't you?" the bolder of the two asked, her cheeks turning pink as her friend elbowed her.

"Yes. And you are?"

At least they didn't say they were her biggest fans. They did, however, ask for photos. Emma acquiesced, grateful she had washed her face and redone her pony tail and mascara. No doubt the photos would be up on Twitter and Instagram before she finished shopping. She gave them her usual plug to support the Reign, the local professional team that had recently completed its inaugural season in the National Women's

Soccer League (NWSL), and then the two girls skipped off. Sure enough, Emma's phone vibrated inside her purse with a series of notifications as she continued down the juice aisle.

Had she ever been that young? These days high school seemed impossibly distant. Even though she was back in Seattle after nearly a decade on the East Coast, she had found that living in the city as an adult was significantly different from growing up in the suburbs. Her current life barely resembled her childhood, not least because her brother lived in DC and her mother had moved back to Minnesota. The only person tying her to the Pacific Northwest was Dani, her childhood best friend, who after ten years in Southern California had taken a job with a Seattle PR firm. They had seen each other often over the years, given US Soccer's proximity to Long Beach where Dani lived and worked after college. But now they saw each other almost daily again, and their friendship had resumed as if they'd never been apart.

Speak of the devil. Emma was about to check out when the text alert she'd picked for Dani—a whistle—sounded. She tapped the screen.

"Call me?" Dani had texted.

"At PCC. Call you in fifteen."

"Better yet, meet at yours?"

"Perfect. See you soon."

Emma wondered if her friend's desire to see her was truly urgent or if her text merely reflected her usual lack of patience with social niceties. With Dani, it was hard to tell.

No one else recognized her as she left PCC and walked to her car, a Subaru Legacy that had been all but given to her by a Bellevue dealership when she signed with the Reign. After anchoring the back line in the last World Cup and Olympics and earning all-league honors first in the Women's Professional Soccer (WPS) league and now in the NWSL, she was a recognizable figure in soccer-crazy Seattle.

Ten minutes later, Emma pulled into the parking garage beneath her building on West Highland. Her general text alert sounded as she was unlocking the door to her unit, followed by three more chimes. A group chat usually meant either the national team or her club, and with Reign pre-season months away and NT training camp starting in a few weeks, it wasn't hard to figure out which. US Soccer was supposed to release the official camp roster that afternoon. Was that why everyone was feeling so chatty suddenly? For a moment she considered leaving her groceries on the counter and checking the federation's website, but she was pretty sure she already knew what it said. Besides, Dani would be here momentarily to discuss the implications.

Emma had just kicked off her Chucks when the buzzer sounded in Dani's signature rhythm. She buzzed her friend into the building and headed into the kitchen to put away the perishables. A minute later she heard Dani push through the unlocked front door, slamming it as she always did.

"So?" the other woman demanded, rounding the corner from the hall.

Head still in the refrigerator, Emma glanced over her shoulder. "So what?"

"You don't know, do you?"

"Apparently not." She kept her tone even despite the fact she could probably guess what had her oldest friend smiling so smugly.

"Here." Dani shoved her phone at Emma, who took it and leaned against the nearest counter.

As she'd expected, the browser was open to a US Soccer story about the upcoming national team training camp. She scrolled through the list of players invited to attend, pausing as she read the name: *Jamie Maxwell*. For the first time during Emma's tenure on the national team, she and Jamie would both be in LA for residency camp.

Toying with her pony tail, Emma shrugged and handed Dani her phone. "And?"

"You can't expect me to believe you have no reaction to the idea of spending two weeks with her."

"It's been almost a decade. Besides, we're both professionals. It'll be fine."

3

Dani's eyes narrowed. "I didn't ask if it would be fine. I asked how you felt about seeing her."

"We've seen each other before, Dan. Don't go stirring up drama where it doesn't exist."

"Another dodge." As Emma stared at her, Dani held up her hands. "Fine, I'll let it go for now—as long as you promise to feed me. As if Mondays don't suck enough, I missed my afternoon coffee break."

They settled on Thai and called in the order. Then, wine in hand, they retired to Emma's living room where large picture windows and a private patio looked out over Kerry Park, the Space Needle, and the lights of downtown. In late November the sun set by four thirty each afternoon, so Emma was used to seeing the city all lit up. Her favorite time of year in her hometown was summer, when the sun didn't set until after nine and the city skyline remained twilit even later. And yet, she always welcomed the return of rain in autumn. This was her first full year back in Seattle. She hadn't realized how much she missed the Pacific Northwest until she'd moved back.

At first she'd rented an apartment not far from here, uncertain where soccer would take her in the future. But then Dani convinced her to check out this listing. One visit and Emma knew—this was it. The view from the living room alone had been worth the condo's exorbitant price tag, an amount paid not by her national team salary—as if—but by her endorsements. As one of the higher paid pro women soccer players in the world, she didn't have to worry about where her next paycheck would come from. Then again, with the trust fund her father had left, she likely wouldn't ever have to worry about affording her more than comfortable lifestyle.

As usual, she and Dani talked about nothing and everything while they waited for their food to be delivered, eventually transferring to the kitchen bar where they spread out the containers of sweet and sour chicken and spicy pad thai. Dani was dating a guy she'd met at a club on one of their nights out in the city, but it wasn't serious. Emma meanwhile had been single for almost a year and wasn't looking. With her schedule, having a relationship took way too much effort.

"You don't have to have an actual relationship to have sex, you know," Dani said.

"So you say."

"Are you sure you're not a lesbian? I've heard serial monogamy is big with the Sapphic ladies."

Emma sipped her wine, trying to decide if she should respond to her friend's jab or not.

"I know," Dani said. "It's the person you're attracted to, not the gender."

"At least you don't call us 'the gays' anymore."

"Not where you can hear me, anyway. Speaking of gay... When's the last time you saw Jamie? Last year at the Olympics?"

She should have known Dani wouldn't give up that easily. "No, I had dinner with her in LA and didn't tell you."

Her friend ignored her sarcasm. "Do you think this means she's back in the pool for good?"

"No idea. I'm not on the coaching staff, am I?"

"Ooh, a bit snippy, are we?"

Emma frowned. "Seriously, Dan, let it go."

"Fine," Dani relented. "But only because you're sick. I'm here if you decide you want to talk about it, okay?"

"You'll be the first to know."

After dinner, they poured more wine and caught up on *Grey's Anatomy* on DVR. Then Dani hugged her and headed out with promises to text as soon as she got home.

"You're still coming to Thanksgiving, aren't you?" Dani asked as she slipped into the hallway.

"Wouldn't miss it," she said, and waved.

Alone again, she refilled her wine glass and put her feet up on the coffee table, watching the lights of helicopters and commercial airliners crossing over the city while Pandora played Adele on Bluetooth speakers. So Jamie Maxwell was coming to December camp. It was hard to believe they would finally be in LA together after all these years. Jamie had worked out with the national team in London before the Olympics the previous summer, but she had only been around for a handful of practices and had gone home to her own flat each night. Residency camp was different. Camp meant two weeks sequestered together in the same hotel where Jamie had ended their friendship nine years earlier. Two weeks of double sessions, team meetings, group meals, bonding exercises, and general hanging out while US Soccer documented their every move. You know, to make things even more interesting.

The modern obsession with cameras wasn't all bad. Emma would never admit as much to Dani, but she'd kept track of Jamie not only via the national team's impressive grapevine but also on social media where she'd been following her for years. It wasn't like she could be considered a genuine creeper, she assured herself whenever she pulled up Jamie's Facebook page, Twitter feed, or Instagram profile. She only checked once in a while to see if their paths might cross. Because as professional American soccer players with a whole slew of friends in common, their paths were bound to cross.

The first time they saw each other again was the summer of 2010, six long years after their friendship blew up. By then Emma had been a pro for two years and a regular on the national team for three, while Jamie was in her first professional season with the WPS after a solid career at Stanford. Emma was playing in Boston that year for the Breakers while Jamie had been drafted by the Bay Area side, FC Gold Pride, at the end of her senior year of college. She hadn't even graduated yet the first time their teams met.

Emma had always thought it fitting that the first time soccer brought them back together they were in California, the state where their friendship had begun and ended. Their reunion in a San Francisco bar after the match had gone better than Emma could have expected. A month later, their second meeting in Boston went just as well, and Emma had even introduced Jamie to Sam, her then-girlfriend, over dinner. With their teams scheduled to meet twice more and Jamie widely considered a shoo-in for the next World Cup, Emma had been sure their renewed friendship would continue to grow that summer. But in July, she heard the news: Jamie had torn her ACL only days before her first scheduled call-up to the senior national team.

Her ACL surgery and recovery took her out of contention for the 2011 World Cup squad. That team played so well—despite losing to Japan in the finals—that the coaching staff decided not to make any significant changes going into the 2012 Olympics. As a result, Jamie didn't make it back into the pool until late 2012. But Emma wasn't around for Jamie's first official call-up. Sidelined by a burst appendix midway through the gold medal victory tour, she'd had to watch from her mother's living room in Minneapolis while Jamie earned her first cap before a huge crowd in Portland during a friendly against Ireland. She'd played beautifully, assisting on not one but two goals in the twenty minutes she was on the field, and Emma couldn't help but be excited for her—and for the team, too. Jamie was still one of the most talented playmakers Emma had encountered, and she had long believed Jamie deserved a spot on the national team, if only she could stay healthy long enough to win it.

Emma had been watching with her mom again a few days later when Jamie started the second half, again against Ireland but in Arizona this time. Watching, too, when an Irish player slide-tackled her at midfield. Jamie's initial scream had echoed throughout the suddenly silent stadium, and as Fox ran the replay on a loop, the sickening snap of her ankle could be heard over the crowd's collective gasp. Emma had held tightly to her mother's hand as they watched the trainers load Jamie onto a stretcher, her lower leg immobilized. That was it for Jamie's first call-up. By the time Emma rejoined the national team for January camp in LA, Jamie was already back in England with her club side trying to make it back from her second potential career-ending injury in two and a half years.

As the months passed, Emma hadn't been surprised to learn that not only did Jamie recover, she went on to post the best stats of her professional career. Jamie had proven before that she was a survivor. Once again her perseverance had earned her a shot at the national team pool, and this time there would be no avoiding being in the same place at the same time.

Assuming they both stayed healthy. It was the off-season in England and even Champions League was on a break, so unless Jamie injured herself skateboarding—she'd posted more than one Instagram video of herself cruising on a long board down a London street—they would soon be together for thirteen intense, fun-filled days and nights at the main US Soccer training center in sunny Southern California.

Please don't let us be roommates, Emma thought, sipping her wine as a helicopter flew past the Space Needle, the whir of its rotor blades a blur against the night sky.

#

When the familiar Los Angeles exchange flashed on her phone a few days before Thanksgiving, Jamie ducked into the kitchen, took a few calming breaths, and managed to say in a voice that didn't tremble at all, "Hello?"

"Jamie Maxwell?"

"This is." She gripped the counter with her free hand, trying to control her heart rate through sheer force of will.

"Carrie Fitzsimmons here, manager for the US Women's National Team. Is this a good time?"

"Yes, ma'am." *Ma'am?* Really?

"Good. First of all, congratulations on another fantastic year at Arsenal. A lot of people on both sides of the pond were impressed with the season you put together, especially after what happened against Ireland last fall."

"Thank you, ma'am."

Out of habit, she painted a circle on the floor with her right toe, relieved as always when the ankle joint operated flawlessly. After that Irish hooligan had destroyed her latest national team dream, she had almost given up. But here she was a year later, stronger and faster than ever and fielding a call from the federation.

"How's that ankle treating you these days, anyway?"

"Fine. No problems."

"And are you match fit?"

"I am. We were up in Scotland a couple of weeks ago for Champions League."

"All right, then. I won't draw out the suspense. You may have heard we're putting together a training camp in LA next month. We'd like you to attend—if you're available."

Jamie made herself pause a beat before replying, "I'd love to attend. Thank you for the opportunity."

"It's nothing you haven't earned. Is your email address still the same?"

"Yes."

"I'll send you the details, then. We need to move quickly to get your travel arrangements made, so don't be a stranger."

"Yes, ma'am."

As soon as they hung up, Jamie sent a group text to her dad, sister, and best friend: "Guess who's going to national team training camp in LA next month?!"

Britt's reply arrived first: "Way to go, stud!"

Meg chimed in ten seconds later even though it was only eight in the morning in Utah: "My awesome baby sister! Woo hoo!!!"

And their dad, probably on the way to work with their mom, wrote, "That's our girl! We love you and can't wait to hear more!"

"So? Did they invite you back?"

Jamie glanced up to see her girlfriend watching her from the kitchen doorway. "Yeah, they did."

Clare closed her eyes briefly and nodded. Then she moved forward and pulled Jamie into a hug, fitting her head under Jamie's chin as she always did. "Well done, love. I'm happy for you."

Was she, though? Jamie wouldn't blame Clare for being uneasy. Her first call-up had come almost exactly a year earlier. Her injury had brought them closer in the end, but for a while Jamie had struggled. Last January in particular had been a dark time, the darkest she could remember since the aftermath of her trip to France ten years earlier. Clare had stayed at her side as she worked to lift herself back into the light, but it had been difficult for them both. And now here she was ready to risk her health and their joint happiness for another shot at the dream that still eluded her.

"It'll be okay," she said, rubbing a gentle circle against her girlfriend's back. "I promise."

As Clare leaned back and gave her a look that said she shouldn't make promises she might not be able to keep, Jamie's phone buzzed again.

"Don't be too long," Clare said, pulling away. "Your tea is getting cold."

"I'll be right there." Jamie smiled reassuringly before glancing back at her phone.

Britt had texted, "The pub. Nine tonight. Be there."

"I'm in!" she replied, and then silenced her phone as she went to finish her afternoon tea.

The Twelve Pins on Seven Sisters Road was only a short bus ride from their flat in Holloway. By the time she got there that night, nearly all the members of the Arsenal Ladies FC squad currently in London were gathered around a table in the Function Room, hastily set aside for their impromptu celebration.

"Well done, Max! Where's the little woman?" Jeanie, their tall, butch center forward, smiled as she clapped Jamie on the shoulder.

"She decided to stay home."

"Smart woman," Britt said, sliding a lager shanty light on beer and heavy on lemonade her way. "Everyone listen up! To Jamie Maxwell, future World Cup champion and Olympic gold medalist, for getting called back up to the show. May you dazzle the powers that be—and for fuck's sake, stay out of the hospital this time!"

A chorus of cheers sounded around the table as Jamie held up her glass, grinning at her friends. "Thanks, guys," she said, trying to memorize the feeling of happiness unfurling inside. If there was one thing sport had taught her, it was to enjoy the good times while they lasted.

This party, unfortunately, couldn't last long. It was a

weeknight, and almost everyone on the team had second jobs that allowed them to moonlight as low-paid professional women footballers. Jamie covered her own expenses by running social media accounts for several players on the Arsenal men's side. The work came with a ton of perks: awesome seats not far from the home bench, and since her job required her to track down game day photos and post-match quotes, access to the locker room. It was a sweet gig as part-time jobs went. Unsurprisingly, most of her teammates weren't as lucky.

By eleven, Britt and Jamie were the only two left. They moved into the main room of the pub as Judy, the owner's daughter, came in to tidy up.

"Good luck in Los Angeles," Judy said, pausing to give Jamie a hug.

"Thanks, Jude."

"You will come back to us, won't you?"

"Don't worry, I still have another year left on my contract."

As they slid into an empty booth, Britt held up her phone. "Speaking of LA, they released the camp roster."

Jamie gripped her glass tighter, knowing what was coming. "So?"

"So no emergency surgery to save you this time."

"Dude, it's not a big deal. You saw us last year. She was perfectly friendly and so was I."

In addition to being her current club teammate and longtime best friend, Britt was also the only person in her life other than her sister—and Clare—who knew of her history with Emma Blakeley.

"A few practices is nothing like residency camp," Britt pointed out.

"Maybe not, but I do have a girlfriend, in case you hadn't noticed."

"This is Blake we're talking about. If you're trying to say you don't find her attractive, I call bullshit."

Jamie wasn't trying to say that at all. In the decade since they'd met at Surf Cup in San Diego, she had watched from

11

afar as Emma evolved from adorable teenager to lovely woman. At twenty, Emma had been the youngest player on the roster at the 2007 World Cup, and since then her international football star had ascended steadily. Her face popped up regularly in fitness magazines, Nike ad campaigns, and articles and social media posts about the national team. As a central defender she wasn't as well known to the mainstream public as the team's leading scorers and legendary goalkeeper. But her girl next door looks and mediagenic personality ensured that she was only a little off-center in nearly every US Soccer marketing campaign. The lead positions were occupied by Jenny Latham, straight, pretty, and a dynamic scorer; Maddie Novak, beautiful and fiery and the team's midfield playmaker; and Rachel Ellison, the current captain and leading scorer— and the only short-haired, out lesbian player the UWSNT had ever known.

"I didn't say she's not attractive, Britt. But we were kids. Or I was, anyway. I'm not sure she ever was." She pictured Emma on stage at her father's funeral reading a eulogy she'd written herself, seemingly collected before the crowd of hundreds only a week after her dad died. At the time Jamie was sure she had never seen anyone or anything more impressive.

Britt touched her hand. "Be careful, okay? You can't afford any distractions, not if you want to make it this time."

"I know. Thanks, B. How are you holding up, anyway?"

"Me?" The goalkeeper shrugged and gave her a lopsided smile. "Okay. I haven't given up *all* hope yet."

Britt often said she'd been born at the wrong point in soccer history. Phoebe Banks, the current American keeper, had held the starting job for nearly a decade and didn't show any signs of slowing down. Her back-ups were almost as good as she was, and despite a few injuries always seemed to make it back in time for the big cycle years.

"Good," Jamie said, "because I'm still rooting for you."

"Fat lot of good that does me."

"I can't help you picked the one position on the field that almost never gets subbed."

Britt rolled her eyes. "Spare me the lecture on field player versatility, will you?"

Jamie reached across the table and tried to flick her arm, but the goalkeeper was too quick.

"You need to work on your hand-eye coordination, son," she said, smirking.

"Is that a challenge?"

"You know it."

"Bring it, then."

"Oh, it has already been broughten."

They played pool and threw darts for another hour, and Britt won almost every contest because Jamie's hand-eye coordination didn't get nearly the amount of work her foot-eye coordination did. After chatting with the pub staff a little while longer, Britt walked her to the bus stop around the corner. As soon as they stopped, Jamie was unsurprised to find herself being lifted off the ground and twirled through the air.

"Seriously, James, I am so freaking stoked for you!" Britt said.

"Thanks, buddy." Jamie pulled away and patted her shoulder. "You guys still bringing the cranberries and pumpkin pie?"

"You got it. Allie can't wait to experience her first American Thanksgiving."

"My family still doesn't believe I can cook, so we have to document the crap out of this."

"You'd think they'd realize by now that we have to find something to do other than binge on Netflix."

During the season, the team practiced at seven thirty each evening, which left plenty of daytime hours to fill. In the last three years, Jamie had taken advanced graphic design courses, studied German and Spanish, and volunteered at a variety of local organizations, including a nearby community kitchen where her fellow volunteers had taught her the art of "cookery," as the Brits insisted on calling it.

"Anyway, I better get home," Britt added. "Hi to your lady."

"Ditto. Later."

Britt waved and spun on her heel, heading for the nearby Tube station. Jamie took out her phone and scrolled through the photos they'd snapped in the Function Room. She found one of her and Britt, arms around each other's shoulders with a couple of teammates smiling in the background, and posted it on Instagram with a caption that read, "I love @BrittCrawdad12 more than she knows—or probably wants to know. Thanks for the awesome night out with fabulous friends. #Shesakeeper #ArsenalLadiesFC"

When the red double decker pulled up only a little late, Jamie slid into the first empty seat she found. As the bus meandered south toward Camden, she scrolled through her feed. A few minutes in and her post had already garnered a couple of hundred likes, mostly from Arsenal fans and her faithful contingent of American followers, who, judging from their comments on her photos—"I can't" and "ILYSM!!!" and "I'm dead"—were predominantly fifteen-year old Tumblr girls who wanted to either be her or be with her. She'd been out since she was fourteen, and despite the pressure on female professional athletes to refrain from using the "l" word, had never tried to hide who she was. Europeans didn't seem to care as much about the queer thing, and since she wasn't that well-known outside her sport, she hadn't attracted many bible-bangers or other haters.

All that could change, she knew, if she became a regular on the national team. She would take it, though. She would willingly withstand almost anything to represent her country at the highest level of her sport. Even share a hotel room with Emma Blakeley, if it came to that.

As if of their own accord, her fingers brought up Emma's feed. She had posted a photo a few days before of herself with fellow national team members Maddie Novak and Jenny Latham, all made up and decked out in Nike gear, supposedly working out somewhere warm and sunny. The caption, "#Nike #NikeStrong #USWNT," reinforced Jamie's suspicion that the photo was part of a shoot, because who looked that good while working out? Which wasn't to say that

Emma and the other two women didn't look good doing most things. But pro athletes tended to exercise hard enough to sweat in buckets, and the image on Emma's feed revealed only the lightest of sheens.

The bus hit a pothole and Jamie juggled her phone briefly. Regaining control, she checked Emma's photo quickly, relieved that her bumbling hadn't resulted in her accidentally "liking" the picture. She didn't need Emma to know that she was creeping her feed on the way home from the pub. At least they weren't strangers on social media. They'd started following each other on Instagram during the Olympics last year and had been Facebook friends even longer, ever since the first time their WPS teams played each other. Their teams had gone out together in the Mission after the game, and she could still remember the way they had watched each other across the bar until finally Jenny Latham, Jamie's teammate at FC Gold Pride, had waved Emma over.

"Emma, this is Jamie Maxwell from the U-23s. Max, say hello to Blake."

To her surprise, Emma had actually held out her hand, eyes uncertain as if she thought Jamie might freeze her out. Jamie had only hesitated a second before reaching out and tugging her former friend into a quick hug.

"It's great to see you," she'd said, smiling as she pulled away.

Emma had smiled back, brow slightly furrowed. "Really?"

"Of course. I can't believe it took this long."

"Honestly, I can't either."

"You two know each other?" Jenny had asked, watching their reunion curiously.

Emma's eyes were still on Jamie's. "You could say that."

They'd found a quiet corner and caught each other up on the past six years, and as the evening wore on, Jamie had felt the tension easing from her shoulders. She couldn't remember why she'd been so nervous about seeing Emma. True, things had ended beyond badly when they were teenagers. But Emma still seemed like the same smart, kind person she'd been in high school, and the connection between them, though frayed, was still there. By the end of the night, Emma was scrolling through her iPhone showing her photos of the woman she'd been dating for a few months. She'd seemed happy, and enough time had passed that Jamie could be happy for her, too.

The next time they'd seen each other in Boston, Emma had brought her girlfriend to the post-match dinner. The group was smaller this time, and Jamie had enjoyed her conversation with Sam, a sports photographer, about LGBT representation in professional athletics. She could see why Emma liked her. Sam was intelligent and attentive. They looked good together, too, a fact that wasn't lost on Emma's many social media followers. She may not be officially out, but she had posted a few photos of her and Sam all dressed up and out on the town. You'd have to be an idiot not to figure it out.

All of that was before the 2011 World Cup made Emma and her fellow national team members household names. Jamie had heard through the soccer grapevine that Emma and Sam broke up not long after the US lost to Japan in the finals. A little while later the WPS folded and Emma moved back to Seattle where she'd been photographed out and about with a bearded, tattooed hipster. Apparently she still favored fluidity when it came to her sexuality—not that her sexuality was any of Jamie's business.

At her stop, she stepped off the bus and walked the short distance to her building with her raincoat hood up and her snapback pulled low, a bottle of mace at ready inside her jacket pocket. Even after three years, London still occasionally spooked her. She didn't think she was meant for gritty urban life. But she made it home without incident and let herself into their flat on the second floor of a terraced house. Inside she dropped her keys on the table near the door, kicked off her boots, and headed into the kitchen.

Clare had left the light on over the sink, and as she drank a glass of water, Jamie surveyed the smallest room of their flat. The refrigerator was one of those tiny English types that looked like a holdout from 1950 but had in fact been manufactured sometime this century. The stovetop was burners only while the oven was mounted at face level above a row of drawers. Jamie wasn't sure how this setup saved space, but it would simplify cooking their Thanksgiving turkey. She hoped.

This apartment had been home for almost a year now, longer than anyplace else she'd lived since college, and Clare's presence was a big part of the sense of well-being she always felt here. While they had spent time apart—Jamie usually went home to California for a couple of weeks in the off-season— the upcoming trip felt different. Residency camp with its constant training sessions, group meetings, and team meals meant being out of touch in a way they hadn't previously experienced.

On the side of the refrigerator was their calendar, and Jamie drifted closer. "Thanksgiving!" was scrawled over Thursday's square in her handwriting, with Clare's characteristic smiley face below. A primary school teacher, she was big on smiley faces. Jamie had always found this endearing, seeing as Clare's smile was the first thing she'd noticed when Britt's girlfriend Allie introduced them at a dinner party eighteen months earlier. Allie and Clare had gone to university together, and Jamie had been fully aware that Britt and Allie were setting them up. But once she met Clare, she forgot to be irritated by their mutual friends' machinations.

Her phone buzzed again, and she turned it off and plugged it into the charger on the counter. Clare had to be up early for school, but she might have waited up. She usually didn't like to go to sleep without saying goodnight.

Jamie headed down the hallway, hopeful when she noticed the light coming from their bedroom. There she discovered Clare propped up against her pillows—fast asleep, book open on her lap, reading glasses perched low on her nose. Carefully Jamie slipped the glasses off and moved the book to the bedside table.

"Goodnight," she murmured, kissing her girlfriend's forehead before turning out the light. "Love you."

Clare sighed and slid lower under the covers. But she didn't say anything as Jamie moved quietly about the darkened room getting ready for bed.

CHAPTER TWO

Emma had always loved returning to training camp after a break. No matter what had happened in the last friendly match, tournament, or cycle, camp always felt like a fresh start. Part of the shine was the younger faces the coaching staff liked to bring in for the longer residencies. Not only did the new kids change team chemistry, but they also kept the returning players hungry. Nothing like riding the bench for a match or two to remind you that your position was only as stable as your fitness, work ethic, and quality of play deserved.

This time, though, as her airplane taxied toward the arrival gate at LAX, there was a different quality to her sense of anticipation. She was looking forward to seeing her friends on the team, but despite her assurances to Dani to the contrary, she was anxious too. For once her pre-camp jitters had nothing to do with what was about to happen on the pitch.

As the plane slowed to a stop, Emma turned her phone on and texted her mom to let her know she'd arrived safely. Out of habit, she checked her Instagram feed. Her teammates had been arriving throughout the day, and there were the obligatory group shots. A certain Arsenal player had yet to arrive by the looks of it... Crap, there went her brain again. Why was it stuck on someone she'd only seen a few times in the past decade? She didn't like worrying about something she couldn't control.

And yet there the worry was, stubbornly persisting.

Everyone else in business class leapt out of their seats the second the plane stopped, but Emma remained where she was, playing on her phone. While US Soccer paid for coach, her frequent flyer miles basically meant free upgrades for life. Like father, like daughter—though hopefully not when it came to heart disease. According to the tests the federation required, she was as healthy as, well, a professional soccer player. Good thing, too—residency camp almost always started out with extensive fitness testing. The beep test with heart rate monitors, forty and one hundred meter sprints with GPS trackers, power analysis of vertical jumps, agility testing, body fat measurement, average VO2 max, and all the other tortures Lacey Rodriguez, the longtime fitness coach for the women's side, could dream up.

As she waited, Emma cracked a new bottle of water and finished her half-eaten energy bar. They would hit the field tonight after dinner "to get the blood flowing," as Lacey liked to say. It was a tradition to put in a light workout on travel days. Helped everyone recover and eased the newbies in right away, before their nerves could get the best of them. Emma wondered if Jamie would arrive before the night session. Players who came from overseas usually needed that first workout the most.

The cockpit door finally opened, and as Emma swung into the aisle, her gaze fell on a figure in coach reaching into the overhead compartment. Emma paused, her eyes on the stranger's narrow hips and lean upper body, clad all in black. There was something familiar about... Oh. *Oh.* As the athletic woman turned toward the front of the plane, Emma looked away quickly, hoping she hadn't been caught. No wonder Jamie Maxwell had been on her mind. For the past two hours she'd apparently been sitting a dozen or so rows back as they sped along at 500 miles per hour six miles above the earth.

A man cleared his throat impatiently—Emma was blocking the aisle. Forcing herself not to look in Jamie's direction again, she grabbed her carry-on and filed off the plane. Inside the terminal she hesitated, debating whether or not to wait. Would she for a different teammate? Obviously. Besides, they would no doubt end up sharing a shuttle to the hotel in Carson, so any avoidance would be short-lived. With a sigh that felt more dramatic than it needed to be, she stepped out of the way of the passengers disembarking behind her, trying not to chew her lip as she watched the crowd for a glimpse of black.

It was no mystery how Emma had failed to register Jamie's presence on the plane. Her flight routine involved boarding at first call, slipping her headphones into place, and leaning against the window, eyes averted to discourage (1) anyone from recognizing her, and (2) those who did recognize her from trying to engage. The "fuck off" vibe she emitted when she wanted to was difficult to miss, or so she'd been told. Had Jamie even known she was on the plane? And if she had, why didn't she say hello?

As she waited, Emma's mind suddenly cast her back to the first meeting between their WPS teams in California three years earlier. She had noticed Jamie during warm-ups, of course. Half expecting her teenaged friend—friendly and a bit coltish—she had instead been faced with grown-up Jamie, whose high cheekbones and tattooed biceps were surprisingly intimidating. When their eyes met across the field, Emma had looked away and then instantly regretted doing so. They were adults, mostly, and professionals. Besides, she'd always hoped they would meet again.

For whatever reason—rookie status, stacked team—Jamie sat the bench that game, so they didn't come face to face until afterward when their teams shook hands. Emma had smiled hesitantly when she reached Jamie, relieved when her former friend smiled back. If she hadn't, Emma might not have gone out to the bar later for the usual post-match socializing. But she had gone, unsure what to expect of their first significant encounter since the week of her father's funeral.

Now as Jamie exited the gangplank and glanced around, Emma watched her carefully. She looked good. Tired and a bit disheveled but strong and healthy, as if she had never been carted off a field and into a waiting ambulance while an entire stadium—and all those watching at home—tried to process the magnitude of her injury.

Jamie's gaze stopped when it landed on her. She halted a few feet away, her eyes questioning. "Hey."

"Hey yourself." Emma forced a smile and bridged the distance, offering the other woman what might have been the shortest hug in the history of hugging. "It's good to see you. Congrats on making residency camp."

Jamie smiled back, but it seemed almost as tentative as Emma felt. "Thanks. It's good to see you too."

"Baggage claim?" she practically chirped, cringing inwardly at her own cloying cheerfulness.

Jamie nodded and they fell into step together.

"So. Same flight, huh?" Emma commented.

"Yeah. Kind of crazy." Jamie was quiet as they neared the end of the terminal. Then she said almost apologetically, "I would have said hi but you seemed like you didn't want to be bothered."

"No, I get it." She glanced sideways. "I actually didn't see you until the very end."

Jamie met her gaze and then looked away quickly, face unreadable. "Right."

Did she not believe her? But that would mean she thought Emma had been avoiding her. Fantastic. This entire encounter was following the worst case scenario script in her head. She didn't get it—there was no reason they should be this awkward. They'd had drinks and even dinner together in the not-so-distant past. On both occasions, though, they had been part of a group, which meant this was the first time they had been alone together since high school.

The last time they'd been in an airport, Emma remembered, she'd flung herself at Jamie and cried all over her jacket. A week later she'd flung herself at Jamie again, this time at a train station, and unwittingly signed the death knell for their friendship. No wonder Jamie hadn't said anything during the flight. Talk about awkward.

And yet, it was too early—and she was far too stubborn—to concede defeat. "How was your flight from London?" she asked, still channeling the same vapidly cheery version of herself.

Jamie shrugged. "Not too bad. We went over Greenland, which was pretty cool. I kept looking for polar bears but no luck."

Emma glanced at her, nearly tripping over her carry-on. Then she noticed Jamie's eyes crinkling at the corners. Apparently she wasn't ready to give up, either.

This time Emma's smile was more genuine. "Very funny."

"As in hardy-har-har?"

"As in looking," she replied, the banter returning easily as if it hadn't been a decade since they'd exchanged those well-worn lines.

In her peripheral vision she saw Jamie smile too, and the sight made her relax slightly. Maybe they could do this after all. And if not, she had kept her distance from other players before. When you routinely threw two dozen or more insanely competitive women from a variety of backgrounds and regions together, there was bound to be conflict.

They were almost to baggage claim when a dark-haired blur crashed into Jamie.

"Oof," Jamie grunted, barely managing to catch the smaller woman. "Easy! I kinda need my sternum."

Angie Wang pulled away, snickering. "Wuss. That's what ice baths are for. I can't believe you're finally here, though. Took you freaking long enough!"

Jamie's head tilted. "Do you mean literally here as in LA or figuratively here as in residency camp?"

Angie whacked her on the shoulder. "Both. Oh, hey, Blake," she added, turning her smile on Emma.

"Oh, hey, Wang," Emma mocked, grinning back.

They hugged, and then Angie reached for Jamie's carry-on and started towing it toward baggage claim. "I volunteered to drive the shuttle when I heard it was you."

"So you can reach the brake pedal, then?" Emma put in.

"Dude, already with the short jokes?" Angie shook her head and glanced back at Jamie, her face brightening again. "By the way, congrats on a killer WSL season. I only wish Britt could be here too."

"Right? Then it'd be like a genuine reunion tour."

Emma followed them, eavesdropping as they chattered on about the third member of their self-proclaimed "bro band," Brittany Crawford, the starting keeper at Arsenal. Britt, who had played at Stanford with Jamie and lured her to England after the Bay Area club folded, was a frequent guest on Jamie's social media feeds, along with her cute Scottish girlfriend, Allie.

Wait. Was it strange that Emma knew the name of Jamie's best friend's girlfriend? But it wasn't like she and Britt were strangers. The lanky keeper had been in and out of the national pool since their youth days and had practiced with the senior side more than a few times. She might not be one of the top five keepers in the country, but she wasn't that far down the list. With three of the top five over the age of thirty, it wasn't impossible to think she might get a shot at a roster spot someday. After all, look at Jamie.

She watched Jamie laugh at something Angie had said and throw her arm around the smaller player's shoulders. The girl she had known all those years ago had been considerably less comfortable with casual physical contact than the woman before her seemed to be—for reasons Emma remembered only too well. As they reached a conveyor belt that had yet to begin moving, she wondered in what other ways Jamie might have changed.

The next two weeks were bound to be interesting, that much was certain.

#

As Angie gave her the lowdown on the schedule for the rest of the day, Jamie stole glances at Emma, who stood nearby, her gaze fixed on the unmoving baggage carousel. When she'd boarded the plane in Seattle after clearing customs and jogging what felt like a mile through Sea-Tac, the last thing Jamie had expected was to see Emma already settled in business class, noise-reducing headphones clamped over her ears, face turned to the window. The federation often placed players together, and with her flight connecting through Seattle, Jamie had been aware they could end up on the same plane. But the team manager hadn't mentioned it, and in the rush to make her connection, the possibility had slipped her mind. Unprepared, she'd paused in the aisle to see if Emma would look her way. When she didn't, Jamie had moved on, not sure if she was more relieved or disappointed. She knew from Emma's Instagram and Twitter feeds that she had been approached by fans in airports and on flights more than a few times since the last World Cup and Olympics. Probably she wanted to be left in peace.

During the flight, Jamie had accommodated that wish, but it hadn't kept her from staring at the back of Emma's head. Even in jeans, a sweatshirt, and ponytail Emma looked photo shoot-worthy. Why wasn't everyone else on board staring at her, too? But the rest of the passengers didn't seem to realize who she was, and Jamie had to remind herself for the zillionth time that women's sports stars usually flew under the radar.

"Are you listening to me?" Angie asked, elbowing her.

Jamie felt Emma's gaze swing back to her. "Light training, dinner, and a meeting. I have a copy of the schedule in my email, you know."

"Ooh, look who's being all high and mighty," the Jersey girl said, holding up her hands. "My bad. Only trying to help. Whatevs."

"I can't believe you still talk like a twelve-year-old boy," Jamie commented.

"The ladies love it. Right, Blake?"

"Freaking irresistible," Emma dead-panned.

Jamie cracked up. "Nice shade, Blake."

Angie glanced between them. "That's right, you guys know each other. How did you meet again?"

Emma looked at Jamie, eyebrows slightly raised as if to say, *This one's all yours.*

"We played against each other in high school," Jamie said,

hoping Angie had a sub-par memory.

No such luck. "That's right. You guys were tight back in the day, weren't you?"

Jamie shrugged, playing it casual. "For a little while. Then this one went off to the East Coast and never looked back."

Emma frowned, and Jamie held her gaze. Technically *she'd* been the one to call off their friendship. But unless they wanted the entire team to know what had gone down between them, they would be better off sticking with the most reasonable explanation of why their friendship had ended: distance and time.

Apparently Emma recognized this fact because after a moment she nodded. "We got back in touch after college, but this is the first time we've been called up at the same time."

"Why—oh, yeah." Angie slapped her forehead. "I almost forgot about your little emergency last year. You thought you were the drama queen with the ambulance in the stadium, Max? Well, this one here freaked everyone out at open training in Connecticut. No one was even near her when she turned completely white and like, collapsed."

This wasn't news to Jamie. A fan had caught the whole thing on video and put it up on YouTube. Apparently Emma's appendix had burst the day before, but she'd ignored the pain, thinking it was only extreme cramps. People routinely died from untreated appendicitis. In fact, the older brother of a girl Jamie had played club with in California had died at soccer camp when the staff misdiagnosed him. What had likely saved Emma, Jamie had read later in *USA Today*, was her incredible fitness level. She'd been hospitalized in serious condition for a few days after surgery but had recovered more quickly than anyone had expected.

"What are we, ninety?" Emma asked, tugging on the end of her pony tail.

The gesture was so familiar that Jamie stared at her, story momentarily forgotten. The last time she'd seen Emma do that had been at the train station in downtown Seattle. Emma had tugged on her hair, and then she'd leaned in and kissed her.

After nearly a decade, Jamie still hadn't forgotten what it had felt like to be kissed by Emma Blakeley. How could she? Emma had been the first girl she'd ever kissed.

Angie scoffed. "What do you mean, are we ninety?"

"This is what my great aunts in Minnesota always do," Emma explained, one corner of her mouth turning up. "They sit around comparing major illnesses and surgeries, competing over who has it worse. 'Oh, geez, Helen, my pancreatitis is worse than your infected boil, I guaran-damn-tee it.'" She glanced at Jamie to share the joke, her gray-green eyes warm.

Clare, Jamie thought. She should text Clare to let her know she'd arrived. It was past midnight in London, but her girlfriend had said she would leave her phone on.

"Excuse me," she said, and stepped away, already scrolling through her contacts.

The carousel began to turn as she finished the text, and soon they were headed out to short-term parking. Emma climbed into the back seat of the van, leaving the front for Jamie. They hadn't made more than brief eye contact again, instead allowing Angie to carry the conversation. Why were things so weird between them? In London last year at the Olympics they'd been friendly, and not once had Jamie recalled their first kiss. *Only* kiss, she reminded herself, half-listening to Angie chatter on about the Southern California traffic and weather as they left LAX. Emma had kissed her once and then gone off to U-19 World Cup qualifiers in Canada where she'd slept with Tori Parker, resident whore of the American youth national pool.

Hmm. Jamie gazed out the passenger window. Perhaps she still had some unresolved anger about the past, after all.

Angie was saying something about roommate assignments when Jamie tuned back in. "Wait, who am I rooming with?"

"Ellie." Angie gave her a significant look.

Holy crap. She was going to room with the national team's co-captain and leading scorer? Britt was going to be so jealous when she found out. Rachel Ellison was a legend. Even people who didn't follow soccer knew her name. She'd arrived on the team a dozen years earlier and had led by example ever since. Most people thought she would pass Mia Hamm's scoring record before she was done, which in and of itself was fairly impressive. She was also the first openly gay player in US Soccer history, male or female. Jamie had met her a couple of times now, including the previous year when she'd been called up. In Phoenix, Ellie hadn't left her side once while they waited for the ambulance. She'd also been the first player to show up at the hospital the next day after Jamie was cleared for visitors. But while the veteran player's support in Phoenix had been incredible, Jamie was happy to be seeing her again under less dire circumstances.

Soon Angie was pulling into the familiar hotel driveway to unload. Jamie took a deep breath before stepping out of the van. She hadn't been here in forever, not since her last under-23 training camp in college. While she'd spent the past few years trying to work her way back from one injury after another, Angie and a handful of their other U-23 teammates had been training with the senior side. At least she would know people—other than Emma—at camp.

Angie waited until she and Emma had retrieved their bags. Then she waved out the window and called, "Later, dudes!" before heading off to park.

"Nervous?" Emma asked as Jamie stood on the circular drive, staring at the hotel entrance.

"A little bit." No use lying; Emma would probably see through it anyway.

"Might as well get it over with." Emma squeezed her shoulder gently and propelled her forward.

At her touch, Jamie felt a nearly forgotten sensation spreading through her limbs. Even after all these years, Emma could still somehow make her feel calm, like herself only better. Then, as they entered the hotel, Jamie's gaze fell on the corner of the lobby where she'd sat that awful night nine years earlier, breaking curfew so that Emma could try to explain why she'd lied about hooking up with Tori Parker. The memory no longer hurt the way it once had, but it did make her step out of

Emma's reach.

Thankfully, Tori had fallen out of the pool in the intervening years. Probably she'd slept with one too many fellow players. Teams were only as good as their chemistry, and whor—*people* like Tori usually weren't good for team cohesion.

"Blake!"

Jamie tried not to stare as an attractive blonde swept across the lobby toward them. Maddie Novak had been a couple of years ahead of Emma at UNC and was now considered the best offensive midfielder in the country, possibly the world. Naturally, Jamie had been star-struck around her in London, Portland, and Phoenix the previous year. It didn't help her tongue-tiedness one bit that Maddie apparently derived pleasure from flirting with anyone remotely masculine. Compared to other queer women, Jamie was a soft butch, but Maddie didn't seem to differentiate.

Speaking of butches—Rachel Ellison was in the lobby too, and as Maddie and Emma embraced, chattering on as if they hadn't seen each other in years, the co-captain came over and gave Jamie a one-armed bro hug, thumping her shoulder enthusiastically.

"Good to see you again, Max. I hear you tore it up in the WSL this season. Nicely done."

"Oh. Yeah. Thanks, man." She tried—and likely failed—to keep the awe out of her voice. Ellie was an American legend, one who would be sleeping in the bed next to hers for *two whole weeks*. Britt was seriously going to blow a gasket. Then again, Jamie might too. One of her assists against Ireland had been a cross to Ellie's head, and she had watched the highlight clip on YouTube a few thousand times to motivate herself during recovery.

At her first national team practice in Portland the previous fall, Angie had told her that newbies on the team always knew they had arrived when Rachel Ellison took an interest in them. Maybe Ellie was only being nice because they were roommates, but Jamie hoped this camp might finally signal the next stage of her national team career.

When Ellie went to hug Emma, Maddie turned her megawatt smile on Jamie. She tried to smile back but was pretty sure her expression more closely approximated a grimace. As Emma shot her an amused look, brow quirking quizzically, Jamie turned away, hoping to at least partially hide the mortified blush she could feel coming on. Freaking Scotch-Irish heritage.

"Here's your room key," Ellie said as if nothing had happened, passing her a key card. "Let's get you settled before dinner, huh?"

"Okay." Jamie watched as Ellie reached down and grabbed her duffle. "That has wheels."

"I'm good," the striker said, throwing the strap over one broad shoulder. "You ready?"

Jamie nodded, relieved—until she realized that Emma and Maddie were trailing them to the elevator. Unbelievable. She was about to ride in an elevator with Emma, Rachel Ellison, and Maddie Novak. For a moment she wondered if she could somehow get a photo or video of the moment to preserve for time eternal, but she caught herself in time and left her phone in her pocket. She was so intent on not making an ass out of herself as the elevator crept upward that she didn't realize Ellie had asked her something until all eyes zeroed in on her. Automatically she looked at Emma. *Help.*

"She grew up in Berkeley but played at Stanford," Emma supplied. "Which I can't imagine your parents took very well," she added, eyes on Jamie. "They both went to Cal, didn't they?"

Jamie nodded and managed to find her voice. "They were all, 'But honey, Cal has a great athletic program. Are you sure you don't want to go to Cal?'"

"Don't let Dierdorf hear you talking smack about Cal," Maddie said as the foursome unloaded on the second floor and headed down the hallway together.

"I would never talk smack about Cal," Jamie said mock innocently, thrilled when the three veterans laughed.

A year ago she'd barely been able to speak around Maddie

or Ellie. Now, with Emma walking beside her along the hotel corridor, everything seemed easier. Before her father died, Emma had been an unwavering fount of support during a year when Jamie wasn't sure she'd ever be happy again. Her anchor, even, as confirmed by the bracelet Emma had given her for her sixteenth birthday. In an impulsive act she had long regretted, she'd thrown the bracelet away the morning after she found out Emma had slept with Tori. A decade had passed, and yet she could still remember how the cool metal had felt against her wrist, tiny engraved letters pressed against her pulse: *I'll be your anchor if you'll be mine.*

She watched Emma now as they came to a stop before doors on opposite sides of the hall. Did Emma want them to be friends again? Was that even a real possibility? She was laughing at something Maddie had said, but her gaze swung back to Jamie as it had always done. Jamie thought she read a similar question in her eyes, and all at once it was too much. This was her chance to finally make the national team. She needed to focus on doing all the little things right—paying attention to coaches and trainers, interacting positively with teammates, making sure she got enough rest, water, and the right kinds of food—not trying to figure out where she and Emma stood, if they stood anywhere at all.

She looked away and followed Ellie into their room. Time to get her head in the game.

CHAPTER THREE

"Grab some water and we'll put what we've been working on into a full-field scrimmage," Melanie Beckett, the defensive coach, said, waving them toward the sideline.

Emma jogged over to the bench and grabbed her water bottle, grateful for the break. Despite her "insane level of fitness," as her brother commented every time he saw her, she was dragging slightly. After two straight days of fitness testing hell, they had at last started to play actual soccer. *Finally*, they had all exclaimed that morning, jubilant—until the coaches started running them into the practice field ground, too.

Out of the corner of her eye, she spotted Jamie a little ways down the sideline wiping sweat from the back of her neck. Jamie caught her gaze, and after a second they exchanged a small smile. Emma looked away first, digging through her bag to find one of her many tubes of sunscreen. It was a lovely, summery, winter's afternoon in LA, and sunscreen was definitely in order, especially for a Seattleite of Scandinavian descent.

Once fitness testing had begun, Emma had been relieved to find that her pre-camp jitters were easily forgotten in the usual blur of raucous laughter and flint-eyed competition. The launch of the new pro league had kept everyone so crazy busy that she hadn't seen her teammates much in recent months. In between measurements and tests, they joked around even more than they normally did, stealing water bottles and occasional items of clothing, choreographing silly dance steps to pop tunes, and teasing each other about everything from musical ability and fashion sense—some of the younger players *still* insisted on rolling their shorts—to nocturnal habits and cooking prowess. Emma had known many of these women since she was sixteen, and while she admittedly loved some more than others, most felt like family. Whenever they came back together, it was almost like they hadn't ever been apart.

As in any family, though, there was usually tension simmering beneath the surface. You only had to know where to look.

When Steph Miller, starting defensive midfielder for the last two World Cups, approached Jamie on the sideline, Emma drifted closer. Before the water break Melanie had been testing the starting defense with different midfield line-ups in a small-sided game, the point of which was to focus on working the ball out of their defensive end. With Steph in the line-up, the starters had struggled to move the ball efficiently through the midfield. But then Melanie had subbed Jamie in for Steph, and the starting unit went on to score three times in a row.

"Nice work out there," she heard Steph tell Jamie. "But maybe take it down a notch, huh? You're making me look bad."

Despite the semi-teasing note in Steph's voice, it was all Emma could do not to snort. Could she be any more obvious in her clumsy attempts at manipulation?

Oh, wait. Apparently she could.

"Are you kidding?" Jamie asked. "No one could make *you* look bad."

A hint of guilt played across Steph's face. "Well, thanks. You're pretty great yourself. It's really good to have you back with us."

Jamie flushed at the praise while Emma resisted the urge to shake her. This wasn't the first time she had out-performed the veteran midfielder. During the beep test Monday morning,

Jamie had come in second overall, handily beating out a bevy of starters who clapped her on the back encouragingly as she tried to catch her breath after the sprint competition. Of the returning players, only Steph had failed to congratulate her. While Jamie hadn't appeared to notice the slight, Emma had. She'd almost been expecting it. During the victory tour the previous fall, Jamie had subbed in for Steph in both Portland and Phoenix. Initially Emma had thought she was wasted at defensive mid. Surely Jamie's creativity marked her as an attacking midfielder, either on the outside or through the center. But to Emma's surprise—and in her entirely unbiased view—Jamie had performed equally as well as the national team mainstay, if not better.

She was guessing that fact hadn't been lost on Steph, either.

Should she intervene? Emma frowned, tossing the tube of sunscreen back in her bag. Would she do so for any other new player, or was the temptation to swoop in and play knight in shining armor specific to Jamie? But that was silly. As an older player and possible future captain, it was her *responsibility* to look out for the younger players. All of them. Doing her part to keep team dynamics positive was nearly as important as coming to camp fit and ready to play.

Emma slipped her water bottle back into her bag and turned in time to see Angie launch herself onto Jamie's back, whooping.

Jamie caught the smaller woman's weight and spun around, brow furrowed. "Does anyone else hear that? A fly buzzing, or like, maybe a mosquito?"

As everyone in the vicinity cracked up, Angie huffed and slid off Jamie's back. "Funny, I didn't hear you laughing the other day when I kicked your ass in the hundred meter."

"No one ever said your tiny body wasn't built for speed."

As Angie lifted her water bottle and squeezed, Jamie ducked out of the way. The stream of water sailed well wide of its target and struck Maddie squarely between the shoulder blades. Emma snickered under her breath as the statuesque blonde slowly turned and fixed her glare on Angie.

"Sorry?" the younger woman offered, hunching her shoulders in a half-shrug.

"Apology not accepted," Maddie all but growled, advancing on her with a distinctly predatory gleam in her eyes.

Emma stared at her residency camp roommate. Maddie wasn't flirting with *Angie Wang*, was she?

"Holy shit," Angie breathed, seemingly frozen in place.

And then Melanie blew her whistle. Break time was over.

"This isn't finished, Wang," Maddie declared, eyes still narrowed menacingly. "Not by a long shot."

Angie skittered away, grinning impishly over her shoulder. "You'll have to catch me first."

"Oh, don't worry. I will," Maddie promised, following her out onto the field.

Well, *that* was weird. Not to mention diverting—she'd completely forgotten about Steph and her little mind games. Fortunately, with ten days left in camp, there would be plenty of opportunity to warn Jamie which veterans to watch out for. And to warn the other newbies, too. Obviously.

Emma followed Jamie and Lisa Wall, the other starting center back, out onto the field. Jamie's years of youth national pool experience had allowed her to fit into residency camp more easily than the average new recruit. Her group of longtime friends—Angie, Lisa, and a couple of others—had played together for the under-20 and -23 squads. When she wasn't with her "bro bandmates," as they referred to themselves, she was often squirreled away in a corner with Ellie, appearing to listen intently as the older player spoke, hands gesticulating passionately. Were they talking soccer? The pros and cons of long-term relationships? Favorite reality television shows? Emma had no idea. And, obviously, it was none of her business. She and Jamie might be making an effort to be friendly, but they weren't really friends. Not anymore. Yet? *Whatever.*

Back on the field, the low hum of conversation faded as the coaching staff divided them into starters and non-starters for the first eleven v. eleven scrimmage of residency camp. The focus, Melanie reiterated as they spread out, would be on transitioning through the midfield. Neither team was allowed to shoot until they had connected a minimum of five short passes, and at least one member of each unit—defense, midfield, offense—had to touch the ball before a goal would count.

Emma, for one, was psyched they were working on transitions. Since Craig Anderson, their New Zealand-born head coach, had taken over and experimented with the line-up—as was a new coach's right and even, most would argue, duty—the team had struggled when it came to working the ball out of their own defensive end. It wasn't that their defense wasn't solid. Emma and Lisa had shared the center ever since the last of the '99ers had retired, and their outside backs were quick and dynamic and could be slotted into almost any position on the field. The same could be said for their formidable cadre of strikers. But with the midfield and front line shifting continually and with so few international matches recently, the team had struggled to develop the chemistry they'd enjoyed under their previous coach.

Once the players were in their designated positions, Melanie joined the other coaches on the sideline and blew her whistle again. The game was on.

Scrimmages between starters and non-starters were always intense, given what was at stake. Knowing this, Emma kept an eye on Jamie. Not in a different way from how she looked after the rest of the team, just, you know, because they were playing in the same general vicinity. The coaches had started Jamie at offensive mid on the opposing team, which meant she and Steph battled for possession directly in front of Emma for the first few minutes. They were surprisingly well-matched—surprising mostly because in the previous exercise Jamie had clearly dominated the older player in both speed and technical ability. At one point, Emma saw Jamie slow incrementally rather than go all in for a fifty-fifty ball. Evidently Steph's attempts to psyche her out had succeeded.

Oh, hell, no, Emma thought, slotting the ball Steph had

tapped to her cleanly up the center to Maddie. This would not do at all. Jamie should be stepping up her play to compete for a permanent spot on the squad rather than laying off a player she admired. The same thing happened fairly routinely in residency camp, but respect in the form of hesitation wasn't a highly valued—or rewarded—trait at this level. Steph had come into camp less fit than usual, complaining to anyone who would listen that her son had started kindergarten and the whole family had been throughout the fall. But even if Steph had come in fully fit, Jamie should be playing her ass off. The national team wasn't a true meritocracy—did such a thing even exist?—but it was close, and this was Jamie's chance to prove her worth.

For a moment Emma paused, questioning her own level of emotional investment. It wasn't because it was Jamie, right? After all, who wouldn't cheer for someone who had worked hard to overcome years of bad luck and succeed at the highest level? Jamie had come into camp as the classic underdog, and despite Emma's previous arguments to the contrary, most people loved rooting for the underdog.

When Craig paused the scrimmage to talk to the opposing team's back line, Emma walked over and tugged on the back of Jamie's pinny. "Hey," she said, keeping her voice low.

Jamie glanced over her shoulder. "Hey what?"

"Stop laying off Steph."

At that Jamie turned to face her. "Who says I'm laying off?"

"I do."

"And how would you know?"

"Because I know you." As Jamie stared at her, Emma tried to reel the words back in. "I mean, I don't know you *now*, but I used to know you, and I don't think you've changed that much. Or at least—"

Jamie set a hand on Emma's shoulder. "No, you're right. It's just, she told me I was making her look bad."

"Don't let her get in your head. All you can do is play your best. Anything less is a disservice—to yourself and to this team," Emma said, repeating the same advice one of the '99ers had offered her at her first residency camp.

"Okay. I will. Thanks."

Emma nodded, aware of Jamie's hand still on her shoulder, her touch surprisingly gentle. And warm. She'd forgotten how much heat Jamie gave off. She was like a furnace, which was partly what Emma had found so comforting about sleeping beside her the week of her father's funeral. Before Jamie arrived, she'd felt chilled all the time. But with her there, she hadn't felt cold at all. Not until she stepped onto the stage and looked out at the hundreds of mourners who were staring at her, waiting for her to deliver the perfect eulogy for the seemingly perfect man who, in reality, was anything but.

Jamie's eyes changed, and she stepped back, her hand falling away as Craig blew his whistle to restart play. Out of the blue the ball came at them, lifted over the top by a newbie defender on Jamie's team.

"Away!" Phoebe Banks, literally the best goalkeeper in the world, screamed.

Automatically Emma pushed off Jamie to leap into the air and head the ball to Ryan Dierdorf, the starting left back. Freaking newbies. What the hell had happened to midfield transition?

"Nice elbow," Jamie said, rubbing her shoulder.

"Get out of the kitchen if you can't stand the heat."

Jamie rolled her eyes as she jogged away, but Emma could see she was smiling.

After that Jamie kicked it back up a notch, and soon the coaches were swapping the lines around. This time Jamie was on Emma's team. The ball started at Phoebe's feet, and within a couple of minutes their side scored on a beautiful through ball that Jamie sent into the eighteen for Jenny to blast past one of the back-up keepers. Jenny hugged Jamie as they jogged back to the center circle, but Emma contented herself with a smile and a high-five.

The less hugging probably the better. At least for the foreseeable future.

#

Like the other days before it, Saturday in Carson was warm and sunny. At four thirty in the afternoon, Jamie sat in the grass at the center of one of the training fields mostly listening to the coaching staff highlight lessons learned in their scrimmage against the under-17 boys' national team, also in residence that week. It was a little embarrassing to be matched up against boys who didn't yet need to shave, but any older and the women's side would be physically outmatched. The reality— that male players would always be bigger, faster, stronger— sucked, but she had long since accepted it. She didn't think it was indulging in biologic predeterminism to admit that even the best female soccer players in the country couldn't get around biology.

And they were the best—not only in the country but in the world, of that Jamie had no doubt. During warm-up and cool-down and in between most drills, the women around her liked to joke around. But once the whistle blew and play began, they morphed into athletic machines with laser focus and unsmiling precision. Jamie could appreciate that. It was how she had always tried to approach the game too. Sometimes she thought that when the time came and she was too old to play at the highest level, she would have to quit cold turkey because there was no way she could see herself playing soccer in a rec league. Coach her kid's team, yes, but play in a beer league? Not likely.

Since her last go-around, she'd nearly forgotten the sheer intensity of national team practices. Despite her pro experience, the speed of play at residency camp was significantly faster than what she was used to. The need to up her own game had come crashing back during the first full-field scrimmage when Emma had all but told her to get her head out of her ass.

That night back in their room, Ellie had echoed Emma's sentiments, though a tad more judiciously. "You can't afford to worry about anyone else," she had said as they lay in the dark chatting before sleep. "You take care of you, and the rest will fall into place."

The captain's words had reminded Jamie of one of Ellie's

early interviews, and it was all she could do to keep from quoting Ellie back to herself. Somehow, though, she'd managed to lie quietly in their shared hotel room and refrain from squeeing at the realization that the person whose breathing she could hear evening out in the bed beside hers was her younger self's biggest idol. She couldn't sleep herself. The old interview that she'd memorized as a teenager kept running through her mind: "A coach once told me that there are only three things you can control: your attitude, your work ethic, and your level of effort. Everything else is outside of your control—coaching decisions, field conditions, weather, teammates, and, of course, referees."

This field-level philosophy dovetailed nicely with Jamie's own sports/life mantra: "Control the things you can and let go of the things you can't." That was what she'd tried to do so far in LA: focus on her own attitude, work ethic, and effort, and let go of the things she couldn't control—Steph Miller's apparent resentment, for one; the look in Emma's eyes when Jamie touched her shoulder, for another. In spite of the occasional hitch, the first five days of residency camp had slipped past in a blur of hard work, afternoon naps, and meals with women she was getting to know some for the first time and others all over again.

She had spent the most time with three of her former youth pool teammates: Angie, a fellow midfielder; Lisa, a defender (because what else would she be with a last name like Wall?); and Rebecca Perry, surprisingly tolerable for a striker. They sat together every morning at team breakfast, cheered each other on in fitness training, and generally had one another's backs. Between practices they napped together in someone's room, and on evenings the team didn't have anything planned, they went out to dinner and watched Netflix until curfew. It was so much like their early days in the national pool that sometimes Jamie felt as though in addition to traveling halfway around the world, she had also managed to journey back in time.

Despite the slightly surreal quality of being back in LA and her near-constant state of exhaustion, she was feeling good about her performance. At the start, she'd had no idea if she possessed even a slight chance at making the team. Now, almost a week in, she was starting to regain some of the blind self-faith that elite athletes usually carry in droves. The last few years hadn't been easy, it was true, and she'd lost some of her previously unshakable confidence. But one good thing about surviving trauma was that it could provide the survivor with perspective. Even if she didn't make the World Cup squad, she still had her health, her family, and a professional soccer career. Besides, she'd already earned a couple of caps with the national team, which was more than 99.99 percent of the soccer players in the world could say.

Beside her, Ellie and her fellow co-captain Phoebe Banks were murmuring quietly as they stretched, slotting their sentences into the gaps in Craig's end-of-first-week speech. On her other side, Angie and Lisa were engaged in a battle to see who could flick the other hardest without gaining the attention of the coaching staff. Jamie was almost certain Melanie, the eagle-eyed defensive coach, had already twigged their game, but Mel didn't say anything as she and Bill, the offensive coach, stood slightly behind Craig, arms folded across their chests. Mel was Jamie's favorite, and not only because she was family. Unlike certain other members of the coaching staff, Mel didn't yell or rant at them. She was calm and thoughtful and had a decent sense of humor. And she seemed to like Jamie, which was always an attractive quality in another person—particularly in one with the power to make or break your biggest life goals.

"So unless you lot have any objections," Craig finally wrapped up, "the rest of the coaches and I think you've earned your day off tomorrow. And that day off begins—" he lifted his arm, pretending to squint at his watch—"right now."

The players immediately erupted in cheers, and if Craig had planned to say anything else, it was lost in the cacophony of thirty women discussing plans for their first day off in almost a week.

"Up for some surfing action tomorrow?" Angie asked, leaning in.

"Hell yes." Jamie pulled her sweaty shin guards out of her socks. "It's been way too long."

Lisa, a native Southern Californian (an identity Jamie generously overlooked), chimed in along with Rebecca, and the plan was set. The water would be cold at this time of year, but that's what wet suits were for. Jamie couldn't wait. Even when it wasn't the best day for waves, she loved being out on the ocean with the sea and sky all around, far from shore without a phone or any other mode of communication. Untouchable.

Before they could leave the field, Ellie and her co-captain called everyone in for an announcement.

"I know some of you want to spend time with friends and family," Ellie said, "but those plans will have to wait until tomorrow. Tonight is mandatory team bonding."

A faint smattering of groans was silenced by a single look from Phoebe Banks, who stood at Ellie's elbow with her hands on her hips. Angie had nicknamed Banks "The Enforcer" and claimed to find her weirdly hot. Banks was straight—or at least she was engaged to a male college soccer coach—but Jamie had always gotten a queer vibe off of her. Then again, most female keepers she knew came off as slightly butch, so probably it was an occupational hazard.

"Don't worry," Ellie added. "It's the kind of bonding that involves dinner and movies. We'll meet in the lobby in an hour, so don't be late."

The mood in the van was cheerful, despite the response to Ellie's pronouncement. It had been a difficult week and most players were ready to chill. For the last five days they'd traveled almost exclusively from the hotel to the training center and back again. A few people had hit the beach one afternoon, but most took advantage of their few hours of free time between sessions to sleep or, in the case of the college-aged players who had been called into camp, to do homework. Jamie remembered her youth camp experiences, cramming in math tests and lab reports wherever she could and dreaming about a life that was entirely devoid of homework. She now had that life, and it was at least as awesome as she had imagined.

An hour later, she was showered and ready to go out with the team. Ellie was ready, too, but she was out on the balcony Skyping with her fiancée. Jamie, meanwhile, had stretched out on her bed with her laptop and started an email to Clare. It was the middle of the night in the UK, so she couldn't call. She wasn't entirely sure Clare would answer even if she was awake. They had only spoken once since Jamie left London, and she was starting to think that Clare was avoiding her.

"Hola, bitches," Angie said, barging uninvited into the room. They had left the metal door latch wedged into the gap, which in camp parlance meant no one was naked and visitors were welcome. "Where's Ellie?"

Jamie nodded at the balcony where the striker was visible through the sliding door. "Chatting with Jodie."

"Aww, they're so cute. That's relationship goals, for real."

"I thought you didn't believe in monogamy anymore?"

"It's fine for other people."

Angie paused in front of the dresser, checking herself out in the mirror. Her black hair flowed loose around her shoulders, partially hidden by a gray fedora. A red skinny tie complimented her black button down and dark gray skinny jeans. Low black boots, dark red lipstick, eyeliner, and a light coat of mascara finished off the look.

Jamie loved Angie, but the whole *playuh* thing she had developed since being dumped by her college girlfriend the previous winter was tiresome. So what if they had girls sending them messages daily wanting to hook up? Half the people Jamie knew outside of soccer had dating apps on their phones and could meet random hook-ups anytime they wanted, too. She had honestly never understood the appeal of sleeping around.

Angie launched herself onto the bed and peered over her shoulder. "Whatcha doin'?"

Jamie minimized her email quickly—but not quickly enough.

"Are you writing to Clare?"

She nodded, bracing herself for Angie's reaction. Instead of teasing her about being whipped, though, Angie only sighed and rested her head on Jamie's shoulder. "That's sweet. You guys are sweet."

"Hold on." Jamie lifted her hand to Angie's forehead. "Are you feeling okay?"

"Shut up," Angie grumbled. "Now come on, get dressed. It's almost time to go."

"I am dressed."

Angie sat up straighter and glared at her. "James Maxwell, you are *not* wearing a hoodie out tonight."

"Why not? It's not like I'm looking to hook up."

"You have a lot to learn about being on this team. It's not about hooking up, it's about keeping up."

"I actually agree with her, Max," Ellie said, reentering the room. She was dressed in dark blue skinny jeans, a gray button down, and a black bow tie, her short hair slicked back. She even had some make-up on.

"But I like this sweatshirt."

The other two ignored her as they ransacked her side of the closet, hauling out black skinny jeans, her favorite red and gray flannel, and her black high tops. Once she was dressed, they dragged her into the bathroom and set to work on her hair and face, brushing aside her protests that she didn't "do" make-up.

When they were done, she stared at her reflection. It didn't even look like her. The deep red lipstick matched her shirt while the mascara emphasized her long lashes, and the concealer they'd brushed on was so light she could barely tell it was there. The extra pomade they had rubbed into her hair made it look shiny but not crusty, and added body while keeping the longer strands out of her eyes.

"Damn, James," Angie said, holding her hand up to Ellie. "You look so good I'd almost do you."

"Totally," Ellie agreed, slapping her palm.

In the mirror, Jamie shot them the bird.

By the time they reached the lobby, most of the other players were already waiting. Jamie glanced around until she found Emma standing between Maddie Novak and Jenny

Latham. She looked beautiful in blue jeans, a loose gray sweater that fell to mid-thigh, and ankle boots, her long hair falling about her shoulders in a cascade of shiny curls. Her eyes caught Jamie's, and all at once Jamie had the strangest feeling, almost like she was about to lose her balance.

Ellie's elbow connected with Jamie's ribs, and she sucked in a breath. "The hell, Ellie?"

"Watch yourself," the older woman said, her voice low. "There are people and cameras everywhere, and you drooling over Maddie is not something you want to have end up online."

"No, I wasn't—it wasn't..." Jamie trailed off. What did it matter if Ellie had picked the wrong teammate? Either way, she was totally off-base. Well, not totally. Emma was attractive. Anyone with eyes could see that. But Jamie didn't have *those* feelings for her, not anymore.

Ellie slung an arm across Jamie's shoulders. "Residency camp is like being at a women's college. Jodie went to Smith in Massachusetts, and she said some of the dorms there were lesbian sexcapades twenty-four seven."

Angie leaned in. "Where are these lesbian sexcapades of which you speak?"

"Other than in your pants?" Jamie quipped, and slapped the hand Ellie offered.

At the restaurant, a warehouse-sized Americana place where the staff had set aside half the dining room for their party, Ellie pointed at her own eyes and then at Jamie, with a subtle nod toward Maddie. Jamie resolved to sit as far from the team captain as possible. This meant she ended up at a table with some of the new recruits, residency camp rookies who, unlike her, had arrived not knowing many of the rostered players. These girls seemed to group her in with the veterans, and she tried not to let that go to her head as she sipped red wine and asked them about themselves. Making everyone else talk was pretty much her go-to move in any potentially awkward social situation.

At one point, Emma and Maddie visited their table on the

way back from the restroom.

"Hey, Jamie," Emma said, smiling.

"Hey." Jamie smiled back, hoping her expression was suitably casual. From across the room she could feel the press of Ellie's gaze.

"You all doing okay over here?" Maddie asked.

While the other women at the table rushed to assure the veterans they were doing splendidly, Jamie sipped more wine, Ellie's words echoing in her head. The idea of her drooling over Maddie was kind of funny. The blonde may have left her tongue-tied on more than one occasion, but it wasn't like Jamie was attracted to her.

As if to mock her, an image of Maddie from the previous year's *ESPN Magazine* Body Issue floated into her mind. Naked. What the hell? Freaking Ellie and her obsession with lesbian sexcapades.

The fly-by didn't last long. As soon as the two starters were out of earshot, one of the newbies declared, "They are so nice! I thought maybe the publicity photos were air-brushed or whatnot, but now I don't think they are."

"They're totally prettier in person," another player agreed. "Did I tell you guys Emma stayed after practice yesterday to help me with my one v. one defending? I thought for sure camp would be cutthroat, but the older players seem really supportive so far."

Jamie wanted to say that it was the coaches you had to look out for and not the other players, but she kept the thought to herself. Steph Miller had proven her wrong with her mind games earlier in the week, and anyway, Jamie was competing with these women for a spot on the team. While she wanted to believe she was basically a good person, she knew the fact that she was older and had already crashed and burned on two previous tries meant that she would have to work that much harder to stand out. There was another residency camp in mid-January and a three-match road trip two weeks later to open the team's 2014 schedule, followed by the annual Algarve Cup in Portugal in early March. At this point, her main goal was to be invited to the January camp so that she would have a shot at making the roster for the February matches. Then if she did well in the friendlies, she might make the Algarve Cup roster, something she'd always dreamed of.

Choosing not to share insight born of experience with her rivals didn't necessarily make her evil. It made her smart, didn't it? Right. She reached for her wine again.

By the end of dinner, she was feeling tipsier than she had intended. Combining utter physical exhaustion with social awkwardness *and* a general inability to hold her liquor had probably not been the wisest of choices. Wait, did wine count as liquor, or was the term reserved solely for hard alcohol? In addition to being a lightweight, she knew practically nothing about booze. She had her reasons for avoiding alcohol, but hanging out with other athletes meant fielding more than the occasional run-in with beer pressure. In high school she'd managed to stay mostly sober most of the time, barring the incident that had started her down the straight edge path. But in college she'd found it significantly harder to avoid drunkenness, especially as a varsity soccer player at an NCAA Division I university. Still, she didn't like to lose control. Tipsy was usually as far as she went.

Even after using the restroom, where she peed for what felt like a full two minutes, possibly longer, her tongue still felt heavy and her head was fuzzy in a mostly pleasant way. When she collided with Angie on the semi-lit sidewalk outside the restaurant, she threw her arms around the smaller woman's shoulders and tugged her closer.

"Hey there, little buddy," she nearly crooned. She loved Angie so much. She had missed Angie, like, totally.

Angie grinned up at her. "Aw, drunk Max is in the house! My favorite!"

"I'm not *drunk*. I'm just so happy to be here with you guys, you know? I just *love* you guys."

"We love you too, Max. Group hug!"

Angie slipped her arm around Jamie's waist while Lisa and Rebecca crowded in, laughing and mussing Jamie's hair while she stood in the middle, smiling so widely her face hurt. Over Lisa's shoulder she caught Emma staring at her from a few feet away, a smile teasing her lips even as her eyebrows arched heavenward. Wait, was "heavenward" even a word? Jamie smiled back at Emma. She was just so genuinely happy. She hoped Emma was, too. Everyone should be, especially people who were as pretty as Emma was.

When Ellie pulled one of the team vans around, Jamie and her friends hustled aboard, smushing into the front row behind the driver's seat. The other three made sure she had the center seat so that she could see out the front window.

"We don't want you getting car sick on us, Max," Angie said, her arm loose around Jamie's shoulders.

"Like in Mexico," Rebecca added.

"Oh my god, that was so gross." Lisa made a face. "You totally puked in your shopping bag."

"I took the clothes out first," Jamie protested. "Anyway, like you remember—you were passed out in the back row."

"To be fair, no one except Britt even knew what happened until we got back to the hotel," Rebecca said, flipping her long, blonde hair from one shoulder to the other.

Why were all strikers blonde? Jamie frowned a little in concentration. Or was it that all *blondes* were *strikers*? Whoah. That was too much for her brain to parse. If only Britt were here right now. Even at her drunkest, the keeper maintained a calm exterior and clear mind that allowed her to answer life's great questions. Missing her friend, Jamie closed her eyes and then opened them quickly, focusing on the road ahead as Ellie guided the van onto the freeway.

They were back at the hotel in a matter of minutes. But instead of retiring to her room alone to potentially drunk— ahem, *tipsy* dial her girlfriend, Jamie found the entire team piling into their room, where Ellie and Phoebe had arranged for a DVD player to be brought up. Right—movie night was happening in their room. In fact, Ellie had asked to commandeer the sleeve of DVD favorites she liked to travel with. Crap. She had totally forgotten.

Good thing she didn't drink that much normally. Her memory was questionable enough as it was. Too many headers, possibly? Or was it a trauma response? One of the things she admired about her girlfriend was that she had a mind like a steel trap. Not that her girlfriend was talking to her right now.

While Ellie and Phoebe wrestled with the DVD hook-ups, Jamie ducked into the hall and scrolled through her phone, trying to remember what time it was in London. Was the UK eight hours ahead or behind? It wasn't like Clare was going to answer either way. She had sent a grand total of three texts in the last week, all in response to messages Jamie had sent. Jamie rubbed her eyes and hit dial, wandering down the corridor as she waited for Clare's line to ring. But the call went straight to voicemail, so Jamie hung up and headed back to the room. She missed Clare. Why was Clare avoiding her?

Except she kind of thought she knew the reason.

In the open doorway she surveyed the overcrowded room, stopping when her eyes fell on the figure leaning against her headboard, iPhone in hand. Emma glanced up and their gazes met, and Jamie stood there looking at the girl—no, the *woman*—who had once been her best friend. Then they had become something indefinable but definitely more, and then they'd stopped speaking altogether until the damn soccer gods had decided to bring them back together. Clare knew all of this in theory, but she didn't know details. The only person Jamie wasn't related to who knew everything was Britt, and that was only because Britt had held her hand through the longest week of her life after she broke up with Emma in this very hotel— or whatever you called it when you told your best friend slash sort of almost girlfriend you never wanted to see her again.

"Max, where's *Pitch Perfect*?" Ellie asked, breaking in on her spiraling thoughts.

Jamie tore her gaze away from Emma. "What?"

"Your movie case." Ellie spoke slowly, enunciating as if she were talking to someone slightly hard of hearing. "Where. Is. It."

Jamie frowned and glanced around, trying not to notice that

Maddie, also seated at the head of Jamie's bed, was whispering in Emma's ear. She didn't know, right? Emma hadn't told her about what had happened between them? More importantly, Emma hadn't told her about France, had she? The old panic started to rise in her chest, mixing somehow with the tide of tipsiness, and Jamie stared at Ellie blankly. She could feel her face flushing, could feel the way her mouth opened and closed like a fish that been ripped from the water. Some dispassionate part of her mind noted the symptoms of extreme anxiety coolly, as if they were happening to someone else. But they weren't happening to someone else. They were happening to her in the presence of the entire national team player pool.

Fuck.

It was Ellie's turn to frown, and she was clearly about to say something when Jamie felt a hand on her arm. She started to jerk away, but then she looked into familiar gray-green eyes and paused as a wave of something that was the opposite of anxiety washed over her.

"Can I borrow you for a second?" Emma asked, tugging her toward the door.

Jamie let herself be pulled, barely managing to ground out to Ellie, "Backpack. Closet."

Emma led her across the hall and into her room where she closed the door and leaned against it. Jamie stopped a few paces in, willing away the tiny pinpoints of light bursting at the edges of her vision as she tried to force air into her starved lungs.

"Can I…?" she choked out, gesturing toward the bathroom.

"Of course. I'll be right here."

She pushed into the mirrored room and shut the door. Then she turned the cold water on and leaned over the sink, splashing her face and trying not to notice the scent of cucumber shampoo hanging in the air. Except cucumber was a soothing scent, one that could be found in assorted aromatherapy products. Jamie had often wondered if it had a doubly calming effect on her—she associated it not only with essential oils but also with Emma, the girl who had helped her through the hardest year of her life.

As the water cooled her body, she meditated, focusing on her breathing and on the image of each word of the meditation falling slowly through the blackness of her mind into an imaginary well. A few minutes of deliberate practice and her heart rate and breathing slowed. *Whew.* The old method of calming her mind still worked. She hadn't had to test it in a while.

After another minute or two, she turned off the water and dried her hands on a white hotel towel. Then she looked at herself in the mirror, noting her red-rimmed eyes and the flush in her cheeks. This right here? *This* was why she didn't like to drink.

With a last scrub of the towel over her now make-up free face, she opened the door and stepped out to meet Emma's concerned gaze.

"Are you okay?"

"I think so." She hesitated. "How did you know?"

"Your face got red and you looked like you couldn't breathe." As Jamie winced, she added, "But don't worry. I don't think anyone else noticed."

"That's good, I guess." Jamie rubbed the hair at the back of her neck. "Thanks, Emma. I mean it. That could have been… Anyway, thank you."

"You don't have to thank me, Jamie."

Emma was looking at her in a way that made her heart rate increase again, and all at once she realized that they were alone together in a room whose furniture consisted mostly of beds. No wonder she could feel the panic trying to reassert itself.

"We should probably get back," she said, gesturing to the hallway.

"Are you sure you want to?" Emma toyed with the tip of the ponytail she had trapped her hair in at some point during dinner. "We could go for a walk, maybe get some air?"

"Ellie would be pissed if we skipped out on mandatory team bonding," Jamie heard herself say. Which was true and yet so not the point.

"Oh, yeah. Right. Back it is, then." Emma opened the door and held it, waiting for Jamie to pass.

Her foot had already crossed the threshold when she paused. "Hang on. Can I ask you something?" She stood half-in and half-out of the room, fidgeting a little as she made herself meet Emma's eyes.

"Sure. Do you want to…?" She waved behind her.

"No, that's okay," Jamie said quickly. "I was only wondering, does Maddie know about, well—"

"High school?"

She nodded, even though that wasn't exactly what she'd meant.

"She knows about you in theory, but she doesn't know it was *you.*"

Maddie didn't know *what* was her? But what Emma may have told her friends about their past relationship wasn't really any of her business, and it wasn't what Jamie was after, anyway. "What about France? Does she know anything about that?"

Emma shook her head. "No. No way, Jamie. The only person I ever talked to about France was my mom. Well, and Sam, my girlfriend in Boston. But I never used your name. She didn't have any idea it was you."

Relief poured into Jamie's chest, and suddenly she could breathe more easily. "Okay. Thanks. That's good to know."

A tiny crease appeared above the bridge of Emma's nose. "Is that what you were worried about? Is that what caused—"

"My first panic attack in three years?" Jamie nodded again. "I think so."

Except that wasn't entirely true. She was pretty sure the anxiety had arisen from a confluence of events—letdown from the end of the first week of residency camp; dread over Clare going underground the second she left London; and, if she was being honest, worry over trying to negotiate a renewed acquaintance with the girl-turned-woman standing before her. But she couldn't tell Emma all of that because they were potential teammates and possible future friends, which meant their relationship existed in the past and, if she was lucky enough to land a spot on the national team, somewhere in the indeterminate future.

"Well, don't worry," Emma said, still holding the door open with one hand and reaching out to press Jamie's forearm with the other. "Your secret's safe with me."

She believed her. Why wouldn't she? Emma had always been so—what was the word Jamie had first coined to describe her? *Conscientious.* Until she wasn't, but even then there had been extenuating circumstances that involved Jamie behaving like a clueless wonder and Tori Parker behaving like the badass girl-whisperer even Jamie could admit she had been.

"Thanks," she said, and smiled a little. "Again."

"Like, completely de nada, dude."

Jamie rolled her eyes and turned away. "You sound a little too much like Angie, *dude.*"

"OMG, that was, like, totes the point."

"Now you sound like Chloe. Are you a *Pitch Perfect* fan?" Jamie asked as they crossed the deserted hallway.

"Are you kidding?" Emma sounded almost offended. "Who isn't?"

The opening scene of the musical comedy was already underway when they returned. Maddie had saved Emma's spot on the bed, but Jamie wasn't so lucky. As she went to find a space on the floor near the balcony, she noticed Ellie give her a questioning look from where she had squeezed onto her own bed with five of the older players draped over and under each other. Jamie gave her a brief thumbs-up, which seemed to satisfy her temporary roommate.

Yeah, this team wasn't gay or anything, she thought as she intercepted the nervous glances her newbie dinner mates were sending Rebecca and Gabe Prescott, an older midfielder, currently cuddling against Ellie's headboard. Were they harmlessly flirting or were they an actual thing? Wasn't Rebecca straight? She would have to ask Angie for an update later.

Her gaze found its way back to Emma, tucked into

Maddie's side on the other bed, Jamie's pillows wedged behind them. Her pillows were going to smell like Emma tonight. Britt's words, the ones she'd carried around like a mantra since arriving in LA, came back to her again: *You can't afford any distractions if you want to make it this time.* At that moment, Emma glanced up and caught her looking. Almost hesitantly she smiled and lifted her eyebrows. *You okay?*

Jamie nodded slightly. *I'm good.* Then she looked back at the screen, letting the opening chords of "The Sign" by Ace of Base wash over her. She hated this song but she loved this movie. 2015 was going to be epic. Not only would the US women be trying for their first World Cup gold medal since 1999 but—wait for it—*Pitch Perfect 2*, the sequel, was coming out in the spring. If she didn't make the World Cup team *and* the Bechloe 'ship actually became canon in *PP2*? It would be debatable which event she would feel like celebrating more.

Ellie waited until after the team had filed back to their own rooms and they were lying in bed, lights out, to ask, "What happened with you earlier? If I you don't mind me asking."

"No, it's okay." She hesitated. Would Ellie get her kicked off the team if she thought she was a head case? "I had a minor panic attack. It's the first one I've had in years, though."

"Ah." There was no judgment in Ellie's voice, only understanding. "Is that why you don't usually drink?"

"How do you know I don't usually drink?"

"It's my job, Max. Besides, your reputation as a lightweight precedes you."

"Oh. Well, yeah. It is one of the reasons."

"And Blake? Where does she come in?"

Where *did* Emma come in? Good question, but one Jamie was far too sleepy and comfy to want to ponder for long. "We were really close friends when we were younger, and I think maybe we could be again one day."

Ellie didn't respond, but Jamie could tell by her breathing that she was still awake. Awake and chewing on something, based on the sound of her covers rustling restlessly.

Ooh, alliteration. Her favorite. Noise when she was trying

to sleep, though? Not so much, not even when the noise in question was made by a certified soccer legend.

"Stop it," she finally muttered into the quiet room.

"Stop what?"

"Thinking so loudly."

The team captain huffed out a soft breath of laughter. "Go to sleep, Jamie."

After a while she did, because Ellie was the boss and not even coaches or referees messed with her. Usually.

CHAPTER FOUR

Unlike her younger brother, Emma had always been a morning person. The same could not be said for Maddie, which was why when Emma's phone alarm went off at six in the morning on their one day off at camp, the other woman cursed colorfully and threw a pillow at her. Emma shrugged the pillow aside and continued flipping through the TV's on-screen guide until she found what she was looking for.

"I'm muting it," she promised as a rainy London stadium flickered into view. Perfect timing—halftime was nearly over. "Go back to sleep, grumpy girl."

"I hate you." Maddie rolled over and sighed loudly, grumbling as she settled back into her pillows.

"Love you too."

Emma unplugged her phone from its charger and sat back against her pillows, waiting for the game to resume. The Premier League website had updates from the weekend's matches, and she clicked through the stories, catching up on the action she had missed. After Manchester United had lost—*again!*—the previous morning, she'd stopped paying attention.

The color green in her peripheral vision caught her attention, and she glanced up as the game came back on. The score was 0-0. Apparently she hadn't missed much. She was hoping Everton would beat Arsenal, and not only because Tim

Howard, the US men's national team goalkeeper, played for the club. With Arsenal currently in first place in the EPL, Emma was pretty much always rooting against them these days, even if she had long considered them her second favorite team.

As the game continued on scoreless, she scrolled through Instagram. Most of the early morning activity originated from the East Coast or international accounts she followed, but a photo from a location a bit closer at hand caught her attention. The image showed two pairs of bare feet resting on a hotel bed, the television in the background tuned to the game she was watching. The caption confirmed this fact: "Go @TheRealTimHoward! Kick some Arsenal booty! #Everton"

Below that photo was almost the exact same shot only from a different angle. That caption read, "Sorry, @TheRealTimHoward. My heart bleeds #Arsenal red!"

Emma hesitated and then, before she could overthink it, clicked the heart icon on both images. Not even a minute later her phone buzzed.

"Are you watching?" the text read.

"Duh."

"Is Maddie asleep?"

"Duh x 2."

"Come over. Door's open."

"K."

Moving as quietly as possible, she changed out of her sleep tank and boxers into sweats and a long-sleeve T-shirt. In the bathroom, she brushed her teeth and applied a minimal amount of make-up. Then she shut off the TV, grabbed her key card, and crept out of the room.

The door was propped open as promised. Emma pushed inside in time to catch Ellie quietly whooping from her spot at the head of her bed.

"Yes! Way to go, Timmy!"

"That was a nice save," Jamie allowed.

"Hey guys," Emma said, smiling brightly at them.

Ellie gave her a quick wave, eyes glued to the game.

"Hey." Jamie smiled up at her, eyes still sleepy. She was lying on her stomach now, head near the end of the bed, a pillow tucked under her arms. She looked adorable—

Emma bit her lip as the thought rose of its own volition. Nope. No way. Jamie did not look cute with her bedhead and black-rimmed glasses. Emma had seen her wear glasses on social media. She had just never experienced it in real life. Jamie certainly did not look simultaneously hot and nerdy, which was definitely not Emma's favorite type of human being.

She dropped down next to Ellie and leaned against the headboard. "Thanks for the invite. Nowhere near as enjoyable on mute."

"Thank that one there," Ellie grunted, nodding at Jamie's back. "It was her idea."

Jamie glanced over her shoulder. "Watching the EPL on mute is so not cool. The commentary is the best part."

"Especially in a scoreless match," Emma agreed.

She was sure they'd had this same conversation more than once, back when they were teenagers and spent hours on the phone "watching" soccer matches together. Their siblings had thought they were crazy at the time, but their obsession with international soccer had paid off. Look where they were now.

The game noise increased exponentially as Arsenal, the home side, barely missed a chance. Jamie shook her head while Ellie and Emma cheered and slapped hands.

"Wait," Jamie said, sitting up and crossing her legs, the pillow on her lap. "Why are *you* cheering for Everton? They beat your boys last week."

Emma shrugged. "National team solidarity. Besides, everybody loves an underdog."

Jamie's jaw dropped. "I've literally heard you say the exact opposite!"

"People change, Jamie."

"Sure they do." Her look turned sly, or what passed for sly on someone with an appealing—er, *noticeable* tendency to wear her heart on her sleeve. "You're just pissed Man U are at the bottom of the heap."

"Ninth is hardly the bottom of the heap," Emma scoffed. "It's not like we're in danger of being relegated."

"Maybe not, but four losses in a row? When's the last time that happened?"

"1961." As Jamie stared at her, Emma added, "What? You know I like statistics."

Ellie frowned between them. "Seriously, guys, what happened to listening to the commentary?"

"Sorry," Emma and Jamie murmured in unison. They exchanged another small smile and Emma thankfully managed not to say something inane like, *Jinx, you owe me a Coke.*

The match remained scoreless until nearly the end. Arsenal finally slotted one past Tim Howard with ten minutes left, and then, in typical Premier League fashion, Everton came back almost immediately to tie it up. The game ended with one goal apiece, much to Jamie's voluble disgust. Emma and Ellie were still celebrating Arsenal's failed bid to go seven points clear at the top of the standings when the door shot open.

"Hola, Jamestown company," Angie said, settling onto the empty bed. "Why aren't you ready yet?"

Jamie scowled at her as Emma and Ellie snickered at the newest nickname. "Because the game got good right at the end. Anyway, when have you ever shown up on time in your life?"

"Dude! That offends my delicate Asian sensibilities," Angie said, holding a hand to her chest.

"Does this offend your delicate Asian sensibilities, *dude?*" Jamie asked, flipping her off.

"Always with the clever comeback."

"Shut it, Wang," Jamie said, purposely mispronouncing her surname the way most stadium announcers did.

"Whatever, Maxi Pad."

At that, Jamie launched herself onto the other bed and pinned Angie to the comforter. "Take it back," she ordered, kneeling on the smaller woman's waist and tickling her mercilessly. "Take it back, you little shit!"

The door opened again and Maddie stepped into the room, eyebrows rising as she took in the scene. "I don't know if I should be relieved or insulted that I wasn't invited."

Emma's gaze flew back to the other bed as Jamie let out a startled squeak and hit the floor. Somehow Angie had bucked her off and was now sitting up, trying to catch her breath and fix her hair at the same time. "'Sup," she said, her voice suddenly half an octave lower as she smiled up at Maddie in a manner clearly meant to be seductive.

Emma glanced back at her roommate to see her smiling almost shyly back at the younger player. Which made no sense because Maddie didn't do anything shyly, ever. *Oh, god.* Emma knew that look.

"Thanks for the game," she said suddenly, rising to her feet. "Have a great day off everyone!" And she reached for Maddie's arm, tugging her toward the door.

But Maddie, apparently, wasn't ready to leave. As Jamie picked herself off the floor and moved to the dresser, grumbling about pint-sized jackasses, Maddie lingered near the foot of the bed, eyes still on Angie. "So, what are you up to today?"

"You know, a little surfing, maybe catch some rays by the pool. You?"

"Spa day," Emma said, answering for her roommate. "Which we're going to be late for if we don't get going. Bye!"

Jamie threw her a quizzical look as she pulled Maddie from the room, but Emma didn't pause to explain. She propelled her roommate across the hall and waited until the door was completely closed behind them to demand, "What the hell was that?"

"What?" Maddie asked, folding her arms over her sizable—for a pro soccer player—chest.

"You know what."

She shrugged. "Nothing, probably."

"Seriously? Did you just say, 'Nothing, *probably*' about Angie Wang?"

"She's kind of cute, okay?" As Emma gasped, Maddie turned away, reaching for her purse on the dresser. "Please don't freak out. Honestly, it doesn't mean anything. You know what a flirt she is."

"Flirt? I heard her telling Lisa she's going through a 'slutty' stage."

Maddie turned back, frowning. "When was that?"

"At the last residency camp."

"Emma, that was six months ago."

"You still have to be careful. The last thing this team needs is relationship drama before the World Cup."

"Thanks, Captain Obvious. I was there for the Tori Parker debacle, remember? If ever there was a prophylactic against teammate romance it was you two."

Stupidly, Emma and Tori had tried to make a go of it her first year of college, but Tori's problem was that she couldn't say no to anyone who wanted to sleep with her. Or maybe she didn't want to say no. It had taken them months to be civil after Emma walked in on her making out with a random sorority girl, and their mutual antagonism—Emma for being played, Tori for being dumped—had put a strain on both of the teams they played on.

"Anyway, don't think I haven't seen you and Jamie eye-fucking," Maddie added.

A native Chicagoan whose grandparents had been Polish immigrants, Maddie was not known for her subtlety. But she was as loyal as Dani and, as a plus, significantly less prone to pseudo-gangster posturing.

"Nice try at changing the subject, but that is not even close to being a thing."

"Uh-huh. Right."

"I'm serious, Maddie," Emma said, staring her friend down. "She has a girlfriend. And even if she didn't, I wouldn't go there. Drop it, okay?"

Maddie blinked at her, the teasing glint in her eyes fading. "Okay, sorry. I didn't mean—"

"It's fine." She released a breath, willing herself to relax. Maddie clearly hadn't guessed that Jamie was The Girl from High School^{TM}, which was how Emma wanted to keep it. The past could still give Jamie panic attacks as the previous night had attested—not something Emma particularly wanted to witness (or trigger?) again. "Are you ready for breakfast?"

Maddie only nodded and followed her from the room. She was quiet as they made their way down to the hotel conference room to meet Jenny and Ryan; reserved throughout the ensuing meal and their Uber ride to Beverly Hills; untalkative even as the foursome checked into their favorite day spa in Larchmont Village. While Ryan and Jenny had signed up for hot and cold stone massages, Maddie and Emma had selected a detoxifying mud wrap followed by a hydrotherapy soak in matching copper tubs.

Emma couldn't quite believe it, but Maddie's silence persisted through most of their treatment regimen. Finally, halfway through the hydrotherapy soak, Maddie set her phone aside and looked at Emma. "Can I ask you something?"

Emma lowered her copy of *Self* magazine. "Can I stop you?"

"Jamie's the girl from high school, isn't she? The one before Tori?"

Damn it. If she hadn't over-reacted earlier, Maddie probably wouldn't have figured it out. So much for no one knowing. "I don't think I can answer that."

Maddie frowned. "You know I wouldn't tell anyone, right?"

"*I* know that, but she doesn't."

"Ah. Gotcha." She paused. "Is it strange to be around her after so long?"

"A little," she admitted. "But it's been a really long time, so it's not like either of us is the same person."

And yet, Jamie didn't seem all *that* different. From Emma's low-key social media stalking, she had thought Jamie might have grown into someone more like Angie. But while she was admittedly more put together and less naïve than her teenage self, from what Emma had seen so far Jamie was still the same intelligent, thoughtful, occasionally goofy girl Emma had fallen in l—No. Nope. Not okay.

"Did she invite you over to their room this morning?" Maddie asked.

"No, Ellie did." Technically that was true, if only because Jamie didn't have her number.

"Huh."

Emma waited, but Maddie closed her eyes and rested her head against the back of the tub. "Huh what, Mads?"

"Nothing."

She knew there was something else on Maddie's mind, but she also knew her friend couldn't be made to speak before she was ready—a trait that drove Emma crazy, but there it was. Instead of dwelling on that which she couldn't change, she tried to focus on generally relaxing in the tub. When that failed, she set her mind to one of the calming exercises the team psychologist had taken them through earlier in the week.

Not even two minutes later, Maddie's phone vibrated. Emma watched as she reached for it, careful to hold it away from the water. Soon a silly smile spread across her face, and she glanced up at Emma, eyes practically glowing.

Before the blonde could say anything, Emma shook her head. "No way. We are not meeting Angie and her little friends at the beach."

"It wouldn't be at the beach. They're heading back to the hotel after lunch to hang out by the pool."

"I'm serious, Maddie. Tell her no."

"Are you sure? You know what swimsuits mean: tattoo porn, babe."

The realization made Emma pause momentarily. She'd seen Angie's and Lisa's tats a few hundred times by now, but not Jamie's. At least, not in real life. From Tumblr, she knew that in addition to her arm bands, Jamie had a black tribal tattoo of a bird in the middle of her back between her shoulder blades. The faintly Celtic-looking design featured wings that fanned out across her shoulders along with tail feathers that trailed down her spine, their arrow-shaped tips pointing away from her heart. Seeing the elegant black lines up close in person would be...

Emma stopped the thought and reached across the narrow space between the tubs to flick Maddie's bare shoulder. Hard.

"Something better, Miss Novak," she said, channeling one of their assistant coaches from college.

The midfielder sighed noisily. "Fine. Sometimes I hate that you're such a control freak."

"Not my fault one of us has to be mature."

"But do we? I mean, we get paid good money to play a game, in case you hadn't noticed."

Emma stared at her friend until she huffed in irritation and typed out a satisfactory reply. Still staring at her phone, Maddie muttered something that Emma's mind unhelpfully translated to, *Ham sandwich.*

"What?"

"I said, you're a *clam jammer.* You know, a female cock blocker?" Maddie held up her phone. "I looked it up on Urban Dictionary."

"You're such a nerd."

"You're such a dork." She paused. "Love you, Ems."

"Love you too, Mads."

#

On the last day of residency camp, Jamie awoke to the sound of soft voices and louder cheering. Blinking groggily, she rolled over to see Emma and Ellie sitting on the other bed, pillows at their backs, to-go cups from a nearby coffee shop clutched in their hands. The television volume was set to low, but even so the crowd sounds grated against Jamie's sleep-sensitive eardrums.

She glanced at the digital clock between the beds. "For fuck's sake you guys, it's barely five."

"You can sleep when you're dead," Ellie said, not looking away from the game.

"Sorry," Emma offered. "I brought you tea, if that helps."

Jamie squinted at the cup beside the clock. Maneuvering herself reluctantly into a sitting position—she was probably the fittest she'd ever been, but after two weeks of two-a-days she was *sore*—she lifted the cup and inhaled the reviving scent of black tea. English Breakfast, her favorite.

"It helps a little. Thanks," she added, smiling at Emma.

Emma smiled back, her gaze seeming to linger on Jamie's briefly before she glanced back at the television. "You're welcome."

After a few sips of the still-hot beverage, Jamie finally focused on the game. Manchester United was playing Aston Villa on the road, trying to recover from their uncharacteristic losing streak. They were already up—the goal celebration by the away fans was what had awakened her. As she blinked at the TV, registering the score, another cry went up from the corner pocket of red-clad spectators. Danny Welbeck had scored his second goal in three minutes.

Emma leapt off the bed and danced around the room, coffee held above her head. "Yes! That's what I'm talking about. Way to go, Danny boy!"

With her arms upraised, Emma's UNC hoodie crept up and Jamie caught a glimpse of red jersey underneath. She frowned. It almost looked like Emma had on the old school United jersey Jamie had sent her for her seventeenth birthday. But no. Surely it was a completely different shirt. She wouldn't have kept it all this time, would she?

The cameras focused on the Aston Villa keeper during the replay, and Jamie couldn't resist saying, "What happened to national team solidarity? Or do you like Howard better than Guzan?"

"Priorities, James," Emma said. "No offense to Brad, of course."

"Of course."

Emma took her seat next to Ellie, and Jamie closed her eyes, drifting off again to the disgruntled roar of the home crowd and the quiet murmur of her would-be teammates' voices. She dozed on and off throughout the rest of the game, only sitting up again at the end when Emma got up to leave and paused beside her bed, hand lightly brushing her shoulder.

"See you at breakfast?" she asked, a soft smile curling her lips.

"Okay," Jamie agreed, still struggling to wake up fully.

As she watched Emma leave the room, Jamie felt Ellie's

eyes on her. But when she looked over at the national team captain, the older woman was already pushing herself off her bed with a tired groan.

"Get moving, kid. Our last day at camp is upon us."

Our last day at camp. Jamie chewed over the phrase as she got ready for breakfast. Would today be her last day ever with the national team? She hoped not. She didn't think it was—she'd played well, she knew she had. The coaching staff had given her plenty of opportunities to prove herself, and even though she was hardly objective, she had a sense that she had done better than most of the other new recruits. Still, she had yet to hear a word about January camp. Would they wait until everyone had gone home to make phone calls? They had to let people know soon, if only to get the best deal on flights.

She and Ellie were leaving their room when the door across the hall opened. Maddie waved at them, yawning. Jamie caught a flash of red behind her and looked closer. Sure enough, Emma was pulling a national team warm-up on over the jersey Jamie's father had helped her buy on eBay a decade earlier.

Downstairs, the four players went through the breakfast buffet line together.

"Nice jersey," Jamie said casually, pretending to focus on the pancakes stacked in the nearest chafing dish.

"Thanks," Emma answered, loading fresh fruit onto her plate. "An old friend gave it to me. It's always been one of my favorites."

Jamie checked the sentimental "aww" that tried to escape her lips. Emma keeping the jersey probably had more to do with her devotion to the United than it did with their friendship. Still, she didn't have to bring it to residency camp, especially not when she knew Jamie would be there. Unless… had she wanted Jamie to see her wearing it?

"Anyway," Emma added as they carried their laden plates to a nearby table, "at least my team won this weekend. That's more than you can say."

Jamie shrugged, sitting down across from Emma. "I'm not worried."

"Why, are you a fair weather fan?"

"The weather's pretty fair in North London currently, to be honest."

Emma's brow quirked as Maddie and Ellie joined them. "I guess if you consider being blown out by Man City fair…"

"Top of the league, Blake. *Numero uno, chiquita.* What are your boys again?" She touched her hand to her chin and tilted her head sideways, pretending to think. "Is it ninth or tenth?"

"Eighth after today," Emma corrected her immediately. "And we're only ten points behind your boys. Besides, there's still a lot of season left."

"Sure there is. You keep telling yourself that."

Maddie looked between them, her eyes narrowed. "You can't possibly be that interested in English football, can you? It's played by hulking brutes whose idea of tactics is wham, bam, thank you ma'am."

Of all the things Jamie had expected to come out of the midfielder's mouth, that had not been it. "You do know the English invented modern football, right?"

"Maybe, but the Brazilians perfected it. I hardly need a history lesson from you, *Rook*," Maddie added, invoking the nickname Jenny Latham had christened her with during their brief time together on the Bay Area WPS team.

"Be nice," Emma chided, frowning at Maddie. To Jamie she added, "Ignore her. She needs at least two cups of coffee in the morning before she can be trusted to interact responsibly with other human beings."

"You say that like it's a problem," Maddie commented, gripping her mug.

"Only for your future spouse—assuming anyone could be convinced to take your cranky ass in lawful matrimony."

Jamie couldn't help but notice Emma's word choice—*spouse*, not husband; and any*one*, instead of any *guy*. Was Maddie not as straight as she seemed? Then again, nothing surprised Jamie anymore when it came to female athletes and sexuality. The whole jock-dyke stereotype existed for a reason, although she would rather kiss a frat boy than admit as much publicly.

Maddie shook her head. "Totally uncalled for, Blake."

"Uncalled for how?" Ellie asked. "Like you'd ever want to get married."

Maddie shrugged. "I haven't ruled out the institution completely. It's the whole rug rat thing I could probably do without."

"Really? I can't wait to have babies with Jodie. That's one of the first things on my post-soccer bucket list."

"Aren't all those nieces and nephews enough for you?" Maddie commented. "I know mine are."

"It's the opposite for me—the Ellison baby arms race only makes me want my own kids more. How many are there in your family now?"

As they compared their large extended families, Jamie felt a foot nudge hers under the table. She glanced up to find Emma watching her.

"You know," she said, leaning closer, "I still can't believe you're such a hardcore *Pitch Perfect* fan."

At dinner the night before, Jamie had somehow found herself confessing that the movie soundtrack was one of the most played albums on her phone. She had also admitted that it was possible her Kindle library contained fan fiction featuring Bechloe, the *PP* fandom's most popular femslash couple. Emma had asked what femslash was, a question that had caused more than one person at their table to nearly spew out their food.

"What?" Jamie said now. "I told you, some fan fiction is better than traditional novels."

"Not that. A capella just doesn't seem like it would be your thing."

"My sister was in a group at Stanford, and I dated their pitch my sophomore year. She was my first serious girlfriend—and for the record, she was nothing like Aubrey."

As Emma's brow shot up, it occurred to Jamie that she had just admitted she hadn't had a serious girlfriend until halfway through college. Yeah, that wasn't something she had ever intended to tell Emma.

"Plus," she added quickly, trying to change the subject without actually changing it, "all the queer subtext in *Pitch Perfect* is totally up my alley."

"Queer subtext?" Emma repeated. "Now this I have to hear."

"Aw, man, don't get her started on subtextual references," Angie groaned, sliding in to the empty seat on Jamie's other side.

"Just because you can't wrap your little brain around queer theory doesn't mean everyone else is as intellectually challenged," Jamie said.

Angie flipped her off and dug into her pancakes, her little moans of contentment making Jamie lean away and Maddie drift closer. *Ew.*

"You were totally a Gender Studies major, weren't you?" Emma asked.

"Minor," Jamie corrected her. "And it was Queer Studies, not Gender."

"Ah." Emma nodded thoughtfully.

Ellie's eyebrows rose. "Blake, you're not thinking of trying to recruit Max to the nerd squad, are you?"

"Why not? She went to Stanford."

"Easy, guys. I have to make the team first," Jamie said, and then wished she hadn't as silence fell around the table. "Sorry. Didn't mean to bring up the elephant in the room."

Emma smiled reassuringly. "We've all been there, so at least it's a familiar elephant. You know, like Dumbo or Horton."

As Angie's face lit up, Jamie elbowed her. "Don't get any nickname ideas, Wang."

"Me? She's the one who compared you to Dumbo."

"Maybe you need to work on your listening comprehension skills," Emma said. "Or is the rumor true?"

Angie eyed her warily. "What rumor?"

"I heard athletes at Florida can earn a degree without ever attending a single class," Emma said.

"Good one, Blake." Ellie nodded approvingly and held up her hand for Emma to high-five.

"Shut it, both of you," Angie grumbled, and launched a piece of muffin at Emma.

Maddie reached out at the last second and snagged the pastry out of the air, smiling suggestively as she lifted her fingers to her mouth and sucked the morsel from them in a way that had everyone but Angie looking away as quickly as humanly possible. The subsequent next-level flirting was hard to ignore, though, and eventually they made sarcastic comments and left the pair on their own. Not that Maddie or Angie seemed to mind, Jamie noticed as she, Ellie, and Emma left the conference room to get ready for practice.

By the end of the final training session that afternoon, Jamie was pretty sure that if she heard one more person mention her on-field chemistry with Emma, she was going to smack them. Already in the past week a coach and several players had commented on the way they supported each other and worked together to create offensive chances. Now, on the last day of camp, Steph had decided to pry into their history.

"You weren't on the same team in the WPS, were you?" she asked, following Jamie off the field.

"No. But we did play together a little in high school," Jamie said, hoping that no one would press her to define *a little*. They had worked out together the two times they'd visited each other her sophomore year, and that was about it.

"I thought you were from San Francisco," Gabe said, stripping off her shin guards as they reached the sideline. A Colorado native, Gabe was a year older than Jamie, so they had played together sporadically in their youth pool days.

"I am."

"If Emma's from Seattle, then how did you guys play together?"

"ODP and the youth pool." It wasn't a complete lie, but close enough that she could feel the heat climbing up her neck. She ducked, pretending to struggle with her double-knotted laces. God, she was such a bad liar. She'd always required elaborate planning to sell even the smallest fib.

Just then, Ellie dropped down on the bench between them and draped her arm across Gabe's shoulders. "Hola, *muchacha*. Want to grab dinner tonight? Bring your brother along, if you want. I haven't seen him in forever."

"That sounds great. He's been asking about you," Gabe said, smiling sideways at the older woman.

Rumor had it that Gabe and Ellie had dated for a while when the younger woman first joined the team. They seemed like good friends now, though, so Jamie wasn't sure if the gossip was true or not. Either way, she took advantage of the distraction to slip away. Another Emma-shaped bullet, dodged.

She was almost to the parking lot when she heard her name being called. Melanie Beckett, the defensive coach, was jogging toward her.

"Hey, Max. Feel like walking back to the hotel with me?" Mel asked.

"Sure," Jamie said, even though she'd been looking forward to hitching a ride back on one of the team vans and taking a nap before dinner. Her flight for London left the following day but didn't arrive until early Tuesday morning, which meant she had a long couple of days ahead.

"How has your camp been?" Mel asked as they fell into step together.

Jamie was conscious of her soccer sandals making slapping sounds against the bottoms of her feet. "Really incredible. The older players have been so gracious, and the competition has been amazing."

"The WSL isn't quite as deep, is it?"

"No," she admitted. "Arsenal's close, though. Practice pushes me sometimes more than league matches. Champions League helps too. Can't beat playing against the best clubs in the world."

The assistant, who was in her early forties and sported the crow's feet typical of middle-aged soccer coaches, nodded. "Have you given any thought to coming back home to play?"

"You mean in the NWSL?"

Mel gave her a look that said she knew she was stalling. "Yes, in the NWSL."

"Well, yeah, of course. It would be great to play near my family and friends again. They obviously don't get to see me play very often."

"The reason I ask is that Craig, Bill, and I think you've made a real case for yourself at camp the past couple of weeks. Now we need to hear from you: How committed are you to playing for this program?"

Jamie stopped on the broken sidewalk and turned to face the national team coach, no longer aware of the traffic rushing by on the wide Southern California street. "I am one hundred percent committed."

Mel smiled a little and nodded. "That's what I thought." She started walking again. "In that case, can I give you some advice?"

"Absolutely."

"Move back to the States," she said bluntly. "Sign with the NWSL and play with and against these women week in and week out. Be available for every training camp and friendly. That's your best avenue to making this squad. Staying overseas makes it that much harder—to be seen by our staff, to bond with the existing pool of players, to develop chemistry with them on and off the field. This camp was a good start, but if you want to be part of this program, you'll have a much better shot if you come home."

"Do you really think I have a chance at landing a permanent spot?" Jamie asked.

She nodded. "I do. As you know, there are a number of players on the bubble for the World Cup. It's always possible for player contracts to be terminated due to retirement or for other reasons."

Jamie nodded, her hand tightening on the strap of her duffel. This wasn't the first time she'd thought about leaving the WSL. It was just the first time that a national team coach had asked her to do so. Why was her gut twisting and her chest tightening? Shouldn't moving one step closer to achieving a life-long dream feel more like joy personified than the beginning of a panic attack?

Mel rested her hand on Jamie's shoulder as they approached the hotel. "I'd like to tell you that you have some time to think about all of this, but you don't. We're hoping you want to come back in January, and ideally you would have the pro league situation worked out by then. As this is the middle of the NWSL's Discovery Period, it's the perfect time to send out feelers. From what I've heard you shouldn't have any trouble finding a team to snap you up. Assuming you can get out of your WSL contract, that is."

Jamie nodded. "I have a year left, but I think I could work something out with the GM. To clarify, you're *not* offering me a roster spot, correct?"

"Correct. What we're offering you is a chance to play yourself onto this team. What you do with the opportunity is up to you. I for one am rooting for you. Your chemistry with some of the starters is unreal for someone who's been abroad or injured as much as you have. That's another thing, Maxwell. We need you to stay healthy."

"That's the plan." As the coach's words sank in, Jamie's heart pounded so hard she could hear it in her ears. She forced a smile. "Thanks, Coach. I appreciate the opportunity."

"Don't thank me yet. The only guarantee I can offer right now is that you have a lot of work ahead of you."

Back in her room a little while later, Jamie stripped and stepped into the shower where she leaned against the tile surround, letting the warm spray soothe her. From conversations with Ellie, she knew there were twenty-four athletes on contract with US Soccer at any given time, and that eighteen of those spots were guaranteed a tier one (premium) salary. In almost all cases, the contract specified that players be allocated to the NWSL. If she came home to play, would she really be in line for one of the coveted roster spots?

It wasn't like she hadn't already known that leaving the WSL for the NWSL would probably be better for her career. But with her contract situation and the timing of her injury the previous fall, she hadn't seriously considered making the move. England—and English football—had been good to her. After her ACL injury, when rumors of the demise of the WPS were flying fast and furious, joining the nascent FA WSL had made sense. But three years made a huge difference. Now what made sense—according to the federation—was coming home.

With this realization came another: Clare was not going to be happy about this latest bit of news. Jamie thought about calling her, but not only was it the middle of the night in London (yet again), it would be immeasurably better to discuss the implications when she got home. The person she wanted to talk to most was Britt, but that was tricky too because Britt lived with Clare's best friend. Even if it hadn't been the middle of the night, Jamie couldn't risk Allie somehow finding out about her conversation with the national team coach before Clare did.

Ellie was packing when Jamie emerged from the bathroom clad only in her bathrobe.

"Hey, champ," the striker said. "Did you leave me any hot water?"

This was an ongoing joke. Trained by the fact that the shower in their flat operated on 50p coins, Jamie took the shortest showers in the history of showerdom, according to Ellie. Meanwhile, the thirty-something captain relied on regular ice baths and long, hot showers to revive her aching joints and muscles.

"Yep," Jamie said, and lay back on her bed, arms under her head.

Ellie eyed her. "You okay?"

"I don't know."

"End of camp letdown or something else?"

"Something else."

"Can I help?" Ellie asked, dropping onto the edge of her own bed.

"Maybe." Sitting up against her pillows, Jamie briefly summarized her chat with Mel.

"Wow," Ellie said when she'd finished. "No wonder you

look shell-shocked. Can't say I'm surprised, though. Do you think you can get out of your contract?"

"I have a clause to let me out for national team service, but I would need something in writing from the federation."

"Carrie Fitzsimmons should have a letter on file from last year when Gabe wanted out of her Tyreso contract."

"Yeah, but Gabe was already officially on the roster."

Ellie waved her hand. "Fitzie owes me. Besides, if all goes well, you'll be on the roster soon, too."

Jamie sat up straighter, staring at her as the beginnings of excitement began to pool in her stomach. Rachel Ellison seemed to want her on the team. *Rachel Ellison* wanted her as a teammate. "Do you really think so?"

"Absolutely, if I have anything to say about it. And if you keep your nose clean and stay healthy. Think you can do that?"

Her grin felt almost painfully wide as she launched herself at Ellie. "Of course! Thank you, man! Seriously."

Ellie patted her back. "Easy, killer. I don't think either of our girlfriends would be happy with you springing an all-but-naked hug on me."

Jamie backed off quickly, tugging on the hem of her robe. "Oops. Sorry."

"For the record, you're not my type."

"As if," Jamie said, laughing.

On one level, she was still semi-amazed by her ability to joke around with the national team captain. But after the last two weeks and especially after her earlier conversation with Mel, she was starting to feel more and more like she belonged on this team. It helped that she had come in with a ready-made group of friends she had known since college. Or in Angie's and Emma's case, since high school.

Then again, *were* she and Emma friends? After the past couple of weeks, it kind of seemed like they might be. For a moment she pictured Clare's reaction to hearing that she and Emma had managed to get past their differences. She wasn't sure which would upset her girlfriend more—learning that she was thinking of moving to the US or hearing that she was becoming friends with Emma again.

Ellie went to take a shower while Jamie got dressed. Angie had said something about going out to dinner in Manhattan Beach with a group that included Steph Miller, among others. Jamie got along with most people, but with a long flight and a huge decision in her immediate future, she wasn't in the mood to deal with undercurrents of tension that she had never quite learned the knack of detecting. Besides, she was genuinely exhausted. A quiet couple of hours on her own to process everything sounded amazing.

Ellie understood her need for space, but Angie, predictably, didn't see it the same way. When Jamie told her she didn't think she was up for a night out, Angie turned away from the mirror where she'd been checking her hair. "Wait, what?"

"I'd rather get packed and go to sleep early tonight," Jamie said from where she sat cross-legged on her bed, folding her laundry.

"But this is our last chance to hang out!"

"Only for a few weeks." She smiled a little as she folded her boy shorts into squares.

"A few...?" Angie jumped onto the bed, disturbing the neat piles. "Dude! Does that mean you're coming to January camp?"

Jamie nodded, grinning. "Mel asked me after practice."

"This is so freaking cool!" Angie punched her in the shoulder. "I knew you were going to make it eventually. I told you, didn't I?"

"I don't have a roster spot yet," Jamie reminded her.

"No, but you totally will. Now you *have* to come out with us. We have some celebrating to do."

"Next time, okay? I have a super long day tomorrow." And almost as long of a night after that, she thought, picturing Clare again.

It took a while, but Jamie finally convinced Angie to accept her refusal—"But only because Imma see you next month"— and leave the room peacefully. Once she was gone, Jamie called in an order of Thai food and finished packing, her mind returning to her girlfriend. She honestly wasn't sure what would happen when she got back to the UK. She couldn't see Clare giving up her job, family, and friends to follow Jamie to America. At the same time, Jamie wasn't about to give up her national team dream to stay in London, either. It wasn't an option, no matter how committed she was to their relationship.

Was that why Clare was avoiding her? Because she already knew how this—how *they*—ended? The thought settled inside her chest, rounding her shoulders and taking the edge off her excitement at being invited back for January camp. Her college coach had a framed quote from Kareem Abdul-Jabbar on his desk that she thought of now: "The good and the great are only separated by their willingness to sacrifice." But was sacrificing her present for an ambiguous future her key to greatness, or would she end up not only disappointed but forever wondering *what if* about Clare?

She heard the assistant coach's voice again: "The only guarantee I can offer is that you have a lot of work ahead of you." And, "Move back to the States. That's your best shot at making this squad."

If moving home could help her chances at playing in the World Cup even a little, there wasn't much of a choice, was there?

The front desk staff called to let her know her food had arrived just as she managed to get her duffle closed around all her new practice gear. Wallet and room key tucked into the pocket of her hoodie—another team issue—she headed downstairs to pay the delivery person. She was almost back to her room when she heard a sound in the vending machine alcove. A sense of déjà vu shadowed her as she slowed and looked in. Sure enough, Emma was standing there in her matching US Soccer hoodie, scooping cubes into an ice bucket.

"It's not out of ice, is it?" Jamie asked. Then she wondered if Emma even remembered their first meeting in a hotel not all that far from this one.

Emma glanced over her shoulder, brow clearing when she saw Jamie. "Not this time, fortunately."

She did remember. It shouldn't have been important, but it was.

"I didn't think I'd run into you tonight," Emma added.

"Me, either. Why aren't you out with those guys?"

She shrugged and tossed the scoop back into the machine. "Wasn't in the mood. What about you?"

"Same."

Emma moved toward the hallway, her voice light. "You're embarrassed about yesterday, aren't you?"

Jamie gazed down into hazel eyes that were simultaneously so familiar and so foreign. "Yesterday?"

"Hello, does six to three ring a bell?"

She rolled her eyes. "Whatever. Arsenal is still on top. You're the one who's embarrassed. Ninth place, Blake."

"*Eighth*," Emma corrected, flashing the dimple Jamie had always loved.

The exchange felt so easy, and as they stepped into the corridor side by side, a handful of memories came back to Jamie—the warmth of Emma's body leaning into hers on the bench by the ocean the night they met, the contact somehow comforting when it probably (definitely) should have felt intrusive; the rasp of her voice over the phone as they lay in bed night after night talking about school and families and the unknowable future; the press of Emma's arms around her waist as Jamie sobbed into her shoulder on a San Francisco beach; the curve of her smile as they gazed at each other across the table in a cozy restaurant that used to be someone's house in Seattle. She had told Ellie that Emma was one of her closest friends when they were younger. Was it really possible she might be again someday?

Another indefinite outcome that depended strongly, Jamie had a feeling, on whether or not she made the national team.

As they paced the length of the hotel hallway, she considered inviting Emma back to her room to share the Thai food currently filling the space between them with its rich scent. Pictured telling her what Mel had said, asking what she thought the way, once upon a time, Jamie had looked to her for advice on every single aspect of her life. But then she remembered how long it had been since Emma had been her first and last text of the day. She remembered the women and men who had come and gone for each of them in the intervening years. She remembered how Clare had asked her the night before she left London, her voice thin and doubtful in their chilly bedroom, "You don't still have feelings for her, do you?"

She almost wished she'd never told Clare that the Emma from high school was the same Emma that graced Nike ads and fitness magazines. If she hadn't, Clare might not have gone AWOL the past few weeks and Jamie might not now be dreading her return home. But the previous summer after her first practice with the Olympic squad, when she couldn't stop chattering on about Angie and Britt and Ellie and Emma, Clare had half-smiled at her and said, "Emma Blakeley? She isn't the Emma you were in love with, is she?"

For a moment, Jamie had only stared at her. Then she'd nodded, and Clare had swallowed hard, her smile falling away altogether.

"Surely not?" she'd asked, voice lacking conviction.

"No, she is."

They hadn't talked about it again. Emma was out recovering from her burst appendix when Jamie got called up a few months later, and she hadn't even been sure that Clare remembered until the other night when her voice rose between them in the dark. Jamie didn't need to ask which "her" she meant. If only she'd learned the art of the compassionate white lie somewhere along the way because then she might not have felt compelled to answer, "She was my first love. I'll always have *some* feelings for her." Before she had even finished she could feel Clare pulling away, in mind if not in body.

Since then, she hadn't been able to do or say anything to narrow the gap that had appeared between them. But at least she could try to keep the gap from widening further.

When they reached their rooms, Jamie nodded toward her door. "I should get back."

"Me too. What time is your flight?"

"Nine thirty."

"Same here. Looks like we're on the same flight again."

Jamie nodded but didn't say anything. It wasn't like they would be sitting together on the plane. Emma was a first class kind of flyer, and she, well, wasn't.

Emma turned away, waving over her shoulder as she disappeared inside her room. "Good night, Jamie. Sweet dreams."

"Sweet dreams to you too," she replied, the phrase automatically bubbling up as if it had been lying dormant all these years waiting for another chance to escape in Emma's presence. Then she ducked into her own room, trying not to notice the slight ache in her chest as she closed the door. It wouldn't always be like this. Then again, she wasn't sure if that was a good or a bad thing.

A few hours later, she was bored with cable TV and running out of willpower, knowing that Emma was presumably alone across the hall. She checked the time—after ten, which meant there was a chance that Clare would be up and getting ready for the school day. She hit the call button and waited, half-expecting to get voicemail again. But for the first time in days, her girlfriend picked up.

"Hello," Clare said, her voice echoing strangely.

"Hey. Where are you?"

"In the loo."

"Want to call me back?"

"Hang on." Jamie waited as the toilet flushed and the water ran. Then Clare came back, her voice cautious. "How did the last day go?"

"Excellent, actually." Jamie paused. Now that they were talking, she might at least give her a heads-up. "I have some good news. They want me here for another training camp in January."

Clare released a deep, whistling breath into the phone. "Does that mean you're not coming back?"

"Of course not. It's like a month away, Clare."

"Don't be upset. I thought that was what you were saying."

Dating a Brit could be infuriating at times. They rarely came right out with what was on their minds and tended to get all squirrelly if anyone even remotely raised their voice. Kind of like Emma's family. What was it she had once said? Something about descending from Scandinavian Minnesotans who, when confronted with a situation that required even a modicum of emotional intelligence, were basically, *Oh, hell no?*

"Anyway, like I said, it's good news," Jamie repeated, picking at a loose thread on the hotel comforter.

"Right." Clare sounded tired. She was a morning person more by necessity than choice. "Well done."

"What about you? It feels like we've barely talked. How's school?"

Clare perked up a little as she chatted about the students she loved and the administrators who occasionally made her life miserable, her stories marked by the dry humor that always reminded Jamie she lived with an Englishwoman. When she described her recent visit home to Cornwall to see her nine-month-old niece, her voice became downright gushy. They discussed the London weather, LA's winter sunshine, and what January camp would mean for their holiday plans. Speaking of which, Jamie realized, she needed to get the exact dates from the team manager and get working on her travel arrangements.

Everything she had to do before the next residency camp suddenly crashed through her mind on a veritable tidal wave of panic. As conversation lagged, she said, "It's getting late here. I'll see you on Tuesday, all right?"

"Are you sure you don't want me to meet you at the airport?" Clare asked, though it was clear from her tone that she was offering more out of obligation than a genuine wish to make the long trek to Heathrow.

"I'm sure. It's your last week of school before break. I'll take the train and see you at home, okay?"

Clare agreed and they hung up a little while later, their goodbyes as stilted as the rest of the conversation. Jamie lay back on her bed, regretting the impulse that had led her to call.

It was hard to believe that only a month before, when another call-up had seemed increasingly unlikely, they had been excitedly planning an American Thanksgiving with their closest friends. What had happened to them? Except she knew. Her national team dream had happened.

When she opened her email, she discovered a new message from the team manager with the subject message "January camp: Jan. 8-15, 2014." Seeing the dates in print suddenly brought home the reality of the invitation, and all at once she couldn't wait to share the good news with Britt and her family. She may not have a roster spot yet, but she'd made the cut for the next camp. Now she just had to keep moving forward, getting better a little bit at a time.

Well, that wasn't all she had to do. Could she honestly sort out her contract issues in three and a half weeks? Figure out things with Clare? Find an NWSL team to take her on? There were nine teams in the league, each of which had two or three national team players. What if she ended up in Kansas City or Houston? After growing up in the Bay Area and living in the UK the last few years, she wasn't sure she'd survive the humidity—or the conservative mindset—of either city. At least she'd know where she would be sooner rather than later. NWSL pre-season started in March, the same as the WSL, so negotiations couldn't drag on too long.

Assuming anyone even wanted her aging, injury-plagued ass on their team. Mel had said she didn't think she'd have a problem, but what if she was wrong?

As another wave of panic washed over her she closed her eyes, inhaling a deep breath. Slowly she released the breath, murmuring the words of the meditation she'd been using for the last ten years: "May I be filled with inner kindness; may I be well; may I be peaceful and at ease; may I be happy." It took longer than usual, but when she finally felt more like herself, she switched to her closing mantra, tattooed in Sanskrit around her right bicep: *Om lokah samastah sukhino bhavantu.* This translated to, "May all beings everywhere be happy and free." She pictured Clare the first time through before focusing on her own image, envisioning herself the way she always did when she meditated—as a young girl still trying to find her way in a world whose darkness she hadn't known to expect.

Everything would work out one way or another. It always did. All she could do was try her best to be happy and, just as importantly, to not make the people around her miserable.

She released a final breath and reached for her laptop.

CHAPTER FIVE

In the back of the van on the way to the airport, Emma watched Jamie and Ellie peer down at Ellie's phone, speaking in low voices she couldn't quite hear. They had been thick as thieves at breakfast, too. What were they planning?

As they approached LAX, Ellie finally held up her hand and Jamie slapped it, and they both smiled widely.

"You are so in," Ellie said, her voice carrying through the van.

Jamie shushed her and glanced around, her eyes meeting Emma's. But Emma looked away—not quickly, as if she'd been caught, but casually and a little off to the side so that it would seem like she hadn't been watching them at all. Camp had gone better than she could have expected, but eavesdropping on Jamie's private conversations probably wasn't the best way to get back in her good graces. Not that she was trying to get back in... No, she definitely was, and for reasons that were probably better left unexplored.

At the airport, they checked their bags and made it through security in plenty of time for their flights. They reached Ellie's gate first, and Emma watched as the veteran striker tugged Jamie into a tight hug, pounding her on the back. Jamie pulled back, laughing, and punched her on the arm. God, they were like little kids. They approached the game—and most other things—with an almost palpable sense of joy, like there was nothing they would rather be doing. Emma loved soccer, but after more than half a decade as a professional, her feelings for the game were nowhere near as pure as they had once been.

Like any other job, being on the national team brought with it a host of difficult situations and personalities that required care to negotiate. In her case, these complications were exacerbated by contractual obligations that specified what she was allowed to say, do, wear. Even, at times, how she could conduct her personal life. And privacy? She'd given up on *that* long ago. The limits playing soccer at the top level placed on her daily life sometimes made her question whether or not it was worth it. Usually the answer came back as a resounding yes. When it stopped doing so, that was when she would have to think seriously about retiring—assuming the federation didn't try to make that decision for her, too.

Jamie stood aside so that Emma and Ellie could say goodbye, but Emma caught her eye. "I'll catch up in a minute."

"Oh." Jamie looked between the two national team players for a moment before nodding and backing away. "Okay. See you, Ellie."

"Later, Max," the striker said.

Emma waited until Jamie was out of earshot to launch her attack. "Spill, Ellison, or do I have to remind you that you owe me for the crappy Secret Santa gift?"

"I don't know what you're talking about," Ellie said, dropping onto a nearby chair and pressing her boarding pass against her chronically jumpy knee.

Emma slid onto the seat next to her. "Come on. What were you and Jamie in cahoots about?"

Ellie regarded her, brown eyes slightly narrowed. "Why do you want to know?"

"Because we were friends once a long time ago and I'm hoping we can be again."

At that, Ellie snorted. "Call me crazy, but I get the feeling the two of you have some heavier history than the average pair of old friends."

"Our history isn't anyone else's business," Emma said, and then chastised herself as she realized she'd invoked "our" in reference to Jamie. There was no *our* or *us*. There was only *they* and *them*: Jamie and her girlfriend.

"That's where you're wrong. Until we win the World Cup, everything that happens on this team is my business."

Emma folded her arms and tried to stare down her longtime teammate. Her practiced bitch face came in handy, as it reduced most people to stuttering messes.

Rachel Ellison wasn't most people, though. "Emma, I'm serious. Jamie's trying to make the roster, and you know as well as I do how the federation feels about inter-squad relationships."

"What?" Emma squeezed her arms tighter against her sides. "I don't—Jesus, Ellie. What are you even…?"

"I love you, Blake, but you don't have the best track record when it comes to team drama."

Was she never going to live down what had happened with Tori Parker? It had been two full World Cup cycles since they'd dated, but given they'd drawn not one but two national pool feeder teams into their soap opera…

"What about you and Gabe? You're hardly one to speak," she pointed out.

"Maybe not, but someone needs to. Don't pretend you were in our room only for the Premier League."

Emma sighed, watching the stream of people in business suits and Disneyland T-shirts streaming through the concourse. "Honestly, there's nothing to worry about. The last thing I want to do is jeopardize her chances at making the team. Besides, she's in a relationship. I would never get involved in something like that."

Her father had cheated on her mother a couple of years before his heart attack, and though her mother had eventually forgiven him, Emma was still estranged from her dad when he died. Now, a decade later, she had considerably more empathy for her father. Turned out relationships—and people—were a tad more complicated than she'd believed at seventeen.

"I know you wouldn't. Neither would she. Jamie's a good kid." Ellie slipped an arm around her shoulders. "I have faith in both of you."

Emma leaned her head against the taller woman's shoulder. "Are you going to tell me what you guys were plotting?"

"Not a chance. It's her news to share or not."

"It has something to do with January camp, though, right?"

Maddie had returned from dinner the night before bursting to tell her about Jamie's invitation to the next residency camp. Emma had almost gone across the hall to offer congratulations, but then she'd realized Jamie could have told her when they ran into each other earlier. For whatever reason, she had chosen to keep the news to herself.

"How do you know she got invited back?" Ellie asked.

"You *are* aware of who I've been rooming with, aren't you?"

"Seeing as I helped make the assignments... But like I said, it's not my news. Ask her, Emma. I have a feeling she'd be psyched to talk to you about it."

"Fi-ine." Emma rose and reached for her carry-on. "Tell Jodie hi, and I'll see you next month, okay? Oh, and happy holidays."

"You too. Be good," Ellie called after her.

Emma waved without looking back. When she reached their gate, she found Jamie slouched in a chair near the window, eyes closed, headphones over her ears. Ellie's words came back to her. *Ask her.* Before she could overthink, she slid into the seat next to Jamie.

As their legs brushed, Jamie's eyes flew open and she sat up quickly. "What the hell, Emma?" she said, pulling off her headphones.

Whoops. Sometimes she forgot how twitchy Jamie could be when it came to personal space. "I'm sorry." She started to reach for her arm and then thought better of it. "I didn't mean to spook you."

"You didn't spook me." Jamie's voice still sounded tough. Then she softened. "Well, maybe a little. I didn't realize it was you, that's all."

This close, Emma could see the freckles that dusted Jamie's nose and cheekbones. Apparently those hadn't faded with time. "Sorry again."

"It's fine. Did you and Ellie have your chat?"

"Uh-huh," she said noncommittally. "You two definitely seem to have bonded. Guess the roommate situation worked out."

"She's been great about trying to help me figure things out."

"What sorts of things?" she asked, trying to appear only mildly interested.

"Team stuff mostly." Jamie hesitated. "I got invited back for January."

"That's fantastic! See? I told you it was only a matter of time until you made it."

"I haven't made it yet, but Melanie says I have a shot. The thing is, she and the other coaches think I'll have an even better shot if I play in the NWSL this season."

The NWSL? That meant leaving the UK. No wonder Jamie had reached out to Ellie. The decision the coaches were asking her to make would impact not only her career with the national team but every single aspect of her life, all without any guarantee she would even make the permanent roster.

"That's major," she said, immediately regretting the understatement. Before she could reel it back in, though, the loudspeaker crackled with an invitation for first class passengers and those traveling with small children to board.

How was it already time to go home? It seemed like she'd only just arrived at LAX to find that Jamie had been on her flight all along.

They exchanged a look, and Jamie gestured awkwardly at the nearby gate. "I guess that's you."

What could she say? That she would rather forego her usual flight protocol to keep talking with Jamie until the last possible moment? Because that was the truth. Now that the time had nearly come to say goodbye, she was beginning to realize how used she'd gotten to seeing Jamie every day. How much she was going to miss—nope. Not going there.

"See you on there?" she asked, reaching for her bag.

"Right." Jamie offered her a small smile. "See you, Emma."

She didn't look back as she joined the small line near the desk and followed a harried-looking woman with two small children onto the plane. Once on board, she stowed her carry-on and arranged herself in the window seat. Only instead of shutting out the rest of the world as she normally did, she kept an eye on the cabin door, watching people file past as the plane loaded. A pair of teenaged girls stared at her, elbowing each other, and she knew she'd been made. But she continued to face forward until, at last, a familiar head ducked through the door.

Jamie smiled at the effeminate male flight attendant who was greeting passengers, and Emma was unsurprised when he smiled back in that knowing way gay men and lesbians reserve for each other. She had witnessed similar exchanges many times, though she'd only rarely been the recipient of such a look. Jamie turned down the aisle, smile fading as she appeared to search the handful of rows between them. When her gaze fell on Emma, she nodded and Emma returned the gesture.

"Hey," Jamie said as she passed, smiling a little as if to say, *Here we are again.*

"Hey," Emma echoed. But she didn't smile as Jamie barely hesitated before walking past. That was it. They wouldn't see each other again until next month. They had compared itineraries at breakfast, and she knew that Jamie would have to run once they got to Seattle. Her brief layover would only allow time for a brief goodbye. Which, probably, was just as well given that Emma's thoughts were threatening to cross into the non-friendship territory.

She blamed the Premier League. If she hadn't started watching EPL games in Ellie and Jamie's room, she might never have begun to find herself remembering how Jamie's voice sounded first thing in the morning, all rough and sweet. Or the way she kicked her covers off before she got out of bed, as if their constrictive presence was the most irritating thing in the world. Or the way she squeaked like a puppy when she stretched, eyes shut adorably against the sunlight pouring into the room.

Emma settled back into her seat, pulling on her headphones and closing her eyes against the images flooding her mind. Maybe this break away from the team would be good. Maybe she would come back in January miraculously cured of inappropriate thoughts, the kind she couldn't afford to have toward someone who might well end up as her teammate for the World Cup. Sure. Because the next three and a half weeks were likely to undo what ten years apparently hadn't. She turned her music up, wishing she was already home by herself instead of preparing to spend two plus hours on an airplane trying to ignore the fact that Jamie Maxwell was sitting somewhere behind her just out of reach.

Take-off went without incident due no doubt to her habitual appeal to any and all supernatural and/or deistic powers that might be in listening range. She didn't hate flying. She hated the take-off and landing parts, that was all.

Once they were in the air, she finally started to relax. The crew had just begun the beverage service when she felt a tap on her shoulder and looked up into the smiling gaze of the flaming flight attendant. He waited for her to pause her music and pull off her headphones before asking, "Is that your friend sitting in economy?" And he pointed toward the rear compartment where the curtain had been pulled back for the beverage cart to pass.

Emma undid her seatbelt and half-rose, glancing over her seat-back to see Jamie seated on the aisle a dozen rows back. Jamie looked up, caught them eying her, and gave a quick if somewhat surprised wave. Emma waved back and nodded up at the flight attendant as she took her seat again. *Tom*, his nametag read.

"Would you like her to sit with you?" he asked. "I noticed you were together at the gate, and since the seat next to you is open…"

"Oh," Emma said, thinking quickly. The smart thing would be to say no. But Jamie obviously knew they were talking about her, and the flight only lasted a couple of hours. What could go wrong?

Tom's knowing smile had started to slip by the time she nodded up at him and said, "That would be nice."

"Are you sure?" he asked. "You don't have to…"

"No, I'd love the company," she said quickly. Perhaps a bit too quickly because his former sly smirk returned in full force.

"I thought so," he said, and winked at her as he sashayed away.

Oh, god, even strangers could see it. The only thing she could hope for was that Jamie would be as clueless as she always had been. But what were the odds, really?

She craned her head around, peering through the gap in the seats as Tom stopped beside Jamie's seat. The two talked briefly and Jamie frowned. Was she going to refuse? That possibility had not occurred to Emma. And even though that outcome would be, you know, *for the best* or whatever, she couldn't help the way her stomach clenched at the thought. But then Jamie was nodding and Tom was pulling her carry-on from the overhead bin and escorting her up to Emma's row. This would be fine. Or maybe it wouldn't, but either way it would be over in a couple of hours.

Dani was never going to believe the upgrade to business class wasn't her idea. Or Maddie, for that matter. Then again, they didn't actually *need* to know, did they?

"Hey." Jamie stopped at her row, brow slightly furrowed. "Are you okay with this? Or would you rather be alone?"

"No," she said. "I think it's a great idea."

Tom helped Jamie stow her bag before she slid into the empty aisle seat beside Emma. Then he gave them another smile and left them to sit silently for a moment, both of them staring straight ahead.

"I've never flown first class before," Jamie confessed after a minute, her fingers on the seat belt that she had fastened as soon as she was seated. "I guess every once in a while there are perks for being queer, huh?"

Emma gnawed on a loose cuticle. "I guess so."

She knew she was probably giving off crazy chick vibes—
yes, stay and *no, don't*—but she didn't have the energy to fight
both her fear—wariness, really—of flying and her dread of
doing or saying the wrong thing with Jamie. She had resigned
herself to the idea of a Jamie-less flight only to now have her
so damned close all of a sudden, their thighs almost touching
despite the roomy seats. It was as if anytime they came near
each other, some sort of magnetic tracking system activated
and Emma found herself drifting even closer, unaware she had
done so until far too late.

Beside her, Jamie rubbed the tops of her legs nervously.
"Are you sure this is okay? Honestly, I don't mind going back
to my seat."

"No, don't. I want you to stay." Some part of her brain
decided that touching Jamie's arm would be appropriate. Her
hand lingered, again without her conscious consent, and then
she pulled it away quickly as she registered the heat rising from
her seatmate's body.

"Oh. Well, okay, then." Jamie lowered her head, toying with
the buckle on the seatbelt again.

Emma clasped her hands in her lap. Great—only two hours
to kill before they were on the ground. Not that anyone was
going to be killed on this airplane that was currently defying
gravity by flying miles and miles above the earth's surface.

"As long as I'm here," Jamie said, tucking one leg under her
so that she could turn sideways, "can I ask you something?"

She hoped her abrupt intake of breath wasn't as obvious as
it felt. "Um, sure?"

"I was kind of hoping to get your perspective on the whole
NWSL thing."

Soccer. She wanted to talk about soccer. *Whew.* "Okay.
What do you want to know?"

"I guess I'm wondering if you think being back in the States
would make that much of a difference."

"You mean for your chances at making the roster?" When
Jamie nodded, Emma hesitated, wondering if she could be
even remotely objective about the possibility of Jamie moving

back. "Did Melanie say it would?"

She nodded again.

"Then yeah, I think you should listen to her. The coaching staff have scouts at most league games. Not only are they keeping an eye on existing players but they're also watching out for new talent. That's how Steph made the pool—she wasn't on anyone's radar until the WPS launched."

"That's what Ellie said, too."

Good to know. Apparently she could do objective.

"Besides," she added, "as a major investor in the NWSL, the federation can call us up at any point and the teams have to comply. That makes players here more attractive than those playing for European clubs that might have a vested interest in preventing an American from joining the national team."

Jamie's eyes narrowed. "I hadn't thought of that."

"Do you think Arsenal will let you out of your contract?"

"I'm not sure. There's still a lot to work out."

And yet, she was obviously leaning toward coming home. She was a West Coast native, and the NWSL liked to keep players close to their hometowns or where they went to college, which for Jamie was one and the same. Was there any chance she could end up in Seattle? Emma rejected the idea almost immediately. Portland was closer to the Bay Area. Wait—*Portland*.

"That's what you and Ellie were talking about on the van, isn't it? Where you would play?"

Jamie shrugged. "Ellie thinks the Thorns might be interested in me."

Who wouldn't be interested in her? Fortunately, Emma didn't say that out loud. There would be no recovering from that particular double entendre.

Tom paused beside them, cocktail napkins in hand. "Hello again, ladies. Can I bring you a drink?"

Alcohol was definitely a bad idea. And yet her brain must have decided otherwise because Emma's mouth opened and she heard what was undoubtedly her own voice enquire, "Do you have mimosas?"

"We do," he said, clearly approving the choice. "Back in a jiffy!"

As soon as he was out of earshot, Jamie nudged her. "Mimosas?"

"It's your first time flying business class," she reasoned. "Besides, you had an amazing residency camp and got yourself invited back. We definitely have to drink to that."

Jamie smiled, shaking her head. "It is pretty amazing, isn't it?"

"It's very amazing. I'm really happy for you. I know how hard you've worked to get back into the pool. You deserve this, Jamie."

"Thanks, Em," she said softly. "That means a lot."

Tom returned, interrupting the moment to place glass champagne flutes on their seat-back trays with an exaggerated wink.

"To kicking ass and making January camp," Emma said, lifting her glass.

"And to hanging out with old friends," Jamie added.

They clinked the flutes together and sipped, eyes on each other. As they drank, it occurred to Emma that simply sitting together on a plane was probably not the antithesis of being good. But sharing sentimental toasts and long gazes over champagne? Bad. Definitely bad.

"So Portland, huh?" she asked, trying to reel their interaction back to the professional side. They were colleagues, after all. Or they might be one day soon. "That would be a big move."

Jamie nodded. "Huge."

Something in her tone alerted Emma. "Do you not want to come back to the States?"

"That's not it. I mean, I love England. The WSL has given me the pro career I always wanted. But for a shot at a World Cup?" She shook her head. "It should be a no brainer."

"Somehow it isn't, though."

"No. I don't know. We're midway through Champions League and I still have a year left on my contract. I don't want to bail on my friends, you know?"

"They're professionals, too. They'll understand this is business, not personal. Won't they be happy for you?"

"Maybe. But I'm not so sure my girlfriend will," she admitted, looking down at the champagne flute.

Emma stared at her. "You mean you haven't told her yet?"

Jamie flinched as if she had suddenly realized she had told someone who might or might not qualify as an ex about a potentially life-altering choice before telling her current girlfriend. "I thought about it last night, but I didn't want to tell her over the phone."

"Right. No, of course not."

Emma released a slow breath. She had nothing to add to this conversational offshoot that wouldn't be self-serving, so she glanced out the window and peered through the clouds to the flashes of green and brown earth below. They should be nearing the Bay Area soon, not that they would fly directly over. But somewhere down there were Jamie's parents. Did they know she was thinking of coming home, or were Ellie and Emma really the only people who had any idea of the enormity of the decision she was facing?

They finished their drinks in silence, both shaking their heads when Tom offered to top off their glasses. The bubbly was making Emma's thoughts skitter about even worse than Jamie's proximity. She pulled an energy bar from her bag, holding up an extra questioningly.

"Protein boost?"

"Hell yeah," Jamie said, tearing open the wrapper. "Thanks. After all the two-a-days, I feel like I'm permanently hungry."

"I know, it's like college pre-season all over again. Only without the heat and humidity, thank god."

The conversation shifted to safer topics then—college experiences, favorite foods to binge on in season, and finally, Jamie's recent cooking lessons. Her face flushed either from the alcohol or enthusiasm or possibly both, she described the community kitchen where she'd volunteered her time and, in turn, learned the art of English cookery.

"I don't know," Emma interjected. "I've had British food. I'm not sure the word *art* applies."

Jamie slapped her arm lightly, actually giggling. Must be the champagne, Emma decided, feeling her own semi-permanent smile creasing her face. She tried to focus as Jamie returned to the topic of community kitchens, essentially restaurants that serve anyone and everyone regardless of ability to pay.

"The one I go to has a motto: 'A hand up, not a hand out.' The volunteers range from professional chefs who donate a little bit of food and time each month, to pensioners who are in there every day."

"It sounds wonderful," Emma said. "I wonder if Seattle has any."

"Probably. I know Berkeley does."

"Aw, I love Berkeley. Are your parents still in the same house?"

Jamie nodded. "I think they're afraid to downsize in case I need to move back in." She sighed. "Sometimes I think I should have gotten a job in my major."

"Which was?" Emma asked, pretending she hadn't been stalking Jamie online since college.

"Design."

"With a minor in Queer Studies."

"Right."

"I didn't know you were an artist," Emma said truthfully.

"I'm not. Not like my mom, anyway. Illustrator is my medium of choice. I'm more of a techie like my dad."

Emma rested her hand on her chin. "I don't think I would have predicted a tech career for you."

Jamie's head tilted. "No? What would you have predicted?"

"I don't know. Maybe sports psychology."

"I thought about it but decided I could always go that route later in life." She paused. "I've never told anyone that."

Emma tried not to smile too widely at that, but it was a losing battle—like most contests that involved Jamie. Instead she changed the subject. "Want to guess what I majored in?"

"Non-profit management with a minor in public relations."

As Emma's eyebrows rose, Jamie grinned. "You're an American hero. There's not much about you that isn't available at the click of a button."

"And?" Emma asked. "Is that what you would have predicted for me?"

"Honestly?" Jamie leaned closer, the magnetic force apparently influencing her, too. "It is."

"I'm not sure if that's a good thing or not."

"Good, definitely."

Emma hummed a little. "Oh yeah? Why is that?"

"Because you're exactly who you seem to be on the surface." Jamie's voice was soft again, and Emma leaned even closer to hear her. "You're a good person, Emma. You always have been."

"How do you know all of this—" her wave was meant to encompass business class, the national team, her various endorsements—"hasn't changed me?"

"I just do."

Her eyes dropped to Jamie's lips, and she found herself wondering if they would taste more like chocolate energy bar or mimosa. Then she blinked, realizing where her champagne-befuddled brain had taken her. *Crap. Crap, crap, crap.*

"Where's the nearest restroom?" Jamie asked, looking away as she unbuckled her seatbelt. "I need to pee."

"Up front. I have to go, too." As Jamie glanced back at her, eyes wide, Emma added quickly, "I didn't mean—I meant after you."

"Oh. Okay. I'll be right back." And she practically jogged away.

While she was gone, Tom stopped by to retrieve their glasses and smile conspiratorially at Emma. "You two are adorable together."

She thought about telling him they weren't *together* together, but instead she allowed herself a giddy moment to imagine what it would be like.

"Thanks," she said, and then shook her head at the both of them as he winked again and moved away.

Once she was on her own, though, the champagne haze started to fade and guilt began to intrude. She made herself picture Clare, Jamie's actual girlfriend, a cute, blonde Brit who worked with kids. She was a real person who didn't deserve to have Emma flirting with her girlfriend. Fortunately, flirting was as far as things could go, seeing as they were on an airplane surrounded by other people. If you ignored the fact that Jamie had apparently thought she was suggesting they join the mile-high club, there wasn't much chance they could get into trouble.

She checked the on-board flight computer. One hour down, one and a half to go before Jamie would slip back out of her life leaving a hole the shape and heft of which Emma remembered only too well.

"Your turn," Jamie said as she paused beside their row, not quite looking at her.

Emma tried to keep her distance as she slipped out, but the plane bounced a little and she stumbled. Jamie steadied her, of course, and Emma wondered if she imagined the sigh the other woman released in the vicinity of her pony tail.

"Sorry," she offered, extricating herself from Jamie's grasp.

"It's fine."

It really wasn't, and Emma was beginning to think they both knew it.

In the restroom, she closed the accordion door and flipped the latch, blinking in the sudden weak light. She leaned closer to the mirror, noting the redness in her cheeks and the bags beneath her eyes that concealer couldn't entirely hide. She hadn't slept well the night before, not that she ever did in a hotel bed. That was one thing she wouldn't miss when her career ended.

She peed for what felt like forever and then washed her hands and patted her face with a damp towel, careful not to smudge her make-up. It was possible that she'd taken more pains with her appearance this morning than she normally would on a travel day, knowing she would be spending part of it with Jamie.

"You, my friend, are screwed," she told her reflection. "But whatever you do, don't try to kiss her this time. Got it?"

She wanted to assure herself there was no need to worry on that count, but she had a feeling she'd be lying.

Afterward, she couldn't remember exactly what they talked about the rest of the flight. Families, definitely. Music. The WSL. The NWSL. Europe versus America, the West Coast versus the East Coast. They talked tactics, first touch, set pieces, and it was just as easy and comfortable as it had been back when Emma was a senior in high school and she would lie on her bed for hours at a time, watching the Western Washington sky change colors while she and Jamie discussed the Premier League, high school life, the Bush presidency, the war in Iraq. At one point toward the end of the flight, they tried to come up with the starting eleven for the US in the 1999 World Cup final match, the game they had both attended as young girls on the cusp of making soccer more than a hobby. They came up with ten names, but with their phones set to airplane mode, they couldn't for the life of them figure out who they were missing.

And then the plane was slowing, and they were looking out the window at the summit of Mt. Rainier jutting up out of the dark gray clouds cloaking the earth from view. The plane circled north all the way to the Canadian border before turning back and beginning the final approach to Sea-Tac. Emma closed her eyes as the plane descended through the clouds, shaking and shuddering with the chop. This was why she hated flying in winter. Give her a sunny summer day and she was happy to fly. Or if not happy, at least not petrified.

Eyes still closed, she didn't move as she felt a warm hand clasp hers. Almost instantly some of the fear left her system as if driven out by Jamie's touch. This was bad, she thought again, but she didn't move her hand away. It didn't mean anything. Jamie was only being nice; any of her other teammates would have done the exact same thing. Well, maybe not Phoebe. But plenty of others.

Jamie let her hand go as soon as they were on the ground,

and neither of them said anything as the plane taxied to the gate. Emma remembered their arrival at LAX two weeks earlier. If someone had told her they would ride home together, that Jamie would hold her hand through the turbulence, she wouldn't have believed it. But here they were, almost friends again after the distance of the intervening years. Or something like friends. Something.

Once the plane reached the gate, they filed off quickly, heading for the row of monitors so that Jamie could double-check her flight information.

"Great," she said, frowning up at the nearest screen. "It's running late."

Emma tried to ignore the sudden rush of hope. "How late?"

"An hour and a half."

"That's not too bad, is it?" Emma said, more pleased than she had any right to be. "Gives us time to grab lunch. Sea-Tac has the best food court."

Jamie chewed her lip, and Emma held her breath. It was only lunch in the company of hundreds of other travelers.

As she stood at the edge of the terminal waiting for Jamie to decide whether or not to say goodbye, she heard a familiar sound behind them: the squeal of a teenaged girl(s). Sure enough, the pair who had recognized her earlier on the plane had stopped and were clutching each other's arms, a woman Emma guessed to be the taller one's mother standing in the background watching.

"Ohmigod," the smaller one said, her braces flashing against her dark skin. "It is you, isn't it? Emma Blakeley?"

Sighing inwardly, she put on her professional smile and nodded at the girls. After all, they couldn't know they were interrupting a more-intimate-than-it-really-should-be moment. "Hi there. Are you soccer players, too?"

She could feel Jamie's eyes on her as she chatted with the star-struck girls, going through the usual questions—"What are your names? What club do you play for? Which school do you attend? Did you know I played at Shorecrest when I was your age?" They did, which marked them as serious fans. When they asked for a picture, Emma consented graciously.

Jamie took the phone they handed over and snapped a couple of shots. "Make sure they turned out," she said.

The blonde girl actually gasped out loud as Jamie unleashed the full force of her smile, and it was all Emma could do not to crack up even though she was hardly one to throw stones.

The dark-haired one rolled her eyes. "I think she'd like a photo with you too. Would that be okay?"

"Me?" Jamie's brow rose.

Emma reached for the phone. "Allow me."

The blonde girl turned red as soon as Jamie slipped her arm around her shoulders, and Emma thought she probably knew the feeling.

"Smile," she said, and took several pictures before handing the phone back.

"Thank you so much," the dark-haired girl gushed, eyes wide as she grinned up at Emma. "You are seriously like my biggest hero. I can't wait to see you play in the next World Cup. We're going to get tickets since it's in Canada. It's going to be like the best thing ever!"

"I hope we'll see you there," Emma said. "In the meantime, come out and support the Reign, okay? That's the best thing you can do to help grow the women's game here at home."

"We will," the blonde one said, seeming to recover at last. "We have season tickets."

"That's great. Make sure you come say hi at one of our season ticket holder events, okay?"

The girls nodded and thanked them again, and then they hurried off with the mother in tow, eyes glued to their phones.

"I hope you're prepared to have your photo up on Instagram and Twitter," Emma said. "Three, two, one..." Right on time, her phone dinged, alerting her to the mention.

"No way," Jamie said, laughing. "You planned that."

She held up her hands. "Not even, I swear. Come on, let me treat you to lunch. It's the least I can do before you get on a plane for another what, ten hours?"

"Nine and a half," Jamie corrected. "Okay, fine. On one

condition."

"What's that?"

"No more booze."

"Deal." She thought about offering to shake on it but recognized the impulse in time as her subconscious mind's ploy to get her to hold hands with Jamie again.

"You know, we were that age when we met," Jamie said as they headed to the food court.

"We were," Emma agreed.

"I don't think I realized what a star you've become. I knew, but you weren't around last year when I got called up, so I guess I haven't seen it in person."

"Okay." She wasn't sure what else to say.

"Those girls looked at you like you were Mia freaking Hamm." Jamie smiled sideways at her. "Turns out you're a badass, Blake."

"Don't sound so surprised. Besides, the tall one looked at you the same way."

"Nuh-uh."

"Yuh-huh. You'll see it when you look at the photos."

She almost told her to get used to it, but she stopped herself. Even though it was almost inconceivable, in reality she knew Jamie might not make the national team. Not because she wasn't one of the best players in the country but because of all the other intangibles that went into the selection process. At least she had a champion in Ellie. And another in Emma, even if she didn't know it.

They decided on Ivar's because it was hard to go wrong with fish and chips in Seattle. The food court was crowded, but they found a table at the edge of the seating area and settled in, carry-ons at their feet. Emma was still chewing her first bite when a college-aged guy approached.

"Really?" she muttered, and pasted on a smile.

"Hi," the guy said, smiling confidently at them. "My buddies and I have a bet going. I said you play for the US women's national soccer team but they say you don't. So who's right?"

"You are," Emma said, and took another bite.

"I knew it! You're Emma Blakeley, aren't you?"

"Right again."

"Could I get a photo with you by any chance?"

She finished chewing and swallowed. "Sure. Feel free to grab us when we're done eating, okay? And thanks for your support. It really means a lot." She smiled to take the sting out of the rejection.

"Oh. Right." The guy backed away. "Have a nice lunch."

"You, too." Emma felt Jamie's eyes on her and waited until the fan was out of hearing range. "What?"

"I didn't say anything."

"I don't like it when people interrupt my meal, especially when it's an entitled frat boy, okay?"

Jamie laughed. "Hangry much?"

She threw a french fry at her. "Just wait. You'll see how annoying some fans can be. But you can't tell them where to go even if you're PMSing or you have a cold or you woke up in a bad mood. Once you're on this team, you can't afford to have an off day in public."

"Poor you. It must be so hard to have people adore you."

"You'll see," Emma repeated.

Aware of the group of college boys watching them, she rushed through her lunch even though she knew it was her last chance to spend time with Jamie for the foreseeable future. Jamie still had two pieces of fish left when Emma balled up her napkin and placed it on her compostable plate. LAX didn't have compost bins. She'd missed Seattle. Living here again was seriously ruining her for any other region of the country. Next month the first friendly would be in Dallas, and she was already bracing herself. Texas was so different from her native Northwest that she felt like she'd entered the twilight zone whenever she set foot outside the hotel there.

"What's your hurry?" Jamie grumbled as Emma stood up to take her trash to the bins.

"You have a flight to catch, in case you've forgotten."

"As if I could forget." Jamie stuffed her last piece of fish in her mouth and followed Emma from the eating area.

They had almost escaped when Emma heard it: "Emma! Hold on a sec!"

Reluctantly she slowed. "Do I have anything in my teeth?" she asked Jamie, smiling perfunctorily.

"No, you're good," she said, and swallowed her last bite.

"Could I get that photo now?" the guy from earlier asked, a bit less cocky this time, his buddies trailing him.

And that was how she and Jamie ended up posing with a college boy on either side of them. Jamie slipped her arm around Emma, and Emma let her even though she knew better. She let her because she wanted it to be Jamie's arm against her shoulders, not the random boy's. She let her because she knew they were going to say goodbye soon and she wanted a photo of the two of them together, not separated by a stranger they would never see again. She let Jamie tug her close and she snuggled into Jamie's side because it was the first picture of them posing together in ten years, and she wanted to look happy. Because she was happy on this, the day they started to maybe, possibly, actually become friends again.

After the photo, they shook hands with the guys and walked across the airport together, headed to Jamie's gate.

"What about your luggage?" Jamie had asked earlier, and Emma had told her it probably wouldn't go anyplace without her. Anyway, she packed anything truly important in her carry-on, after learning the hard way on a flight home from Russia that suitcases sometimes escaped, especially when they contained expensive shoes and designer purses.

When her phone lit up, she bit her lip. Probably it wasn't a coincidence. Quickly she swiped her screen and saw she had a new text from Ellie. Without reading it, she shoved her phone back in the front pocket of her zip-up hoodie. She wasn't about to let the other woman ruin her final few minutes with Jamie. They were being good, even if the anecdotal evidence on Twitter and Instagram suggested otherwise.

At the gate, they checked the flight's status. Nothing had changed; Jamie still had forty minutes before take-off.

"Could you watch my bag for a second?" she asked, nodding toward a nearby restroom.

"Go for it."

While she was gone, Emma checked social media mentions. Sure enough, the girls from their flight had tagged her—and Jamie, too. Apparently they really were serious fans. The college boys, on the other hand, had only tagged Emma. She peered at her phone screen, noting the way she and Jamie were angled slightly toward each other, how Jamie's dark hair contrasted with her honey blonde ponytail, the way her hand cupped Emma's shoulder while Emma's fingers rested on Jamie's hip. There was a sense of easy intimacy about them, a level of comfort not typically seen in new teammates. Or maybe that was her wishful thinking.

"That one turned out," Jamie said, leaning over her shoulder.

Emma had been so caught up in her phone she hadn't noticed Jamie's return. She almost turned the screen off, but then decided that would be even worse than getting caught staring dreamily at their photo.

"Yeah," she agreed, "except for the fact those guys apparently go to USC."

Jamie made a face. "Boo. But why don't you like USC?"

"Because Dani went to UCLA. Gotta be loyal to the bestie."

"Are you guys still friends?"

"Yeah. She moved back to Seattle a little after I did. We live a few blocks apart now, even closer than we did in high school."

"That's awesome. Tell her I said hello." She paused. "If that's not weird."

"It's not." She glanced at the time on her phone. Time to say goodbye. *Aargh.* "So anyway," she said, looking everywhere but at Jamie. "It was really nice having you as my seat buddy."

"Yeah?"

She nodded and took a breath, finally meeting her gaze. "I'm glad the soccer gods decided to bring us back together, Jamie. I missed you."

"I missed you too, Emma," Jamie admitted. Then she looked away, curling the edges of her boarding pass together. "I guess I should probably call my girlfriend and let her know about the delay. But thanks for lunch and for walking me to my gate."

"You're welcome." She started to reach toward her, then stopped and glanced around to see if anyone might be watching them. But so what if they were? There was no reason she and Jamie couldn't be friends. She stepped toward her, releasing a long breath as Jamie's arms closed around her. She'd nearly forgotten—Jamie's hugs had always made her feel like someone had injected liquid peace into her veins. She pressed her face against Jamie's neck, inhaling her scent that, thanks to their celebratory cocktail, was tinged with the distinctive fragrance of oranges. Jamie's arms tightened briefly and then released, and Emma remembered what she'd said: She needed to call her girlfriend.

Right.

"Have a good flight," she said, forcing herself to pull away.

"Thanks. Have fun in Minnesota. Tell your mom and brother I said hi."

"I will. Tell your family I said the same."

They stood watching each other, the peace of their hug somehow lingering between them. Then the loudspeaker crackled with an update, and Emma jumped a little.

"That's my cue," she said, even though she had no idea what the airline representative was saying.

"Wait." Jamie held out her hand. "Give me your phone."

Emma paused before handing it over, remembering the last time they'd done this at the edge of a road in Del Mar a few steps from the hotel where her father and Jamie's mother had been waiting. She watched as Jamie typed in her number and sent herself a text. It didn't mean anything. It couldn't. *Be good*, Ellie had said. And she wanted to, she did, but this was Jamie, the first girl she'd ever loved.

"There," Jamie said, handing her phone back. "Now we can talk before camp. I mean, if you want to."

"I want to." She backed away before she could say anything more incriminating. "You have to let me know what you end up deciding, okay?"

"I will."

She waved a little, still backing up. "See you, James."

"Later, Em." She smiled at last, eyes crinkling at the corners as she watched Emma go.

And then Emma was turning and walking away, careful not to look back. It was harder than she'd expected, this taking leave of Jamie. At least she hadn't kissed her. Even with the added complication of a champagne buzz, she had managed to keep things friendly and professional. Mostly. That was a good sign. She could do this. She could be Jamie's friend. Assuming Jamie would let her.

As she neared baggage claim, her text alert sounded. Her heart leapt insanely, but when she checked the screen, it was Ellie's name flashing at her. Clearly she was not about to be ignored. Emma clicked on the message thread.

Ellison, one minute ago: "Please tell me you're not still with her."

Ellison, twenty minutes ago: "#Blakewell? WTF Emma? You were supposed to be good!"

Emma stopped walking so suddenly that the elderly couple behind her almost tripped over her carry-on. "Sorry," she murmured, stepping out of the stream of harried travelers to huddle against a wall, staring at her phone.

Blakeley. Maxwell. *Blakewell*. A handful of hours on their own in public and they had already been 'shipped. Christ. This was the kind of thing that sometimes made her want to hide out in her apartment and only come out for practices and games.

Another text from Ellie popped up, this one with a link to a Tumblr account Emma recognized as belonging to a college student from New York who claimed to be her biggest fan. The girl certainly worked fast. She had already posted screen captures of the Twitter photos of Emma and Jamie posing separately with the girls from their flight and together with the group of guys from the food court. But it was the accompanying text that made Emma wish she was on her couch curled up under a blanket bingeing on *Orange is the New Black*: "It would appear that after spending two weeks at camp together, Blake traveled home to Seattle accompanied by gorgeous (and gay as fuck) Jamie Maxwell. Looks like a new 'ship in the building to me... #ahem #USWNT #Emma Blakeley #Jamie Maxwell #Blakewell #you heard it here first."

Emma glanced around, but no one seemed to be paying her any attention. Sometimes it was hard to remember that being stalked online didn't equate to being stalked in real life. If you were lucky.

Her phone rang as she rode the escalator to the ground floor. She peeked at the screen, debated a moment, and finally hit answer.

"Her flight was delayed," she said in lieu of a greeting. "I was only being nice!"

Ellie exhaled in annoyance. "Jesus, Blake. You know better than to pose *next* to her. The fan always goes between you. What were you thinking?"

"I'm sorry, okay? It won't happen again."

"I know they say there's no such thing as bad PR, but the last thing she needs right now is to be splashed all over the Interwebs with you."

"Ellie, come on. You know how the fans are. If it's anyone's fault, it's the federation's for putting us on the same flight. Look at us. We were always going to be 'shipped. Am I right?"

The striker laughed reluctantly. "You're so full of shit, Blake."

Emma smiled, glad she'd distracted Ellie from the warpath even momentarily. "Which reminds me—why should the Thorns get her instead of some other equally deserving team in the Pacific Northwest?"

"Jamie and I need time to work on our chemistry, which obviously is not an issue for the two of you."

"You're hilarious."

"Not trying to be funny. Did you at least warn her about

the impending WOSO meltdown?"

Crap. Stupid champagne. "Um, no?"

"Fine, I'll take care of it. But you two are on official radio silence until next camp. I'm serious, Emma. I don't want to see you liking her Christmas photos or her training videos or anything. Got it?"

"But Elle..."

"But nothing. You need to calm this shit down, and the only way to do that is to refrain from feeding the fan thirst."

She scowled at her phone before returning it to her ear. "Fine. Why are you going all mama bear over her, anyway? Is it because you think she can help you break the scoring record, or is there more to it?"

"The thought might have crossed my mind. But mostly she reminds me of myself at her age. There was no one like me on the team back then. They were all a bunch of straight-looking girls with ponytails (no offense), and everyone kept telling me to tone down who I was, to grow out my hair and stay in the closet. It was a rough period in my life, and she shouldn't have to deal with that. No one should."

Emma slowed near the baggage claim desk. "I didn't know it was like that for you."

"What am I going to do, bad-mouth the people who gave me the chance at having the life I always wanted? Besides, they meant well. In their own way, they were trying to protect me. Who's to say they were wrong? Things have changed a lot in the last few years."

"Thanks to you." She knew it hadn't been easy on Ellie. She claimed she stayed off social media for years because she was technophobic, but Emma was pretty sure her avoidance had more to do with being bullied online—and in person—for most of her career. For that matter, most of her life.

Ellie dodged the compliment as she always did. "More like because of gay marriage."

"Still, thanks for looking out for her."

"I'm not doing it for you, Blake."

Emma rubbed her eyes, suddenly tired. "I know. Hey, I

gotta go find my bag. I'll talk to you soon, okay? Keep me posted on the contract negotiations."

"I will. Remember, radio silence."

"Aye-aye, captain."

She turned off her phone, resisting the urge to check her and Jamie's Twitter mentions. She already knew what she would find. Fuck, it was starting again. This was why she couldn't have nice things. At least she was home for a few days before she had to fly out for the holidays. Time to hunker down and hide out.

As she stepped up to the baggage claim counter, she remembered her warning to Jamie about fan harassment: *You'll see.* Apparently she was going to see sooner than either of them had anticipated.

CHAPTER SIX

Jamie shouldered her duffel and tugged her carry-on behind her as she reached the front of the taxi line. The London morning was rainy and dark, and she'd been planning to take the train home from Heathrow. But with US Soccer footing the bill, she figured she might as well get home sooner—not to mention drier.

"Do you give receipts?" she asked the driver who got out to help with her bags, and he nodded, his teeth a white flash against dark skin.

"Yes, receipt," he said in a heavy accent as he placed her duffel in the trunk.

Jamie thanked him and slid into the back seat. Another immigrant from North Africa, probably, trying to make a better life for his family in the West. London was filled with people from other places. That was one of the things she'd always loved about living in the British capital. Hang out at Leicester Square for half an hour and you were likely to hear conversations in half a dozen languages.

"Where to go?" the driver asked, turning down the sound on his radio.

"Holloway, please."

As the cab pulled away from the curb, Jamie relaxed in the warm interior. Finally, after what felt like the longest day ever, she was almost home. Returning to economy for the second leg of her trip had been less than pleasant, but at least she'd had a window seat near the front of the plane. She couldn't sleep, her mind too busy trying to process everything—January camp; Clare's reticence; Ellie's offer to talk to the Portland GM on her behalf; and Emma. She probably should have said no when the flight attendant offered to upgrade her to first class, but it was FIRST CLASS, and anyway, she hadn't wanted to hurt Emma's feelings. The same excuse didn't hold for why she had accepted the mimosa. Really, though, Emma's seemingly genuine excitement over her invitation to January camp had been difficult to resist. A voice in the back of her head had noted darkly that the flight might be her one and only chance to celebrate—lord knew Clare probably wouldn't be toasting to her successful residency camp anytime soon.

Slouched down in the back of the cab, Jamie pulled out her phone. She'd set it to airplane mode while waiting in line to board, but as soon as they landed, she'd switched it back and watched in stunned silence as it blew up with notifications. The people seated in her row, a twenty-something French couple who lived in South London and had previously attended a women's football match—more rare to find in Europe than America—had laughed at the cascade of sounds that spewed from her phone before she'd quickly set it to silent.

"What is that about?" Eva, the woman, had asked, squeezing Jamie's arm for easily the hundredth time since they'd exchanged names.

"My friend and I agreed to a photo with some football fans at the airport," she said, turning the screen so the other two could see the picture of her with Emma and the USC guys.

"*That* is your friend?" Michel said.

"Put in your tongue, sweetie," Eva said. "*Mais oui*, she is very attractive. And popular, it would seem."

Jamie shook her head. "I didn't think anyone would recognize me."

"You and she are a pair of angels together." Eva glanced at her husband. "*N'est-ce pas*, Michel?"

He nodded. "*Exactement*."

When they asked her for her number while waiting in line at customs, she politely declined, using the excuse that the team owned her phone and she wasn't allowed to distribute the number widely. Stereotypes existed for a reason, and this particular French couple was a bit too handsy for her comfort. Talkative, too. Thanks to them, she hadn't had a chance to text Clare yet to let her know she'd arrived.

As the cab headed toward the city, Jamie opened her message app and stared at the list of new texts. One from Clare, two from Ellie, one from Angie, one from Britt—and one from Emma. She closed her eyes briefly, remembering how she'd practically stolen Emma's phone from her right before they said goodbye. That must have been the mimosa's doing, as it had been when she'd held Emma's hand on the plane and hugged her for the photo. She wasn't sure which was worse— holding her hand during turbulence or tugging her close to keep her out of her fans' clutches. *Christ*. What would Clare think when she saw the photo? But Jamie knew what she would think. What was worse, she wasn't entirely sure her girlfriend would be wrong, not after the last twenty-four hours.

The question came back to her again: *You don't still have feelings for her, do you?* If Clare asked her that same question now… Damn it. Why did Emma have to be so great? Why couldn't she be hostile or rude or even simply neutral? Instead, every time Jamie had turned around the last couple of weeks it had seemed like Emma was there to help her negotiate team personalities, to tease her about her borderline obsession with *Pitch Perfect*, to get her through a panic attack. Although, to be fair, Jamie wouldn't have had the panic attack if it weren't for Emma. But it wasn't even like she had treated Jamie any differently from the rest of the team. Fame and success in the world of international soccer hadn't turned her hard or self-involved, and as far as Jamie could tell, she was still driven to take care of the people around her. Whether or not she had anyone to take care of *her* was… not a question Jamie was in any position to worry about.

Sighing, she tried to push Emma from her mind as she read Clare's generic *safe flight, text me when you land* message and sent a quick reply to let her know she was on the ground. Britt and Angie were next, both razzing her for her sudden popularity on social media. Britt also asked her to get in touch once she got home so they could "talk," which sounded uncharacteristically serious. Ellie's most recent text promised good news to relate after a phone call to the Thorns' GM. Jamie started to fist pump, but her surge of excitement quickly faded as she scrolled up to Ellie's earlier text: "Have a good flight and don't worry too much about the #Blakewell stuff. We can talk about how to handle it when you're back on the ground."

#*Blakewell*? What the hell was—oh, *shit*. Clare was going to kill her.

The voicemail icon blinked and she checked the log. Ellie had left her two voicemails, one at the beginning of the flight and one in the middle. Portland was eight hours behind London, which meant it was roughly two in the morning there. She left the voicemails untouched for now; it wasn't like she could call Ellie back anytime soon. Besides, there were more pressing things to attend to.

She switched back to her texts again, staring at Emma's name in bold. What had Emma texted her about? Had she seen the Blakewell thing and wanted to kill Jamie too? Not that it was solely her fault, even if she had been the one to initiate the pose for the frat boy's photo. Emma could have pulled away, but instead she'd burrowed closer, her hand on Jamie's hip equally possessive.

Her finger hovered over Emma's name. Somehow texting felt like more of a transgression than letting Emma pay for lunch or drinking airplane cocktails together. Well, maybe not more than drinking together. She stared at the bolded message another few seconds before giving in to temptation. The message was long, and she could hear Emma's voice in her head, low and slightly raspy: "Hey there. You're probably over Greenland right about now. Hope some polar bears grace you with a sighting this time around. By the time you get this, you'll either have seen the Tumblr craziness—"

Tumblr. Of course.

"—or you're about to, so I wanted to say I'm sorry that me dragging you to lunch resulted in a fan meltdown. When I told you earlier that you would see what I meant about some of our fans, I didn't mean today. Ellie feels very strongly that you and I should not be in touch on social media until this dies down, but you can text or call me anytime. Congratulations again on everything. I'm really happy for you, Jamie. And good luck with the Thorns. They would be lucky to have you. Hope to talk to you soon!"

Jamie reread the message a few times, smiling reluctantly at the image of polar bears and, well, pretty much the whole thing. It was so *Emma*: equal parts teasing, caring, and ego-boosting. Which was why she should close her message app and think of something else—for example, how she was going to explain to her girlfriend why the Internet had decided to freak out over an imaginary relationship between her and the first girl she'd ever kissed.

The forty-five minute cab ride seemed to fly past as she scrolled through Twitter, Instagram, Tumblr, and L Chat. The women's soccer fandom had indeed blown up while she was over the North Atlantic. Someone had cropped the college guys out of the photo, leaving her with her arm around Emma's shoulders and Emma leaning into her side, their heads and bodies angled toward each other. No wonder the lesbian fans of the national team—and they were legion—were flipping their lids. They looked about as coupley as you could get without actually being a couple. She only hoped Clare was currently too busy at school to have noticed.

Her eyelids felt exceptionally heavy as she paid the driver and headed into the flat. An hour of sleep would make everything more tolerable, she decided, kicking off her shoes and dragging her bags to the bedroom. One hour, and then she would face the chaos.

Groaning, she collapsed onto her side of the bed. Her last traitorous thought before sleep took her was that it was nearly morning in Seattle.

"You *are* here," someone said in a relieved tone. Then it changed. "For fuck's sake, Jamie, I thought you were lying dead in a ditch somewhere. Why haven't you answered your phone?"

Jamie blinked slowly, trying to remember why Ellie would be yelling at her. Was she late for training? Then she realized she wasn't at the hotel and the angry person had an English accent. Quickly she rolled over and sat up, rubbing her eyes. Clare was the voice, not Ellie, because she was at home, not in LA. Everything came flooding back—Emma, the first class flight, the flirty Frenchies, L Chat, Tumblr, Blakewell. *Fuck.*

"Why aren't you at school?" she asked.

"Because it's half past four. I've been trying to reach you all afternoon." She was standing in the door to their bedroom, arms folded across her chest, perennial smile noticeably absent. She looked pissed.

Still, maybe she'd only been worried when Jamie hadn't responded.

"Sorry, my phone must have died," she offered, smiling tentatively up at her girlfriend. "Come give me a hug? I missed you."

"Obviously." The word dripped with sarcasm.

Jamie's smile faded. "Do you want to tell me why you're so angry?"

"Are you fucking serious right now?" Clare turned on her wool-socked feet and padded away down the hallway.

As the sound receded, Jamie slipped out of bed. So much for her usually reliable internal clock. She should have plugged in her phone and set an alarm, though to be honest, she felt significantly better rested after the day of napping. At some point that she didn't remember, she'd stripped down to her boxers and undershirt and crawled under the feather down comforter. Now she paused to pull on fleece sweats and socks and a soft wool sweater Clare had given her on her last birthday. Except Clare called it a jumper, a word Jamie had previously reserved for a dress worn by small children. Another of her cute British quirks.

Too bad Clare was currently in any mood but cute.

Jamie followed the sound of clattering dishes to the kitchen where she found her girlfriend making afternoon tea. Usually this time of day was relaxed and casual, and Jamie would stop whatever she was working on to join Clare for a cuppa in the living room. She thought about going up and hugging her from behind, but she wasn't convinced Clare wouldn't smack her if she tried. Instead she leaned against the counter and waited.

At first Clare ignored her to focus on buttering toast and preparing tea in her favorite teapot, part of a simple, white porcelain set that she had inherited from her grandmother a few years before Jamie met her. The pink and yellow roses on the side were chipped and faded, but the signs of use added charm, Clare always insisted. Jamie had grown up seeing her own grandparents only a couple of times a year, so she thought it lovely that Clare had been so attached to hers. Then again, England was only eight hundred miles from tip to tip. It made sense that families had an easier time bridging that kind of distance than in the US where the miles could measure in the thousands.

Clare took a bite of toast without looking at her. Then she sipped her steaming hot tea—and promptly whirled to spit it into the sink. "God damn it," she exclaimed, her voice unusually thick as she slammed her cup down, and only then did Jamie realize she was crying.

"Hey," she said, stepping forward. In two steps she had crossed the tiny room and was pulling Clare into her arms, her chin against the smaller woman's soft cloud of hair. She smelled familiar, like black tea and strawberry jam. "What's going on? Talk to me."

"I told myself I wasn't going to cry." Clare buried her face in Jamie's sweater. "Fucking fuck."

Jamie ran her fingers through Clare's hair the way she knew she liked. "Can you at least give me a hint?"

"Do I actually have to?"

Jamie hesitated. There were two options here, so she went with the easier one. "I told you, I don't have to go back until January."

Clare pushed away from her, eyes red-rimmed and wide. "Really? That's what you're going to lead with after making a fool of me for the entire world to see?"

"What are you talking about, Clare?"

Her girlfriend wiped her eyes. "You tell me. I wasn't there, was I?"

She folded her arms across her chest and leaned back against the counter again. "I take it you've seen the photo."

"Yes, I've seen the photo. God, what bloody cheek! I honestly can't believe you right now, Jamie."

"I'm not being 'cheeky.' Nothing happened. We were on the same flight and got lunch together when my connection was delayed, and then some fans recognized her. That's all."

Clare was already shaking her head. "She was your first love, Jamie, and you've spent two weeks in California with her. What am I supposed to think when I see a photo of you posing together like the most perfect couple ever?"

"You're supposed to think you can trust me. I told you, nothing happened." Unless you counted having a drink or holding hands during a bumpy landing. But none of that was important, was it? Shoshanna, her old therapist, had always said that thoughts didn't matter. Actions did.

Brow furrowed, Clare stared at her. "I want to believe you, I do, but there's already fan fiction being written about the two of you." She shook her head. "It's disgusting. It really is."

Fan fiction about her and Emma? Jamie frowned. Femslash stories were supposed to be about fictional characters, like Beca and Chloe from *Pitch Perfect*, or Elsa from *Frozen* and Merida from *Brave*, one of her other favorite pairings. Fan fiction wasn't supposed to be about real people, was it?

"It's called fiction for a reason," she pointed out. "Just

because some random stranger wants Emma and me to be together doesn't mean we are."

"Random stranger? I don't think you understand how big this is. That Tumblr post was reblogged more than a thousand times, Jamie. A *thousand*. And that doesn't even include all the Twitter and Instagram mentions."

Wow. She had apparently missed a few things by sleeping the day away. "I'm sorry, Clare, but you know as well as I do that I can't control what football fans say or do. This comes with the territory of being openly queer in the national team pool. If they weren't shipping me with Emma, it would only be someone else."

"But it *is* Emma." Clare reached for her tea cup. Her voice sounded quieter now, and the eyes she turned back to Jamie were less angry. "All day I had to walk around school wondering if my friends and family had seen the posts of my girlfriend with one of the ten most beautiful football players in the world. Did you know she made that list? How am I supposed to compete with that?"

Jamie stepped closer. "You're not. It's not a competition. You're my girlfriend and she's someone I work with. That's it."

"I wish I could believe you," she repeated, her voice even quieter now.

Jamie wanted to be angry with Clare for not having faith in her. But in reality, she couldn't pretend that she hadn't felt drawn to Emma at camp, just as she had the night she saw her standing at an empty ice machine in a hotel near San Diego all those years ago.

Clare was watching her, and Jamie rubbed a hand across her face. "What do you want me to say? That I don't have any feelings for her at all? I already told you I can't do that. I'll always care about Emma, just like you'll always care about Jess. But I love *you*. I'm in a relationship with *you*. For the last time, I did not cheat on you. Whether you believe that or not is up to you."

"Can you guarantee that you won't? Can you promise me that if you make the national team, you won't fly off to Canada or Texas or Brazil and fall in love with her all over again?"

"Jesus, Clare, can you guarantee that if I'm away for a week or a month, or longer even, that you won't meet someone else? That's not how this works. There are no guarantees, and you know it."

Clare's eyes narrowed. "Longer than a *month*, Jamie? What does that even mean?"

Jamie rubbed her palms against the soft fleece of her sweats. *Crap.* She hadn't meant to let it slip like that. "It means there are some things we need to discuss. I was hoping we could talk over dinner."

"Tell me," she said, and shook her head. "I'm tired of waiting."

This was not how their reunion was supposed to go. Maybe she hadn't figured out how it should go but this was definitely not it. Clare was looking at her so warily, her brown eyes bleaker than she'd ever seen them. But she didn't look surprised, and Jamie suddenly remembered that Clare had been avoiding her calls for the last two weeks. Maybe this was how it was always going to go.

"Fine." She gave in. "But can we at least do this in the living room?"

Clare nodded and walked out, leaving Jamie alone in the tiny kitchen. She tried to will away the tight knot in her stomach as she poured a slug of tea into her favorite mug, a plain red one with "Stanford" written on the side in all caps. Laurie, her college girlfriend, had given it to her their first Christmas together, and it had traveled with her ever since. Briefly Jamie closed her eyes, inhaling the steam and trying to convince herself that they could still fix this. People made long-distance relationships work all the time, didn't they? The fact that she was probably almost definitely moving back to America didn't mean they had to break up, right?

In the living room, Clare was already curled up on the sofa under a fleece blanket Jamie's parents had sent them as a house warmer when they moved in together. Technically, Jamie had moved in with Clare, since she'd had the flat long before they met. Jamie's name had never been on the lease, a point that had never really seemed to matter. Now it felt symbolic—as if her presence here was only ever going to be temporary.

"Can I sit with you?"

Clare nodded, hands wrapped around her cup. Jamie sat next to her and tucked herself under the blanket. The flat was chilly as usual. They had tried turning up the heat, but there was another flat above theirs in the terraced house and the extra heat only escaped upward.

"So," Jamie said, wondering where she should start. "I already told you camp went well and that they invited me back."

"Yes, and I am genuinely happy for you about that part," Clare said, touching her hand.

"Thanks." She tried to lace their fingers together but Clare pulled hers away, not meeting her gaze. Jamie lowered her chin and continued on with the story of her conversation with Melanie, ending with Ellie's offer to talk to the Thorns GM and hook her up with her agent.

Clare shifted away from her on the couch. "Portland. That's in Oregon, isn't it?"

Jamie nodded.

"And when would you need to be there?"

"I'm not sure. It might not even be an option if I can't get out of my contract—"

"When, Jamie?"

She toyed with the fleece blanket. "Soon. Pre-season starts in March."

Head bent and tea cup cradled to her chest, Clare didn't speak for a little while. When she finally did, her words weren't at all what Jamie was expecting: "Rachel Ellison is the one who stayed with you until the ambulance got there, isn't she?"

"Exactly. If I played on her team, I would have her to mentor me. Plus they won the league championship, and more than fifteen thousand people attended some of their games. The club is affiliated with the MLS franchise in Portland, which means they have better resources and management."

Clare reached for her hand again, tracing the tanned skin near her wrist. "You know I wouldn't want to stand in the way of your football dreams, right?"

Jamie paused, swallowing against the rising lump in her throat. She had a feeling she knew where this was going. Honestly, they'd been headed in this direction since the moment the national team manager had called to invite her to December camp.

"Right," she said finally, her voice low. "I would never want to stand in the way of your dreams, either, Clare."

She nodded. Then she pulled away and tucked herself into the corner of the sofa, turning so they could face each other more easily. "So. You might have noticed I've been a little distant lately."

Jamie gripped her mug in both hands. "You haven't been that subtle."

"That's fair. But I had my reasons."

"Other than me spending the last two weeks with Emma?"

Clare frowned at her bitter tone. "That was part of it, yes. But it was more that I've been doing a lot of thinking about what I want out of all of this. And the thing is, well, I don't really know anymore."

Jamie hunched her shoulders. "Yes, you do. Just say it."

"I'm trying. This is difficult for me too, Jamie." She looked down at her hands and released a breath. "But I guess that's the whole point. Somewhere along the way it got too hard."

"What got too hard?"

"This. *Us.* You missed my sister's wedding *and* my parents' anniversary party. Not to mention all the school events and the other things you've missed. I never know where you're going to be when, and now you say you're moving back to the States…"

"I'm only thinking about it," she argued. "It's not a done deal yet."

"But that's the entire point. Nothing is ever a *done deal* with you. I never know if you're going to show up for my life or not. For *our* life."

"That's not fair. I can't help it if football is unpredictable."

"I never said you could. I recognize that a lot of this is out of your control, I do. But that means football dictates my life too, Jamie. I'm not getting any younger. I'll be thirty soon—"

"You're twenty-eight."

"And in two years I'll be thirty and Lila will be three. I want my children to play with their cousins, not have them as babysitters. But if you make the national team, in two years you'll have just come off the World Cup and be trying to qualify for the Olympics."

"I told you, making the national team is still a big *if* right now."

"You would take the spot if they offered it, wouldn't you?"

"Of course. It's all I've ever wanted." As Clare looked down, Jamie realized how that sounded. "I mean, it's not *all* I've ever wanted. You're amazing, and I feel lucky to have you in my life, you know that."

Clare shook her head. "But *I* don't feel lucky, Jamie. That's what I'm telling you. I want someone who's all in. I want a wife and kids and a home—"

"I want those things, too."

"Sure, but they're not a priority right now. I don't want to have to explain to my children why their mum can't be home for their birthday or their school concert or any of a thousand other important moments. I don't want them to stumble across fan fiction about their mum and one of her teammates. I don't want them to see me like I was today, doubting you, doubting us. Doubting myself."

Her words were spoken without malice, but Jamie felt the accusation anyway. She set her mug on the coffee table and stood up, squeezing the back of her neck with both hands. "I get that being involved with a professional athlete is difficult, but Jesus, Clare, I was a football player when we met. None of this is new." She dropped her arms to her sides, shaking her head.

Clare rose and set her hands on Jamie's hips as if to hold her in place. "I know it's not new, but I didn't realize what living with an athlete would be like. I'm sorry, Jamie, but I want to be settled. You're lovely, and I wish things were different. But at the end of the day, I want someone who's here with me in body *and* heart, someone who would never even think of giving up what we have for a chance at a World Cup. Can you honestly say that's you?"

Jamie looked down, and Clare's hands fell away.

"You can't, can you?"

She didn't want Clare to be right, but not admitting the truth didn't make it any less true. She took a breath, looked into her girlfriend's eyes, and shook her head.

"That's what I thought." Clare sniffed and turned away, hugging herself.

"I'm so sorry." Jamie hesitated, and then she put her arms around Clare from behind. Her girlfriend leaned back into her and covered her face, body shaking with the force of her sobs. Jamie felt her own throat tighten. "I'm so, so sorry, Clare."

They stood together, Jamie wishing she could figure out a way to fix this, to fix everything. There had to be something she could do, didn't there? But if there was, she couldn't imagine what it might be.

When Clare's sobs finally abated, she turned and took Jamie by the hand and led her toward the bedroom. There, they undressed each other slowly. Naked and trembling, Clare tugged Jamie toward the bathroom where she turned on the shower and inserted enough coins in the receptacle to keep the water hot for a long while. Then they stood under the soothing spray, bodies loosely pressed together.

Was this it? Were they over?

Trying not to think, Jamie slowly washed Clare, running the wash cloth over every inch of her skin, memorizing her already familiar body. When she was clean, Clare took the cloth square and washed Jamie in return. They rinsed the soap from each other's skin, fingers and lips lingering over sensitive spots. Jamie cupped Clare's breasts in her hands, feeling the weight of her girlfriend's flesh, mind struggling to accept that this might be one of the last times she touched her like this. A month ago they had enjoyed Thanksgiving with their closest friends, and Jamie had felt closer to Clare than to any other person on the planet. Now they were, what? Planning their break-up?

Later, after the water finally cooled and they'd crawled naked into bed, they made love slowly, eyes closed against the ending they both knew was coming. Afterward, Jamie felt Clare's fingers painting the lines of her phoenix tattoo, and she knew: Clare was saying goodbye. When the brush of fingertips against her back had ceased, Jamie shifted, pulling Clare against her side and holding her tightly. As Clare's tears dripped onto her shoulder, she let go and cried too. Cried for the pain she was causing Clare, for the pain she was causing herself by walking away from another person she had thought might be—could be?—in her life for good.

Cried for not wanting the life they'd imagined together enough to stay.

Night had fallen by the time they made dinner and sat at the dining room table, talking through next steps. Jamie checked her email, and sure enough, Carrie Fitzsimmons had sent her a copy of the letter Ellie had suggested she use to secure release from her Arsenal contract. It would take a few days to figure things out with the club, and Clare agreed that Jamie should stay in the flat until she left for the States. But Clare might head down to Cornwall to visit her family earlier than planned, and perhaps Jamie could move up her travel dates? Drawing things out through the holidays would only make it harder on them both. Jamie agreed to be out before Christmas, feeling almost numb as they discussed details of their break-up as if they hadn't lain in bed naked and crying together only an hour earlier.

Were they really doing this? Was she really leaving Clare and Britt and her other friends and teammates because one of Craig Anderson's assistants had said they might, possibly, maybe if she was lucky offer her a place on the national team? There didn't seem to be any other choice, though. She couldn't stay. Even if she'd wanted to, Clare had already made up her mind. She didn't want to be a footballer's wife. And honestly? Jamie couldn't blame her.

That night, they lay awake in each other's arms. Clare cried again and Jamie held her, trying to accept that their relationship had gone from seemingly happy to utterly doomed in such a short time. It wasn't that they didn't love each other. Sure, they bickered like all couples did about silly and not-so-silly things, and personally, Jamie would have been thrilled with a bit more sex. But they were happy together, weren't they? Or at least, she had been. She thought of Laurie, her college girlfriend. They had loved each other too, but in the end it hadn't been enough to keep them together either. What was wrong with her that she cared more about soccer than the people in her life?

No wonder some of her friends swore off relationships with non-athletes. Only fellow pros could understand—and accept?—blind devotion to a game that could injure you, destroy your confidence, ruin you in multifold ways. The thing was, it could also enrich your life the way few things could. Being on a team provided you with instant friends who shared your same sense of purpose. Committing to a common goal was as addictive as any number of chemical substances. And, in some cases, nearly as damaging to the rest of your life.

Still unable to sleep at midnight—late afternoon West Coast time—Jamie longed to talk to someone other than Clare about the sudden, rapid-fire unfolding of events since she'd touched down in the UK. An image of Emma appeared in her mind, but she closed her eyes, willing it away. She knew she shouldn't have spent so much time with her. And yet, there was a reason she'd sought Emma's advice on her professional future, a reason she wanted to call her now. If the brain was a muscle and not an organ, she would have called it muscle memory. As it was, the heart was the only muscle in the body that also doubled as an organ, and clearly she would be better off not dwelling long on that symbolism.

When they were younger, Emma had been her go-to friend for an entire year. The most important year of her life, in fact, as she'd struggled to put her mind and body back together after the assault in France. Without Emma she didn't doubt she would still have recovered, but having her there to call or text or email at any time of the night or day had made her feel so incredibly cared for. Emma had been there for her by choice, not out of obligation like her family. When Emma's father died suddenly, Jamie had gotten a chance to support her in return. And she had done so until their friendship ended.

Years later, she had come to understand that Emma had pushed her away the only way she knew how—by "cheating" on her with Tori Parker. It wasn't cheating, though, as much as it might have felt that way to Jamie. They were friends and nothing more, despite the kiss they'd shared, despite the fact that Jamie was utterly in love with her. She had never told Emma how she felt. Instead, knowing that Emma was leaving for college soon, Jamie had dated other girls in an attempt to get over her. When she found out about Tori, she told herself it was the lying she couldn't forgive and summarily banished Emma from her life. But at some level she had always known it was the fact that Emma had chosen to be with a girl who wasn't *her* that had hurt so desperately.

Now that they were back in touch, she wanted to be friends with Emma. She had missed her ever since the moment they had stopped talking, and being together at camp had reminded her of how much she had always loved being around Emma. But that was the keyword—love. Could they be friends, or would there always be something more between them?

Her soon-to-be ex-girlfriend shifted restlessly in bed beside her, almost as if she could hear Jamie's thoughts. Yeah, this was definitely not the right time to be pondering that question.

She waited until Clare's breathing was so even she knew nothing short of a gas main explosion would wake her. Only then did she slip out of bed, pull on sweats and faux fur-lined slippers, and head for the kitchen. She unplugged her phone from the charger and carried it to the couch where she opened her message app and began to respond, at last, to her texts.

First she sent her parents and Meg a group message letting them know she'd gotten home safely and would be in touch about her holiday plans soon. She had texted her parents to let them know she'd been invited back to camp, but they didn't know anything about her NWSL plans. From prior experience, she knew it was better to leave that reveal until she had something definite to report. Her mom in particular tended to get swept up in the drama of when—*if ever, honey?*—Jamie was planning to move home. It would be cruel to dangle the possibility of Portland, the closest NWSL team, in her face and then have to revoke it if those plans didn't work out.

Next she wrote Angie and Britt to say that the social media situation was under control. Sort of. Not to worry. But maybe she and Britt could meet for lunch the following day?

When she got to Ellie's message, she hesitated. Then she hit dial, not bothering to check her prepaid international minutes. Clare had blown her off so much during camp that she should have plenty left.

"Max, my man," Ellie answered, sounding ridiculously cheerful.

"Sorry, I would have called sooner but I totally crashed when I got back this morning. And then my girlfriend came home a few hours ago and decided to break up with me over the Blakewell thing, so..."

"What?" Ellie yelped. "Are you serious?"

Jamie closed her eyes and leaned back on the couch. "No. We did break up, but mostly I think it's because we realized we're not on the same page. She wants a normal life with babies and a mortgage and a wife who has a regular job, and I want—"

"A World Cup," Ellie finished for her.

"And, you know, Olympic gold, if that's not too much to ask."

"Shit." Ellie's voice had deflated. "I'm sorry to hear that. She sounded great."

"She is, just not for me apparently. Or more to the point,

I'm not great for her."

She sighed, snuggling under the blanket. Tomorrow was going to be another rough day. She was not looking forward to telling Britt she was leaving, or to trying to track down Charity, the Arsenal GM. Neither of them would be happy she wanted to transfer midway through their Champions League campaign. The quarter-finals were set for the end of March, and their chances at advancing would be stronger with her in the lineup. Not that she was irreplaceable, but most of their set pieces revolved around her and anyways, it was always risky to mess with team chemistry, especially when it was working.

Ellie seemed to perk up a little: "Does this mean you're coming back before January camp?"

"That's the plan—assuming Arsenal lets me out of my contract."

"They will. They can't afford to piss off the federation, not if they ever went a shot at another player in the pool."

Ellie's confidence was reassuring, and they talked the business of football for a little while. Ellie filled her in on the talk she'd had with the Thorns GM, who was more than willing to schedule a meeting with Jamie. She talked about the Thorns set-up and philosophy, and offered advice on how to prepare for the meeting, which she said was "all but in the bag."

And then, inevitably, Ellie said, "By the way, what happened to keeping your nose clean?"

Jamie stalled. "What do you mean?"

"Um, hello, Blakewell?" The national team captain sounded more exasperated than angry, though.

"Nothing happened, I swear." She hesitated. "Or I guess I *did* hold her hand at one point, but only because the landing was bumpy and she's afraid of flying. You know, because of her uncle."

There was a corresponding silence at the other end before Ellie asked, "Since when is Emma afraid of flying? And what happened to her uncle?"

Whoops. Apparently Emma's uncle's plane crash wasn't common knowledge among national team members. Good to know. "Never mind. She's totally not. Forget I said anything."

Ellie sighed. "Max, you're killing me here."

"The point is, we're friends and that's how we're going to stay."

"At least everyone agrees on that."

Jamie paused. "And by 'everyone,' you mean you and me, right?"

"And Emma."

Jamie blinked, focusing on the street light flickering on and off outside their—*Clare's*—flat. "You talked to Emma about me?"

"Jamie. Do you know how many times that original Tumblr post got reblogged?"

"So what did she say?" Jamie asked, trying to keep her voice casual. And failing—she could almost hear Ellie's eye-roll through the phone.

"She said the same thing you did, only without the hand-holding, fear-of-flying bit."

"Oh. Well, good." Jamie pushed away the whisper of disappointment at the back of her mind. She already had enough to worry about. The less relationship drama in the next few months, the better.

"Jodie's on her way home from work, so I should get going. Are you okay, kid?"

"I'm fine. I'll keep you posted on my plans, okay?"

"Let me know ASAP what happens at your end. If all goes well, we can set up a meeting with the Thorns management before January camp."

"*We?*"

"Well, yeah. You didn't think I'd let you go through all this alone, did you?"

She blinked at the tears suddenly stinging her eyes, unsurprised by her own weepiness. It had been a freakishly long couple of days. "Thanks, man. I really appreciate everything you're doing."

"You're welcome. Hang in there, okay? You'll be home soon."

"Right," she agreed, even though she currently felt homeless in every sense of the word.

The call ended, and Jamie sat in the dark, watching lights glint through the window. At least her parents would take her back. They always did. It was just, at some point she hoped they wouldn't have to. At some point it would be nice to have a lease in her own name, or even, someday, a mortgage like her friends from college who had gone to work for Google and Microsoft. Her Facebook feed featured a steady stream of engagement announcements and work anniversaries—one of the risks of going to a university full of overachievers—and here she was nearly four years later about to ask her parents if she could move back in. Again.

A car horn sounded in the distance, faint but strident. Their street was quiet, but only a couple of blocks away buses and motorbikes zipped along the Seven Sisters Road in spite of the late hour. She was going to miss this flat, this street, this city. She had grown up so much since arriving in this foreign land, sight unseen, for a shot at the soccer career that had seemed increasingly out of reach. Arsenal had taken a chance on her and given her back her dream of playing professionally not once but twice—her club insurance had paid for her ankle surgery and rehab, even though she'd been injured during a US match.

Despite her early obsession with the Premier League, an English football career definitely wasn't anything she'd expected. When she graduated from Stanford, she'd been certain that her life was unfolding as it should. At twenty-two, she was a regular on the U-23 national team, a paid professional in the best women's league in the world, and had just received her first call-up to the senior national team. Then a defender from the Washington Freedom had slammed into her from behind, and she'd uttered what one of her teammates called the "ACL scream" as she fell. She'd known as she lay on the ground, clutching her knee, that her season was over. For a few dark days that fall, Jamie had considered giving up on soccer. But thanks to Britt, a new door had opened.

Some people say you make your own luck. As a professional footballer, though, Jamie wasn't sure it was quite that simple. Admittedly, some teams did seem to possess an almost magical energy that elevated them above all others. In 2011, the Japanese earthquake and resulting tsunami and nuclear disaster pummeled the island nation only four months before the World Cup. When Japan defeated the US favorites in the finals, even the American coaches and players seemed resigned to the fairytale ending for their disaster-plagued foes. Jamie remembered watching Emma's interview later on YouTube, her heart breaking for the exhausted defender who had looked more perplexed than anything else. At least Emma had made her penalty kicks, both in the quarters and in the finals. Ellie and Steph Miller couldn't say the same.

Her phone vibrated, and she opened her messages. Her older sister had texted: "#Blakewell? The more things change… Apparently you and I need to chat, kiddo. Call me when you wake up."

Jamie texted back. "I'm awake. Wanna Skype?"

"Yes! Give me five."

Why did everyone call her kid? Not Emma, though. Except wasn't there that one time she'd called her "bean pole" or something similarly embarrassing? *Crap.* She should *not* be thinking of Emma right now, only she couldn't help that her brain kept conjuring memories. It was like Emma was a favorite old song that she'd rediscovered and played constantly for the last two weeks, and now the melody was looping through the back of her mind, ready to leap forward whenever she let her guard down.

As she waited for Skype to alert her, Jamie tried to plan out what to say to her sister. Meg had been the first person Jamie had told about Clare, the first member of the family to fly to London to meet her new girlfriend shortly after Jamie moved in with her.

"This one's a keeper," she'd told Jamie when Clare was in the kitchen. Then she said in the very next sentence, "But does this mean you're never coming home?"

"We don't really talk about the future," Jamie had told her, and her sister had rolled her eyes.

"Of course you don't."

Meg, more of a planner by nature, had long considered Jamie's preference to go with the flow a personal affront.

Skype beeped at her and Jamie hit accept, smiling in spite of herself as Meg's face came into view. "Hola, big sis."

"Hey James. What are you doing up? Isn't it late there?"

"My body is stuck on West Coast time."

"I still can't believe you didn't let Mom and Dad come see you at camp. And now you're blowing us off to have Christmas with your British in-laws, aren't you?"

Jamie blinked as tears pricked her eyes. She didn't have British in-laws anymore. What were Clare's parents going to think about her suddenly walking away from their daughter? Would she ever see them or any of Clare's other family members again?

On the small screen, Meg's affectionate smile turned to a frown. "What's wrong? Is this about Emma?"

"No. Well, not really." She took a breath. "Clare and I are breaking up."

"Oh, no." Meg set her chin in her hand. Her hipster glasses were sliding down her nose and her messy bun was hanging in shreds about her face, and she looked so worried and so familiar that Jamie was hit by a wave of homesickness.

"Yeah," she said, and sniffed, swiping at her eyes.

"Because of the online shit storm?"

"No. Or, I guess it might be part of it. But mostly I think we realized we're in different places, you know? She's ready to get married and settle down and have kids, and I . . ." She trailed off.

"You, what?"

"I'm coming home, Meg. I'm coming back to play in the NWSL."

"No way!"

"Yes way. Assuming everything works out." Quickly she summarized the events of the past few days, including Ellie's offer to get her in with the Portland team. "But don't tell Mom and Dad yet," she added at the end. "I don't want to get their hopes up in case it doesn't work out."

"Oh, so it's okay to get *my* hopes up?"

"Well, yeah. When are you and Todd going home?"

"We're driving out this weekend." She squinted at the camera. "What about you? What are your plans?"

"I told Clare I'd be out by Christmas."

"That's only a week away."

Jamie covered her face with one hand. "Don't remind me. At least I don't have that much to pack. Most of the stuff here is hers." It was possible the last part came out more bitter than she intended.

"Don't worry," Meg said. "You'll get through this. You know, if you do end up in Portland, it's a pretty cool city."

"Right? I could do worse. Like, Kansas City worse. That's in, what, Missouri?" She shuddered.

"Perish the thought. The land of Mormons is bad enough. Either way, I'll help you move, okay?"

"You have to teach. And aren't you supposed to be finishing your dissertation?"

Meg sighed dramatically. "One can only hope."

They talked about Meg's class schedule at the University of Utah where she and her husband were both PhD candidates in music education. At a lull in the conversation, Meg said, "Are you going to tell me what happened with Emma?"

"There's nothing to tell."

"Tumblr would respectfully disagree."

"Since when has Tumblr done anything respectfully?"

"Valid point. I did see the photo, though."

"So did Clare. I know it looks bad, but nothing happened."

"I know. You're not the cheating type."

"Tell my girlfriend—sorry, my *ex*-girlfriend—that." She toyed with the tag on the fleece blanket. "But, I don't know, I think I could feel something more if I let myself. Which I'm totally not going to do."

"Because...?"

Jamie scowled at her sister through the phone's camera. "Because I'm just getting out of a serious relationship and I don't need to jump into something else? Besides, I need to focus on soccer if I'm going to make the team I've wanted to be on since I was ten."

She didn't mention that Emma apparently wasn't interested in anything more than friendship, at least according to Ellie. She didn't feel like admitting that one out loud, not even to her sister.

"Oh. That makes sense. And here I was thinking you were being a chicken because it's Emma Blakeley."

"Thanks a lot, Meg. And on that note, I'll see you when I see you." Jamie's thumb hovered over the red receiver icon.

"No, wait! I'm sorry, I shouldn't have said that. I've had too much coffee and not enough sleep the last couple of nights trying to get grades done. Forgive me? Please?" she wheedled, making a funny face that used to make Jamie laugh when they were little.

Reluctantly she moved her thumb away. "Fine. But try not to be such a douchebag, will you? This is not the easiest time for me, seeing as I am in the process of dismantling my life as I know it for an uncertain outcome."

"You know what they say about change."

"Change is inevitable; growth is optional?"

"I was going to say, 'Change is inevitable, except from a vending machine.' But we can totally go with yours."

When they hung up a little while later, Jamie lay back under her blanket feeling a tiny bit better. Knowing she would see Meg and Todd, the coolest brother-in-law ever, at the end of the coming week made it easier to face what she had to do in the interim.

If Emma was a melody at the back of her mind, Clare was the album she had listened to nearly every day for the last year and a half. Jamie was going to miss the way her girlfriend got excited or teary-eyed when she talked about the kids in her class; miss her calm confidence when they played Monopoly or Cranium with Britt and Allie; miss the way she smiled across the table when they were having dinner at home alone, just the two of them.

And yet here she was, the metaphorical ink on their break-up not even dry, and she was already thinking about Emma. Clare had treated her with nothing but kindness their entire relationship. Surely she deserved better.

Jamie opened her messages app, scrolling down the list until she reached Emma's text. She reread the message and typed a quick reply: "Thanks for checking in. No worries. I won't hold the entire fandom accountable for the actions of a few. Have a good holiday, and I'll see you at camp next month."

Before she could change her mind, she clicked send. She waited for a few minutes, but Emma didn't write back. Maybe she was busy, or maybe she recognized the text for what it was: a thoroughly impersonal reply that said without actually saying it, "Don't call me; I'll call you." She and Emma had both told Ellie there was nothing between them, but Clare hadn't been all wrong, had she?

She turned off her phone and lay back on the couch, curling up on her side, hands folded together under a throw pillow. She had made a mess of things with Clare. The least she could do would be to get through the next few weeks without doing anything else to disappoint her. Emma may have been her first love, but Clare had been the first woman she'd lived with, the first person she'd considered having kids with. The first person she'd imagined herself proposing to.

She didn't want their break-up to be in vain. If she was going to sacrifice their relationship at the altar of professional soccer, she had damned well better make sure she made the national team, which meant no distractions of any kind. As Clare had said, football dictated her life right now. At least for a little while longer, she owed it to herself to let it.

CHAPTER SEVEN

If LA felt like a foreign country compared to Seattle, then Minneapolis felt like a different world. It wasn't the multitudes of tall blondes that always threw Emma. Seattle had plenty of those, especially in the Ballard neighborhood, which locals still sometimes referred to as "Little Scandinavia." No, it was the higher rate of obesity in the Midwest that she noticed every time she traveled to her mother's homeland. Seattle's culture revolved around REI and coffee. The point was to look like you had just finished climbing a mountain as you sipped your coffee, even if you hadn't set foot outside the city in weeks.

Since her mom had returned to the land of her youth, Emma had noticed she'd become increasingly sedentary. Now every time she came to visit she made it her personal mission to get her mother exercising. This Christmas was no different. The afternoon Emma arrived, she pestered her mom until she agreed to go for a walk around Lake Harriet, conveniently located across the street. Emma and her brother still called their mom's lake view property the "new house" even though she'd lived there for two years. It was hard to picture her there on her own, but her schedule at the University of Minnesota children's hospital meant she rarely had time to be alone. Besides, one of her sisters and a handful of college friends still lived in the Cities, while June, her other sister, was only an hour away in Rochester.

Apparently being on her own was even less of an issue now that Roger, her recently divorced "friend" from college, had started hanging around. It had only been a few months, but already he was on his way to being upgraded to "partner" status, she confided shortly after Emma arrived.

"You can't call him that," Emma told her mom as they bundled up in down coats, balaclavas, fleece-lined mittens, and other assorted winter gear.

"Why not?"

"Because you're misappropriating the only term people in same-sex relationships can call each other in what, like thirty-seven states still?"

"You know same-sex marriage is legal here, don't you?"

"It is in Seattle too, Mom. Washington was one of the first states to approve gay marriage by popular vote."

"And Minnesota was one of the first to vote down a ban."

Emma stuck her tongue out as she picked out a second scarf. "You're never going to convince me that Minnesota is better than Washington, so you might as well give it up."

"I know, you're nothing if not loyal to your home state. But I have hopes you and your brother will come around," she said in the flat, nasal accent that had reemerged in full since she'd moved back to her home state.

"You're the one who complains about the weather here."

Her mom pulled on a hat with ear flaps and buckled them together under her chin. "I'd forgotten how hard it is to get out when the temperature is thirty below. I'm nowhere near old enough to do circuits of the Mall of America."

"Dress warmly and keep moving," Emma told her. "How bad can it be?"

Ten minutes later as they walked the trail around Lake Harriet, Emma realized that her mother, a native Minnesotan, *may* have been right.

"What did you say the temperature is?" she asked, teeth chattering despite the multitude of layers adorning her wildly shivering body.

She thought her mother said, "Fifteen below, not counting the wind chill." But the ear muffs on top of the scarf on top of the wool beanie made it difficult to be certain. At least her ears were warm. *Ish.*

Whatever the temperature, it was cold enough that Emma suggested they turn back on the spot. Even then she worried that they might die before they could reach the house. The air was so cold it hurt to breathe, which she had experienced before when running in Boston. But they weren't running. They had too many layers on to effect more than a medium-paced walk.

"Okay, you were right," she admitted a little while later as they disrobed in the mud room between the house and garage. "It is too cold to go for a walk."

Instead of saying *I told you so*, her mother only hugged her and suggested warming up in the kitchen with hot chocolate.

"How was residency camp?" she asked a few minutes later as she putzed around the kitchen. "Was it good to see your friends?"

Emma sat at the breakfast bar, elbows on the countertop. "It was a little long, to be honest, especially considering we didn't play a match. I can't remember the last time we went this long without a friendly."

"How's the new coach?"

"He's, um, good. I think." Unlike some of her teammates, Emma was reserving judgment for now. She didn't feel like she'd seen Craig in action enough to form an opinion—which Phoebe and Steph claimed was the problem to begin with.

"You can tell me how you really feel, honey. I promise not to leak it to the press."

Emma shook her head, smiling at her mother. "Honestly, I don't know yet. He's different from Marty, that's for sure. I think we all felt that the month-long residency camp before the World Cup was overkill, especially when we were trying to play our pro seasons too. But Craig's approach is the exact opposite so it's been difficult to get a rhythm going. It takes a ton of training time—and match time—to develop the kind of chemistry we're going to need going into the World Cup."

Her mother placed a steaming mug of hot cocoa in front of her. "Did I hear there was a new player at camp? Perhaps a certain midfielder from Northern California?"

Emma shot her mother a look. "You know you did."

"And how was that? It was your first residency camp together, wasn't it?"

She had never been able to hide much from her mother. Not that she wanted to. Even before her father's death, they'd always seemed closer than her other friends were with their mothers. Her mom claimed that dealing with sick and dying children at work every day gave her a perspective most parents didn't have, but all bias aside, Emma thought she was simply a better mother than most.

"It was hard in some ways," she admitted, "but good in others."

"Difficult how?"

"Well, you know, she doesn't seem like she's changed all that much."

"And that's a problem because…?"

Emma sighed and muttered, "Because she has a girlfriend."

"Ah." Her mother sipped her hot chocolate. "Sounds like little has changed in the Emma-Jamie saga."

"It's been ten years, though. Shouldn't something have changed by now?" Emma lamented. "Oh, before I forget, she said to tell you hello."

"That's sweet. Tell her hello back."

Not for the first time since the day #Blakewell blew up, Emma considered sending a quick text to Jamie. But Jamie's reply had seemed fairly clear. *See you at camp*, she'd written. Not, *Talk to you soon* or any other open-ended statement. Apparently once the champagne wore off, she'd regretted the impulse to trade numbers. Emma shouldn't have been surprised by the hundred and eighty degree turn. That was what happened when you flirted with someone already in a relationship.

"Anyway," she said, leaving her phone in her hoodie pocket where it belonged, "even if she didn't have a girlfriend, it's not like anything could happen."

"Why not?"

"Because we might end up being teammates. Remember the Tori fiasco?"

"I do, but you and Jamie are adults, not teenagers. Besides, you're both professionals. You wouldn't allow your personal life to affect the team."

"It doesn't matter how mature or professional we are. An inter-squad relationship can be really distracting, which is why the federation frowns on them. At our level team dynamics have to come first."

"Oh, honey." Her mom shook her head. "You create more obstacles for love than anyone I've ever known."

"This is not an obstacle I'm 'creating,'" Emma said, frowning. "Do you know how long it's been since the '99ers won the World Cup? Fourteen and a half years, Mom. Rarely does a day go by that I don't think about what happened in Germany. When we walked off that field in second place, I felt like my heart had been ripped out of my chest and trampled by a thousand pairs of cleats. Canada might be my last chance at a World Cup title. There's no way I would do anything to jeopardize our chances."

"Honey, you have two gold medals, a national championship, and countless other titles to your name. Are you telling me that you won't feel like your soccer career is complete if you don't win a World Cup?"

"That's exactly what I'm telling you. We're the United States. We're supposed to be the best in the world, and yet someone else has won the last *three* World Cups." As her mother stared at her, Emma shook her head. "You don't understand. I don't think you can."

"I do understand. You're your father's daughter, Emma, which means nothing you do will ever be good enough in your own eyes. Be careful not to apply those expectations to anyone else. That's the quickest way to push away the people you love."

"I don't expect other people to be perfect," she said,

tapping her foot against the stool she perched on.

"Really? When's the last time you had a partner anywhere in the picture?"

"That's more about timing than anything. With my travel schedule, all I want to do when I'm home is curl up and watch TV." As Dani liked to say, to her *Netflix and chill* meant just that, literally.

"Other women on your team don't seem to have that problem," her mom pointed out.

"That's because most of them are in relationships with people they met in college. Starting something new is almost impossible when you're on the road as much as we are. But speaking of partners," she added, hoping to guide the conversation away from her profound lack of work/life balance, "does Roger know you've vowed never to remarry?"

"No," her mom admitted, ducking her head in a way Emma was pretty sure she'd never seen.

"Does that mean you might change your mind?"

"I think it's fair to say I'm no longer quite as *wedded* to the idea of permanent widowhood, yes."

Emma smiled at the pun before reaching over to touch her mother's hand. "Good. Dad wouldn't have wanted you to be alone for the rest of your life. He would have wanted you to be happy."

"You think so?"

Emma nodded. "I do."

"He wouldn't want you to be alone either, you know."

She pulled her hand back. "Mom, I'm twenty-seven. I have plenty of time to find someone and kick out a house full of babies."

"A house full, huh? That's what I like to hear. But don't wait too long. I want to be able to get down on the floor and play with my grandbabies."

Emma sipped her hot cocoa. "You should have thought of that before you moved to the land of cheese curds and cold-ass winters. As if I'm ever bringing my babies here."

"Young lady," her mother said, laughing. "As long as you're

under my roof you will show Minnesota a little respect."

"I'm kidding. I can tell you're happy here."

"I *am* happy here, hypothermia-inducing temperatures aside." Her mom squeezed her hand, and they sat in the warm kitchen, sunshine filtering in through the snow-covered branches outside.

Emma understood why her mother had returned to Minnesota. Her parents had never lived there together, which meant this place held memories for her mom of a time before her dad. Emma was a little envious of her mother in that respect. Being back in Seattle was sometimes difficult precisely because it was the city she'd grown up in. Golden Gardens had been the site of sunny beach afternoons and cool evenings around a bonfire, of swimming and sailing in the cold waters of Puget Sound. Seattle Center, on the other hand, was problematic. Whenever she went to a WNBA game at Key Arena, she entered and exited on First Avenue so that she wouldn't have to walk past Fisher Pavilion where hundreds of mourners had gathered to celebrate her father's life and legacy shortly after he died.

Here, though, there were no memories of her father to contend with, positive or negative. They had visited Minnesota when she was growing up but only in the summer and never this particular corner of the Twin Cities. The holidays, often difficult for families who had lost someone, were a little bit easier here in this new house and a neighborhood where, as far as Emma knew, her father had never set foot. He still featured prominently in their holiday reminiscences, of course, and her mother always offered up a prayer for him at Christmas Dinner, but his ghost didn't lurk in the shadows of every room. They missed him, but not like in the beginning.

The first Christmas after he died had been, predictably, the hardest. Emma had been in Thailand at Thanksgiving for the U-19 World Cup, so Christmas 2004 was her first major holiday at home without him. Christmas Day was hard enough, but then she awoke the following morning to the news of the tsunami in Asia and the holiday took an even darker turn. She spent hours watching online footage of the destruction of Phuket, Thailand, where the US side had played all of its group matches only a month before, and somehow it seemed unsurprising that the earth had shifted and the ocean had risen up to obliterate the incredibly beautiful, vibrant beach community she had fallen in love with.

And yes, maybe she had been a tad angsty, but she was back in Seattle for the first time since August and she missed her dad—and Jamie—like crazy. School and soccer and the national team had kept her too busy to think about who might be missing, but that week she'd had nothing but time on her hands—a situation she'd vowed to avoid if possible in the future.

A few years later when the earthquake off the coast of Japan triggered its own deadly tsunami, she'd found herself reliving those first dazed days after the 2004 tsunami that was somehow indelibly connected in her mind to losing her father and, to some extent, Jamie too. Similarly, the 2011 tsunami would forever be linked to the national team's loss to Japan in the World Cup finals. That one had been easier to take in theory because at the end of the day, soccer really was only a game, and how could the US players begrudge the Japanese women the most joyful moment of their lives so soon after some had lost homes and loved ones in the tsunami? How could they be sorry that a grieving nation finally had some good news to latch onto, an inspiring story of overcoming the odds to help them rise from literal ashes?

Except that she *was* sorry. Placing second to Japan was far worse than watching from the stands as the US lost to Germany in the 2003 World Cup semi-finals; worse even than being on the bench when they were blown out by Brazil in the 2007 World Cup semi-finals, her first major tournament. She would forever regret Japan's victory in Germany because, as she'd told her mother, it meant that she might not ever know how it felt to be a World Cup champion. Was that selfish? Perhaps. But as the national team psychologist had said more than once, they had a right to their feelings about any loss, win, or tie, even if it wasn't how they thought they should feel.

In a year and a half, barring injury and natural disaster, she would have another shot at the title. And while her father's absence from her life was permanent, apparently Jamie's didn't have to be. January camp was only a couple of weeks away. Maybe they would find a way to salvage something from the ashes of their former friendship, too.

Assuming Jamie wanted to. Blowing her off via text at the holidays was hardly an encouraging sign.

"More hot chocolate, honey?" her mom asked.

"Sure. Thanks, Mom."

"You're welcome. It's good to have you home."

It was good to be there, too, though it didn't feel entirely like home. One good thing about Minnesota was all the sunshine. The scenery wasn't bad either, even if it was too cold to enjoy in the winter except through a double-paned window.

Emma's brother Tyler and his fiancée, Bridget, flew in from DC on Christmas Eve. Emma and her mom met them at the airport and then whisked them off to Rochester where Aunt June was hosting a large family get-together. There were cousins Emma hadn't seen in years except on Facebook, along with older relatives who stared and whispered about her as if she couldn't hear them. She was used to having people watch her in public and at assorted events. But in her mother's sister's home on Christmas Eve? Not her favorite, frankly.

When her mom suggested they leave before the evening church service, Emma and Ty (self-avowed "heathens" that they were) agreed readily. They drove back to the Cities along the dark highway, the flat, snow-covered earth awash in starlight as they sang Christmas carols at the top of their lungs and laughed about the odder of their Minnesota relatives. Ty had grown into a lean-faced man with a gorgeous head of hair, just like their dad, and a similar drive to change the world. A political analyst, he had met his fiancée a year and a half earlier at the DC-based think tank where they both landed after graduating from separate East Coast institutions. Bridget wasn't like the cheerleader and sorority types Ty had dated all through high school and college. She was pretty enough, but she cared more about the outcome of the civil unrest in Sudan than about her hair or make-up. She was a keeper, which was why Emma and her mom had both been thrilled when Ty called to tell them at Thanksgiving that he was going to ask her to marry him. This was their first time doing the holidays together. After Christmas in Minnesota, they were planning to head back to the Boston suburbs to ring in 2014 with Bridget's family.

Back at the house, they popped popcorn, put in *Love, Actually*, and lay around the living room, enjoying each other's company and the cheesiest of holiday movies. At one point, their mom excused herself to call Roger, who was spending the evening with his grown children in Anoka, leaving Emma with her brother and his fiancée snuggled up on the couch. They were adorable together and obviously very much in love, and it occurred to her that somehow, everyone in her family had someone but her. Even Dani was starting to get serious about Booty Call Guy, as Emma still mentally referred to Derek, press officer for the Mariners.

Was her mom right? Did she create obstacles to keep love at bay? If so, then she was a big ole cliché: the girl who lost her father and couldn't bear the thought of losing anyone else, so she held people at arm's length to make sure she didn't have to risk feeling that way ever again. That, or choose emotionally unavailable people to get involved with. That was what she'd done in high school and college, again and again. She finally broke the pattern with Sam. Or rather, Sam made her break it by being so amazing that Emma had forgotten why she usually scheduled her love life as rigidly as she organized her daily work-outs and caloric intake. At least, for a while. Then the hectic nature of a long residency camp in LA combined with a long WPS season, the failed World Cup bid, and crazy fan stalking in the aftermath of Germany, and Sam was gone.

Emma had never told her family why Sam left—she hadn't

wanted to worry them—but for once she hadn't been the one with commitment issues. She couldn't blame Sam, though. Her first (and only to-date) serious girlfriend's announcement that they needed to break up had arrived almost predictably on the heels of the latest Twitter attack by a particularly disturbed male "fan" of Emma's. This same man had targeted Sam on multiple occasions with kidnapping and rape threats, among other violent fantasies shared in one hundred forty characters for all of Sam's friends, family members, and co-workers to see. They had reported him each time, but that hadn't stopped him. He merely created a new account under another fake identity so he could go after her the next time another photo of the two of them surfaced.

The final straw had been different, though. This time he'd described in vivid detail how he would stalk and kill her in front of Emma, thereby releasing her from Sam's "sick obsession." The police officer they spoke with in Boston explained that they could try to track him down through his Internet service provider, press charges, and obtain a restraining order. Or they could try to become invisible and wait for him to fixate on some other target, which was what happened in most cases like this. Either way he suggested they arm themselves in case he broke the pattern of the majority of social media stalkers and decided to approach them in real life.

"*Arm* ourselves?" Sam had repeated, her hands clenching and unclenching spasmodically as she stared across the cluttered desk. "Do you mean get a gun?"

"That might be good to have in your home. But I would definitely recommend getting mace, for starters."

Emma had sat there in silence as the officer droned on about steps they should take to protect themselves, wondering how she'd gotten from the vibrant green of the soccer field to this gray, dingy room.

The officer gave them a handout, and Emma had skimmed it: Remove home address on personal checks and business cards; place real property in a trust and list utilities under the name of the trust; utilize a private mail box service to receive all personal mail; file for confidential voter status or register to vote utilizing mail box address; and on and on. One of the items further down the list had grabbed her attention: *Get a new driver's license with the new mail box address on it.* Seriously? She'd glanced at the revision date at the bottom of the page, July 2009, and wondered how many times the list had been given out since it was created. How many women had followed these steps to try to convince themselves that they were safe?

Safety was an illusion, though. As a female professional athlete, she understood that better than most.

"I can't live like this," Sam had announced when they got back to Emma's apartment that evening. "I'm sorry, Emma. I care about you but I hardly ever see you and now this? It's too much."

Emma had sat on the couch watching as Sam packed up the few items she kept at the loft. Of course it hurt. Of course she had hoped Sam would miss her enough to reconsider. But in a way she'd been almost relieved to be on her own again. The online harassment had been so much worse when she was with Sam, far worse than when she dated Will the year after she and Sam broke up. She didn't worry that he would get stalked, didn't worry that some random person would leap out from a Seattle doorway and stab him Monica Seles-style. No one had ever threatened him for being with her, as far as she knew. It was as if the crazy dudes who fantasized about her went ballistic at the thought of her with another woman, especially a slightly butch, gender non-conforming woman like Sam.

That description fit Jamie, too. Jamie, who she'd last seen in the airport about to catch a flight to Heathrow. Jamie, who had held her hand and taken her number and then neglected to even text her. Emma glared at the screen as Emma Thompson's on-screen husband flirted with his personal assistant. For the first time ever, this movie was hitting a little too close to home. Why did it have to be set in London, of all places? She should have known it would only remind her that Jamie was probably sound asleep in her flat that was no doubt all lit up with Christmas lights, curled happily in slumber around her girlfriend trying to eke out as much quality time before she headed off to America and they had to live through Skype and stolen weekends and holidays the way other national team members did with their spouses and significant others.

It was better to be alone, honestly, than to try to make something work in the narrow spaces that playing for club and country allowed; better to be unattached than to have to worry that some nut job was waiting around the corner to pounce on the woman she'd had the gall to fall in love with. She wrapped her blanket tighter around herself and tried not to feel quite so much kinship with the lonely and very fictional Prime Minister of England who found himself falling for someone he worked with. Hollywood had written the ending to this particular story, so the excessively heterosexual and potentially mismatched couple would end up together in the end. In real life, it wasn't quite as easy as that. Watching people hug and kiss their hellos at airports was all well and good, but half of all marriages still ended in divorce, and for professional athletes the rate was even higher.

As her brother giggled—*giggled!*—at some private joke and kissed the top of Bridget's head, Emma threw a handful of popcorn at them. "Hey! Knock off the PDA."

"Scrooge much?" Ty said, eating the popcorn that had landed within reach.

"Be nice to your sister," Bridget said.

"Yeah, be nice to me," Emma echoed. "Glad to see someone is keeping you in line, Ty."

Bridget smiled. "It's a tough job but someone's got to do it."

"Shh, you guys," Ty said. "I like this part."

On screen, the kid who'd lost his mother was practicing the drums twenty-four/seven in an attempt to impress the girl he loved. It reminded Emma a little of how her brother had thrown himself into skateboarding after their dad died, learning trick after trick until he was so good he got scouted by a West Coast brand. Jamie had taught him a few tricks when she'd come up to Seattle for the funeral, and at first Emma had thought he might have a crush on her and that was why he was working so hard on ollies and kick flips. But then she'd realized that with her heading off to college and their mom devoting even more time than usual to her pediatrics work, Ty had been the only one not busy enough that he wouldn't have to notice how much he missed their dad.

How did everything tonight come back to Jamie? No matter what she'd told her mother, she wasn't sure what was going to happen if Jamie made the national team and they had to spend weeks upon weeks together away from their regular lives, training and playing matches together and possibly even sharing a hotel room at some point. For a moment she allowed herself to imagine what Christmas might look like if things were different. Would she and Jamie ever be wrapped around each other on the couch in her mom's living room watching *Love, Actually*? Singing carols on the dark highway and relating the inane conversations they'd overheard at the party? Waking up to each other on Christmas morning, the frost on the window pane sparkling in the Minnesota sunshine while they snuggled in bed, waiting for the rest of the house to wake up?

God damn Hollywood, she thought, glowering at the television screen as the eleven-year-old boy raced through the airport, trying to track down the girl he was in love with before she flew off to America. It was an impossible myth, this notion of romantic love, one they were told starting from birth, practically. And yet, even though she knew that the movie version of love and real life love were different beasts, even though she honestly believed she was better off on her own at this particular point in her life, she still wished she had someone beside her to share Christmas Eve in her mother's new house on the frozen tundra of Minnesota.

#

By the time Jamie cleared customs at the San Francisco Airport, it was already mid-afternoon on Christmas Day. With her backpack over one shoulder and her carry-on rolling behind her, she walked into the main hall of the international terminal to find her entire family, including Todd, waiting for her. As she shook her head at the sight, half-laughing, she felt the tears that were never far off these days clouding her vision. She blinked them away and watched as Meg handed the large hand-written sign she'd been holding ("Welcome home, Jamie! Best. Christmas. Ever.") to her husband and set off toward her, skirt billowing in her wake.

Just before Meg reached her, Jamie realized she probably should drop her bags, since her sister showed no signs of slowing. Meg slammed into her, hugging Jamie as tightly as any teammate ever had.

"Did I nail it?" she asked, laughing as she pulled back. "That's how soccer players greet each other, isn't it?"

Jamie pressed a kiss against her sister's forehead and picked up her bags in one hand, continuing toward their parents with her arm around Meg's shoulders. "Totally. Well done."

Their parents were standing together, matching smiles curving their lips as they watched their girls approach. Their mom was the first to break away and pull Jamie into a tight hug.

"You're back," she murmured, and Jamie could hear the choked-back tears in her voice.

"I'm back," she confirmed.

Her dad moved forward and enfolded them in his arms, and then Meg joined in, too. Jamie saw Todd standing a little ways away, and she jerked her chin at him.

"Get in here, bro. Family hug time."

They opened their arms and he joined in, and the Maxwells and the Kirschoffs stood in a huddle at the edge of the main hall while strangers moved about them enacting their own touching reunions.

Eventually they took the escalator to baggage claim, chatting as they waited for the carousel to kick into motion. Jamie had had her final meeting with Arsenal management the day before and filled her family in on the deal that would loan her to an NWSL team yet to be determined—on the condition that she come back for Champions League. That meant she would be in London during the NWSL pre-season and again at the end of the NWSL regular season. She was fine with the deal because it meant she would have the best of both worlds—NWSL, which was far more competitive than the English WSL, *and* Champions League, which brought together the best of the best in European club football.

Assuming an NWSL team signed her, Jamie's combined season would last nine months, which was all any football player wanted, anyway. The men worked ten months out of the year, and played thirty-five (MLS) or forty-five (Premier League) matches in that time. But in the US, as in the UK, the women's league operated on an abbreviated summer schedule with only twenty-four regular season matches. Champions League, which ran in the fall and spring, offered additional opportunities to train and play.

"So you're not back for good, then?" Jamie's mother asked.

"No, I am. I just have the chance to go back and play Champions League if I want to. That is, if Arsenal makes it next year. Only the top two WSL finishers each season go on to Champions League."

"Any word on Portland?" her father asked.

"I have a meeting with the GM on the third of January. Ellie says it's looking good."

He shook his head. "Rachel Ellison going to bat for my kid. It boggles the mind."

"I know," Todd put in. "You're bringing me all sorts of street cred. Even music majors know who she is."

"Soon everyone's going to know who you are too," Meg said, smiling.

Please, God, Jamie prayed, *don't ever let my parents discover Tumblr, L Chat, or fan fiction.* They worked for a software company, though. The odds they wouldn't somehow stumble across all manner of mortifying speculation seemed fairly low.

Maybe she would have to hold a family meeting about it. "*So, guys,*" she imagined herself saying. "*I am officially banning you from Googling me. If you insist on breaking the ban, you must never speak to me of what you find.*"

She knew how her mother would respond: "*Why, sweetie?*

What are you worried about us seeing?"

Probably she should break her no-heavy-drinking rule beforehand. That way she wouldn't have to remember the conversation later.

The house was the same as ever—white icicle lights hanging from the gutter at the front of the house, the perfectly decorated Christmas tree framed in the living room picture window. Inside it smelled of eggnog and spices, pumpkin pie and turkey. Her mother had roasted the turkey that morning, and as soon as they got back to the house, she and Meg went into the kitchen to work on Christmas Dinner. When Jamie offered to help, they shooed her out.

"You know, I'm not a bad cook anymore," she said, watching them from the dining room doorway.

"We know. We saw the Thanksgiving pictures," Meg said. "But you just moved halfway across the world. Relax, okay? Let us make dinner for you."

"Fine," she muttered, and stalked out of the kitchen. She'd dozed on the way home from the airport and woken up cranky, and even though she knew she shouldn't take her mood out on her family, she also knew there wasn't anyone else to take it out on.

Her dad and Todd were in the living room, the usual Christmas Day football game on, and all at once the scene was so heterosexist—the women in the kitchen making the meal while the men watched sports and drank beer—that she wasn't quite sure where she fit. On Thanksgiving they'd all chipped in together in the kitchen, and everyone had been equally happy with the lesbian film they'd watched on Netflix after dinner. That was one advantage of a same-sex partnered life: You didn't have to behave in a certain way just because that was how things had always been done.

"You joining us?" her dad asked, smiling up at her from his favorite recliner.

"In a little bit. I think I'm going to go for a run first. It's what the national team always does on travel days. Supposedly it helps with jet lag."

"By all means, go," her dad said. "You don't have all that long before you have to get back on another plane."

"Actually," she said, "I was thinking of driving up to Portland. It's not that far, and as long as the mountain passes aren't bad, it shouldn't be too treacherous."

He frowned. "Oh. Well, okay. Did you want to borrow the car or were you thinking of renting one?"

"Neither. I sold my scooter before I left London and I already had some money saved. I was thinking I might buy a car this week."

"A car?" He considered the idea for a moment before nodding. "That makes a lot of sense now that you're back. Your mom and I can help."

"Dad, I'm twenty-five. I can buy my own car, okay?"

He held up his hands. "Only trying to help."

"I know." She drifted closer and squeezed his shoulder. "But you've done enough. More than enough."

From the couch beside her, Todd cleared his throat. "You know, Meg and I were thinking about getting a new car. In case you haven't gotten our Christmas present yet, Tim."

Her father laughed, and Jamie shook her head.

"Worth a try." Todd shrugged and turned back to the football game.

Upstairs in her room, which was unchanged except for the sewing table that had taken the place of her old desk, Jamie dropped onto the bed, phone in hand. She opened a new text message and then paused. This was it: her last contact with Clare until she went back in March for Champions League. They had agreed on a clean break. No texts, no emails, no phone calls unless they had to discuss details of the move. In March, if they were ready, they would meet for coffee to gauge where they were at. They both wanted to stay friends ultimately. It was in the lesbian contract, after all. Besides, Britt was one of Jamie's best friends, and Allie and Clare worked together. They didn't want to make it any more difficult for their friends than it already was.

Britt had taken the news well. Apparently Clare had been talking to Allie about her doubts for a while now, and Allie had dropped plenty of hints while Jamie was in LA. In fact, Britt was probably less surprised by the break-up than Jamie had been. The NWSL move hadn't come as a shock, either. Britt had fielded offers herself and hadn't ruled it out completely. She even had a meeting planned with DC in mid-January when she came back to the States to participate in a mini-goalkeeper camp at US Soccer headquarters. She was one of eight keepers invited to the mini-camp set for the week after residency camp. Depending on what the coaches said, she'd told Jamie, she might consider a move back to the US as well. But Jamie knew it would take more than a tepid offer to get her to leave Arsenal and, more to the point, Allie.

Jamie's phone had gone to sleep while she sat on her bed trying to figure out what to write. Finally she turned it back on and typed, "Arrived safely. Hope you're having a good Christmas with your family. Take care, and I'll talk to you in a few months. XO." She paused, deleted the "XO" at the end, and then put it back in before hitting send.

There. That was that. No more Clare. No more "we" or "us," no more afternoon tea dates, no more holidays in Cornwall. They were officially done now, and there was no chance that Clare would change her mind or that Jamie would move back to London. Her sister had once said that a relationship didn't end if it didn't end badly—referring to her friendship with Emma, if she recalled correctly—but that wasn't the case here. She and Clare had ended their relationship on more of a technicality, really, and yet there could be no doubt that their lives would be moving forward separately.

Her friendship with Britt was slipping away too. She knew they would always be the kind of friends who could talk or visit and feel like they'd never been apart. After all, they'd known each other for more than a decade and had been teammates for all but one of those years. But there would be no more match day drinks at The Twelve Pins before making their way to UAE Stadium to watch Arsenal take on Chelsea or Liverpool or Man City. No more larks about London, no more double dates with their girlfriends, no more quiet afternoons hanging out at one flat or the other while Britt read whatever historical mystery series she was currently obsessed with and Jamie messed around in Illustrator. No more long bus rides to various corners of the UK, no more mystery meat pub suppers on the road, no more shared hotel rooms in four hundred year old buildings. Although perhaps that last bit was just as well, given Britt's snoring issues.

Tears threatened but she blinked them back again and rose from the bed. Time to go for that run. The fitness coach would be pleased. Thoughts of Lacey reminded her of training camp, which, inevitably, led to Emma again. She was in Minnesota with her family, a recent photo on Instagram had confirmed. As Jamie changed into work-out gear, she thought about texting her. She could use Christmas or the move as an excuse. But if she told her she was back earlier than expected—last Emma knew, Jamie wasn't coming home until January camp— then she would have a lot of other things to explain, too. Better to maintain silence on all fronts. They would see each other in LA soon enough. Two weeks to the day, to be exact.

Not that she was counting.

Some things apparently never changed.

A week later, Jamie was eating sushi with her parents at a restaurant on the San Francisco waterfront a few hours before New Year's Eve fireworks were scheduled to light up the city. Meg and Todd had headed down to San Diego to ring in 2014 with his family, but Meg's best friend from high school, Becky—or *Becca*, as she liked to be called now—had moved back to the Bay Area the previous year and was at the other end of the table with her wife and parents. Kyle, her younger brother, was normally around for the holidays too, but this year he was back east with his girlfriend's family. The pair had met at Penn and now worked together on Wall Street, much to his sister's disgust. Their parents, Michael and Ruth, still taught at Cal (political science and chemistry, respectively) and seemed stunned that their youngest child had grown up to become a financial analyst at a brokerage house.

"He admitted he would vote Republican 'if not for the social issues,'" Becca had said scathingly on their way into the city that evening. "And to think he used to accuse *me* of not being black enough. Chump."

As their server stopped by to top off their tea, Jamie glanced over and caught Becca and Rhea exchanging a smile. They were cute together, with their matching urban, almost punk hairstyles and hipster glasses. Becca had shocked the hell out of Jamie when she came out shortly before leaving for her freshman year at NYU, but Jamie had adjusted to the idea by now. She'd been invited to their wedding two summers ago, but she'd had a match. Out of all the events she'd had to miss over the years, she had always regretted missing Becca's wedding in particular. Not only had she wanted to celebrate the marriage of one of her oldest friends on the planet, but she also knew it might have been her only chance to experience a swanky lesbian beach wedding in Provincetown. Rhea's family was old money from Maryland, and had been happy to go all out for their only daughter.

Becca caught her looking and picked up her phone, nodding at Jamie's lying on the table.

"R and I are plotting our escape," the text read.

"There is no escape. Fireworks with the folks, remember?"

"Three hours until they start. Or we could go out afterward?"

"No. I turn into a pumpkin at midnight."

Becca smirked as she typed, "Is pumpkin British slang for bottom?"

"It's a Cinderella reference!"

"Whatever you say, Princess."

Jamie sent her a pig emoji and pointedly set her phone back on the table. Meg had recently accused her of going overboard on the emojis, but she couldn't help how much she loved the new phone their parents had gotten her for Christmas. It was too much and she'd told them so. But at least they hadn't tried to give her a car.

Becca, however, wouldn't take no—or an animal emoji—for an answer, which was how Jamie ended up a little while later outside the Lexington, the sole remaining lesbian bar in the city. Becca and Rhea preferred El Rio, but the NYE party there was already sold out. As they waited in line to get in, Jamie weighed all the reasons this little jaunt was a bad idea. She actually loved queer clubs, the only place in the world outside of Pride weekend where same-sex PDA ran rampant, and San Francisco had provided the backdrop for some particularly memorable escapades back in college. But she'd been younger then and not as worried about pinging US Soccer's radar for the wrong reasons. Then there was the fact that Becca had said to her during the short BART ride from the Embarcadero, "The best way to get over someone is to get under someone else."

Or, like, *not.*

As they showed their IDs and paid the cover, Jamie remembered the last time she'd been at the Lex. She and Clare had come to Berkeley for a holiday during a brief break the previous fall between Champions League tournament legs. They'd had so much fun that week, cut out of space and time, and had come into the city on the next to last night of their trip to "dance their booties off," as Clare had put it. This was a month before Jamie broke her ankle, and they were still decidedly in the honeymoon stage. Jamie remembered dancing pressed as close as they could get, tipsy from mojitos and unable to keep their hands off one another. It seemed like forever ago now.

Inside, she followed Becca to a cocktail table in the corner while Rhea braved the busy bar. Drinks were their treat, Becca had insisted on the ride over, which was good because Jamie hadn't budgeted the night out and her savings had taken a major hit with the down payment for the three-year-old Kia hatchback that had recently become her first official car. She was always doing things late—first (consensual) sex at nineteen; first senior national team cap at twenty-four; and now, first car only weeks before her twenty-sixth birthday.

Becca leaned in to be heard over the music and said, "What's your type, anyway? Girly girls?"

Jamie shrugged. "Pretty much. Although I like an edge, too."

Clare appeared ultra-feminine, but underneath the penchant for make-up and dresses was a take-charge teacher. That was why Jamie knew Clare would never call her up saying she'd made a mistake and wanted another chance. Even if she thought those things, which Jamie doubted, there was no way her pride would allow her to admit as much.

Then there was Emma. During training or a match, she had a swagger that was completely different from the way she carried herself in the rest of life. Someone on Tumblr had once called her the butchest femme they'd ever seen, and Jamie thought the description was perfect.

"Where did you just go?" Becca asked. "Or do I even need to ask, *Blakewell?*"

"Shut it."

"Oh my god, I'm right, aren't I? You were totally thinking about Emma Blakeley!"

Jamie rolled her eyes, ignoring the comment. It was unfortunate that Becca had been around the year she and Emma were friends. When Emma came to visit for New Year's, Jamie had brought her to the waterfront for the fireworks show—as Becca had reminded her when she, Meg, and Jamie went to dinner a couple of nights earlier.

Before Becca could press further, Rhea materialized out of the crowd, juggling their drinks. They made room for her and stood around the table, sipping their cocktails and people-watching. Other than the bar, the most crowded area in the club was the dance floor where women of all shapes, ages, and sizes gyrated to the music. Currently the DJ was playing Flo Rida's "Good Feeling." As Jamie's gaze wandered the room, she noticed a redhead leaning against a pillar at the edge of the dance floor, mixed drink in hand. She looked a little like Emma, with curves and muscles equally visible beneath her tank top and short skirt.

"Nice," Rhea said, following her gaze. "Do you need a wingman?"

"No, I'm not looking."

"Why? You're single, aren't you? Why not have a little fun?"

Jamie pondered the question. After Laurie, her college girlfriend, had left to join the Peace Corps, Jamie had thrown herself into soccer and hadn't dated for a few months. Then, over the next year and a half, she went through a handful of relationships in short order. Each time she broke up with one girl, she immediately found another one to date. And every time without fail she somehow convinced herself that she was falling for the girl she was seeing, even though as soon as it ended she realized that she hadn't been. Britt had accused her of serial monogamy. At least she'd been monogamous. That was more than could be said for some of their friends—like Angie's college girlfriend, Shay. They found out later that Shay had been dating other women on the side nearly the entire time she was with Angie.

At this point, Jamie knew herself well enough to recognize that she would rather be with someone than be alone. But maybe she should try the alone thing, or at least not date seriously, for a while, given how uncertain her immediate professional/geographic future was. Most of the people she'd dated in college had picked her rather than the other way around. Half the time she'd been so flattered by the interest that she'd simply gone along with it. At some level, despite the years of therapy, she still saw herself as damaged. She'd talked to other rape survivors and knew she wasn't the only one who struggled sometimes with feeling worthy of genuine love.

But she *had* survived, and Rhea was right: She was single. No reason she couldn't enjoy herself for a few hours.

As Wiz Khalifa and Snoop Dogg started rapping about getting drunk and smoking weed, Jamie finished her Tom Collins.

"Yo, old married ladies," she said, grinning sideways at the other two. "Let's dance."

Becca set her glass down with a thump. "Come on, Rhea. Time for us *old married ladies* to show this skinny white girl how it's done."

Jamie hummed along with the music as they approached the dance floor. In straight clubs, too often she felt out-of-place among the women in their tiny skirts and heavy make-up, not to mention the guys who eyed her short hair and tattoos suspiciously. When it came to hetero, meat-market kinds of places, she usually steered clear of crowded dance spaces where men who felt threatened by anyone remotely gender non-conforming might "accidentally" place a well-aimed elbow into her ribs or back. But at a place like the Lex, when she got elbowed by a man it was usually because he was tripping on E and showcasing his impressive dance skills a bit too enthusiastically. At the Lex, the women in tiny skirts and heavy make-up were all but guaranteed to be queer or trans or both.

The DJ, a bald woman covered in tattoos, kept the music going fast and furious, and Jamie soon lost herself in spinning and bouncing between hot, sweaty bodies in the center of the dance floor. A few minutes in, the redhead and her friends joined the throngs not far from Jamie and hers. Another few minutes went by, and suddenly Jamie found a cloud of red hair in her face and a firm ass pressing against her. When her hands automatically fell onto the encroaching hips, the other woman glanced over her shoulder and smiled, her eyebrows rising in a clear question. Jamie hesitated. Dancing with complete strangers was so not her thing. If not for the alcohol coursing through her veins, she probably would have backed away already. But she was feeling good and loose, and it was New Year's Eve. And as Rhea and Becca had pointed out, she was single. She took a breath and smiled back with a slight squeeze of the stranger's hips.

They danced like that for a while, the redhead's back against Jamie's chest, Becca and Rhea grinning at her and the crowd cheering each new beat. When she closed her eyes, Jamie ended up remembering the last time she had danced here, Clare gyrating against her, arms around Jamie's neck, her own palms tugging Clare's hips closer. Then her eyes opened and she remembered she wasn't here with Clare. For a moment the muscles in the stranger's shoulders reminded her of Emma again, and she let herself pretend it was Emma whose hips were swaying beneath her hands, Emma whose eyes and lips shone under the spinning lights. Then she pushed her once and possibly future teammate from her mind. Fantasizing about someone she couldn't have was a terrible idea for too many reasons to count. And yet, it was better than mooning over Clare. At least, she thought it was.

She danced until, even with her button down tied around her waist, she was hot and sweaty. Then she signaled the redhead that she needed a break.

"Want company?" the other woman shouted into her ear.

Jamie shook her head. "Sorry, I can't. Happy New Year!"

The redhead nodded, her eyes only slightly disappointed as she whirled back to her group of friends.

Bottle of water in hand a little while later, Jamie leaned against a pillar surveying the room as she cooled down. New Year's brought out all types, from pierced dykes in leather and hipster chicks like Becca and Rhea to sporty lesbians and sorority types. Becca had been right to drag her here. It was good to remember that while the woman she'd thought might be The One had gotten away, there were still plenty of other fish in the sea.

The evening passed in a whirl of lights, hot bodies—in every sense of the word—and heavy beats. Jamie danced a few more rounds with Rhea and Becca, who even after five years together danced like they were honeymooners. It was sweet but a little hard to take given her own current flailing at life and love, so Jamie spent more time leaning against a pillar at the edge of the dance floor than dancing. At one point she thought she saw two sporty types watching her from a nearby table, but when she stared back, they quickly looked away. Had she imagined the look of recognition in their eyes?

A few minutes later the pair approached. "Excuse me," the taller one said, leaning in. "Are you a soccer player on the national team?"

Holy crap. Someone had recognized her. "Not exactly. I'm in the pool, though."

The taller one nudged her companion. "Told you so." Then she smiled and held out a hand. "Chris Bennett, and this is Beth, my girlfriend. I think I saw you play in college. Stanford, right? I played basketball at Cal, so we probably know some of the same people."

Turned out they did. It was hard to talk so close to the DJ booth, so when they invited her back to their table, Jamie agreed. The next half hour passed agreeably as they talked about life in Berkeley, women's college sports, and soccer. Chris and Beth had been together since college and had been season ticket holders for FC Gold Pride, Jamie's first professional club.

"Sorry," Jamie said. "I heard they didn't give deposits back after they folded."

"It wasn't a big deal," Chris assured her. "We were just bummed we didn't get to see you guys play again. You ended up overseas, didn't you? It was cool to see you back in the pool for Ireland last year."

"Although not so cool to see you go down again," Beth added.

"Tell me about it."

They asked her about the national team schedule and what she thought her chances were at making the roster, and she played it safe and answered vaguely before changing the subject to Stanford's perpetual dominance of PAC-12 basketball.

When Becca and Rhea caught her eye from across the bar a little while later, Jamie flashed them a thumbs-up. Time to head to the waterfront to meet up with their parents.

"I have to go, but it was great to meet you guys," she said, meaning it.

"Is there any way we could get a picture with you?" Chris

asked. "That way we can say we knew you when."

She hesitated briefly, remembering how the Internet had exploded the last time she'd posed for a fan photo. But then she said, "Sure," and stood between the two women as they snapped a couple of quick selfies.

"But maybe, if you don't mind, don't mention the name of the club if you post it?" she asked as the couple checked the photos. "Obviously I'm not in the closet, but I also don't want to give the federation any reason to look elsewhere."

"No worries," Chris said, nodding. "I totally get it. Thanks for hanging out. It means a lot."

"Thank you," Jamie said, hugging each woman in turn. "Tell Cara hello next time you see her."

"Better yet, we'll tag her on Instagram."

"Sounds good. Happy New Year!" she said with a last wave. "Good luck with the team!"

Their encouraging words still rattling around her head, Jamie followed Becca and Rhea out into the chilly San Francisco night. It was bizarre to think that she had fans, people other than her friends and family who were hoping to see her suit up in a national team jersey. Twice she had thought that dream crushed, and now all of a sudden it was back, almost within reaching distance. She wasn't sure what she would do if she crashed and burned a third time.

Her phone buzzed while they were on the train. Chris had uploaded the photo to Instagram and tagged her and Cara, the old college buddy. The caption read, "Look who Beth and I ran into out on the town celebrating New Year's Eve? #CalBearsRule #FCGoldPride #USWNT"

That last hashtag had Jamie wincing a bit because she knew the federation's social media mavens would be monitoring it closely. She stared at the photo, but she didn't look drunk, only flushed and happy. What would Clare think if she saw it? Not that it mattered what her ex-girlfriend thought. What would Emma—? She stopped the thought before it could form completely.

"What happened to the redhead?" Becca asked as they

waited for the train back to the waterfront. "One minute you were dancing with her and the next you disappeared."

"I was thirsty." As Becca waggled her eyebrows, Jamie slapped her arm. "For water, asshat."

"I apologize for my wife," Rhea said, corralling Becca and tugging her close. "That pig emoji is perfect when it comes to this one."

"Hey." Becca narrowed her eyes at them. "No ganging up."

"Oh, so you can dish it out but you can't take it?"

Becca reached across Rhea to flick Jamie—her traditional method of inflicting abuse on her younger brother and anyone else who pissed her off—but Jamie's reflexes saved her and she danced away, her laughter drowned out by the screech of an approaching train.

Twenty minutes later they were parked on a blanket at Rincon Park as colorful lights exploded overhead, music blasting accompaniment on nearby speakers. Jamie gazed up at the sky, the Bay Bridge and city skyline glowing in the background, and watched the fireworks rise and fall only to be replaced by more new shapes and colors. Their two families had come to this show—or watched it from Indian Rock in Berkeley—every year that she could remember. Even after she moved to London, she came home each winter, purposefully timing her trip for the holiday season. As far as she knew, she'd never missed a single New Year's Eve fireworks on the Bay.

Came home—the phrase repeated in her head, and she realized: London had never felt like home, not really. She loved the city, yes; loved her girlfriend and friends and teammates there, even loved her job more than anything else she'd ever done except maybe those first giddy weeks with FC Gold Pride at the end of her senior year of college. But London and the WSL had always felt temporary. Or rather, she had always felt temporary there. Now, sitting on a blanket at Rincon Park flanked by her parents on either side, her UK life seemed almost like it had never happened.

Her dad slipped his arm around her shoulders and leaned closer. "Happy New Year, kid. I hope 2014 is your best year yet."

"Thanks, Dad," she said, resting her head on his shoulder.

The coming year certainly had the potential to be the best yet. She might end up playing for the Portland Thorns; Arsenal might make it past the quarterfinals of Champions League for the first time in several years; and she might win a roster spot on the national team in time to play in the 2015 World Cup—on the top-ranked team in the world, no less. Then again, she could fail on all fronts and end up living at home with her parents pursuing Plan B—a graphic design job at Google or some start-up that didn't even exist yet. She had gone to Stanford, so while failing at international soccer was an option, failing at life most decidedly wasn't.

An image of Emma flashed into her mind, and as soon as the fireworks ended, she pulled out her phone to check her Insta feed. There were NYE photos from all over the country and even the world, given that the West Coast was one of the last spots in the western hemisphere to hit midnight. Sure enough, Emma had uploaded a photo of her and Dani on a balcony overlooking Seattle with the city skyline behind them, fireworks shooting off the top of the Space Needle. There was a man's arm resting on the balcony railing next to Emma, but he had been cropped out of the photo. Was she dating someone? The caption—"Happy New Year!"—gave nothing away.

She almost clicked the heart below Emma's photo. Almost commented with a smiley face and a quick message of well wishes for the coming year. But then she remembered Ellie's injunction on contact between the members comprising Blakewell; remembered that Clare hadn't unfriended her on social media (yet?); and instead she put her phone away. To distract herself, she chatted with Becca's parents as she helped pack up the blankets and plastic wine glasses they'd been bringing to the waterfront to toast the fireworks for at least the last decade. But then she found herself thinking they were probably the same glasses she and Emma had sipped sparkling cider from the year Emma had come to visit her for New

Year's, and she realized that Emma was far more entrenched in her life here than she had ever been in London. If Jamie played for Portland, she and Emma would see each other regularly whether she made the national team or not. There would be home and away matches in each other's cities, with parties and overnights likely because everyone in the NWSL knew everyone else and what was a game without a night out afterward?

At least 2014 would be interesting. No doubt about it.

CHAPTER EIGHT

"Are you creeping your girlfriend's Insta account again?"

Emma looked up as Dani slid back into the seat across from her. They had just finished dinner at their favorite pub on top of Queen Anne, and while Dani used the restroom, Emma *may* have pulled up Jamie's social media accounts.

"I'm not creeping anyone's Insta," she said.

Without warning, Dani reached out and swiped her phone, holding it up in one hand and repelling Emma's counter-reach with the other. "Oh, sorry, I meant Twitter. I was gone for three minutes. Seriously?"

"She was supposed to meet with the Thorns today. I thought there might be an announcement."

"And you know this how? I thought she blew you off."

"Ellie texted me. I'm curious about where she ends up, that's all."

Dani sipped her beer. "You keep saying you don't want anything to happen, but the fact you're stalking her says otherwise."

"I'm not stalking her."

"Swear that on the next World Cup and I *might* believe you."

Emma leaned her elbows against the table. "Okay, maybe I'm stalking her, but only a little."

"Is that like being a little bit pregnant?"

"Oh my god, don't even joke about being pregnant this close to the World Cup."

"You'd have to actually have sex to worry about that, Emma. You know, with a guy?"

Which was a valid point.

"At least the fans seem to have calmed down," Dani added, sliding her phone back to her.

"Thank god."

Without additional fodder, the women's soccer fandom had backed off the idea that Blakewell was an actual thing. Multiple sightings of Jamie at a club in San Francisco on New Year's Eve combined with Emma's photo of the Seattle fireworks had helped convince Tumblr they weren't a couple—especially the photo that showed Jamie grinding with some chick who was definitely not Emma. Or her long-term girlfriend, for that matter. As soon as Emma saw the posts on New Year's Day she'd texted Ellie, who had confirmed that Jamie had moved back to the States. Permanently.

"If you want to know what happened," Dani said, "why don't you text her? Or better yet, call? She did give you her number, after all."

Emma fixed her with a stare. "You're not helping."

"This is me helping. I told you before you haven't seemed happy since you broke up with Sam."

"And I told you that it's because we lost the World Cup, not because I lost Sam. I don't need a person in my life, Dan. I can be happy on my own."

"That's right, I forgot. Ice Queen Blakeley doesn't need anyone."

"Dude, you haven't called me that since high school."

"*Dude*, it's not my fault you're reverting. You have camp again in less than a week. What's the plan? Are you going to try to avoid her again, since obviously that worked so well last time?"

"I don't know. I haven't really thought about it." She swirled her phone around the polished wooden surface of their small table. "Can we talk about something else? How's Derek?

Or better yet, how is your adorable nephew?"

Dani started to protest at the subject change, but then she caved as Emma had known she would and pulled up photos of her nephew in Woodinville, a chubby one-year-old with a mouth full of teeth and still not a hair on his head.

Later, after another beer and more of the kind of easy conversation that came of being friends since grade school, they pulled on their puffy tech jackets and walked home together, pausing outside Dani's building to hug goodbye.

"I'll see you tomorrow, right?" Dani asked, keys dangling from her fingers.

"You got it," Emma said, squeezing her affectionately.

As Dani disappeared into the brick apartment building, Emma headed home. Booty Call G—er, *Derek's* sister was in town from Santa Cruz, and the following evening would be Dani's first time meeting a member of his family. Since the sister was apparently a big soccer fan, Dani had thought having a USWNT starter along for dinner and drinks might help make a good impression, though Emma was under strict instructions not to mention their early AYSO years when Dani proudly answered to the nickname "Thunderfoot."

On a whim, Emma took the long way home, cutting down to Highland Avenue and walking past the well-heeled homes with their circular drives and expansive views of the city. At Kerry Park, crowded with tourists and locals on a non-rainy Friday night, she paused and looked out over the city. The Space Needle was still flying the "2014" NYE banner overhead, along with the Twelfth Man flag for the Seahawks. As the Seahawks had become increasingly successful over the past few years, the city had become exponentially more fanatical about their NFL franchise. The Seahawks regularly drew more than 65,000 fans to Century Link Field while the Sounders averaged somewhere around 40,000 fans in the same stadium. Meanwhile, the first season of the NWSL had been considered mildly successful with an average attendance of 4,200 people per game, and the players were grateful and appreciative for even that amount. Emma didn't believe that the NFL and MLS had a better sporting experience to offer its fans. But their games were so much shinier and flashier than what the NWSL could offer that even she understood the draw.

Emma turned away from the view she loved and headed home. Trying to answer the decades-old question of why men's sports succeeded and women's sports didn't not only in America but the world over was an exercise in futility. She couldn't expect society and culture to change quickly. Look how long African Americans had been fighting for their civil rights, and police brutality and racist voting laws were still huge problems. Look how long queer people had been fighting, for that matter, and gay marriage was only now on its way to gaining popular support. In the context of people being denied their constitutional right to state protection and recognition, it seemed like an exercise in entitlement to bemoan the lack of support for female athletes.

And yet, she knew for a fact that sports had saved plenty of girls and women, black and white and brown. Jamie for one. Soccer had kept her out of her own head at a time when being inside her head might have destroyed her, Jamie had once told her. Emma knew what she meant. Every time she stepped on the field, she surrendered her sense of self. That was one of the things she loved about soccer—it was inarguably a player's game. Forty-five minute halves and no timeouts meant the players on the field had to do their jobs without substantial involvement by a coach. They had to know each other, had to trust each other, had to communicate and move in tandem together.

Sometimes she wondered what she would do after soccer to keep that team feeling in her life. Or even if there was anything she *could* do to keep it.

Normally Emma didn't have trouble ignoring the worry that she could slip in the shower and lay unconscious and bleeding—or worse—for a day or two before anyone noticed.

But for whatever reason, be it that the people she was closest to seemed to be finding potential life partners all at once or only that she had started yet another new year without someone who belonged solely to her, she was having a harder time than usual right now enjoying her own company. It didn't have anything to do with not hearing from Jamie. Nothing to do with seeing those pictures of her grinding with a super hot redhead. Like, nothing at all.

As the days leading up to January camp crawled by, she found herself out and about more than usual. This led to more fan interaction, but she was okay with that because hey, at least that meant she had someone to talk to, right? As pathetic as that sounded inside her head, it felt even worse as she strolled along Broadway two days before she flew out, window-shopping on an unseasonably sunny afternoon.

"Emma?"

She turned, her professional smile giving way to a genuine one as she recognized Will standing before her, his brown eyes as warm as ever. "Oh my god, Will!" He opened his arms and she didn't even hesitate before stepping into them. They may have only been together for eight months, but he had become one of her favorite people ever in that short amount of time.

"I thought that was you," he said, once they'd pulled back to regard each other. "How are you?"

"I'm good. What about you?"

"I'm good, too. Great, even. I'm—well, I got engaged."

Of course he had. But she kept the smile in place because he was a lovely man and she did want him to be happy. "Congratulations. That's wonderful news."

"Thanks." He glanced at his phone. "I have a little time right now. Would you, I don't know, want to grab coffee?"

"Absolutely," she said. "I would love to."

As they headed down the block, Will told her about the woman he planned to marry. Her name was Gianna, she was a twenty-nine year old graphic designer at Amazon, and they'd met online. Honestly, he had been a little leery of the online dating thing, but the local service he'd used swore by their algorithm. Now so did he.

At Vivace's, Emma's favorite café on Capitol Hill, they carried large ceramic mugs of drip coffee to a retro Formica table by the window. Her father had first brought her here during his thankfully brief separation from her mom, and she'd been coming back ever since. No matter what else she'd thought about the man, she had always admired his taste in coffee.

"So when did you shave off your beard?" she asked Will once they were seated.

"It's been a while. Maybe if you ever messaged me like you said you would…"

"Maybe if you logged into Facebook more than once a year…"

"Yeah, that's not going to happen."

She sipped her perfectly brewed dark roast, savoring the deep, intense flavor. "Well, either way, smooth looks good on you."

"You would think that."

"What's that supposed to mean?"

He took a bite of chocolate chip cookie. "You know what it means. I told you when we broke up, Emma, I think you prefer women. Not that I blame you. I prefer women, too."

When they called it quits, he'd pointed out how frequently she'd complained about the details of dating men: his beard scratching her face; the annoyance of birth control pills; the constant worry that she could get pregnant accidentally and miss a World Cup or the Olympics or an NWSL season. Before that conversation she had never stopped to think about how the constant grumbling had made him feel because, well, *feelings*.

"Was I really that awful?" she asked now.

Will shook his head. "I didn't mean it like that. But let me ask you this: Which was easier, dating me or dating your ex in Boston?"

"What does that have to do with anything?"

"It's sort of the point, isn't it?"

"Honestly, I'm not sure what the point is." She offered him a smile to soften her words. "I just know it's nice to see you."

"It's nice to see you, too. In real life, that is. I saw online that you were in the Twin Cities for the holidays. How was the land of cheese puffs and frozen cow pies?"

"Hello, they're called cheese *curds*."

"I don't really have anything to say to that."

She laughed and swallowed more delicious coffee. "It was fun. My brother was there with his fiancée, who is awesome."

Will pretended to be shocked. "Then there *is* a Blakeley who isn't commitment-phobic?"

She smacked his arm. "Shut up."

"Ow. No need to resort to violence, jock girl. How's your mom doing?"

They drank their coffee and talked, and it was nice. They had always gotten along well. That was never the issue. The problem was that he'd wanted more from her than she was prepared to give—time, affection, future plans. After Sam, she'd returned to her old relationship ways, scheduling dates around practice and gym time and keeping her professional and personal lives carefully separate. And Will had let her, at least for a little while.

He asked about soccer, and as she described the previous month's residency camp, she consciously tried not to talk about Jamie. She thought she was doing pretty well, too—until Will's head tilted and his lips pursed.

"Wait. The new midfielder's name is Jamie?"

"Um, yes?" *Crap.* Why was she so terrible at this?

"Jamie, as in the girl from California?"

Emma nodded, squinting at him.

"That's good, isn't it?" Will reached across the table to touch her hand. "You always said you hoped she would be back in the pool."

The fact that she had "always said" anything about Jamie to him was news to Emma. Faintly unwelcome news, given the current not-speaking, not-actually-friends thing Jamie seemed intent on doing.

"Right," she said, her tone noncommittal.

At this, he pulled his hand back and shook his head at her in an affectionate, slightly exasperated way that reminded her of her mother—*You put up more obstacles to love than anyone I've ever met.* She wasn't the one who had pulled a runner this time, though, was she? Which was poor consolation, if she thought about it.

A little while later Will checked his phone and said in a voice that sounded sincere, "I wish I didn't have to go. It's been really great catching up."

"I know what you mean. I'm so glad I ran into you," she said, and she genuinely meant it, too.

He rose and pulled on his wool pea coat, eyes fixed on hers. "You know, you *could* call me sometime. I think we would make good friends, Emma."

"I know. You're right. I'll try, okay?"

"Okay." But he sighed in the old way, like when he used to tell her he wished she would say what she meant. The problem was, she wasn't always sure what that was.

Now she rose and let him pull her into another warm hug. He gave awesome hugs, just like Ja—she cut off the thought, forced her mind back to the present. Turning her face toward his neck, she inhaled the nearly forgotten scent of the cologne that his mother sent him every Christmas. She hadn't seen Will in nearly a year, and she was realizing that she had genuinely missed him. He was such a good guy, smart and kind and athletic in a non-contact sport kind of way. If things had been different, if *she* had been different...

He kissed her forehead. "Don't be a stranger, all right?"

"I won't. And congratulations again. Happy New Year, Will."

"Happy New Year, Emma."

He carried his dishes to the counter and headed for the entrance. A moment later he was back out on the street waving at her through the window. She waved and watched him stride away, his shoulders braced against the wind that had picked up while they sat inside the yellow-walled coffee shop, offering up bits and pieces of the lives they'd built without each other.

As she worked on draining her giant mug—because no drop of dark roast should ever go to waste—she texted Dani: "Ran into Will. Got coffee. He's engaged."

"Ooh. Vivace's?"

"That's all you have to say?"

"You could be engaged too if you wanted, according to your Twitter mentions."

Emma laughed and sent Dani a middle finger emoji.

"Rude," came her best friend's reply. And then, "My place later?"

"I thought you were hanging out with Derek tonight."

"My girls come first. By which I do not mean my boobs, you understand."

"Naturally. By which I do not mean au naturel."

"Good one, Blake."

"Thanks!" She added a smiling emoji.

"It's called sarcasm, Emma."

"Whatevs. Later."

She set her phone aside and wrapped her hands around the mug, mind buzzing with the pleasant jolt of caffeine. It really had been nice to see Will, if not a bit disconcerting. Was he right? *Did* she prefer the company of women? She usually didn't think of it in those terms. She'd once heard the human body compared to a car—what was on the outside was interesting and usually what made people notice each other in the first place. That was certainly true for Emma. But what kept her coming back was who someone was inside—their sense of humor, their strength, their willingness to care for others. Their essence.

Will did have a point, though. What she'd had with him had been different from what she'd had with Sam. She and Sam had both loved sports, so they'd spent their free time attending live sporting events or lying around at one of their apartments watching soccer, football, hockey, basketball, and even, one memorable time, curling. Those Canadian women could really throw a good rock. But while Will didn't mind sports and was a big Sounders supporter, he'd grown up in Boise where football was king and boys like him—smart and techy and a tad clumsier than average—were definitely not. That was one of the reasons he loved Seattle: There were more men like him than he'd even known existed.

The sex was different, too. With Sam, she'd been more vulnerable, more intimate, possibly because she'd trusted her in a way she had never seemed to let herself do with the men she'd been with. In Boston during the off-season, she and Sam would spend entire weekends together having sex and snuggling, raiding the fridge and then having more sex. Will worked long hours at a downtown tech firm, and on the weekends, he couldn't wait to escape the city for hiking and nature adventures. They'd had a more traditional sex life, and given the fact they only saw each other a couple of times a week, things in that department had seemed a bit more predictable than when she was with Sam.

She thought back to college, the last time she'd seriously dated a guy. Brent Mulvaney, a Virginia boy who had seemed so sweet at first and then turned out to be jealous and possessive—similar to Justin Tate, her second-biggest high school regret, although minus the homophobia. At least with Will she'd finally picked a good man. So why wasn't that enough? Had it just been timing? Would she be ready to let someone in if and when she finally won a World Cup title? Or was it that at some level she'd been waiting ever since Sam walked out to see if the soccer gods might finally make things right?

Maybe she didn't prefer women in general. Maybe she preferred one woman in particular.

She rose and deposited her mug in a bin meant for dirty dishes. As she pulled her jacket on and walked outside into the cold, sunny day, Dani's question from the other night came back to her: *Are you going to try to avoid her again?* She pictured the photo of Jamie dancing with the woman in San Francisco, her hands on the redhead's hips. Jamie was probably on the rebound, which meant that avoiding her right now would definitely be the sensible thing to do.

Sometimes Emma hated that she was nothing if not sensible.

#

Flying might have been better after all, Jamie thought as she shoved her bags in her and Ellie's hotel room and jogged back down to the conference room. Thanks to freeway traffic, she'd missed the team dinner, only arriving in time for the first official meeting of January camp. She paused in the doorway, trying not to feel nervous as she surveyed the packed room. She belonged here. Really.

"Max," Angie called, waving her over to the row where the U-23s were seated.

She waved back and started over, almost stopping when she realized that the only open seat was at the opposite end next to Emma. Emma, who was either genuinely captivated by something on her phone or purposely ignoring her. In all fairness, she probably deserved the cool reception. After all, she was the one who'd insisted they exchange numbers and then didn't text or call for a month. Not exactly the best way to get their fledgling re-friendship off the ground.

Jamie smiled as Angie, Lisa, and Rebecca jumped up to hug her and slap her on the back. Maddie and Jenny offered enthusiastic smiles and waves, but Emma barely even nodded at her before returning to her phone.

The coaches came in just as Jamie slid into the seat next to Emma. She took a breath. "Hey."

Emma glanced up but didn't quite look at her. "Hey. Welcome back."

"Thanks." She hesitated as Emma gazed stoically at the front of the room where the coaches were getting settled around a long table. "How were your holidays?"

"Fine. You?"

"Good. I moved back to the States."

"Portland, right?" Emma's tone was polite.

"Eventually. For now I'm staying with my parents in Berkeley."

The last time Jamie had mentioned her hometown, Emma had gushed about how much she loved Berkeley. Now she only nodded, gaze still trained on the coaches' table.

The meeting began, and though Jamie tried to focus on the front of the room, she couldn't help watching Emma out of the corner of her eye. She looked cool and casual in a dark green Nike tank top, her hair knotted in a sleek bun, her shoulders all rippling and smooth despite the unflattering fluorescent lights of the conference room. They were close enough that Jamie could feel the heat rolling off Emma's body, and she folded her arms across her chest to resist the temptation to lean closer.

"I'm sorry I didn't call," she murmured as Craig handed the mic to Lacey for a description of the evening's workout session.

Emma looked at her quickly and then away again.

"Or text," Jamie added.

A muscle in Emma's jaw twitched, but that was it.

"I wanted to. Honestly."

Out of the corner of her eye she saw Emma shake her head. "They why didn't you?" But before Jamie could trot out her litany of excuses—breaking up with her girlfriend, moving halfway around the world, going car shopping for the first time in her semi-adult life—Emma added, "No, forget I said that. We're teammates, Jamie. You don't owe me anything."

Jamie blinked at the unexpected pain trying to crawl its way into her throat. *We're teammates.* That wasn't all they were, was it?

"We should listen," Emma added, her eyes trained on the coaching staff again.

"Right. Of course."

She leaned away from Emma, putting as much distance between them as their chairs allowed. She couldn't blame Emma for wanting to keep things professional. After all, she wasn't the one who had reached for her hand on the airplane, or stolen her number, or proceeded to ignore her as one year ended and a new one began. For that matter, Emma wasn't the one who had given up on their friendship all those years ago. She couldn't be expected to keep waiting around for Jamie to figure out what she wanted.

The meeting was the same as every other training camp meeting she had been to since entering the national team pool a decade earlier. Good thing, too, because she was currently having trouble focusing on the droning from the front of the room. Still, Ellie was frowning at her from a few rows up, which reminded her that this camp was another try-out for the national team. The Freaking National Team. *Control the things you can and let go of the things you can't,* she told herself. Attitude, work ethic, and effort—check. Former best friends who apparently weren't interested in being anything other than teammates? Not so much.

As soon as the meeting was over, Emma slipped her arm through Jenny's and headed for the door. Jamie lingered near their seats, watching her vanish into the hall. This was not the start she'd envisioned on the drive down. At the end of the last camp they'd been sipping champagne and grabbing lunch together, and now Emma wouldn't even look at her. Well done. Yet another disaster to add to the growing list.

"Trouble in Blakewell paradise?" Angie asked, wrapping her arm around Jamie's neck.

"Fuck off," she replied, her tone more tired than annoyed.

"No, seriously, it's legit hard to piss off Blake. What'd you do?"

"No, seriously, fuck off."

"Geez, James. No need to get your panties in a bunch."

"I'm not. They're not. Anyway, how was your break?" she asked, heading toward the corridor.

"Better than yours, sounds like. Sorry about Clare. I liked her."

"Thanks," Jamie said. "So did I."

She'd been looking forward to camp as a welcome distraction from the break-up. Apparently she'd expected too much.

Angie elbowed her. "Challenge accepted, by the way."

"What challenge is that?" Jamie asked, even though she was pretty sure she didn't want to know.

"Getting you laid. I'm an excellent wingman."

"I am so not hooking up at team camp."

"Chill, dude. I meant on the last night. We usually have it off, and you need rebound sex. The sooner the better."

Jamie ducked into the stairwell. "Yeah, I'm going to have to say no to that one."

"Too bad Britt won't be here by then for keeper camp," Angie continued as if she hadn't spoken, "or we'd be back in business, for reals."

"Still wouldn't happen," Jamie said as they climbed the stairs, the cement stairwell echoing with female voices.

"Why not? Crawdad and I are awesome wingmen."

"Even if that was actually true, her girlfriend is Clare's best friend."

"Oh." Angie nodded as they reached the second floor. "I feel you."

They were halfway down the hall when Jamie heard a male voice call her name. She turned to see Bill, the offensive coach, approaching, his mouth its usual unsmiling line. Was she in trouble for missing dinner? It wasn't like she could help the traffic situation.

"Later," Angie said, and squeezed her shoulder before skedaddling away.

"Yes, coach?" Jamie forced her wired body into a relaxed stance, legs slightly apart, arms loose at her sides.

"Heard a rumor that you'll be with the Thorns this season," he said, a slight smile softening his wide, square jaw.

"Oh, yeah, that's right."

"Well, good," he said, and slapped her arm. "Glad to have you back on this side of the pond, kid."

And then he walked away, his shoulders ramrod straight again, jaw solid as steel.

Had she imagined that? But no. That had really happened. At least the coaches were happy to see her, even if certain other people who should not be named most definitely were not.

Jamie wasn't exactly *upset* that January camp was only eight days long. The first friendly match—assuming she made the roster—was set for the end of the month, which gave her a week in the middle to firm up her long-term plans. She still had to find a place to stay in Portland, and even though Ellie had offered up her spare bedroom, she doubted Jodie, her fiancée, would be thrilled to share their house indefinitely. The meeting with Thorns management had gone better than she'd expected, with Ellie and her agent there as more than moral support. They'd even agreed to Arsenal's terms—time off for Champions League this March and again the following spring as needed. Somehow she'd managed to get her personal and professional life sorted in the three and a half weeks Melanie had given her.

Well, almost sorted.

After the first day, she'd thought maybe Emma would stop avoiding her. She had truly believed they were past the awkward, fake smiling stage. In fact, she was sure they had been; there was photo evidence from Seattle that proved as much. But every once in a while she caught Emma watching her across the breakfast buffet or the practice field with a look that sucked the air out of her lungs. In those moments, she recognized that beneath the pseudo-friendly façade, Emma's feelings weren't neutral any more than hers were.

"I thought your Tumblr nickname was lesbian catnip," Angie murmured to Jamie on the second day when Emma hesitated near their table before carrying her lunch plate to the opposite end of the room.

Ellie reached out and slapped the side of Angie's head.

"Ow," Angie said, glaring at the older woman. "What was that for?"

"Being a douchebag."

Which, Jamie thought, was fair.

Fortunately, Emma didn't treat her any differently during practice. On the pitch their connection was just as strong, and she even coached Jamie up a couple of times when they were on the same side, offering her tips on how to tailor her play to the coach's expectations or how to read the players on the opposite side. She did it for everyone, Jamie knew, so it didn't mean anything. But still. At least Emma was being professional. It was Jamie who was struggling. December camp had gone well partly because she'd felt like she had nothing to lose. This time she had everything to prove.

On the third day of camp, she woke up hours before the alarm was set to go off and couldn't get back to sleep. She lay in her hotel bed staring at the paint whorls on the ceiling, trying to fight through the anxiety and doubt that had her stomach acid doing its best to escape through her esophagus. It wasn't like this was an entirely new experience. On mornings like this, she felt like her feet were mired in tar, except it wasn't her body trapped in the black, sticky substance but her mind, and she was never sure how to shift her mindset. Normally she used meditation to combat the occasional negativity, but on days like this, with tar mucking up her veins and clouding her mind, she couldn't get clear enough to start. As her mind spun furiously, conjuring every possible worry it could find to dwell on, she could only try to ride out the wave and stay as far away from other people as possible. Otherwise the barbed quills that had taken up residence in her skin sometime in the night would sting the soft flesh of anyone unlucky enough to get too close.

Keeping her distance, unfortunately, wasn't a realistic option considering she was basically living in a hotel with twenty-seven other women she was required to interact with for sixteen of every twenty-four hours.

A longer than usual shower helped clear the fog of exhaustion but failed to make a dent in her sense that the world was a shittier place than usual. Though she tried her best to stay quiet at breakfast, she couldn't seem to stop herself from snapping at Rebecca and Lisa when their food fight spilled over onto her: "Why don't you guys grow the fuck up already?"

There was a pause, and then Lisa whistled. "Looks like someone woke up on the wrong side of the bed."

"Look out, everyone," Angie added, glancing around the table. "Better steer clear of Max today."

They were right, but that didn't stop Jamie from flipping them off as she stomped away with her still half-full plate. If she could have, she would have taken off to the beach or a forest or a mountain and run until she dropped. But she couldn't flee, so instead she got ready for practice and clamped her noise-canceling headphones over her ears, hoping the other players would take the hint.

As the van rolled down the wide LA street, Jamie leaned her head against the window and closed her eyes, right leg jumping faster than the beat in her headphones. She knew that the people around her were not the threat. She knew that she was safe. She knew that anxiety was a feeling that couldn't actually hurt her. She knew all of these things, and yet still sometimes the old terror overwhelmed her subconscious mind and there was nothing she could do but wait for the feeling to subside.

The jitters stuck with her through the morning session and into afternoon practice, and she could only watch as if from a distance as her brain misfired again and again. Her reflexes were slow, her focus non-existent, and what was worse, she knew that everyone else could see it, too. The other players, the coaches, her friends, the newbies who she was in direct competition with. They all knew she was having an off day precisely when she couldn't afford one.

The anxiety swirled and morphed inside her brain, distracting her on the soccer field where usually nothing did, until she started to wonder why she'd ever been called up in the first place. Maybe she didn't belong here, she thought as she waited in line for her turn at a crossing drill. Maybe there was a reason other than injury that the federation had never offered her a contract, she worried as she half-listened to Mel coaching up her team in a small-sided scrimmage. Maybe she simply wasn't good enough, she thought, chewing her cuticles as they paused for a water break. And always in the background as she worked on taking the ball out of the air cleanly, as she analyzed her mark's body language, as she moved off the ball for one teammate or another, was the same question that had plagued her since the last camp: What if walking away from

London—and Clare—was the wrong decision?

At the end of her least successful practice in recent memory, she threw her cleats in her bag and stalked from the field while the other players were still chatting and laughing in the warm afternoon sunshine. She had just passed the parking lot—she was way too worked up for a van—when she heard someone call, "Jamie?"

She knew that voice. She'd heard it at different times of the day and night, tear-filled and tipsy and happy and angry, scared and elated and sweet. She'd heard it in her dreams for years before finally getting over it. Before finally getting over *her*. Clenching her fist around the strap of her team duffel, she slowed and stopped.

"What?" she asked, eyes narrowed as Emma neared.

"Can I walk back to the hotel with you?"

The question was so far from what she was expecting that Jamie could only stare at her. *What the fuck?*

"Please?" Emma added, eyes lowering, fingers fiddling with the strap on her matching team bag.

Jamie was tempted to tell her where she could go, but that was about as unprofessional as one teammate could get with another. Although, was it really less professional than ordering mimosas and flirting? Or, for that matter, asking for someone's number and then never calling them?

"Suit yourself." She started off down the sidewalk, not waiting to see if Emma would follow.

They walked in silence for a few minutes, not a comfortable silence but a heavy one filled with the weight of things unsaid. Jamie waited for Emma to speak, but the other woman walked beside her, staring down at the sidewalk and clearing her throat softly every so often. Was she nervous? Jamie couldn't remember the last time she'd seen Emma Blakeley unsure of herself.

When she couldn't stand the silence anymore, she blurted the first thing that came to mind: "What's up with Maddie and Angie?"

So far the two had been even flirtier than at December

camp, and Jamie was seriously starting to wonder.

Emma's head came up. "Didn't Angie tell you?"

"Tell me wha—" Jamie cut herself off. "No way. Are you serious?"

Emma nodded. "They spent the weekend before camp at Maddie's condo in Palm Springs."

"You've got to be joking."

"Nope. Believe it or not." And then, as Jamie's mind was still struggling to absorb that piece of news—although looking back, if she hadn't been so caught up in her own drama she probably would have noticed—Emma added, her voice lower and huskier than usual, "I'm sorry."

It was Jamie's turn to glance quickly at her. "What?"

"I said I'm sorry." Emma looked steadily back at her, forehead slightly creased.

"For what?"

"For being such a dick to you this week. You don't deserve it."

Jamie couldn't stop the snort that erupted.

Emma's forehead smoothed out. "What? You know I have been."

"No argument here," she allowed. "So why stop now?"

"You seem like you're not having the best day, and I wanted to make sure it wasn't because of..." She trailed off, gesturing awkwardly between them.

Jamie felt herself bristle. "Don't flatter yourself. People can have bad days all on their own, you know."

"Right." Emma's hand returned to worrying her bag strap. "Well, okay, then."

They walked in silence again, as far from each other on the sidewalk as possible without Emma falling into the street. Jamie speeded up, tempted to hide out in her room for the rest of the day. But there was still team dinner to get through, followed by another meeting in the conference room. Or was it virtual reality training tonight?

The hotel was in sight when Emma grasped her arm, forcing her to stop. "Jamie, wait."

She barely resisted the urge to rip her arm away. "What, Emma? I tried to apologize the first day but you didn't seem interested. Do you feel sorry for me or something? Because I don't need your pity."

And there were the quills, flying out before she could stop them at the one person in LA she really didn't want to hurt.

Emma's brow furrowed again, but her voice came out gentle. "I don't pity you. You've always been one of the strongest people I know."

The admission made Jamie's throat tighten, but she swallowed down the threat of tears. "So what then? Do you want me to say it's fine if you don't want to be friends? Is that it?"

Emma's voice came out so quietly Jamie almost couldn't hear her over the sound of traffic speeding past. "No. I was going to say that you were right before. I *was* upset about the break. You were the one who wanted us to exchange numbers, and then it was like you dropped off the face of the earth."

Jamie squinted at Emma, unaccustomed to such straight-forwardness after dating a cagey Brit for so long. Her anger receded a little as she took in the way Emma was watching her, lips pursed, shoulders tense.

"That totally makes sense. Again, I'm sorry I didn't get in touch. Things have been kind of—intense, I guess, the last few weeks."

"Ellie mentioned you broke up with your girlfriend."

Jamie rubbed her palm over the soft, shaved hairs at her nape. "Yeah."

"Was it—did it have anything to do with the Tumblr thing?"

"No," she said quickly. "We split up because of the distance. Her future's there and mine is here, so..."

"Of course." Emma paused. "I'm sorry it didn't work out."

"Thanks." Jamie felt a little better now that they were talking, but she could still feel the noxious tension twisting under her skin. She nodded toward the hotel. "Want to keep going?"

"Sure," Emma said, and started walking again. "I need to shower before dinner."

Jamie fell into step beside her. "Best news I heard all day." The response emerged from some back corner of her brain, sneaking out while she focused on keeping any remaining quills firmly in check.

Emma laughed, and for the first time all week, the smile she aimed at Jamie seemed genuine. "I can't believe you remember that. My dad used to say that to me and my brother."

For a moment, Jamie forgot about the anxiety creeping through her bloodstream. "I'm sorry. I didn't mean to—"

"No, it's okay. It's kind of nice. I don't have that many people anymore who were around before he died." She glanced sideways at Jamie. "For the record, I would like us to be friends again. It's just, I don't know if I can handle the on again off again thing, not after what happened when we—well, before."

So she'd been right. The less-than-neutral look in Emma's eyes *had* been hurt. "What are you saying?"

"I'm saying that if we decide we're going to do the friends thing, you can't just back out again. Neither of us can." Emma paused, the worried crease back again. "What do you think?"

She wasn't supposed to make big decisions on days like this. She was supposed to hide out from humanity, not have important discussions with people, especially not people named Emma Blakeley. But it wasn't like Emma was giving her a choice. She nodded slowly. "I think you're right."

"You do?"

"Yeah. I'm in—if you are, I mean."

Emma gave her a shy smile that almost made Jamie forget she'd woken up on the wrong side of the bed that morning. "I'm in." She stopped walking and held out her hand.

After a moment, Jamie shook it gingerly, feeling her tension recede as she pressed her palm against Emma's. A handful of memories came sweeping back, of sunlit bedrooms and glass-walled pavilions and train station platforms, but she pushed them away. Those memories were from a long time ago, when they were entirely different people. Or mostly different, anyway.

The rest of the short walk was quiet, but Jamie thought it was more a thoughtful type of silence than the earlier oppressive kind. At the hotel they took the stairs to the second floor where they parted ways, heading back to their rooms in opposite directions.

Before they got far, though, Jamie turned back and called, "Emma?"

"Yeah?"

She jogged back to face her, nearly overwhelmed by another sense of déjà vu. The night they'd met, Emma had called back to her and they'd met in the middle of the hotel corridor as their disapproving parents looked on. Now it was only the two of them—and half a dozen unseen but easily heard teammates lurking behind nearby closed doors.

"Thanks for coming after me today," she said when they were a few paces apart. "You didn't have to."

"I know, but I wanted to."

Jamie's brow rose skeptically. "Really?"

"Well, no." Emma gestured between them. "But I wanted this to be better. I like you, Jamie. I don't want to have to pretend I don't."

"I like you too." And then because even on a good day this conversation would feel like too much, she added, "Despite the fact you're a manure—sorry, a *Man U* fan."

"That's United to you, Rook."

"Whatever." Jamie raised her hand. "See you, Blake?"

Emma slapped her palm. "Later, Max."

As she headed off down the hallway again, Jamie tried to quiet the tingle that had moved from her hand, up across her shoulder, and down into her chest. It wasn't hope. She couldn't afford hope. She needed to be thinking about her attitude, work ethic, and effort, especially after such an awful training day.

Back in her room she threw herself onto her bed, grateful that Ellie was apparently occupied elsewhere. This way she could be on her own to process—or sulk, as the case may be.

Before she could decide which, her phone vibrated, signaling a new text message. Her heart rate picked up, even though it could be any number of people texting her. But it wasn't any number. It was Emma.

She stared at the notification, allowing herself to feel the flickering ball of warmth in her chest at the thought of Emma on her own bed a few doors down, thinking of her. Then she clicked.

"Hi," blinked out at her.

She smiled and shook her head. "Hi."

"Thought I'd try the friends thing."

"Good idea."

"I think we're going to be fast friends," Emma sent, followed immediately by a winking emoji.

Jamie laughed at the *Pitch Perfect* reference and then paused. Laughter on a quills kind of a day? Practically unheard of.

"Why do you always get to be Chloe?" she typed.

"Um, hello, alt girl..."

"I'm sunny! Well, usually."

"One word: tattoos."

Jamie thought about it. "Valid." Then she typed, "Thanks for earlier," and hit send quickly.

The response came back equally fast. "You're welcome. Nerd."

"Dork."

The next message took a little longer: "Maddie says Netflix in our room tonight. If you're up for it."

"Cool." Though she should probably see how dinner went before inflicting her company on anyone.

"Assuming you can play well with others," Emma wrote. Then, "Lol!"

"Guess we'll have to see," Jamie replied, adding a wink emoji.

"Sounds good. See you at dinner?"

"I'll be there."

After a minute her phone screen dimmed, and Jamie leaned back on her bed. No great mystery as to why she should suddenly feel less like throwing metaphorical daggers at the world. Earlier, when they were walking, Emma had asked if her standoffishness could have triggered Jamie's mood. And, despite her assurances to the contrary, maybe it had. Now that they had talked, now that they had voiced a mutual wish to be real friends again, the dark cloud that had followed her around all day was dissipating. She could still feel the emotional hangover her bouts of anxiety had a habit of leaving in their wake, but the feeling was growing fuzzier, easier to combat. If the light in Emma's eyes when Jamie said she liked her too had something to do with driving away the darkness, who did that hurt?

No one, she decided as her body relaxed further, the jitters fading to a dull murmur under her skin. Absolutely no one.

CHAPTER NINE

Emma walked down the brightly lit corridor, headed for one of the many training rooms at Home Depot—no, *Stub Hub* Center. The sponsor had changed the previous year, and she still had to remind herself of the training center's new name. Practice had ended a little while earlier, but she'd stuck around to work on penalty kicks. Now she was hoping it had been long enough that she wouldn't have to wait in line for a spot in the tub reserved for ice baths. Her body ached in a way that always reminded her of preseason at UNC her first year, when she and Jamie had stopped talking and she and Tori had started dating and everything was new and her body had *hurt*, despite the pre-preseason workouts she'd diligently put in.

"Yo, Ems," Maddie said as Emma entered the training room. She was already ensconced in the large pool in the usual ice bath uniform of compression shorts and sports bra.

"Yo, Mads."

Maddie, who had been a junior when Emma started at UNC, had introduced her to the practice of soaking in a cold bath to boost recovery time. For that alone the midfielder had earned her undying love. It had helped that the Chicagoan had also revealed her own bisexuality early on that first fall and offered to help Emma navigate the perils of coming out at a university in the southeast, a region not generally known for its embrace of non-heterosexuals. Emma couldn't remember hearing anyone use the term "homosexual" non-ironically before moving to North Carolina.

"Come on in," Ellie said, glancing up from her phone. "It's positively balmy."

Just then a timer went off, and Phoebe climbed out of the tub, water dripping from her muscular physique. "All yours, Blake."

"Thanks," Emma returned, dropping her bag and stripping out of her practice jersey and training shorts.

She was about to step in when she heard a sound behind her—Jamie had paused inside the training room doorway and was now looking at her, eyes slightly wide. Or, rather, looking at her mostly bare back. Emma waved a little and slipped inch by inch into the water, hoping her own blush could be passed off as ice-bath-induced. Jesus, she'd forgotten how cold fifty-eight degrees actually felt. And yet the cold felt so good, too.

"What are you doing here?" Phoebe asked Jamie.

Jamie offered the keeper a slight smile. "Taking an ice bath."

"Aren't you a little young to need one?"

"Leave her alone, Phoebes," Ellie said without looking up from her phone. "She's older than she looks."

Emma settled fully into the water, glad Ellie had shut the keeper down so that she didn't have to. She preferred not to cross Phoebe unless completely necessary. The older woman didn't take kindly to challenges from players who hadn't been on the team as long as she had—which meant anyone other than Ellie, at this point.

As Jamie stripped down and approached the tub, Emma kept her eyes on the far wall. They had been doing the friends thing successfully for a couple of days now, sitting together at meals with friends and hanging out after dinner. She didn't want to ruin the progress they'd made by ogling Jamie's admittedly lovely lats. Or, say, her tattoos.

"Do you want me to set a timer?" Jamie asked.

Oops. "Yeah, that would be great."

"For how long?"

"I usually do six minutes."

Jamie set the time and climbed in beside her. Unlike Emma, though, she didn't lower herself a little bit at a time. Instead she submerged her body completely and then burst upward, gasping. "Fuck!"

"You said it." Ellie smiled as her phone vibrated. "And that's my cue. See ya, kids."

"Mine too," Maddie said as they both escaped the tub and reached for towels. After a quick rubdown, they stepped into soccer sandals and followed Phoebe toward the door, towels wrapped around their waists. At the last minute, Maddie turned back and snagged the van key from Emma's bag.

"Hey! I'll be done in like five minutes!"

"You could use the exercise," Maddie said, winking as she ducked into the hall. "Don't do anything I wouldn't do!" Her laughter, accompanied by Ellie's shushing and Phoebe's questioning tone, floated back to them as Emma looked at Jamie and realized that they were alone. Half naked. In a tub of really, really cold water.

"Looks like we're walking back," Jamie commented.

"Looks that way." Maddie and her transparent matchmaking—Emma had never met anyone as unsubtle in her life.

"How are you sitting there so calmly?" Jamie asked, swimming away from her into the middle of the pool.

Emma took advantage of her turned back to examine her tattoo. It was beautiful—dark and elegant, the bird's wingtips arcing over her toned, perfectly symmetric shoulders. She had read somewhere that Jamie had designed it, and not for the first time she found herself admiring her talent. Art was something Emma admired but had next to no skills in herself.

Jamie glanced back, eyebrows lifted, and with a start Emma realized she was waiting for an answer.

"Experience," she said quickly. "Besides, I love ice baths."

"Weirdo."

"Says the woman currently sitting in an ice bath."

"Yeah, but I don't *love* it."

"You say that now…" Emma focused her eyes on Jamie's so that she wouldn't be tempted to let her gaze linger elsewhere, and in a moment she forgot the lure of water beading on her delicate clavicle, of her lean muscles and the smattering of moles on her forearms. Jamie's cheeks were flushed from the cold and her blue eyes were sparkling like a super gay version of a Disney princess, which, Emma thought, should really be a thing, and her lips were curling up into the smile that Emma had always lov—*Wait*. But no, that was exactly right: the smile she had always loved.

Well, shit.

Emma had never been one to fall in love easily, not after her first high school boyfriend broke her heart. Will had said it first, three months into their relationship. Sam had said it first too, after only six weeks together. In both cases, Emma had waited a little while to be sure before saying it back. But with Jamie, they'd already exchanged those three anything-but-innocuous words. Admittedly they had never talked about what either of them meant, but Emma at least knew what she had meant at her end: She had been in love with Jamie, even if she hadn't held out much hope of being with her.

And now? If she was honest, she knew what she hoped now, deep inside her stupid, stubborn heart. But that didn't mean Jamie felt the same or that the timing was anywhere close to being right.

"Okay, this sucks," Jamie said, her teeth chattering audibly. "Tell me a story, please? Anything to distract me from this icy torture."

Emma shook her head, trying to focus. "What kind of story?"

"I don't know. I'm too cold to think."

She went for the easy laugh—her mother's relatives and their antics. Soon she was telling Jamie all about Christmas in Minnesota, focusing on the party at her aunt's house where her multitudes of relatives had discussed hot dish recipes, ice hockey, and how someone's boss's cousin's sister-in-law had her identity stolen on the World Wide Web, dontcha know. She didn't mention that her relatives had treated her like an exotic stranger, or that she'd felt lonely watching *Love, Actually*. She definitely didn't mention that she'd thought of Jamie and missed her.

"And bursitis, right?" Jamie put in. "They talk about their bodies falling apart, don't they?"

It took her a second to realize that Jamie was referencing their conversation at LAX the previous month. "Right. Can't forget those pesky joint capsules."

With Jamie's encouragement, she set out to recreate a typical conversation between her Great Aunt Olga and Great Uncle Aner, two of the eight siblings who had grown up on a farm near Upsala. They had a habit of complaining about the "new" stoplight that had been installed in the 1980s and that they still blamed for "all that traffic." Right. In a town of 427 people. In addition to their varied complaints, they would randomly say things like, "Remember that girl? You know the one, went down to the Cities that one time?" And all the old people in the room would nod, knowing which girl the speaker meant. Inevitably someone else would chime in with a scintillating response like, "She never did come back," followed by more group nodding.

When the buzzer went off, Jamie literally leapt out of the tub. "Oh my god! How do you guys do this after every practice?"

"It's not after *every* practice," Emma said, laughing at the way Jamie hopped around the training room, rubbing a towel over her frigid skin.

Emma left the tub considerably faster than she had entered it and reached for a towel. Jamie turned her back to change out of her wet clothes, and even though Emma thought she should tease her about her shyness—after all, they had both been naked in front of dozens if not hundreds of different teammates over the years—she was just as happy to turn around herself to change into dry sweats and a clean T-shirt.

Behind her Jamie cleared her throat. "Are you…?"

"Decent? Yep."

As they faced each other, Jamie asked, "Want to walk back together?"

Emma smiled at her. "I would love to."

Jamie smiled back and they walked down the corridor in silence, arms brushing every so often even though the hallway was more than wide enough for two, nodding at assorted athletes and coaches they passed. The training center was home to other national programs, and at any given time there might be tennis players and swimmers, to name a few, in addition to soccer players of all ages. Being an elite athlete was the norm here.

As they approached the main entrance, Emma caught sight of Steph Miller's husband and son resting on a couch in the lobby. Steph must be with a trainer. Did that mean she was injured...?

"Hey champ," Jamie said, waving at the little boy.

"Jamie!" Even though they had only met in December, Brodie jumped off the couch and launched himself at her. "Will you kick the ball with me? Pleeease?"

Jamie glanced at Emma as the boy tugged her toward the door. "Do you mind?"

"Not at all. Have fun." Emma sat down beside Geoff, Steph's husband. They had met in college at Southern Methodist where he was on exchange from Australia. He'd transferred to be with her, and a dozen years later they seemed as committed as ever. "Hey, G."

"Hey, E."

"You okay with that?" she asked, gesturing toward the lawn outside where Brodie had dragged Jamie.

"Don't worry. By now I'm used to playing second fiddle to two dozen aunties. How was the ice bath?"

"Cold." She pretended to shiver.

"I'll bet. So. That's my wife's competition, huh?" he asked, watching through the wide windows as Jamie dribbled away from Brodie, giggling.

"Is that what Steph's been saying?"

"No, simply an observation," he said mildly, pushing up his glasses. A sociologist at UCLA, Geoff was about as far from the stereotypical flamboyant, beer-guzzling Aussie as one could get. "She's pretty great, though, isn't she? And not just at soccer."

"Who's pretty great?" a voice asked from behind them.

Emma glanced back to see Steph emerging from one of the many hallways. Geoff rose and pecked her cheek. "Hey, hon. How was the massage?"

"Good. Where's Brodie?" And then her gaze fell on the pair carousing outside. "Oh. So that's who you were talking about."

By now Emma was standing too. She watched Steph, noting the smile that inched onto the other woman's face as Brodie leapt onto Jamie's back and she carried him around the perfectly manicured lawn, dribbling the ball helter skelter. And she realized: "You like her, don't you?"

"She's all right." Steph glanced at her. "But you obviously think a lot of her. Why is that, Emma?"

She took a breath and willed her body not to react. She considered Steph a good friend, admired her strength and passion, and adored Brodie, who had grown up around the team. But at the same time, she wouldn't put it past Steph to do whatever it took to hang onto her roster spot. While there were always younger, faster, stronger players in the running, once a player hit thirty the competition intensified. Steph and Ellie had recently complained that the most common question reporters asked them—other than the ubiquitous, *Do you think you'll win the next World Cup?*—was, "How much longer are you going to play?"

If Steph continued playing the way she was currently, Jamie was a real threat. Jamie knew it, Steph knew it, and so did everyone else connected to the pool.

"We've been friends a long time," she said, her gaze fixed on Jamie and Brodie.

"That may be true, but I don't look at anyone from high school the way you look at her."

Geoff made a slight noise at the back of his throat and

walked away without another word, heading outside where Jamie and Brodie had collapsed in a heap on the bright green grass, giggling so loudly Emma could hear them from inside.

"We should probably get going if we don't want to miss dinner," Emma said, barely keeping the bite out of her voice.

Steph's gaze softened. "Look, I'm saying this as your friend, not because I'm afraid of…" She waved outside. "My career isn't going to last forever, but hers? It's still getting going. Be careful, okay, Emma?"

"I will," she said. But as they walked outside into the warm winter evening, she couldn't help thinking it was a little too late for caution.

"Do you two want a ride?" Geoff asked as they approached, Brodie now hanging around his neck, soccer ball under one arm.

"That's okay." Jamie retrieved her bag from the walkway. "I wouldn't mind a walk. If that's okay with you, Em?"

She nodded. "Thanks anyway, Geoff. See you guys at dinner?"

"We'll be there." Steph started to turn away, but at the last moment she stopped to smile at Jamie. "Thanks for hanging out with Brodie."

Jamie's eyebrows rose momentarily. "Oh, yeah, no problem. He's a good kid. Aren't you, Bro?" she added, holding out her fist.

The little boy bumped his fist against hers, giggling as Jamie opened her hand and made a whooshing sound.

"Boo yah!" she said, completing the ritual.

"Boo yay!" he replied.

At the street, the little family turned one way while Jamie and Emma turned the other, strolling along the sidewalk lit by lamps stationed at regular intervals. Jamie's display of adorableness with Steph's small fry was making it difficult for Emma to effectively push down her stupidly stubborn feelings. Which she should definitely do—after all, as Steph had pointed out, Jamie's future on the team wasn't secure, and there was a World Cup coming and… Huh. She knew there were more potentially good reasons she wasn't supposed to think about Jamie in that way, but she couldn't seem to remember them, not with the woman in question walking so close beside her along the warm pavement.

"You have a fan," she observed.

"He really is a good kid."

The question that popped into Emma's head next was so ridiculous she almost snorted at her own cheesiness. There was no way she could ask Jamie if she wanted kids one day. Or, well, she *could* ask her that, but what if the answer was no? Actually, yes would be nearly as tricky because then Emma's subconscious would probably go off conjuring images of Jamie holding a smiling baby with blue eyes and chubby knees and...

"What about you?" she asked quickly, trying to divert her wayward mind.

"What *about* me?" Jamie echoed, nudging her shoulder teasingly.

"Sorry. I mean, what did you do on Christmas?"

"I moved." She looked down at the sidewalk. "My flight got into San Francisco on Christmas Day."

"So when did you and your girlfriend...?"

"The day I got back from camp. We were planning to spend Christmas with her family, so she left early."

Emma frowned. There she'd been in Minnesota surrounded by family while Jamie was alone in London on Christmas Eve, getting ready to dismantle her personal and professional life. Beside her she saw Jamie shiver. Still chilled from the cold water, perhaps? She'd always been a skinny thing. Honestly, she probably didn't have enough body fat to keep her warm.

She slipped her arm through Jamie's and leaned into her side. "I'm sorry. That must have been really hard."

Jamie's eyes flew to her face. Still, she didn't pull away. "It wasn't easy," she admitted. "Fortunately Britt was around for a while before she headed home for the holidays. But I think it was the right thing to do, for both of us."

The right thing. Emma wasn't sure she knew what that was

anymore, assuming she ever had. What she had believed would be right for herself, for Jamie, for the team, definitely didn't involve the two of them walking down the street together, arms linked, strides perfectly in synch. It didn't involve Jamie blushing at the sight of her in a sports bra or her fantasizing about skimming her fingertips over Jamie's tattoos. It didn't involve her heart rate increasing at the slide of Jamie's skin against hers, or at the sense of what could only be relief at having her this close finally. *Finally.*

And that was okay, she decided as the hotel came into view. She didn't have to know what they were doing or where they were headed. It was enough that they were together like this now, and they weren't turning away from each other anymore. Enough that they really were becoming friends again, even if this bubble didn't extend past residency camp. They were here and they were both trying, and that was enough.

Maddie, however, evidently didn't think it was enough.

After dinner they decided to watch a movie again, and this time it was only the four of them—Emma, Maddie, Angie, and Jamie. A coin flip meant Maddie and Angie got to choose. Emma rolled her eyes when Angie held up *Pitch Perfect.* Predictable. While Emma watched Jamie connect the laptop to the television and start the DVD, the coin toss victors curled up together on Maddie's bed.

"Mads," Emma said, giving her roommate a look.

"Ems," her friend drawled, lazily running her hand over Angie's hair.

"All set," Jamie said as the opening scene began. She straightened and turned away from the TV, and then paused as she caught sight of the seating arrangements. "Oh. So that's how it is."

Emma shrugged. "Totally your call. You can either sit with me or risk being accidentally caught up in their PDA. Which, seriously, no judgment if that's your thing."

"Ha, ha." Jamie threw herself onto the bed next to Emma and arranged the pillows behind her back.

"It isn't PDA if we're in an actual hotel," Angie pointed out.

"No one can exactly tell us to get a room, am I right?"

"Of course you're right, babe." Maddie kissed her cheek with a resounding smack.

"Keep your lips to yourself over there," Emma instructed, fixing her gaze on the television. But it was no use. She could still see the couple on the other bed in her peripheral vision.

"So in addition to being the grammar police, now you're vying for the role of kissing police, too?" Maddie asked.

Jamie snickered. "Grammar police? Clearly some things never change."

"I can't help it if I'm more linguistically gifted than the rest of you." Emma held up a hand as Angie opened her mouth, knowing where the younger woman's mind had gone. "Not a word, Wang, or I will kick you out of my room."

"*Our* room," Maddie said, smirking.

They finally settled down to watch, and as usual everyone laughed at the questionable humor and sang aloud with the assorted a capella performances. Also as usual, the other three rolled their eyes when Jamie got excited each time Chloe and Beca shared a "homoerotic" interlude, as the Queer Studies minor insisted on referring to the lesbodrama moments seeded throughout the movie. Or when she went on a rant about the marginalization of queer characters in mainstream media, which everyone agreed was an important issue but *maybe* something they could wait to discuss after the movie ended.

Half an hour in, Emma found herself watching the woman sharing her bed—*er*, sitting beside her more than the actual movie. And watching her, she found, made her want to move closer. So she did, ignoring Jamie's look as she leaned against her.

"I'm cold," Emma finally murmured as Jamie continued to stare pointedly at her. "Maddie likes AC and you're a heater, okay?"

Jamie smiled a little. "Apparently some things really don't ever change."

During the riff-off scene, Jamie slipped her arm around Emma. She was watching the screen so intently that Emma wasn't sure Jamie was even aware of her hand rubbing up and down her arm, but honestly, she didn't care. The gentle touch soothed her, and she leaned her head against Jamie's shoulder, suddenly cast back to the week of her father's memorial service when she'd experienced the lowest lows and the highest highs of her life, sometimes all within the same sixty seconds. The pain of losing her father was still with her now, but as Jamie had promised, a callus had formed over her heart in the years since he'd died. The high of being with Jamie that week, on the other hand, the fragile joy she'd felt falling asleep in her arms each night was coming back ever more vividly. She had always known at some level they would find each other again, even in the in-between years when she worried they wouldn't. Or maybe she hadn't known. Maybe she had simply hoped, and that hope had carried her along to now, when she and Jamie curled together in a California hotel room watching *Pitch Perfect* as their friends snuggled on the next bed over.

It was almost unbearably sweet, this moment, and Emma wished it could go on and on. Instead it insisted on doing what all moments do. Too soon the team curfew hour was upon them, and Jamie was slowly extricating herself from Emma's side. As their eyes met, Jamie reached out as if she might touch her cheek, or possibly only push back the hair that had escaped from her messy bun. But she didn't make contact. Instead she stopped herself and turned away, hopping off the bed as quickly as she had vaulted onto it. And that was that.

Except it wasn't.

Later, after Emma had walked Jamie to the door and they had gazed at each other for a long moment before Emma pulled her into a hug, after Angie and Jamie had said goodnight and Emma had closed the door behind them, Maddie finally voiced the questions her eyes had been asking all evening.

"So I know I'm not supposed to know about high school, but you know I do, right?"

Emma removed her ear plugs and lifted her eyeshade. They had turned the lights out a few minutes before, and she had actually started to think she might be allowed to fall asleep without the third degree.

"Right."

"And last I knew, you were fairly adamant that nothing could happen there."

"I know." And she did know. She knew that it was dangerous for her and for Jamie to pretend that cuddling could ever mean less than it always had; to pretend that hugging each other was no harm, no foul. But somehow she couldn't seem to stop herself whenever Jamie came close. She wanted to touch her, and unless Jamie pushed her away—which she was pretty sure hadn't ever happened—she didn't *really* see the problem.

"Then what are you doing, Emma? Because it doesn't look like nothing from where I'm sitting."

She considered Maddie's question. "Honestly? I don't have any idea."

"You don't?"

"No. In theory, we're trying to be friends."

"And how's that going?"

"Fine. If you don't count the constant urge to hold her hand and tell her how pretty she is." There was the whole being in love with her thing, too, but she didn't plan on admitting that to anyone yet, not even to Jamie. Especially not Jamie.

"Been there done that." Maddie paused, and her voice changed. "Hold on. Where's the calendar?"

Emma sighed. "Why do you need a calendar?"

"Because Emma Control Freak Blakeley admitted she's winging something. Gotta be a first."

"You couldn't just be nice, could you?"

"It's like you don't know me at all."

Emma repositioned her earplugs and slid the eyeshade back into place. "I'm going to sleep now."

"Sweet dreams. I'm sure they will be."

She held up her middle finger, smiling as muffled laughter rose from the other bed.

But saying she was going to sleep was one thing. Succeeding at the undertaking was another matter. In the dark everything looked different. Along with the occasional rattle of the windowpanes from a passing truck, with the sporadic sound of water moving between walls came the thoughts she would rather avoid. In her bed that smelled of Jamie—cinnamon and a hint of coconut, maybe—Emma remembered all the reasons they weren't supposed to be together. She remembered Sam and the police station, the faceless harassers on Twitter and the look on Sam's face as she left the loft for the last time. She remembered France and the way Jamie had cried all over her sweatshirt the day she shared what had happened to her shortly before they met. She remembered Tori and the veiled comments she was still fielding nine *freaking* years later. She remembered her commitment to the team, and she remembered telling her mother she would never jeopardize team chemistry so close to the World Cup.

But then she pictured Jamie, with her soft smiles and her warm eyes. Jamie, who only a few days ago had looked at her like she wished they never had to see each other again. That look had nearly killed her. If she could, Emma would have taken back those first few days of camp when she had been so concerned with her own feelings that she hadn't stopped to think how her behavior might impact Jamie. And while Jamie had insisted that her off day had nothing to do with her, Emma wasn't sure that was true. She got it, she really did. Jamie *could* have been having a bad day all on her own because there are some things that people don't ever get over—like being assaulted in the back room of a bar, or losing your barely middle-aged father to a heart attack before you had the chance to forgive him. But as soon as they'd made up, as soon as they'd decided to move forward, Jamie's shoulders had relaxed and her smile had come back.

Ignoring her was impossible, and avoiding her only made things worse. Clearly there was only one good option. The fact that it aligned with her deepest hopes, well, that was purely coincidental.

And while yes, their wounds would always be with them, that didn't mean they couldn't be happy. With enough time and healing, with an adequate supply of love and joy, most human beings could get past most things. You still carried the memory of pain in the back of your head, and it was still ready to leap to the forefront if anything else traumatic or awful happened, but for the most part it lay dormant, a reminder of what you had survived—like surgery scars or, in some cases, tattoos. You carried it with you, and if you were lucky, somewhere along the way you found people willing to help shoulder the burden.

She *was* lucky—soccer had brought her not only her closest friends and current career but Jamie. Jamie, who still looked at Emma sometimes the way she had all those years ago—like everything someday would be okay. Or, even better, the way she had tonight while they cuddled in her hotel room: like everything already was okay.

#

Jamie knew she was playing with fire. Or, more precisely, with her future on the national team. Teammates weren't supposed to date. There wasn't an actual line item on the federation's contract, Ellie had told her when she oh so casually broached the subject, but involvement with a teammate was actively discouraged. In her own defense, it wasn't like she had a choice. When Emma wasn't speaking to her she'd played like crap, and now that they were doing something that could loosely be termed friendship (if friendship involved corny daydreams about going on dates and, say, adopting a rescue mutt together), she was playing well again. In fact, she was playing "awesomely," which she knew because Mel had pulled her aside and told her as much.

If she was in trouble either way, she might as well do what made her happy off the field while simultaneously helping her kick ass on it.

Four days down, four to go, Jamie told herself at breakfast the morning after she and Emma watched *Pitch Perfect* with Maddie and Angie on what had felt suspiciously like a double date. Instead of reassuring herself, though, acknowledging the ever-present countdown only made her feel worse because if she didn't make the team, when would she see Emma again?

Not, how would she deal with the let-down for failing to achieve a life goal but how would she deal with having her excuse to see Emma ripped away?

Yeah. So much for being focused on soccer.

Scenes from the previous evening came back to her as she sat down at an empty table and tried not to watch Emma in her adorable flannel pajama pants and pink bunny slippers making her adorable way through the breakfast buffet line. At first, she'd tried to hold herself separate from Emma the night before, aware that they were reclining ON EMMA'S BED. TOGETHER. But once Emma had snuggled up against her, she'd rapidly acquiesced to the other woman's touchy-feely tendencies. A few days into their reclaimed friendship and Emma was as handsy as she'd ever been—and Jamie was as okay with her handsiness as *she'd* ever been. Which was highly okay. No use pretending otherwise. She was highly okay with most things involving Emma Blakeley.

Her level of okayness was apparently evident to others, as she discovered when Maddie slid in across from her and declared, "Before Emma gets here, I want to know one thing: What are your intentions with my friend?"

Jamie stared at her. "Wha—what?"

"You heard me, Max. Because if you hurt her, I will end you." And Maddie narrowed her blue eyes, one eyebrow arched in the pose Jamie had witnessed on the cover of more than one magazine.

"I don't have—I don't really..." But before she could force out a suitable grade school response like *none of your freaking business*, Maddie lost the battle she was apparently waging with her own face and smirked.

"No—did you do it without me?" Angie dropped her plate on the table. "Dude, you said you were going to wait!"

"Sorry, babe, had to strike while the iron was hot."

"Ew," Emma said, sitting down beside Jamie. "Hot irons— I told you not to talk about your BDSM stuff before I've had my coffee. Seriously, Maddie."

"BDSM?" Angie's forehead creased.

"Ignore her. She's joking," Maddie said.

"Right." Angie peered down at her bacon.

"Honestly, Ange, I'm not into that kind of thing. Not that there's anything wrong with it. What consenting adults choose to do is between them."

"Oh, sorry." Emma sounded genuinely worried. "Have you guys not had the branding talk yet? My bad. I just assumed. You usually have by this point."

Maddie wasn't laughing anymore, and it was all Jamie could do to keep from squeeing and confessing her undying love— not *literally*, of course—to Emma for flipping the table on the bodacious blonde.

"Emma," the blonde in question said, "stop trying to freak out my girlfriend."

Jamie watched as Emma frowned slightly. "Honestly, Mads, shouldn't you have told her about your— *predilections* before you made it official? I would have thought you'd have learned after what happened with Parker."

"Parker?" Angie's head shot up. "As in, Parker Van Howell from the men's team?"

Maddie ignored her, gaze sharpening on her friend. "You saw me messing with Jamie, didn't you?"

Emma shrugged and took a sip from her coffee mug. "Maybe."

"You are such a bitch."

"Takes one…" Emma winked, and Jamie finally let herself giggle.

"So wait," Angie said. "There's no sexytimes branding and no Parker, right?"

Maddie huffed. "Trust me, you would know by now if there was."

Angie's face relaxed as she let out a pent-up breath. And then, unexpectedly, she started laughing. "Damn, Blake," she said, and held up her hand for a high five. "You're sneakier than I thought. You almost had me."

Emma slapped her palm. "I won't point out how quick you were to believe the branding thing, Wang."

Angie shrugged, her lips quirking. "Knowing this one, would it really be a shock?"

"Good point." Emma glanced at Jamie. "Eat up, Rook. You need to put on some weight if you're going to keep up with the big dogs."

Jamie rolled her eyes and turned back to her food. At least Emma hadn't called her a bean pole this time, she thought, and eagerly shoveled a forkful of roasted potatoes into her mouth. For a moment there with Maddie glowering at her from across the table, she'd almost lost her appetite. But it had rebounded quickly. It usually did.

Maddie wasn't finished, however. When Jamie reached the van for practice a little while later, she paused, looking in through one of the open rear doors. Usually she and the U-23s sat in the first row, with Emma driving and Maddie controlling the radio from the passenger seat. But today her seat was taken.

"I think you're in my spot," she said, frowning at Maddie.

"Take mine, Rook." Maddie nodded at the seat next to Emma. "I didn't think you would mind shotgun. Consider it an early birthday gift."

"Yeah, this way you won't get car sick," Angie added, waggling her eyebrows.

So that was the plan. Which, if she thought about it, wasn't such a bad plan.

"Well, thanks," she said, trying not to seem too excited at the change. She opened the front passenger door and glanced in at Emma. "Can I...?"

"Of course. Maddie wouldn't allow anyone else to take 'your' seat."

"So you're okay with this?" Jamie asked, climbing in.

"Totes." Emma smiled at her and it was all she could do to restrain a giggle. Jesus, where had that even come from? "Even though Maddie and I *were* the longest van buddy couple on the team—until Yoko there had to come along and break us up."

"I heard that," Angie said. "Enough with the racism, Blake. Not all Asians look alike, you know."

"Or do they?" Jamie asked over her shoulder.

Angie flipped her off while the players around them snickered.

As Emma pulled the van away from the curb, she lowered her voice. "What did Maddie say to you at breakfast, anyway?"

"Nothing." Telling Emma that Maddie had given her the best friend lecture would just make things awkward between them. It wasn't like they were dating. *Yet*, her mind insisted on whispering.

Emma's eyebrows rose. "Didn't look like nothing."

"I'll tell you about it at some point. Just, not now. Okay?" Right. Because being mysteriously lame was always better than going with the truth.

"Okay. Whatever."

The van turned onto the main road and Emma stared out the windshield. Jamie fiddled with the radio controls, wondering if she should reconsider her stance, as it turned out not telling Emma might be more awkward than broaching the subject Maddie's prank had raised. Although, as she imagined Emma throwing her head back and laughing wildly when Jamie told her, or even worse the moment of silence before she patted her hand and told her sympathetically that she didn't feel *that* way about her, that they were only friends, remember, she was glad she'd kept her silence.

At the training center they piled out of the van and headed for the practice field. While Emma went to get her ankle taped, Jamie grabbed a seat on one of the benches to go through her sunscreen regimen. She had a 60 SPF roll-on bar for her face and neck; 15 SPF spray-on for her arms and legs, and 30 SPF lotion for her ears and the top of her head. Once, during youth camp in Texas, she'd neglected her part, and by the end of the week she had burned her scalp so badly that it peeled, giving her the look of someone with a particularly nasty case of dandruff. Never again, she had sworn. Especially not with the cameras that followed their nearly every move.

When she was ready, she glanced around for Angie, her warm-up partner. But in keeping with the day's theme, Angie and Maddie were already warming up together a little ways away, passing the ball back and forth with quick, skilled touches. No way. Angie had ditched her for her girlfriend. Again.

"Seriously?" Emma paused beside her. "Are they actually doing this?"

"Apparently."

Why were her friends and family members always trying to set her up, anyway? Her sister had given Laurie, her college girlfriend, Jamie's phone number, and Britt and Allie had introduced her to Clare. Did no one think she was capable of finding a girlfriend on her own?

Hmm. Probably she shouldn't dwell on that question.

"Do you want to warm up together?" she asked despite the fact it was obviously what Maddie and Angie were angling for.

"Sure," Emma said, toying with her ponytail.

Crap. Emma only played with her hair when she was nervous or uncomfortable.

"We don't have to, you know," Jamie said. "I can totally find someone—"

Emma's hand on her arm stopped her. "No, don't." She smiled, her hand lingering on Jamie's bare skin. "I want to."

"Okay, then."

"Okay, then," Emma echoed. "I'll grab a ball."

And that was how she and Emma became seat buddies and warm-up partners—because their best friends at camp were dating and apparently thought they should be, too.

On the docket that afternoon was a "Fitness Update" meeting, but when the players showed up as instructed to the designated conference room, Lacey assigned them to small groups for a "friendly competition." As if any of them were capable of approaching a contest with something other than ruthlessness. It wasn't just soccer, either. Bowling, pool, obstacle courses, paint ball, mini golf—you name it, and the women on this team would find a way to fight almost to the death.

From youth camp and the U-23 team, Jamie knew that it wasn't unusual for the coaches to interrupt their two-a-days for a different sort of activity, one that would allow the staff to evaluate their leadership skills, creativity, and teamwork off the pitch. During her years in the national pool, she'd participated in relay races, soccer tennis tournaments, swimming contests, and other competitions, and had emerged from each feeling rested by working different pathways in her brain. The games also allowed players who might have little contact on the field to work together, another important step in creating team cohesion. And then there were the bragging rights that were up for grabs. You could never underestimate those among a group of women who hated to lose almost more than anything else in life.

Today's gladiator-in-training competition was a scavenger hunt, and somehow Emma and Jamie ended up on the same team with a mix of veterans and newbies. Emma was quickly voted team leader, and they looked through the list of challenges and associated time limits, divvying them up based on personal strengths. It was Emma's idea to check off the most esoteric items on the list by enlisting the aid of the hotel's front desk staff.

"Hey Gloria," Emma said, smiling at the woman in her white collared shirt and tasteful gold jewelry. "How's your day going?"

"Good, Emma," the woman said, smiling back. "What can I do for you ladies today?"

"We were wondering if you might be able to help with this little contest." Emma held out the list emblazoned at the top "MISSION USWNT: Chasing Gold." As Gloria looked it over, she added, "Any ideas where we might find a beach ball? And, say, a crab or a fish?"

"Hmm. Does it have to be an actual fish, or would a fish-shaped flotation device do?"

"Flotation device!" Five voices shouted at once.

Gloria laughed. "You've come to the right place, my friends. Our lost and found has almost anything you might need in the way of beach supplies."

Emma grinned at Jamie and hooked their arms together.

"Stick with me, kid," she murmured into her ear as they followed Gloria around the side of the desk and through a door marked "Employees Only."

And it was a cheesy line, maybe, but Jamie shivered anyway at the feel of Emma's breath on her neck, warm and intimate. "I intend to," she murmured back. She knew the look she gave Emma wasn't really a look one friend would—*should*—give another. She knew that Avery, the back-up keeper, was watching them with raised eyebrows, and that Jess, one of the newbies, was staring at them like they were a train wreck. Maybe they were and maybe they weren't, but at that moment she didn't care. She wanted to be the one Emma looked for each time she entered a room, the one Emma seemed to reach for almost unconsciously whenever they were near each other. What was more, she wanted Emma to be the one she texted in the middle of a team meeting, the one she sat with at breakfast quietly before either of them had had enough caffeine to converse. She wanted them to belong to each other equally and undeniably. And the truly great thing? She was starting to think that one day sooner rather than later they actually might.

They won easily; their scavenger hunt team name wasn't Nerd Squad for nothing. Later, as the results were tallied and the level of their winningness was revealed, the other groups complained about how unfair it was to have Emma paired with Jamie *and* Avery, who had graduated from Stanford while Jamie was still in high school.

"They're the closest to Ivy League we have," her U-23 buddy Lisa pointed out, arms folded across her chest. "Plus Jamie's a beep test ace, so she definitely should have been on a different team."

The other players chimed in irritably, and Emma nudged Jamie where their team stood at the front of the room, slightly removed from the fray. "Aw, look, everyone wants you on their kickball team."

Jamie laughed under her breath. "Says the pot to the kettle."

"They're only jealous because we make a good team." And she smiled into Jamie's eyes again, the usual unspoken undercurrents passing between them.

"You really do," Avery said, leaning in to interrupt the moment. "How long have you guys known each other, anyway?"

"Ten years. More than a third of my life," Jamie volunteered.

"It is, isn't it?" Emma shook her head. "I can't believe it took us this long to—" But she stopped as Ellie and Phoebe began to snipe at each other about cheating on the swimming leg of the challenge and Lacey finally intervened, calling an end to another USWNT bonding incident turned near bloodbath.

This long to *what?* But Jamie wasn't an idiot, nor was she the same young girl who had first asked Emma to go for a walk all those years ago. She knew what Emma meant, and as they accepted grudging congratulations for winning the competition and found seats together for the fitness update Lacey was determined to squeeze in before dinner, she couldn't believe it had taken this long either.

CHAPTER TEN

The last training session of January camp was in the books. Emma stuck the key in the ignition, scrolling through her phone as she waited for Jamie. It was still strange not to be sitting with Maddie. They had been van and bus buddies since joining the national team, which was why she had let out an audible gasp a few days before when Maddie waved semi-apologetically at her before sliding into the back seat next to Angie. But then Jamie had ended up sitting with her, and any ire she might have felt toward her roommate mysteriously melted away.

Soon Jamie tugged open the passenger door, bag over her shoulder, and Emma watched her slight wince as she pulled herself up and into the seat. She had noticed Jamie limping a little at the end of their full-field scrimmage, but she hadn't wanted to ask about it in front of the coaching staff.

"You okay?" she asked now.

"Yep."

She lowered her voice. "You're totally not, are you?"

"Nope."

"Quad or groin?"

Jamie's gaze flew to hers. "Groin," she whispered. "Was it that obvious?"

"I don't think so." She paused, glancing in the mirror to

make no one was eavesdropping, but the other players were either dozing or on their phones except Maddie and Angie, who were caught up in their own little world as usual. "Is it bad?"

"I hope not." She dropped her chin against her chest and groaned a little. "Sometimes I wonder what I did to piss off the soccer gods."

Emma hid a smile. Jamie's obsession with soccer deities was oddly endearing. "I doubt it was anything you did. Luck isn't something you can control."

"This from the woman who believes 'everyone makes their own luck.'"

"My mother believes everyone makes their own luck," she corrected. "I'm a bit more on the fence about the whole thing."

"On the fence, huh?" Jamie shook her head. "I am so tempted to make an inappropriate joke right now, it isn't even funny."

"That's because biphobia *isn't* funny," Emma said, mock-glaring at her.

"It's a little bit funny." As Emma slapped her arm, she held up a hand. "I take it back. It's not funny in the least."

"Damn straight it isn't." Emma watched Jamie out of the corner of her eye as the last member of their van group climbed in and slammed the back door. "I said, *damn straight* it isn't."

"I see you, Blake," Jamie said as she pulled her phone from her bag.

"Whatever." Emma checked her mirrors and pulled out of the parking lot. "That was funny. I'm funny."

"Funny *looking*, maybe..." Jamie flinched away, laughing as Emma tried to smack her again. "Hey, concentrate on the road!"

"I can multitask, you know." But she relented, allowing her hand to curl briefly instead around Jamie's forearm before placing it back on the steering wheel. "RICE when we get back, okay?"

"Yes, ma'am."

A few minutes later they parked in the lot in front of the

hotel and piled out, talking amongst themselves. Maddie and Angie waited for them and they crossed the lobby together, Jamie chatting with Angie, Emma trying to distract Maddie from Jamie's faint limp. Instead of taking the stairs, Emma stopped in front of the elevators. She didn't miss the grateful glance Jamie shot her.

Apparently neither did Maddie. "What was that look?" she demanded the second their door was closed.

Damn it. "What look?"

"Jamie isn't injured again, is she?"

"That's a question for Jamie." Emma averted her gaze as she crossed the room and dropped her bag on the partially unmade bed. Now that camp was all but over, there would be no more afternoon napping. Pity, really.

"She's hurt, isn't she? Fucking Christ. That was so not part of the plan."

Emma turned on her. "So there is a plan! I knew it."

Maddie flipped her ponytail over her shoulder. "What? We just wanted to have someone to go on double-dates with in Portugal."

Which, actually, sounded lovely. Before she could get caught up in daydreams of exploring the whitewashed fishing villages and sandy coves of the Algarve region with Jamie at her side, Emma stripped out of her sweaty practice jersey and grabbed a change of clothes from the dresser. "You and Angie became a 'we' awfully fast, didn't you?"

Maddie flopped onto the bed by the window. "Only if you call a year and a half fast."

"A year—" She stopped halfway across the room. "What are you talking about?"

"Apparently Angie has had a crush on me since London."

"No way."

"Yes way."

Emma's eyes narrowed. "And you?"

Maddie sighed. "Also since London."

"Why didn't you tell me?"

"Would you have told you?"

She paused. Valid point. "I guess I'm happy for you, then?"

"Gee, sound a little more sure there, Emma."

Obviously she owed one of her closest friends more than tepid support. But Maddie dating Angie was complicated for all sorts of reasons. "You can't tell her what happened in high school, okay?"

Maddie frowned. "I wouldn't. I promised, remember?"

"I know." Emma hesitated again, watching her across the room. "Are you sure you want to go down this road? I mean, it is *Angie* we're talking about."

"I'm sure."

"I don't know if I trust her, Mads."

"You don't have to trust her." Maddie's voice took on a deep, smooth timbre, as if she were channeling Morgan Freeman or some other much-revered film actor. "You only have to trust me."

Emma rolled her eyes. "So cheesy, Novak."

"You love it."

"I do," she admitted. "Okay, fine. I'm happy if you're happy. Better?"

"A little." The other woman winked lazily. "I have a few suggestions on how you could be happier, too…"

"Fuck off, Maddie."

"That's what she said."

"And on that note, I'm going to try to shampoo that image from my brain."

Emma ducked into the bathroom and turned on the shower. Craig had given them the night off, and tomorrow there were only a couple of meetings before camp officially closed. Given the lack of training sessions in their immediate future, the captains had decreed that tonight was a mandatory team bonding session, the kind that involved dinner, drinks, and dancing. She was looking forward to getting dressed up and going out. It had been a grueling couple of months, and they could all afford to let off a little steam. An image of Jamie sipping her mimosa on the plane flashed into her mind, and for a moment she let herself remember her post-cocktail fantasy of kissing chocolate protein crumbs from Jamie's lips.

Probably she should go easy on the alcohol tonight. It wasn't that she didn't trust herself around Jamie. She just really, *really* didn't want to do anything to screw up her chances at making the team. Despite her rough start to camp, Jamie was playing incredibly well. Although if she had pulled her groin, Emma distracting her might be the least of her worries.

Still, maybe Jamie would be able to nurse her leg back before the first friendly in two weeks—assuming she made the roster for the road trip. Ellie had said her chances were good. Bill and Melanie had slotted Jamie into the starting line-up even more this time around than in December, and Ellie thought they were grooming her to eventually fill Steph Miller's shoes as the veteran player drifted closer and closer to retirement. Or rather she'd said she *hoped* Jamie would take Steph's spot. Usually Ellie got what she asked for—the perks of being not only a team captain but also the player most expected to break the international scoring record.

Emma lathered her skin with body wash and then stood beneath the hot spray, eyes closed as the suds rinsed away. The Algarve Cup was only six weeks away. Would Jamie be along for the international tournament the '99ers had affectionately deemed the Golf and Wine Cup? Portugal in March was always beautiful, and the Algarve region was one of the more romantic spots the national team visited, perfect for long, moonlit walks and daytrips to hidden beach coves… She sighed and reached for her shampoo. Could she be jealous of Maddie and Angie? Yes. Yes, she could.

Right. She should definitely go easy on the alcohol tonight.

She didn't go easy on the alcohol that night. She meant to, but as soon as they reached the bar a bunch of them jammed into a wide, semi-circle booth to drink to Jamie's birthday, and Jenny had to go and buy tequila shots for the whole table. Except for Tina Baker, the last of the '99ers to retire, who was in town visiting her in-laws and also, incidentally, eight months pregnant.

Jamie shouldn't do shots, though, should she? Not after what had happened at the last camp. Beside her in the booth Jamie hesitated, brow furrowed as if she was also remembering her first panic attack in however many years, and Emma knew what she had to do. She pointed at the dance floor and announced loudly, "Oh my god, you guys, is that *Craig* over there?"

As soon as everyone's heads were craned around, Emma grabbed Jamie's shot and pounded it back, forcing herself to breathe through the burn in her throat without coughing. *Christ.* That was way too much tequila in way too little time. As Jamie reached for her hand under the table, she wasn't sure which made her blood sing more—Jamie's skin pressed to hers or the alcohol suddenly rushing through her veins.

"Max," Jenny said suddenly, her eyes on the empty shot glass in front of Jamie, "when did you do your shot?"

"Oh. Uh, just now. That is…"

Emma gripped her hand tighter, willing Jamie to stop rambling. Obviously her fibbing skills still needed work. Jenny looked between them, her gaze sharp and suspicious. But then Tina made a sound and touched her belly, distracting everyone.

"You're not about to go into labor, are you?" Maddie asked.

"Why would you even say that?" Jenny shook her head.

"Because once you've had a baby," Maddie explained, her tone clearly indicating her opinion of the striker's intelligence, "all it takes is a sneeze for baby number two to pop out. Or three, for that matter."

Tina laughed. "No worries, it's only a kick. This little girl has some power in her legs, though."

"Damn right she does." Ellie's smile managed to be both sweet and proud. Tina had asked her that afternoon to be the latest Baker Baby's godmother, Emma knew, so her possessiveness was understandable. Ellie's love for all things baby was widely known. Emma wouldn't be surprised if she got pregnant the second she retired. Unlike Tina and Steph, who had brought their young children on the road with the team every chance they got, Ellie had decided to wait until she was done with soccer to pursue procreation.

Emma leaned back next to Jamie as the conversation drifted to due dates and birth plans, stretch marks and post-baby workouts. Someday that would be her, she hoped, with the giant belly and the excited look and the sore, tired feet. Although she might already have that last one covered.

"Thanks, by the way," Jamie murmured.

With a start, Emma realized they were still holding hands. Touching Jamie felt so natural, as if it was something she'd done every day for years. "You're welcome. I'd say anytime, but I think two shots are my limit."

"You doing okay?"

"Fine. A little fuzzy but in a nice way."

"You're nice," Jamie nearly whispered, her forehead brushing Emma's.

Before Emma could respond, Tina startled again. "Geez! Apparently she likes Mexican food." She reached for Jamie's free hand almost blindly and placed it on her baby bump. "There, feel that? That's our future soccer girl."

Emma heard Jamie's breath catch, saw her eyes widen, heard her reverent, "Oh my god..." She squeezed Jamie's hand again, her mind suddenly tripping over a fantasy of a cute house higher up the Queen Anne hill, of herself sitting on a porch swing with Jamie beside her, one arm over her shoulders, the other extended toward her belly... She shook her head a little, trying to banish the mental slideshow. Quite the specific daydream, complete with fully formed details. How long had her subconscious been working on that one?

"You have to feel this," Jamie said, dragging Emma's hand across her own stomach to reach Tina's. "It's amazing!"

Emma placed her palm carefully on her former team captain's taut abdomen and waited. Sure enough, a slow movement soon tickled her palm, followed by a swift jab. "Doesn't that hurt?"

"No. It feels strange at first, for sure, but it doesn't hurt. The gas, on the other hand, feels like a freaking heart attack."

Emma pulled back as the conversation shifted again, dipping her chin almost to Jamie's shoulder. "Cool, huh?" she murmured.

"Cool doesn't even begin to cover it," Jamie responded, her eyes clear and shining.

A quiet moment passed between them, and even though Emma could feel Jenny's eyes on them, and Ellie's too, she couldn't bring herself to care who witnessed the emotion threatening to burst out of her. It wasn't fair that anyone could be that radiant. Because really, didn't Jamie realize how difficult she was making this whole not-kissing thing? Her gaze dropped to Jamie's lips, but even as Jamie's chin tilted infinitesimally toward her, Emma reminded herself that this wasn't the right time or place, not when they were surrounded by teammates and she was burping up tequila. Given how badly she'd botched their first kiss, she wanted to get the second one right.

Their hands remained connected even after the moment passed, and Emma could have happily sat there all evening leaning into Jamie's side and chatting with their friends if Maddie and Jenny hadn't pulled her forcibly from the table and dragged her to the dance floor. And yeah, it was their thing to dance together whenever they got the chance, which wasn't all that often these days, but still. They were leaving tomorrow and it wasn't like Jamie could dance, not with her injured leg. If it wouldn't have raised too many eyebrows, Emma would have ignored her two best friends and stayed holed up in the booth beside Jamie all night. As it was, she let herself be led away, shooting Jamie a last regretful, semi-apologetic glance over her shoulder.

Except who was she kidding? It totally wasn't the last time she looked at Jamie. They had only been on the dance floor for a few minutes when Maddie took her hand again and steered her to the bar to buy a bottle of water. As Maddie dealt with the bartender, Emma's gaze wandered. Jamie was sitting between Tina and Ellie now, and as Emma watched, Jamie glanced toward the dance floor. She examined the crowd intently, the crease in her brow deepening.

Emma pulled her phone out and texted: "Three o'clock." Even from here, she could see Jamie's phone light up on the table in front of her. Jamie pulled it closer and frowned again. And then, all at once, her forehead cleared as she glanced over at the bar in time to catch the goofy smile Emma could feel plastering itself to her face.

Maddie chose that moment to lean in, effectively blocking her view of the booth. "Jesus, Blake. Are you trying to broadcast it to the whole world?"

In the face of overwhelming odds, she went with denial. "Broadcast what?"

"How much you'd like Jamie to do a different type of holding, you know, than the midfield kind," Maddie suggested, waggling her perfectly shaped eyebrows.

Emma snickered. "That was terrible even for you."

"Like you could do any better."

"Pssht." She wasn't honorary captain of the nerd squad for nothing. "How about taking it to her box? Slipping it between her legs? Bending her like Beckham?" As the last pun emerged from her mouth, Emma frowned. That was beyond rude. Actually, they all were. *Freaking tequila.*

Meanwhile Maddie was snorting her amusement. "'Bend Her like Beckham' would be an awesome porno title. I'm totally tweeting those."

Emma deeply regretted her own overly competitive nature for approximately the zillionth time in her life. "If you do, Maddie, I swear—"

"I'm kidding. You're so easy. Seriously, though, keep your eyes to yourself unless you want your little secret getting out."

"Did somebody say 'secret'?" Angie piped up.

Really, it wasn't that surprising that the tiny midfielder had materialized seemingly from nowhere. Angie was hard to keep track of in a crowd even when Emma was sober.

"Hmm, I think you're hearing things again," Maddie said.

"Why is it that only seems to happen when I'm around you?"

"Because you only have ears for me?"

Angie shook her head. "Oh my god, you are such a dork."

"You know you love me."

"Lucky for you I do." Angie smiled up at Maddie, her eyes softer than Emma could remember ever seeing them.

Okay, so maybe they *were* kind of cute together.

Emma tugged Maddie toward the dance floor. "Come on. I need to dance off the tequila."

"Good call." Maddie pulled Angie along. "Let's do this!"

"What are we doing?" Emma heard Angie ask.

"Clam jamming."

"Jesus, Maddie!" Emma let go of her friend's hand. "I will pay you good money never to use that phrase again."

"Clam jammer, clam jammer, clam jammer," Maddie sang out, Angie giggling in her wake.

So much for being cute.

Jenny's decision to partake in the dancing portion of the evening's entertainment soon brought a couple of former frat boys turned business consultants sniffing around. Normally Emma would have been fine dancing with the clean-cut guy who smiled at her, his eyebrows lifted questioningly. But tomorrow was Jamie's birthday *and* the end of January camp, and over the random guy's shoulder she could tell Jamie was actively trying not to look at the dance floor, her shoulders hunched as if that would protect her from having to see Emma dance with someone else. If their positions had been reversed, she knew how she would feel.

So she shook her head at the guy in the collared shirt, who simply shrugged and moved on to one of the newbies whose name was currently escaping her mind. She glanced back at the booth, and even though Jamie wasn't looking at the dance floor, her shoulders had relaxed and she was smiling at something Ellie was saying, and Emma knew she'd seen her shoot down her would-be suitor. Crisis, clearly, averted.

Over the next twenty minutes, she danced enough to sweat out quite a bit of the alcohol or at least help her body metabolize it faster. Maddie assisted in the sobering-up process, plying her with water that helped cool her heated skin and flush the spinny feeling from her head. But all that liquid had a predictable effect. When she saw Jamie and Lisa head for the restroom, she grabbed Jenny, pulling her away from her dancing partner.

"Come on. I have to pee."

Jamie and Lisa had already disappeared into stalls by the time they reached the bathroom. Emma followed suit, only once she was seated, it took longer than she expected to relax. Apparently the thought of Jamie with her pants down somewhere only a few feet away was affecting her already impaired brain function.

When she reemerged, Jamie was at the sinks. They looked at each other's reflection for a moment, eyes holding, and then Lisa joined them.

"That guy was totally cute," her fellow defender said as she washed her hands. "Why did you diss him? Are you seeing someone in Seattle?"

"No," Emma said quickly. "Just wasn't feeling it."

"Gotcha." Lisa sighed, fussing with her hair. "I miss Andre."

"Where is he right now?"

"New Orleans. But he'll be home soon."

Lisa's longtime boyfriend was a jazz musician who was away from home almost as much as she was. Emma remembered those days. She didn't envy her fellow defender the distance in her relationship.

Emma washed her hands, checking herself in the mirror. Her cheeks were flushed either from dancing or tequila or both, and her hair was coming out of its bun. Jamie, meanwhile, didn't meet her eyes again as she dried her hands.

"See you out there," she said with a slight wave, following Lisa toward the door.

As Jamie left the restroom, Emma gazed after her, wishing she could—well, wishing lots of things, none of which were immediately obtainable.

"What the hell is that look?" Jenny asked, startling her.

Emma hadn't seen her approach.

"Nothing," she said, glancing back at the mirror to fix her hair.

"Honestly, can no one on this team keep it in their pants?" Jenny complained as she turned on the water. "It's like the World Cup is making you all lose your lesbian minds. It'll be sixteen years next summer, Emma, remember? We were in elementary school the last time this team won."

Technically, she'd been in middle school, but whatever. Emma glanced around. Fortunately no one else appeared to be paying them any attention. "Jen, this is not the time or the place…"

"Babe," her friend replied, tugging her toward the door, "that is exactly what I'm trying to tell you. Maddie too. Sheesh. No wonder people think we're all gay."

"Because we are?" Emma followed her out into the noisy club.

"You wish."

"No, I think *he* wishes," Emma said, nodding at the businessman who had perked up when he saw Jenny.

"I know, right?" The striker slipped her arm through Emma's, tugging her flush against her side. "Gotta give our public what they want."

Used to Jenny's semi-drunken flirtation—what went on in sororities, anyway? Maybe she should have joined one at UNC after all—Emma leaned into her and smiled even as her eyes sought out Jamie. There she was, back safely with Ellie and the other veterans.

"Sorry, babe," she said, giving the striker's arm a squeeze. "You're on your own tonight."

"What…?" Jenny followed her gaze. "Oh, fine. Go get your birthday girl."

"Thanks, Jen."

"Yeah, yeah. Love ya, Blake!" And off she went to flirt with her conquest for the night.

"Mind if I sit down?" Emma asked when she reached the booth, waiting until Jamie nodded to slide in beside her. "It's way too hot out there."

"I'm pretty sure the only thing that's too hot is you," Jamie murmured, half-smiling.

Beneath the table, Jamie's hand found hers again, and Emma bit her lip as their fingers wove tentatively together. She could feel her pulse racing at Jamie's compliment, which was silly because Jamie had been teasing. But maybe, just maybe there was something else beneath her smile, an edge that said she wasn't really teasing at all.

"Happy almost birthday," she murmured, her mouth close to Jamie's ear.

"Thanks." But Jamie's eyes dimmed and her smile turned lopsided.

Emma thought she was probably thinking that after tonight there was no guarantee they would ever be like this again—out celebrating the end of national team camp with their friends and teammates. Curfew was still a few hours away, though, and Emma was determined to enjoy the time they had left together. Because while Nike's slogan *life is short* might be a cliché, it was also accurate.

She shifted closer on the padded bench and tucked her ankle under Jamie's carefully, offering her injured leg a resting place. "Okay?"

Jamie nodded, her smile evening out again. "Better than okay."

"Good," Emma said, and settled in, trying to pick up the threads of a conversation that seemed to revolve around the best time in the World Cup cycle to get pregnant.

When curfew did arrive, Emma's head was clearer (which was good) and she and Jamie were surrounded by their friends on the hotel elevator (which was bad), and the grown-ass women around them were giggling because they were almost late getting back from the club. As soon as the elevator opened on their floor, Ellie sent Angie on a reconnaissance run. Melanie and Craig's doors were closed and the lights were off, the petite midfielder soon reported back, at which everyone heaved relieved sighs and headed for the corridor. The last

Emma saw of Jamie was her backwards glance as Ellie tugged her down the hallway toward their room.

"Come on," Maddie said, slipping her arm through Emma's. "You'll see her in the morning."

Easy for her to say. Angie was going home with her so they could hang out for the next couple of weeks until the team reconvened in Texas. Still, there was no way to see Jamie that didn't involve breaking rules and interrupting sleep patterns, neither of which were remotely her thing, so she only harrumphed and let herself be led away yet again.

Later, while Maddie and Angie texted for a while, Emma lay in bed staring at the dark ceiling as she replayed the evening in her mind. She and Jamie had held hands and almost kissed. In public. In front of half the team and whoever else might be watching! What had she even been thinking? She grabbed her phone and did a quick search on Tumblr and L Chat, but fortunately there was nothing new on the Blakewell tag. *Whew.* She would have to be more careful, though. *They* would have to be more careful, assuming they... well, if they were going to be a "them" around other people. Especially if they planned to do so around strangers with camera phones and Tumblr accounts.

What were they planning, though? She had to be crazy for even considering dating another player in the pool. But Jamie wasn't just another player, and Emma didn't only want to date her. She remembered the look in Jamie's blue, blue eyes the moment after they had both held their hands to Tina's belly to feel her baby kick. The last time Jamie had looked at her like that, Emma had been on the cusp of leaving behind the West Coast—and her—for college back east. *I don't think we get to keep each other,* Jamie had texted a few days after Emma had kissed her for the first time. And she'd been right. They hadn't gotten to keep each other. Instead they had gone off and led separate lives, following different paths that eventually led them here. Back to Southern California, back to each other.

As she lay in the dark, thinking about what had been and what still might be, she remembered something that had happened in the in-between years while they were apart. Jamie was on the under-20 national team when Tina Baker, still in her prime, had taken time out from a USWNT game in the Bay Area to be "interviewed" by the young national team hopeful. US Soccer had filmed their conversation and uploaded it to YouTube. Emma, captain of the U-23 side at the time, must have watched that video a dozen times at least, her heart expanding each time Jamie ducked her head in response to a compliment Tina offered.

The video had ended with Tina pulling Jamie into a hug and telling her that one day she would be there playing with the senior side. Jamie had shrugged and said, "Maybe," to which Tina had replied, "I'm serious. You'll be here and I'll be watching from the sideline."

Earlier tonight when Tina had showed up at the hotel, husband and two boys in tow, she'd hugged Jamie and said, "See? I told you your time would come."

Jamie had smiled and blushed like she had in the old marketing video, and it had been all Emma could do not to wrap her arms around her and hold on tight. Because honestly, if anyone deserved to have their dreams come true, it was Jamie.

#

The groin pull, Jamie realized the following day, was worse than she had thought. The pain was bad enough that a half hour into her drive home from camp, she had to divert to Pasadena where she let herself into her aunt and uncle's backyard and stretched out on a lounge chair, her leg elevated, an ice pack wrapped to her inner thigh. Some birthday this was turning out to be. First she'd had to say goodbye to Emma, not knowing when (if? But no; after last night, definitely *when*) they would see each other again, and now she was stuck in Pasadena for god knew how long. When she'd called from the freeway, her aunt had offered to come home early to meet her, but Jamie had insisted she didn't mind waiting. Armed with her laptop, movie case, and a mini-cooler full of Gatorade, she would be more than fine hanging out on her own for a few hours. In fact, she could use a little alone time to decompress from the last few days.

Talk about a roller coaster—on the one hand there was the injury, but on the other there was Emma. As much as she'd wanted to kiss Emma the night before, she was just as glad now that their first grown-up kiss wouldn't be in a crowded booth in an LA club, Tina Baker's pregnant belly pressed against her other side. Not that hanging out with a soccer legend was bad, per se. At one point she had wanted to pinch herself because she was sitting in a booth with Ellie, Phoebe Banks, and Steph Miller, flanked on one side by Tina, who she had grown up admiring, and on the other by Emma, who was holding her hand under the table. Talk about surreal. But then she'd felt Tina's baby kick, and she'd forgotten to be star struck as she grabbed Emma's hand and placed it on the retired player's abdomen. Gazing into Emma's eyes while the baby kicked against their curved palms hadn't felt strange at all but rather so, so perfect. In Emma's eyes she thought she glimpsed the type of future that she had never even thought to let herself dream of.

Which was slightly terrifying, if she was being honest. Because what the hell were they doing, anyway?

That had been the thought flashing in neon against her mind's eye as soon as she woke up. Then she'd tried to sit up and all thoughts of Emma had—however briefly—faded as her leg seized and she had to focus on not letting out a gasp of pain that Ellie would hear.

She was lucky she had family near LA. Each time she'd tried to lift her foot from the gas pedal or the brake, the pain had been so intense she'd felt slightly sick to her stomach. And that was after a day of the RICE protocol—Rest, Ice, Compression, and Elevation—not to mention popping extra-strength ibuprofen like candy. To get through the short drive to Pasadena she'd had to resort to using her right hand to support her quad every time she needed to accelerate or decelerate. Clearly the six-hour trip back to the Bay Area wouldn't be happening anytime soon.

Christ. She couldn't believe she'd managed to get herself hurt again. Except that the muscle pull wasn't really her fault. If fingers were to be pointed, the obvious target would be Taylor O'Brien, the little bitc—Jamie caught herself. Taylor wasn't a bad person. At least, Jamie didn't think so. She was young, a college senior still, and tended to do most things a bit, well, *intensely.* Taylor liked to tackle, pass, run, shoot, and (again) tackle at approximately a hundred miles per hour, which meant control was not always her strong suit. During the previous morning's practice, Taylor had slammed into Jamie when they went up for a fifty-fifty ball. Forcing herself to pop up as if nothing were wrong, Jamie had tried to walk off the blow. But the contusion that had formed at the edge of her shin guard had instantly—and alarmingly—numbed her left leg from mid-shin downward.

When she went back to her room after lunch armed with a bag of ice, she'd finally gotten a chance to survey the damage in detail. An already purpling blotch the size of her palm occupied the space between her knee and ankle, and her lower leg still felt oddly numb, as if the nerves were hesitant to engage.

"What the hell?" Ellie had said when she saw the bruise. "When did that happen?"

"This morning."

"Obviously, Max. I meant how? Who did that?"

"I don't know."

Ellie's eyes narrowed. "Was it Steph? Please tell me it wasn't Steph."

"It wasn't, okay? Chill, dude. Soccer is a contact sport."

She snapped her fingers. "O'Brien! It was that freaking kamikaze, wasn't it?"

"I can neither confirm nor deny the charge."

"Seriously? Blake's right. You do belong on the nerd squad." And Ellie had walked away, grumbling about national team "infants."

Jamie wasn't sure if she'd meant her or Taylor. Either way, the characterization was a bit unfair. They may be competing for the same position, but it wasn't like the girl had meant to hurt her. Jamie had personally watched her bowl over a handful of other players, including veterans, in her semi-manic attempts to prove herself to the national team coaching staff. And yeah, maybe Jamie *should* have sat out the final afternoon practice like Ellie had suggested. Maybe then she wouldn't have been overcompensating and injured her other leg. But hindsight and all of that. At this point what was done was done.

She knew she should be feeling worse about the whole injury thing. After all, Melanie had told her that she needed to stay healthy if she wanted a shot at the team. But in between paralyzing moments of terror that she was losing her best chance at a spot on the national team were dreamy flashes of the previous night when Emma had squeezed into the booth beside her to take tequila shots so she wouldn't have to and, oh yeah, *held her hand.* Maddie and Jenny had dragged her away, it was true, but Emma had eventually ditched them to come back and hang out with her for the rest of the night, which had been sweet. And amazing. And so, so awesome.

Her talk with Ellie hadn't been so bad, either. While Emma danced, Ellie slid around the table and took her spot, pressing almost as close as Emma had before asking in a low voice camouflaged by the music, "Okay, I've held off long enough. What exactly is going on between you guys?" And she'd nodded toward the dance floor where half the team was rocking out to a Drake and Rihanna remix.

"Honestly?" Jamie had watched Emma spin around, her dimple evident from across the room. "I have no clue."

"Let me rephrase then: How do you feel about her?"

She'd looked down, turning the empty shot glass over and over, but it couldn't tell her whether confessing the truth was a good idea or a really terrible one. "Well, so I might possibly, sort of, I don't know, be in love with her?" She peered at Ellie from the corner of one eye, bracing for the lecture the national team captain was sure to level at her.

Instead, Ellie had nodded. "I thought so. You should tell her, Max."

Jamie's head whipped around. "What?"

Ellie smiled, her eyes gentle. "Trust me when I say that genuine love is rare. If you're lucky enough to find it, you owe it to yourself to grab hold and not let go."

"But you're the one who said teammates aren't allowed to date."

"Officially, it's my job to say that. But unofficially, as your friend? Let's just say I 'ship Blakewell."

She winked and Jamie punched her arm, unsure which was more exciting—that Ellie had given them her blessing or that she had called Jamie a friend.

A moment later Jamie's smile faded as Steph leaned across the table and half-shouted, "Why aren't you dancing with your little buddies? Are you injured again?"

"No," Jamie said quickly, and offered the excuse she had prepared for this very situation. "Just a crappy dancer."

"Yeah, you do not want to see this one try to bust a move," Ellie said, making a face.

Jamie knew she was trying to help, and she appreciated the gesture, but at the same time she wished Ellie wouldn't be quite so nice because the captain—her *friend*—had no idea that Jamie had lied to her face earlier. It wasn't like her roommate wouldn't notice the buckets of ice she was schlepping to their room, so when Ellie asked her about it, she claimed it was for her bruised shin and then proceeded to ice both legs under the covers. She didn't want to lie to Ellie, but she also hadn't wanted anyone to find out about the groin injury until she'd had a chance to assess how bad it might be.

"Oh. Well, good," Steph said, toying with the straw in her mixed drink. "We need to keep you healthy. I'm not going to be around forever, you know."

Jamie had stared at her in shock, automatically looking around for Emma. The spot she'd occupied on the dance floor was now vacant, and try as she might, she couldn't pick Emma's honey-blonde hair or red scoop-neck blouse—not that Jamie had memorized what she was wearing or anything—among the hordes of dancers. That's when the text came through, and instead of being embarrassed that Emma had caught her looking for her, she was only relieved to spot her safe and sound with Maddie at the bar.

Shortly after that the random dude had tried to dance with Emma, and Jamie had watched, relieved again, as she shot him down. Her heart rate was still slowing when Phoebe Banks decided to offer a shock of her own: "You're friends with Britt Crawford, aren't you?"

Jamie had almost glanced around to make sure that the legendary keeper's gaze was fixed on her. Context clues indicated it had to be—it wasn't like Ellie or Tina were great friends of Britt's.

"Um, yes?"

"Tell her to transfer to the NWSL. England isn't doing her career any favors."

"I couldn't agree more," Ellie chimed in.

"I thought the WSL had come a long way in the last couple of years," Tina said.

"It has," Phoebe admitted grudgingly. "But you know how fierce the keeper competition is at this level. I'm not going to be around forever either, you know, so it would be smarter to be back here where the federation can keep an eye on her."

"Remember when we played in Sweden," Tina said, "the summer before I got pregnant with Carter?"

Ellie started laughing. "I haven't thought about that in years. Remember the castle they rented out for us?"

"That place was legit haunted," Phoebe said, sounding peeved.

"So you said, Banks." Tina rolled her eyes, and Jamie was amazed by her cheekiness—until she realized that even Phoebe Banks wouldn't smack a pregnant lady.

As the conversation shifted to Swedish food and currency, Jamie tuned out to send Britt a quick text: "Dude!! Rachel Ellison and Phoebe Banks say they think you should move back to the US so the coaches can see you play more! Oh, and so do I!"

Emma had returned to the booth a little while later to sit

next to her again, and their hands had linked under the table of their own accord, fingers curling together. As midnight approached, Jamie had thought the entire evening might be the best early birthday present she'd ever received.

Good thing her pre-birthday had rocked, since the day itself was falling well short of perfection.

She sat up and glanced at her phone resting on a nearby patio table. The urge to text Emma or, at least, stalk her on Instagram was nearly overwhelming. Instead she opened her laptop and set to work in Illustrator, trying to bury her mind in her latest tree design. She loved drawing trees. To her, there was something so calming about them, both aesthetically and spiritually. For as much as she hated standing still, that was what trees did for their entire life. Patiently. Happily, even, as far as she could tell. This latest design had roots that extended deep underground in a slightly altered reflection of its branches. If she ever managed to finish it, she wanted to have it tattooed on her leg, with the roots disappearing across her ankle and under the bottom of her foot—a visual reminder of the necessity of staying grounded.

When her text notification went off a few minutes later, somehow she wasn't surprised to see Emma's contact photo flash across the screen. The picture was of the two of them on the team van a few days earlier, messing around on their phones as they waited for stragglers. Jamie had been laughing at something on Instagram—a funny dog video, if she remembered correctly—and Emma was leaning close and looking at her with the softest smile Jamie had ever seen. Maddie had snapped the candid shot and texted it to both of them with the caption, "A rare sighting of Blakewell in its natural habitat."

She pulled up Emma's text. "How's the leg, birthday girl?" Before she finished reading, another alert sounded. "Not that you should be checking this while you're driving." Another buzz heralded the third message: "Eyes on the road, Maxwell!"

Smiling even though no one could see her, Jamie typed back, "Don't worry. I'm not texting and driving."

"Good. But where are you if you're not driving?"

"My aunt and uncle's house in Pasadena."

There was a slight pause before her phone buzzed again. "From Thanksgiving?"

"The same."

Jamie had a brief flash of sitting at her cousin's iMac in her pinkalicious bedroom ten years earlier downloading a photo of Emma in her Manchester United jersey. Emma had worn that same jersey only a couple of days earlier to watch an EPL match in Jamie and Ellie's room. When Jamie mentioned she was surprised Emma still had the jersey after all these years, Emma had smiled and told her that the shirt was lucky—even if it *had* come from a diehard Arsenal fan.

At that, Ellie had grunted. "You gave her the jersey, Max? Is that what I'm hearing?"

Jamie had pulled her gaze away from Emma's smile. "Yeah. In a moment of obvious weakness."

"To be fair, you didn't know you'd end up playing for Arsenal," Emma had pointed out.

Which was true. She hadn't known how any of this would turn out. Still didn't. Because if her chances at making the national team were slipping away, where did that leave her and Emma?

"Where are you?" she typed.

"On the tarmac. Your leg hurts too much to drive?"

She didn't even think about lying. "Yep. I think it's more than a minor strain."

Her phone rang a second later.

"I'm so sorry," Emma said, her voice low. In the background the sound of airplane engines was steadily rising.

"Me too. Don't you have to go?"

"In theory." Emma paused. "You should have called me. I would have driven you home, you know."

"You would have?"

"Of course. I know how you feel about Southern California."

"You don't always have to do that," Jamie said, closing her

eyes and readjusting the ice pack. "You know, follow something sweet with a joke?"

Emma was quiet. "I know. Sorry."

"It's okay. Anyway, at least it's warm here. Better to lay out by the pool than stew in my bedroom."

"Did you call your parents yet?"

"Not yet. I think I'm in denial."

"Right." She hesitated, and the background din got louder. "We're taking off. I really should turn off my phone."

She pictured Emma with her eyes closed, fists white-knuckled in her lap, teeth worrying the inside of her lip. Too bad she couldn't be there to hold her hand this time.

"Have a good flight," she said. "And don't worry. Everything will be all right."

"Isn't that supposed to be my line?"

"I think it's supposed to be both of our lines."

Emma laughed softly. "You're probably right. Thanks, Jamie. I miss you."

Her heart melted a little. "I miss you too. Call me later?"

"I will. Bye."

"Bye." Jamie listened until the call died, and then nearly jumped as her phone vibrated against her cheek. Emma had texted a line of emojis, in among which Jamie noted a birthday cake, an airplane, and, if she wasn't mistaken, a bag of ice. She leaned back on the lounge chair, a smile teasing her lips because seriously, who even has an ice bag emoji on their phone?

Her phone buzzed again. "Take care of your leg. And happy birthday!" Another emoji followed, one that had her blinking behind her sunglasses, wondering if it was her eyesight or her brain short-circuiting because it looked like Emma had sent her a kiss-blowing emoji, the one with one eye shut and a tiny heart emerging from pursed lips. She squinted harder. Yep. That was exactly what Emma had sent her.

She hesitated, and then she typed, "Safe flight. Text me when you're on the ground." She added the same kissing emoji, clicked send, and waited. Sure enough, Emma replied one last time with a thumbs-up.

For a moment, she gave into temptation and let herself relive the moment the night before when Emma had leaned into her in the booth, her body tantalizingly close, her eyes on Jamie's lips. She had been sure Emma wanted to kiss her, and even worried—hoped?—she might. But she was glad they had backed away from that particular precipice. Emma had been more than a little tipsy, that much Jamie knew both from the way she had swayed as she walked away from the booth and from the grimace she'd offered at breakfast this morning, her eyes all squinty, the shadows beneath them darker than usual. She had sipped Gatorade throughout their team meetings and lunch, and the electrolytes must have helped because by the time they said goodbye in the hotel lobby, Emma preparing to board the airport shuttle, Jamie getting ready to drive home, she had seemed more like herself.

The rest of the team was already outside, so Jamie had wrapped her arms around Emma's waist and pulled her close. In return, Emma had wound her arms around Jamie's neck and rested her head on her shoulder, and they had simply stood together, unmoving in the empty hotel lobby while the rest of the team bustled around outside.

"I'll see you soon," Emma had murmured.

Jamie had shivered at the feel of Emma's breath against her skin and held tighter, feeling Emma's arms squeeze back in response.

"I hope so," she'd said, and then she was pulling away to smile down at Emma. Her future with the national team might still be up in the air, but even so, she'd felt as if her life was on the verge of clicking into place. Not only was she about to start her (second) American pro soccer career, but she and Emma were hugging each other almost as if the years of not speaking had never happened.

"I know so. Happy birthday, Jamie," Emma had said, her slow smile warming every inch of Jamie, inside and out.

And yes, it was cheesy to actually think such a thing, even cheesier to admit to herself that she had thought such a thing, but she didn't care. Standing in the circle of Emma's arms, she'd felt too good to do anything but gaze into her familiar eyes and smile. They were back in the same time zone, and they had promised to make this—whatever was between them—work. Which meant they would.

So yeah, she might be injured again and her national team future was still unresolved, but as she sat on her aunt and uncle's patio tracing Emma's contact photo, she figured that things could be worse. She smiled a little, remembering how Emma had once told her it was her mother's Minnesotan family's motto: *Could be worse*. Emma had even had a picture book with that title on the bookshelf in her childhood bedroom, a book Jamie had leafed through early one morning while Emma slept beside her, honey-colored hair spilling across the pillow. So much had happened since that long ago morning, and yet Jamie could still remember the angle of the light through the blinds, the soft puffs of Emma's breath beside her, the way her own heart skipped and tripped every time she looked away from the picture book and let herself stare down at the girl she had only just realized she was in love with.

She'd been so clueless then, a lesbian in name only. She hadn't even kissed a girl before Emma, so no wonder she hadn't known what to do with the grieving girl who clung to her each night like she was the only thing keeping her afloat. Emma had been so patient with her, so gentle, knowing as she did what it was that made Jamie freeze whenever anyone came too close. Or anyone else, anyway. Right from the start, Emma's kindness had slipped under her skin, passing through her bloodstream and into her heart until Emma's limbs felt like mere extensions of her own. Probably she should have known there was something more between them the night they met, but she hadn't. It had taken months for her to accept that what she felt for Emma extended beyond the bounds of friendship. This time around it hadn't taken nearly as long.

But knowing how she felt and knowing what to do with those feelings were two very different things. She had hoped she would join Emma and the rest of the team in Texas to take on Canada, but with her leg as screwed up as it obviously was… There was literally *nothing* she could do but wait and see. Well, she could continue to RICE and see if a sports med doctor would hook her up with some ultrasound and e-stim next week after the swelling had gone down. She could also continue to take the absolute maximum allowed amount of NSAIDs. The joys of soccer—she would probably still be able to walk in a decade (she hoped), but whether she would have a stomach lining left was anyone's guess.

She turned off her phone and went back to Illustrator, determined to lose herself in shading tools and EPS settings. At least she hadn't hit traffic on her way up to her aunt and uncle's house. Otherwise she might still be sitting on a crowded freeway manually lifting her leg every time traffic lurched forward and she had to shift her foot between the brake and gas pedal.

If not for that kiss-blowing emoji, she might have started to doubt what had happened at the club the night before, might have second-guessed her interpretation of Emma's intentions. But the tiny red heart had confirmed that she hadn't imagined anything, as Emma had to have known it would. And now Jamie could only rest in the shade of her aunt and uncle's patio drawing trees and trying not to think about another kiss, one that had happened so long ago that it, too, felt almost like a dream.

CHAPTER ELEVEN

"Fucking FIFA!" Ellie said, pushing to her feet and pacing out of the camera's range.

Emma felt the same, but she stayed in front of her laptop. Amy Rupert, a legendary '99er who had gone on to law school after soccer, was doing them a huge favor taking a break from work on a weekday afternoon to participate in their group video chat.

"Thanks for trying, Amy," Steph said. "We appreciate it."

"Of course. I wish I had better news."

"Why are they refusing to even discuss laying sod over the turf?" Phoebe asked.

"I'm not sure. It's not that expensive—less than five percent of the projected men's budget this summer in Brazil, from what I've heard."

To Emma, using sod over the artificial turf on the Canadian fields approved for the 2015 World Cup seemed like a no-brainer, but then again this was FIFA, who had proven time and again that there really might not be any brains involved in the decision-making process.

"Do you have any suggestions on where to go from here?" she asked.

The former national team captain's shrug was apologetic. "I'm still working on a few angles. I have an email from Scotts

Lawn Care that mentions they might be willing to provide sod for the stadiums for free—but FIFA would still need to pay to outfit the training facilities, so I'm not sure how far that will get us. I know that as an attorney I'm probably expected to say this, but assuming we can get enough players to sign on, our best shot might end up being legal action. The Executive Committee already granted Canada their special disposition. Frankly, they're playing the odds that you guys won't boycott."

Those odds were definitely in FIFA's favor. Refusing to play at their highest profile international event because football's governing body had decided all of the games would be played on artificial turf would be shooting themselves in the foot, and healthy feet were a requirement in their line of work.

"Bastards," Jenny said, her voice as bitter as Ellie's. "They would never try to make the men play on turf. Can you imagine?"

"The meltdown would be catastrophic," Ryan Dierdorf agreed. "Everyone knows artificial turf hurts more when you dive."

The other players on the chat snickered at the dig, but their faces reflected their collective frustration. It wasn't a secret that FIFA was an old boys' network that didn't value women's soccer. Though notoriously cagey about its financials, the governing body had recently admitted to only spending fifteen percent of its annual budget on the women's game. Their argument was that women's soccer didn't draw the same crowds as men's, but Emma's feeling was that if you didn't build it, no one would come. Or, as Amy put it, there could be no return on investment where there wasn't an investment in the first place.

"Actually," Amy said, "that'll probably be the basis for our main argument if this does end up in the courts. By allowing the World Cup to be played on turf, FIFA is treating female players like second-class citizens. They shouldn't be allowed to continue getting away with it."

The conversation devolved then into highly personal insults about the sexist, misogynistic FIFA president, a member of the old European football guard who genuinely believed women didn't belong anywhere near the pitch. It was bad enough to encounter that sentiment within the general public, but to witness it being passed down from the top of the sport's international governing body? Disheartening and disenchanting, to mention only a few disses.

Amy finally put an end to the bitch session. "While I've enjoyed the opportunity to rant as much as you guys, I do have one more recommendation to offer, if you'd like to hear it."

Ellie, who had returned to join in the slam fest, nodded. "Fire away."

"Funny you should use that terminology because that's exactly what I'm suggesting you think about: firing your current player's union reps."

Emma heard more than one gasp over the Skype airwaves. Jack and Sara, their longtime union reps, were more like friends than advisors.

"I thought you liked them?" Ellie said.

"I do like them. I'm just not sure they're representing your interests as well as they should be. It was under their watch that the memo of understanding got passed last year, and there's still no collective bargaining agreement on the books even though both parties agreed there would be by now."

"Do you have someone else in mind?" Steph asked.

As the former president of the Women's Sports Foundation and a partner in a New York corporate law firm, Amy was a powerful advocate. But she had said more than once that she was too invested in the national team's success to be an objective player representative.

"I can think of a few people I could put you in touch with. It may seem premature, but this is the time to start thinking about these issues. If you win the World Cup—sorry, that is *when* you win the World Cup next summer you'll be perfectly situated to capitalize on your higher profile. It's worth thinking about in advance in order to position yourselves as well as you possibly can."

They ended the chat a few minutes later, and Emma sat

back on her couch, trying to process everything that had been discussed. She knew they were lucky to have someone like Amy on their side. To the outside world they were elite athletes fortunate enough to be chosen to represent their country internationally. But behind the scenes, they were women in a male-dominated profession where their careers and working conditions were controlled by people who didn't always have their best interests at heart. Playing for the federation—and for FIFA—was far more complex than it she had anticipated.

Her phone buzzed beside her laptop and she grabbed it, half-expecting Jamie's name to blink up at her from the screen. They had been in near constant contact the last twenty-four hours while Jamie hung out at her aunt and uncle's house waiting for her parents to pick her up and Emma did laundry and caught up on foundation work and otherwise tried to keep occupied during her brief foray into normal life. It wasn't Jamie, though, and Emma ignored the swoop of disappointment as she answered the call.

"Dude," she said, resting her sock-clad feet on the coffee table. "That was intense, wasn't it?"

"I was going to call it a freaking disaster."

Ellie still sounded pissed, and Emma couldn't blame her. This would be the older player's last World Cup unless she somehow defied nature and her own body to keep on through another four-year major tournament cycle.

They chatted briefly about the conference call, and then Emma said as casually as she could manage, "So have you heard from Jamie?"

"We texted a couple of times. Why?"

"Just wondering."

"Emma..." Her tone was mildly threatening.

"What?"

"You know I can't tell you anything about the roster."

"I only wanted to know if you told Craig about her leg."

"What do you mean? I thought it was only a bruise."

Ellie didn't know about the groin pull? Then again, healing time for a muscle strain could be difficult to predict. Probably

Jamie was trying to move forward and hope for the best. So was Emma, really.

"Emma," Ellie said as she remained quiet, "is the bruise not healing?"

"No, the bruise is fine." Which was perfectly true. "How are things going with you and Craig, anyway?"

"Don't get me started. Male coaches are so—*male* sometimes, you know?"

"Uh-huh." Personally, Emma could see both sides. Craig may not have the most open communication style, but then again Ellie and Phoebe weren't enamored with the idea of having to report to any authority figure, let alone a middle-aged man from a foreign country known more for its scenery than its soccer.

"It's not like he doesn't know the game," Ellie added, "but I honestly wish Jo had taken the job when they offered it to her."

Jo Nichols had been their interim coach after Marty returned to the German women's pro league, and most of the players had wanted her to stay on. As a former national team star, director of player development, and coach of the U-16 and U-23 sides, she knew everyone inside and outside the federation. More importantly she understood the politics, both at the national and international level. Craig, on the other hand, was a relative outsider who had come to the USWNT by way of coaching pro soccer, first in Sweden and later in WUSA and the WPS. He knew the game, but was that enough?

According to Ellie and Phoebe, it wasn't nearly.

"Do you really buy that she turned it down because she didn't want to leave Virginia?" Emma asked.

"That *is* the official statement. But would you want to coach this team?"

"Not a chance."

The job wasn't easy, by any means, which Jo as a former player had to know better than possibly anyone else in the coaching pool. Take twenty-four of the most competitive women in the United States and then ask them to eat, sleep, and work together for weeks at a time while competing for playing time—that alone was enough to break most team managers. Not only that, but as the top team in the world, the pressure to win was immense. The federation didn't just demand success; they demanded near perfection. Like Amy Rupert, Emma was planning to go in a completely different direction after her tenure on the national team ended. Hopefully that unknown second career was still a ways away, though. She had too much soccer left in her to walk away anytime soon.

They chatted for a little while longer—Ellie's fiancée was in Paris for work and they had managed to completely miss each other on their travel day, so now they would be going two and a half weeks without seeing each other.

"That's rough. But at least you live in the same—" Emma started. Then she stopped herself. Whoops.

"I knew it! What happened after the bar? Did she sneak out? Because she was there when I went to sleep and there when I woke up."

"Of course she didn't sneak out. That's not her style and you know it."

"You didn't deny that something happened, Blake."

"It didn't. We hugged, Ellie, that's it. Only now I wish…"

"You wish what?"

"I wish I had stayed in California with her." As Ellie stayed silent, Emma added, "Isn't this where you usually warn me to stay away from her?"

"Don't quote me on this, but honestly? I think you guys are good for each other."

Emma straightened up on her couch. "You do?"

"Yeah, I do. She's calmer and more focused when you're around, fairly difficult states to achieve when you're on the bubble."

Emma could still remember her own transition days, when she was the youngest player in the pool and she wondered if every new invitation to train with the senior side would be her last. It had been a while since she'd felt the kind of uncertainty—and self-doubt—that Jamie was currently living with.

"She's good for you too," Ellie added. "You're lighter around her, softer somehow. But I do have a warning. Do you want to hear it?"

"Fire away," Emma said, which reminded her of a certain scene in *Pitch Perfect*, which in turn reminded her of Jamie...

"If you're going to do this, you have to do it. You can't start and then suddenly stop. You have to make it work, and that's a lot of pressure on a new relationship."

Hadn't Emma said something similar to Jamie? Except they weren't in a new relationship, and not only because they weren't technically in a relationship. By now they had known each other an impressive number of years—more than a third of their lives, as Jamie had pointed out. In that time they had seen each other at their best and worst, and even now, there was a strong bond of friendship underpinning whatever romantic feelings they may or may not be having. In fact, they were more friends than anything else—though she suspected that would change as soon as they found time to be alone together away from the team. Or, well, she *hoped* it would. Like, a frighteningly intense amount.

"I get it," she told Ellie. "But I'm not in this for a fling and neither is she."

"I know. Not your guys' style." She paused, and then she said, the smile evident in her voice, "You do know the women's soccer fandom is going to melt down if Blakewell is confirmed, right?"

Emma groaned. "You had to go and ruin it, didn't you?"

The thought of the inevitable invasion of privacy awaiting them was almost enough to make her vow never to date again. Actually, no it wasn't, she decided, remembering the moment she and Jamie had said goodbye at the hotel. Jamie had hugged her, and Emma had burrowed into her chest, enveloped by her heat for a long moment that passed far too quickly. When they'd finally stepped apart, the smile Jamie had given her had been nothing short of luminous. And that smile? It was worth almost anything.

Just before she and Ellie hung up, the older woman said, "We have ten days before we have to be in Texas. If you really wanted to see her you could. It's not like she's in freaking Paris."

Which was true, Emma thought after the call ended. She could book a ticket to San Francisco fairly easily. The question was, would Jamie want her to?

Her mind spinning with possibilities, she rose from the couch and went to assess her kitchen cupboard situation. Downtime between camps and friendlies was always the same—strategic shopping combined with take-out so she wouldn't be left cleaning moldy leftovers out of her refrigerator the next time she stopped over in Seattle. It was Friday, and Dani and a couple of girls from the Reign had invited her out, but she hadn't caught up yet on her sleep from camp. Hotel living was something she never seemed to get used to. Even with ear plugs and an eyeshade, she still slept restlessly. Besides, she was in the middle of a good book, and the idea of curling up on her couch in her PJs with a glass of wine to read the night away sounded like heaven. She hadn't mentioned the reading part of her evening plan to Dani because then her friend would ask what she was reading, and Emma definitely did not want to admit that she was halfway through a *Pitch Perfect* multi-chapter fan fiction that Jamie had recommended.

Normally cooking dinner and listening to her favorite tunes while reading on her comfy couch in her amazing condo made her happy, but tonight she couldn't avoid the feeling that something was missing. Even Beca and Chloe and their adorable fake-engagement alternate universe couldn't hold her attention, and finally she admitted defeat and reached for her phone.

"What are you up to?" she texted.

She didn't have to wait long for the answer: "You know, dancing a jig around an outdoor fire with my aunt and uncle."

"Dork."

"Okay, the outdoor fire part is real but the dance is more

freestyle than a specific jig."

"I say again, dork." Emma pulled the blanket up around her waist and smiled at the glowing screen. "Cool about the fire though."

"I had nothing to do with it. Turns out I would be useless in the zombie apocalypse: zero survival skills."

"You can run fast."

"True. Not currently, but normally for sure."

"Even with your sub-par fire-lighting skills I would totally want you on my apocalypse survival team."

"Aw, thanks."

"Assuming we were in LA where heat was not required."

"Thanks rescinded."

"I feel like I should make sure—you're not actually dancing, right?"

"Dude. No."

"Right. Just checking."

"What are you doing right now?"

"Snuggling on the couch with a good book."

"A literary classic kind or...?"

"The latter." She took a photo of her iBook app open to the fan fic and texted it to Jamie.

Her phone rang a second later, and Emma tried not to light up too much before remembering that no one could see her semi-ecstatic response to Jamie's face on her screen. The photo was the one Maddie had taken of them on the van. Jamie was laughing and Emma could almost hear her surprisingly high-pitched peal ring out, and her heart promptly melted inside her ribcage.

Ridiculous that the thought of someone else laughing should make her so happy, but there it was.

"Hey," she said softly.

"Hey. What do you think of the story?"

"You were right. It's really good. They're so *happy*."

"I know. I love that about fan fiction. It's nice to take a break from real life, isn't it?"

Emma hummed a little. "Very nice."

Jamie paused. "So. Another glamorous night in Seattle, huh?"

"Incredibly glamorous. My PJs have sparklies."

"They do not."

"No. But they could."

"Okay, but *should* they? I feel like sparklies would come off in the night and end up stuck to your forehead. Or possibly the inside of your nostril."

Emma laughed. "Good point. How's the leg?"

"About the same as it was this morning."

They chatted a little while longer about what they'd been up to since they'd last spoken, and all the while Emma could hear the low murmur of voices in the background. Finally she said, "I should let you get back to your family."

"I guess. Can I call you a little later?"

"You can call me anything you want," she said, her voice purposefully raspy.

Jamie released a breath. "You're channeling your inner Chloe, aren't you?"

"Totes."

"And on that note… I'll talk to you later, dork."

"Later, nerd." She hesitated. "Miss you."

Jamie's voice quieted. "I miss you too."

"'Kay, bye."

"Bye."

The call ended and Emma leaned back against the pillows again, noting the expansive warmth once again overtaking her chest. Jamie missed her. Jamie was feeling this, same as she was. For a moment she recalled Ellie's words—*If you're going to do this, you have to do it*—and she felt her stomach flutter. Could they do this? Better yet, should they?

Nothing had happened, she reminded herself, and it might stay that way. But Ellie's other words came back to her, too: *If you really wanted to see Jamie, you could.* Jamie had talked to her parents the previous night, and the current plan was for them to drive down Saturday, drive her home Sunday, and get her in to see a sports med doctor on Monday, who would hopefully okay her for physical therapy. However the diagnosis turned out, Emma could be there with her. Assuming Jamie wanted her to be.

She picked up her iPad, navigating away from the happy, drama-free world of fan fiction to the Alaskan Airlines website. Wouldn't hurt to investigate flight options, would it?

#

Jamie's parents were awesome. Like, seriously. On Saturday, they postponed a dinner party they'd planned in her honor—former soccer parents who'd wanted to see her before she moved to Portland—and drove down to Pasadena. Britt, who was at the mini keeper camp at Stub Hub this weekend, managed to borrow a goalkeeper coach's car and get away for a few hours, and they spent Saturday evening barbecuing and drinking cocktails that Jamie and Britt mixed just like in the old days when they hosted Stanford soccer parties at their off-campus apartment.

It was great being with her best friend, however short the visit had to be, and it was even kind of sweet to see the two middle-aged couples enthusing over their empty-nest lives. She had spent so much time away from home since high school that she'd rarely gotten to see this side of her parents and their closest relatives. Someday she hoped she and Meg and their spouses would enjoy evenings like this one, sharing secret BBQ sauce recipes and chatting about trips they were finally free to take now that they didn't have to worry about college tuition payments. And when she said "spouses," she meant Todd and Emma.

Jesus, she was smitten. How had that happened so quickly? They hadn't even kissed yet and she was already planning how they would spend their middle age together.

A little before ten, she limped out to the driveway with Britt. "Thanks for coming, dude. Seriously, it means a lot."

"I'm psyched it worked out," Britt said, as she stopped beside the car. "But tell the truth—Emma's the one who's been blowing up your phone all night, isn't she?"

Jamie tilted her head. "How did you know?"

"Maybe because I've known you for so long." She paused. "Or maybe because I cracked your passcode while you were in the bathroom. I can't believe you still use your birthday!"

"What? It's not like most people know it."

"Right, because it isn't available on your player profile page or the roster for any team you've ever played on."

"Shut up," Jamie said, laughing. She thought about shoving the keeper but realized it would only put a strain on her already unhappy leg muscles.

"Seriously, you seem happier than I expected," Britt commented.

She leaned against the car, crossing her arms. "I know. I'm injured again, and Clare and I only broke up a month ago, and yet here I am..."

"You don't have to feel guilty. You made the right decision for you, and Clare is doing fine." She hesitated and then said, "I think she might be seeing someone."

"Really?" Jamie stared at her. "Who?"

"Do you remember Susan, that teacher from the eleventh form?"

Jamie nodded. She knew exactly who Britt was talking about. Susan used to tag along on their group dates, seemingly unconcerned that she was the fifth wheel. Jamie had teased Clare more than once about the other teacher's crush on her.

No wonder Clare had let her go so easily.

"How long has—?" She stopped mid-question. The answer didn't matter. She was the one who had left London, after all. She couldn't begrudge Clare the opportunity to find someone who made her happy, even if the thought of her dating so soon after their break-up made her stomach twist slightly. It wasn't like Clare was the only one already moving on. "Never mind. Tell her I said hello when you see her, okay?"

"I will. So Emma, huh?"

"Yeah." Jamie remembered their conversation at the Twelve Pins the week before Thanksgiving. "You were right. Being at residency camp is a whole different kind of intense. Can we say I'm distracted and leave it at that for now?"

Britt eyed her for a moment and finally nodded. "Of course. But if you want to talk after camp, you know, in the few hours of daylight we share on a daily basis... Let me know, okay?"

"I will. Now tell me about keeper camp. How's it going?"

They stayed on the driveway a little while longer, the day's heat still rising from the sunbaked pavement, while Britt filled her in on goalkeeper camp. Like Jamie, she had received words of encouragement from the coaching staff that included a recommendation to come back to the States and play professionally here.

"Wow. That's major," Jamie said. "Have you made any decisions?"

"Not yet. I'll meet with DC next week and then head back to England to talk everything over with Allie."

"If you need a sounding board, let me know. I'm sort of in the unique position of having recently gone through the same thing."

Britt nodded. "I will. But get this: Allie already said she might be willing to try out America for a little while."

"No way!" Jamie smiled broadly. "Dude, that's awesome!"

"*Might* being the key word," Britt said, but she was smiling too.

"Keep me posted," Jamie said, holding up her hand. Britt slapped it, and Jamie pushed away from the car. "You better go if you want to be back for bed check."

"Going AWOL with a coach's car does seem like bad form," Britt agreed.

They hugged, and Jamie pounded her friend's back. "Go kick some keeper ass, okay?"

"You got it. Take care of your leg. And happy birthday again, bro!"

She slipped into the car, started the engine, and drove away, waving out the open window. Jamie waved back until the car turned at the end of the street and moved out of view. It was a little chilly away from the chimineria, so she retraced her steps to the back patio. So Clare was seeing Susan. Interesting. Even more interesting was why the news only caused her a mild pang of regret.

Jamie was entering the back yard when her phone lit up with a text from Emma—"I'm tipsy! Wish you were here! Dani says hi!" accompanied by a selfie of her and Dani at the country bar Dani's boyfriend had dragged them to. Funny—the thought of Emma dancing with random cowboy types made her far more jealous than the thought of Clare dating Susan.

"Have fun," she texted back. "Wish I was there too." And then she added the kissing emoji they'd ended every single text conversation with (not like she had read their text thread more than once in the past few days or anything) since her birthday.

Yep, she was definitely smitten. Fortunately, she thought as Emma's reply came back with half a dozen kissing emojis, the feeling appeared to be completely mutual.

The following morning they had brunch on the patio and headed out, Jamie's mom driving the family car, her dad playing chauffeur in hers.

"Are you ready?" he asked, adjusting the mirrors at the end of his brother's driveway.

"Ready," she said, waving out the window at her aunt and uncle who stood on the front stoop, arms around each other's shoulders.

They backed out of the driveway, following the Forester through the quiet neighborhood and out onto the main road. Soon they were cruising along the 210 toward home, Jamie's foot propped on the dash and a bag of ice bandaged yet again to her right quad. She was starting to think she would be fine if she never heard the clink of ice cubes ever again.

"I've been meaning to ask: What did your coaches say when you told them you were injured?" her dad asked, keeping an eye on her mom maneuvering through the four lanes of semi-heavy traffic ahead of them.

"Oh. Um, well, I haven't told them yet."

His head swiveled quickly in her direction. "What do you mean you haven't told them?"

"It happened on the last day, and I wasn't sure at first how bad it was so I didn't say anything."

"And now?"

"Now what?"

"Obviously it's pretty severe if you can't drive, Jamie."

She shrugged. "I guess so. But it might just be moderate, in which case I could be fine for the friendlies."

He didn't speak for a little while, but she could see his wheels turning. Unlike her mom who privileged passion over lucidity, he preferred to present a fully formed argument. Jamie had inherited his disposition, so this strategy usually worked better on her than it did on her sister, who, like their mother, considered herself a member of the "temperamental artist" ranks.

"The coaches have to announce the roster for the road trip soon, don't they?" he finally asked.

"Any day now."

"How do you think they're going to feel if you don't tell them what's going on and then can't play once you arrive in Texas?"

"That's assuming I make the roster."

He gave her a look that clearly communicated displeasure, but she wasn't sure if he was more disappointed in her lack of positive self-talk or her myopic focus.

She sighed. "Fine, I'll call them. Happy?"

"Of course I'm not happy. I know you've been waiting for an opportunity like this since you were a little girl. But I also know that hiding the truth from your coaches is not only something I wouldn't expect from you, it could also hurt you in the long run."

He was right. She knew it and he knew it. Still, she chewed the inside of her cheek and thought about her options as the freeway twisted and turned past the foothills and up the treacherous Grapevine. But no matter how she did the math, her dad was still right.

When they saw signs for the Fort Tejon rest area, they called her mom and told her to go on ahead. Then they pulled in to the mostly deserted parking area and Jamie pulled on a fleece to combat the mountain chill. At least there wasn't any snow right now. They'd postponed visits with the Pasadena clan more than once thanks to the California Highway Patrol's tendency to close the Grapevine at the first hint of snow or ice. Phone in hand, she limped over to a picnic table where she gingerly settled herself on the bench, making sure her injured leg was fully supported. Amazing how you didn't realize how necessary a muscle group was until you all but shredded it on the soccer field. She scrolled through her contacts, pausing when she saw Ellie's name.

"Max!" the older woman answered, her voice cheerful as usual. "What's up?"

"Not much."

"Where are you?"

"On the Grapevine. I, um, decided to spend a few days with my aunt and uncle in Pasadena."

"I thought you were going home so you could get your stuff together for the move? The road trip isn't going to leave you much time to get settled before the Algarve. And once we're back from Portugal, pre-season will be well under way."

She sucked in her cheeks. "You say that like me going to Portugal is a done deal."

Ellie huffed out a long breath but otherwise remained silent.

Jamie's own breath caught. "Oh my god. *Is* it a done deal?"

"So I'm guessing you *haven't* talked to Craig. He said he'd be making calls this weekend, so I assumed..."

Holy shit. She had made the roster. She had made the fucking Algarve Cup roster! Her heart rose and then, just as quickly, dropped. Not that it mattered much now. She was still injured and her father was still right.

"No," she admitted. "I haven't talked to Craig yet."

"In that case, let's pretend this conversation never happened. Call me back after you talk to him, all right?"

"Wait! Don't hang up. I need to ask you something."

"As long as it has nothing to do with the roster you may or may not have made..."

"It does but not in the way you think."

Jamie could almost hear Ellie's brow furrow. "Okay then, what?"

"Remember how I got hit at practice on Tuesday morning and you said I should sit out the afternoon session?"

"Uh-huh," Ellie said slowly.

"Well, I should have listened to you. In fact, I really, really wish I had."

"I'm not going to like what you're about to tell me, am I?"

"No." Jamie took in another deep breath. "I pulled my groin at the last training session."

At the other end, Ellie paused. "You're not kidding, are you?"

"Nope."

"And that's what you were icing, not the bruise?"

"Yeah. I'm sorry I didn't tell you. I thought at first it might be minor, you know?"

"Right. How bad is it?" Ellie asked, her voice clipped.

"It's not good. My parents came down last night from Berkeley to drive me home."

"Jesus Christ, Jamie, why didn't you tell me?"

"I should have. That's my bad. But in all honesty, I didn't realize how severe it was. I thought I could rest and ice it for a few days and that would be enough."

"You have to call Craig before he calls you. Otherwise... Just do it, okay? Hang up and call him right now."

"Okay." She paused. "I'm really sorry, Ellie."

The older woman's voice softened. "What are you sorry for?"

"Letting you down. Again." Jamie felt her throat tighten as she stared out across the pastureland lining the freeway in this part of her home state. "You've been nothing but good to me and now I've gone and screwed it all up."

"You don't have to apologize, Jamie. And you didn't let me down. You pulled a muscle, that's all. It happens. If a muscle strain meant the end of every player's hopes and dreams, there wouldn't be a national team. Call Craig and go home and do some PT, and before you know it you'll be back on the field. Okay?"

Control the things you can control, Jamie thought, nodding even though Ellie couldn't see her. "Okay. I can do that. Thanks."

"You're welcome. Keep me posted."

They hung up, and then, before she could lose her nerve, she hit the call button next to the national team coach's name. She'd made the roster. That had to mean something, didn't it?

He didn't answer. Her call went straight to voicemail, which meant he was probably on the phone making someone else's day—or breaking their heart. She left a short message asking him to call her, and then she hung up and waited, rubbing her arms to stay warm in the cool, clear air. She could see her dad in the driver's seat reading the newspaper he'd picked up that morning when he went out to refresh her Gatorade stash. Or rather, she could see the newspaper through the windshield, his pale hands grasping the sides. He was a news guy. Like Bill Clinton back in the day before the news migrated online, her dad used to read several newspapers before work each morning, a couple at home and another one or two on the train into the city, depending on how his commute went.

Even now he still loved a good Sunday newspaper despite his iPhone and iPad and any number of other ways he had of accessing the news online. Jamie preferred to get her news filtered through Tumblr or Twitter. She only followed people of like minds. Otherwise, she found, the world was too depressing. As in it literally possessed the power to sink her into depression. She may have gotten past the assault in France, but she would always have to be vigilant about her mental state; otherwise she risked a return of old PTSD symptoms. No matter how long she went between PTSD triggers, she always worried they would come back. Probably because at some point, they always did.

Especially when she had been neglecting her self-care checklist—like she had during the last couple of weeks. Closing her eyes, she inhaled through her nose and began to count her breaths. *More meditation less medication.* Although in reality she was lucky—she hadn't ever needed to rely on medication to keep her emotions in balance. She had always had soccer to do that. Turned out kicking the shit out of a small, leather sphere at every conceivable opportunity was a fine way to relieve tension and express oneself.

"Thinking," she murmured to herself, trying to make her mind a smooth, blank space where the words of her mantra would be free to float and coalesce.

The phone buzzed while she was in the middle of her second time through the prayer of St. Assisi, one of her meditation go-tos. She opened her eyes and released a final breath, and then hit the call accept button. "Hi, Coach."

"Hello, Jamie. I was just about to call you." He sounded remarkably upbeat, more so than she had ever heard him. Which only made what she had to say harder.

"I thought you might be," she said, and steeled herself. Might as well rip the Band-Aid off. "Unfortunately, I have some bad news. I pulled my right groin at the last practice and it hasn't healed as quickly as I was hoping it would."

He paused. "Okay. That's surprising. Have you seen a trainer yet?"

"Not yet. I honestly thought rest and ice would fix it, but I think I might have underestimated the degree of the strain."

"So, not minor, then?"

"No. I don't think so."

"Right." He paused again. "Well, then I suppose that changes things, doesn't it?"

"I don't know," she said, only barely remembering that she wasn't supposed to know anything about the roster.

"When can you see a trainer?"

"Tomorrow."

"Right then. Why don't you call me after you have an official prognosis and we'll go from there. Sound good?"

None of this sounded good. "Yes. I'll give you a call as soon as I know anything."

"You do that. In the meantime, keep off that leg."

"I will," she promised.

Her dad was refolding the newspaper when she limped up and slid into the passenger seat. "Any news?" he asked.

"Not really." She checked her watch. Time for more ice. "Craig wants me let him know what I find out at the appointment tomorrow."

"That makes sense." He hesitated and then squeezed her shoulder. "You did the right thing, honey."

"I know."

But as her dad pulled on his seat belt and checked his mirrors, she wondered what would have happened if she hadn't told Craig the truth. Could she have rehabbed her leg in time to play in Texas? If not, could she have passed off the injury as a new one that occurred during pre-match training? Except Emma would know. And as tempting as it was to do anything and everything to make the roster, she wouldn't be able to look Emma in the eye if she made it under shady circumstances. Or herself for that matter, a day or a week or a month down the road.

So yeah. She'd done the right thing. The only thing she could do, actually.

Fucking Taylor O'Brien.

CHAPTER TWELVE

Her cell phone woke her, and for a moment Emma sat blinking against the lamplight trying to figure out why her hotel room had a couch exactly like the one in her living room. Her phone buzzed again in its spot on the coffee table and she realized what was happening. Rising up on one elbow, she grabbed her cell and held it to her ear.

"'Lo?" she croaked, and sucked in a tiny bit of drool.

"Hey, stranger."

It was Jamie. "Hi!" she exclaimed, struggling to sit up. Jamie was on the phone and she was at home and her entire life came sweeping back suddenly as she focused on the Space Needle beyond the living room window, glowing against the night sky. She'd been dreaming that she was on an airplane plummeting toward the water, and she was bracing herself for impact... *Damn it*. Not that old nightmare. What the hell?

"Were you asleep?"

"No." She pressed her fist to her forehead. "Yes. Are you home?"

"Yeah, we got back a while ago. Didn't you get my text?"

Emma checked her phone. "Oh, yeah. There it is."

"Don't tell me—tequila?"

"Not this time," she said, smiling. "It was more business than socializing. I think I'm still getting caught up from residency camp."

The Reign management had held a pre-pre-season meeting so that the returners could meet the handful of new players acquired in the off-season. Normally they wouldn't have a meeting quite so early, but with Emma and Gabe about to take off on national team duty, they decided to sneak it in. The team had gone out, but Emma had begged off. She didn't tell Jamie that she'd skipped the pub crawl so that she wouldn't miss a chance to talk to her.

"In that case, I'm sorry I woke you up. Do you want me to call you tomorrow? Or, you know, like, whenever?"

"No!" She dialed back her enthusiasm. "Your timing was perfect, actually. You saved me from a bad dream."

"That's no good. Do you want to talk about it?"

"I don't know." She ran a hand over her ponytail, feeling the strands that had worked themselves free. "Do you remember the nightmare I started having after my father died?" She felt ridiculous as soon as the words were out. There was no reason Jamie would remember something so minor.

But: "About your uncle's plane crash? You still have that dream?"

"Not very often," she admitted. "Only when…" She trailed off as she recognized the pattern. The nightmare tended to recur at moments of emotional upheaval—when they lost the 2011 World Cup; when she and Sam broke up; when she and Will stopped seeing each other; when she and Jamie stopped speaking the first time.

Was that what she was worried about? That now that camp was over, Jamie was suddenly going to vanish the way she had when they were kids? But *kids* was the key word. Messed up kids, at that. Presumably they were in different places in their lives now.

"When what?" Jamie asked.

"When I'm especially tired," she said. "I think all those weeks of double sessions combined with the holidays are finally catching up with me. I'm no spring chicken, you know."

"Right. Because twenty-seven is ancient."

"It is. You'll see."

"I'm sure." Jamie paused. "Can I ask you something?"

Emma closed her eyes, blocking out the Seattle skyline. "Yes."

"How are you these days about your dad? In general, I mean."

"Fine," she replied automatically, and then stopped to think. "Or mostly good, I guess. Every once in a while something bad happens and I totally regress. Like, everything bad that has ever happened in my life comes rushing back, and I wish I could go to bed for a day. Or two. Three, tops."

Jamie hummed in agreement. "Sometimes I think that saying, 'what doesn't kill you makes you stronger,' is bullshit. There are things that make you weaker, that take so much of your energy you need time to yourself every once in a while to recover."

"Exactly." She smoothed the blanket across her lap, tracing the snowflake pattern. Her mother had sent her the fleece blanket and matching pillows from Minnesota where, unlike Seattle, snow was not uncommon. "Can I ask you something?"

"Of course."

"How are you now with what happened in France?"

"You know, despite the whole panic attack thing last month, I'm good. It took a lot of therapy and a lot of years, and I'm not perfect. It still comes up, but nowhere near as much as I thought it would."

"Well, that's good, isn't it?" Emma asked, genuinely happy to hear this. Over the years she had wondered and worried for Jamie, and to hear now that she was in a good place and had been for a while was so, so great.

"Totally. It's funny. Sometimes I think that what happened helped shape who I am, and because of that I don't regret it. Other times, though, I would give anything to take it back. Kind of depends on the day."

Emma knew what she meant. "Do you think you recovered so well because of your therapist? What was her name, again?"

"Shoshanna. Yeah, she was awesome. I still call her every so often. But my first girlfriend in college helped a ton, too."

"The a capella girl?" Emma almost called her "the pitch," but that felt too close to name-calling. Which, if she was honest, wouldn't have been a *complete* stretch. Someone else had been Jamie's first girlfriend, someone who was not and never would be her.

"Yep. Laurie was amazing. We're still friends, even though she lives in New York and we don't get to see each other much."

Of course she was still friends with her ex. She was probably friends with all of them. How many—she stopped the thought. She didn't think she wanted to know how many women Jamie had dated. "You're such a lesbian."

"Or as the Tumblr kids would say, 'Gay as fuck.' What about you? Are you and Sam still in touch?"

"We're Facebook friends, but that's about it." Sam had wanted to put distance between them, and Emma had understood. She had kind of wanted that herself. It was hard to come back from someone telling you that if you wanted to be together, you probably should think about stocking up on mace. Oh, and maybe a firearm while you were at it.

"What about Tori?" Jamie asked.

"Tori?" she stalled, reaching for her water bottle. For some reason, her throat was suddenly dry.

"Come on, Emma. Everyone knows about you guys. You were basically the go-to example for why players in the youth pool shouldn't date." As Emma sighed and hid her face, Jamie added, "Not that I minded hearing you'd broken up."

"It was such a disaster. I'm not even sure why I tried to make it work with her, except that I wasn't in a very good place."

"How long did it take you to get to a good place?"

"Who says I ever did?"

"I don't know—by the time the soccer gods finally got their acts together, you seemed pretty good."

"You and your soccer gods." Emma leaned back against the couch cushions. "Aren't you ever worried they'll steer you wrong?"

"They brought me back to you, didn't they?"

Emma touched her lips, feeling the curl of a smile.

"Sorry," Jamie said quickly. "Can I blame ibuprofen for my descent into cheesiness? Like, maybe all the Advil I've been popping has softened my brain?"

"If that's the case, then I think you should keep taking it."

"Yeah?"

"Definitely."

The silence grew between them, but it was a comfortable silence with undercurrents Emma didn't think she'd mind getting swept away in.

Sheesh. Who was being cheesy now?

"I almost called you over Christmas break that first year, you know," Jamie said.

No, she most definitely did *not* know. "Seriously?"

"Seriously. I followed the under-19 World Cup online, and when the tsunami hit a few weeks later, I really wanted to call you. Especially when I saw that video of the beach in Phuket."

Emma knew the video she meant—the one that showed the older European couple who had almost made it to safety when the final wave, the biggest one of all, crashed onto land and buried them under a wall of water and debris.

"It seemed stupid to hold a grudge," Jamie added, "when you didn't miss that by much."

"I know." She chewed her lip. "I almost called you, too."

"You did?"

"Well, yeah. I was home for winter break and I—well, I missed you."

"So why didn't you then?"

"Because you told me not to. Why didn't *you?*"

Jamie paused, her breathing shallow over the phone line. "I think I was afraid you'd gone off with Tori and forgotten about me. Which, as it turns out…"

She lowered her voice even more. "I didn't forget about you, Jamie. I could never do that."

"No?"

"No."

"Well, good, because I don't think I could ever forget you either. Though not for lack of trying."

Emma laughed a little. "Ditto." And then because she had been waiting all day to find out, she said, "Can I ask you something else?"

"Shoot."

"So punny." Emma hesitated, trying to figure out how to broach the topic. Finally she decided to rip off the Band-Aid: "You said in your text that your conversation with Craig didn't go well."

"No. It went pretty much how I expected it would."

As Jamie recounted the conversation she'd had that morning with Craig from a rest stop along I-5, Emma listened quietly, her heart sinking. She still didn't know the head coach all that well, but she'd spent enough time with him by now to know that his subdued response to Jamie's news did not bode well. He hadn't assured her that an injury wouldn't affect her chances at making the team. In fact, he'd clearly stated that the groin pull—and the way Jamie had hidden it, possibly? But maybe that was only in Emma's head—*did* change things.

"He said I should give him a call once I have a prognosis, though," Jamie finished, "so maybe it'll work out. Maybe the doctor will clear me and I'll be on my way to Texas next week."

Emma may not have known the national team coach well, but she knew Jamie. She could hear the note of bravado in her voice, could tell she was trying her best to look on the bright side. But was there a bright side in any of this? They both knew how this went. So many players over the years who could have performed brilliantly for the national team never got a chance. Instead they fell out of the pool due to a second or third ACL tear, a stress fracture, a chronic injury. Those were the risks of playing at this level. You pushed your mind and body far and fast with little rest or recovery time, and sometimes your mind or body—or both—said, "No. Stop. Enough."

That was the reality of their profession, of the crazy, unstable life they had chosen with eyes wide open.

"So doctor tomorrow?" Emma asked, trying to infuse

positivity into her own tone.

"That's the plan."

"Good. I'll keep my fingers crossed for you."

The conversation eased back and moved on then, shifting to previous injuries and then circling back to youth national team travel experiences. They'd covered assorted adventures at the U-20 World Cup in Russia (Emma) and were on the Pan American Games in Brazil (Jamie) when Emma must have dozed off, because she jolted awake at the sound of a siren, momentarily disoriented for the second time that evening. Slowly her awareness returned, and she realized that she was warm and safe in her own living room, an old Bonnie Raitt album playing softly on her iPad, iPhone headphones still tucked into her ears.

She turned the screen on, intending to shut her phone down for the night, but before she could hit the power button she heard it: a faint sigh repeating rhythmically in her ears. She looked at her phone and realized that her call to Jamie was still active, one hundred twelve minutes later. They had fallen asleep listening to each other breathe, like when they were teenagers and on the phone late at night, sleep-starved from soccer and studying and the hormonal swings of sixteen- and seventeen-year-old girls.

She stayed where she was a little while longer, listening, and then finally she forced herself to end the call.

"Good night, Jamie," she murmured softly, finger hovering over the brightly lit screen. "Sweet dreams."

Getting back to sleep wasn't as easy as falling asleep on the phone had been, and she lay in her bed watching the lights of the city try to filter through her blinds, thinking about Jamie's future and, by extension, her own. Would a pro career and a brief byline from the previous year's Victory Tour—*two caps, two assists*—be enough for Jamie? Emma doubted it. It definitely wasn't enough for her as far as Jamie was concerned. She wanted to stand beside her on the podium in Canada and watch her face light up in joy, in relief, in gratification when they hoisted the World Cup trophy as a team. She wanted to watch Jamie's eyes crinkle at the corners as Angie opened a bottle of champagne and sprayed it all over their shrieking, laughing teammates. She wanted to dance with Jamie at the post-match family and friends celebration, to flit around the room, hands connected and lips occasionally connected too, knowing they were in a safe space where no one from the outside world could see or touch them.

But coaches were the team bosses, and even though sometimes—often—the decision they made wasn't what she wanted, she still had to find a way to live with it. That was another reality of their profession, of the crazy, unstable life they had chosen, and no matter how strongly she wanted Jamie on the team, despite how damned hard Jamie had worked and how *deserving* Emma might believe she was, at the end of the day she would have to accept whatever the coaches decided and get back to work because she had long since accepted that she was powerless when it came to player selection decisions. She was fortunate to be on the national team, and she would do almost anything to keep her own dream alive—even if it meant having to watch Jamie lose hers.

That didn't mean she wasn't hoping for a shift in the heavens, a realignment of the stars—or at least the federation—that would give Jamie another chance. She didn't often pray, didn't believe in a benevolent white-haired old guy who was sitting somewhere in the sky keeping tabs on the human race twenty-four/seven. She didn't believe in God, not really, but she did believe in the power of positive thinking. So she squeezed her eyes shut tightly and called up the visualization techniques she had learned as a teenager in the youth pool and carefully honed over the years. Only instead of envisioning herself performing optimally in a game-like scenario, she pictured Jamie. She saw her recovering from this latest injury without complications and going on to an awesome pre-season with Portland and a solid showing in Champions League. She imagined the federation coaches watching her set the NWSL single-season assist record with Ellie as her teammate, pictured Craig picking up the phone and inviting Jamie to a future residency camp. Then she envisioned Jamie sitting down with the federation and the player reps and signing her name to a US Soccer contract, her beautiful eyes alight with happiness.

And when she was done envisioning the perfect beginning to Jamie's USWNT career, Emma imagined Jamie in her living room, curled up beside her on the couch sharing a carton of pad thai or a tray of salmon nigiri, wine glasses within arm's reach on the coffee table. They would be talking and laughing as they had always done, and in mid-sentence one of them would stop, lean forward, and press her lips to the other's. Because they wanted to, and because, finally, they could.

Emma opened her eyes in her quiet bedroom in her quiet condo and smiled. It could happen. For years she'd waited and wondered, but now she knew. She loved Jamie, and she wasn't going anywhere.

#

Jamie wasn't sure when Emma had once again become the first person she spoke to in the morning, the last voice she heard at night. But whenever and however it had happened, on Monday morning it seemed perfectly natural to roll over in bed, kick off the sheets, and turn on her phone. She yawned as she waited for it to fire up, remembering why it was so imperative that they talk first thing this morning. Emma had a video chat later with the board of a children's medical research charity she was involved with, and Jamie had her doctor's appointment after lunch. They would be lucky to speak much once the day got going.

It didn't occur to her to question the constant need to talk to Emma. That was just a given at this point.

"Morning," she said when Emma picked up. She stifled a yawn, blinking in the cool darkness of her bedroom. The sky beyond her window looked gray and foreboding, so she snuggled down into her covers, trying to hold the day at bay for as long as possible.

"Morning, sleepyhead," Emma replied, a smile in her voice. She sounded disgustingly awake—probably because she'd gotten up at five to meet with her trainer before the conference call. Chat. Whatever a group video chat was called.

Group video chat. Duh.

"So how does the whole conference call thing work?" she asked. "Do you use Skype, or is there a different software program involved?"

Emma laughed. "Is that really the burning question keeping you up at night?"

Jamie squinted, because of course there were more important questions keeping her up: *Will I make the national team? Will we make it past quarter-finals in Champions League? Do you love me?*

Emma seemed to read her silence because after a moment she briefly explained the process, ending with, "The main office is in New York, but that's the beauty of the Interweb, as Ellie calls it."

"Skype is a beautiful thing," Jamie agreed, "even if Microsoft bought them out."

"The first time I ever heard of video-conferencing was from you. But by the time Skype got going, we—well, I was in college by then."

"And we weren't speaking."

Emma paused. "Right."

"I'm sorry about that," she said, rubbing her fingers against the stitches in the quilt her grandmother had made her a quarter of a century earlier. "For ending things the way I did. I definitely could have handled everything better."

"You don't have to apologize, Jamie. You had to take care of yourself. I always understood that, even if I hated losing you."

At that moment, she was grateful for the distance between them. If Emma had been standing in front of her, she might not have been able to ask, *"Did you hate it?"*

"Are you kidding?" She stopped. "Wait, did you really think I was fine with never talking to you again?"

"No. Not really," she told Emma. "But at the same time I wasn't sure. Sometimes I thought I imagined our friendship.

Like, what would someone like you be doing with someone like me?"

"What the actual fuck?" Emma drawled, sounding like one of the many college kids in the pool. Taylor O'Brien, for example.

Jamie laughed softly. "Maybe you didn't know this, Emma, but you were pretty freaking impressive as a high schooler."

"You weren't so bad yourself—except for the skateboarding while stoned thing. That spooked me, I have to admit."

"I wish I could say it only happened that one time..."

"But seriously," Emma said, "it was incredibly difficult for me to let you go. Ask my exes."

"What do you mean?"

Emma told her how she'd recently run into her ex-boyfriend, Will, who Jamie was unreasonably happy to hear was engaged to be married. "Apparently I kept mentioning you, because he ended up asking me if the newbie named Jamie in the national pool was the same girl I'd told him about from high school."

Jamie tried not to let the grin overtake her face. Her voice would give her away, and she sort of didn't want Emma to know how adorable she found it that she was doing the same exact thing Jamie was: slipping her name into conversation at every little chance, sometimes even when there wasn't a legitimate reason.

She squinted up at her ceiling where the stars and planets still stuck firmly in the patterns she and her dad had laid out when she was younger. "Clare had the same reaction after Britt and I practiced with you guys in London."

"Seriously?" Emma asked.

"Yeah. Apparently I couldn't stop talking about you, either." She hesitated. "I think that's why she struggled so much with me being invited to residency camp."

"Because of me? But we were barely even speaking at that point."

Jamie pointed her toes toward the ceiling. "I know. But she

knew how I felt about you in high school, and I think she worried that spending so much time around you might bring everything back."

Ask me if it did, she thought, even as she was terrified by the possibility.

But Emma only murmured something that sounded like, "Oh, yeah, right." Then, more clearly, she said, "You know, I don't think I ever told you how sorry I am for the way things turned out, either."

"Nah, we're good. You did email me that one time."

Emma huffed a little, as if she didn't want to laugh but couldn't help it. "I'm trying to apologize here, Maxwell."

"I know, *Blake*, and apparently it's my turn to tell you that you don't have to. I was so utterly clueless back then, which couldn't have been easy for you. Plus your dad had just died. If you're not allowed to go a little crazy then, when are you?"

"Grief is not a good excuse for lying and cheating."

"It may not be an excuse, but it's a fairly compelling reason. Besides, you know you didn't actually cheat on me, right? We weren't together and you didn't have to tell me about Tori if you didn't want to. Coming out is different for everyone. If you weren't ready to tell me yet, you weren't ready. That's not something I should have been angry about."

"But it's not that I wasn't ready to come out to you. Really. I think I was just scared."

"Of what? Did you think I would be upset about you being bi? Because, you know, some of my best friends are bisexual."

"Ha, ha." Emma was quiet. Then she took an audible breath. "No, I was scared that you'd realize how I felt about you and, I don't know, we wouldn't be friends anymore. So instead I let you find out in the worst possible way and lost you anyway."

Jamie lowered her voice. "How did you feel about me?" She had wanted to know the answer to this question for ten years and wasn't about to let the chance to learn the answer slip away.

"Jamie…"

"Would you rather I go first? Because I'll say it if you want me to."

Emma's voice was practically a whisper. "You know how I felt."

"Do I?"

The words came out in a rush: "I was in love with you."

Her throat tightened and Jamie closed her eyes, trying to block out everything but the sound of her heartbeat rushing in her ears. "I was in love with you too."

"You were?"

She opened her eyes. "Oh my god, how could you not know that?"

"You weren't exactly an open book," Emma pointed out. "Besides, you cut me off and then never spoke to me again. For all I knew it was easy for you to walk away."

"I honestly think it was one of the hardest things I've ever done."

"Same." She paused. "Did you know I got my first tattoo the week you stopped talking to me?"

"No." Jamie frowned a little, picturing the tattoos she knew Emma had. There was the requisite bicep tat, which in Emma's case was a tribal band with geometric markings. Her version of the always-popular script on the ribcage read *RISE* in flowing letters just below her heart. And then there was the field of flowers inked on her right shoulder blade, an artist's rendition of a meadow near Mt. Rainier according to the article Jamie had read a few years ago.

Huh. She seemed to know a lot about Emma's tattoos. "Which one?" she asked.

"You haven't seen it before. Not many people have."

Before she could ask why, her phone buzzed: Text message from Emma Blakeley. With attachment. "Did you send me a naked pic?" Her heart rate picked up again at the thought.

"You wish. Open it."

The attachment was a close-up from an artist's portfolio of a compass tattoo, and Jamie studied it. "That kind of looks like the necklace I gave you."

"That's because I asked the artist to use it as the basis of the design."

Jamie felt a surge of strong emotion—was it relief? Gratitude? All those years she had worried that Emma had turned to Tori because she hadn't cared about *her* enough, only to find out that she'd had a tattoo of the spiral sun Jamie had given her permanently inked into her skin.

She cleared her throat. "What about the compass?"

"Sailors used to believe that a compass tattoo would protect them in rough waters and make sure they returned home safely."

A memory glimmered at the back of her mind. Emma's dad had taught her how to sail when she was young, before his surgical work had taken over and he'd all but vanished from his kids' lives. "You got it for your dad, didn't you?"

"Yeah." Jamie heard her swallow. "And for you."

Jamie didn't say anything, just stared up at the same ceiling she used to gaze at back in high school when she would talk to Emma for hours on end about classes and soccer and teammates and friends, everything except what she had wanted so badly to say: *I love you. I miss you. I would give anything to be with you.*

"Emma, what are we doing?" she asked, and then couldn't breathe as the words hung between them like a row of Japanese lanterns that, given the slightest encouragement, would burst into flames.

"I don't know. Being friends?"

"This isn't how I am with my other friends."

"Oh thank god."

Jamie couldn't prevent the short laugh that escaped. "Thank god?"

"I'm not like this with my friends either."

"Okay, then."

"Okay."

They were both quiet, and then Emma said, "I have a question for you."

Jamie waited, but the question didn't come. Was she

nervous? Should Jamie be nervous too? "I have an answer," she tried joking, and then wanted to smack herself. That was what she had told Emma not to do.

"I don't have to be in Texas until next Wednesday," Emma said, her voice growing stronger as she spoke, "and I was thinking—I owe you a visit."

"You do?" Jamie practically breathed into the phone, not even caring that she sounded nearly as delighted as she felt.

"I do. I never got a chance to see you before I left for North Carolina, so I was wondering—any chance you feel like having a visitor?"

"I would love a visitor," Jamie said. "Like, a ridiculously insane amount."

"All right then. I'll look at flights tonight and call you?"

"Perfect."

And it was. Even though Jamie was pretty sure how her day was going to go—the doctor would confirm her diagnosis of a moderate strain (or worse), and she would have to tell Craig and hear him explain why she wouldn't be going anywhere with the national team anytime soon—even though the sky was gray and she was stuck in her parents' house in the very definition of the phrase *in limbo*, Emma was planning to call her tonight to talk about when she could come see her. Even more, Jamie had finally asked the question repeating on loop through her mind, and Emma had sounded relieved when Jamie admitted her feelings went beyond friendship, too.

Soccer was certainly the be-all and end-all of her professional life, but as much as she had believed it constituted her entire life, she was starting to think she might have been a little bit, very much wrong.

CHAPTER THIRTEEN

Jamie scrolled through her phone as she sat on a bench outside Cal's medical center waiting for a city bus. She had just met with the team physician for the university's soccer program, a man who was normally booked up well in advance. But Becca's parents, the Professors Thompson, had called in a favor last week and voila, an appointment had magically opened up. He had indeed confirmed what she already thought—the muscle strain was officially of the moderate variety. The good news was that with rest and physical therapy, it should heal completely in a few weeks. The bad news was— same.

Campus was only a mile and a half from home, and normally she would walk. But she was on strict instructions to rest her leg for the next forty-eight hours before beginning PT on Wednesday—"assuming you want it to heal," the doctor had joked. She'd smiled back because he was doing her a favor and also because he had seemed excited to meet her. Apparently he'd Googled her and read an article on ESPN.com that claimed she might be the next greatest thing ever to happen to the national team.

She should probably read that article, she told herself, navigating to Google. Maybe even tweet the link to the national team coaching staff? That would totally help her chances at becoming an NT regular. Before the bitterness could take too deep a hold, she closed the browser window, opened her contacts, and pressed the call button.

Emma's voice vibrated into her headphones: "I was just thinking about you. How did it go?"

Almost immediately Jamie felt herself relaxing. Emma sounded warm and caring. She also sounded too far away. "Not so great. I'm supposed to be calling Craig right now."

"But you accidentally dialed me instead?"

"Something like that."

Emma paused, and her voice lost its teasing lilt. "You won't be ready in time for Texas, will you?"

"Probably not. They don't even want me to start PT for another couple of days."

"Shit. I'm so sorry, Jamie."

"Melanie basically said I needed to be injury-free if I wanted to make the squad, so…"

"That's ridiculous. It's a contact sport! We're bound to get injured."

"Yeah, but some of us more than others, huh?"

Emma sighed but didn't argue. "This sucks."

"I agree." She hesitated. "I miss you."

"I miss you too. Like, a ridiculously insane amount."

Sitting on a bench in Berkeley chatting with Emma up in Seattle was almost too familiar. Apparently she'd been more right than she realized when she told Clare she would always have feelings for Emma.

"Will you call me after you talk to Craig?" Emma asked. "Even if it isn't good news?"

"Of course. But are you sure you want me to? I could text if you'd rather."

"No—unless you'd rather?"

She stopped the *of course not* waiting to trip from her tongue. "Either one."

"In that case I vote call. Then we can open ESPN3 and find something to watch together. You know, like maybe curling."

"What the hell, Blake? We're not Canadian."

"No, but it's really awesome. I swear. Give it a chance."

Jamie smiled a little. "Wouldn't you rather do something

else with the rest of your day?"

"Seeing as I'm currently in my pajamas…"

A text alert sounded, and Jamie opened a photo attachment that showed Emma in plaid flannel pants and a battered UNC hoodie, her hair in a messy bun, glasses slipping down her nose.

"I feel like all that's missing is your retainer," she said.

"You think you're joking and yet my retainer is literally sitting on the table by my bed."

Jamie laughed. "Sounds like we have an ESPN3 date later."

"Awesome. My favorite."

"Thanks, Emma," she added. "Seriously."

"You don't have to thank me."

Which was becoming something of a recurring theme between them.

As a bus neared, Jamie checked the route on its digital sign. The winter afternoon was chilly but she was tempted to wave it past. After spending the last three years in a foreign city playing and working for one of the best football clubs in the world, she was going a little stir crazy watching Netflix and doing puzzles in her childhood bedroom. Still, she couldn't delay calling Craig forever, and she'd rather not have that particular conversation in public. She stood up and flagged down the bus, fishing in her jacket pocket for her mother's bus pass.

"Hey, I should probably hang up. I'm about to get on a bus."

"Does that mean you'll be home soon?"

"Fifteen minutes, tops."

"Okay. Good luck. Call me after you talk to Craig?"

"I will. See you, Emma."

"Later, James. And remember: Everything will work out, one way or another."

"I know," she said, and sighed. "It always does."

They hung up and Jamie stepped aboard the bus, limping up the three steps to the seating level. She ran her pass through the correct slot and nodded at the driver before moving past and collapsing in the first seat she could find. Strange how much effort everything suddenly required when you were in pain. She wished she were still chatting with Emma as the bus meandered along the streets of her hometown and she tried not to think about the phone call she was about to make. Right now her national team dream was still alive. Somehow she had a feeling that it wouldn't be for long.

Back at the house, Jamie struggled up the front steps. Once inside she shed her jacket and stepped out of her sneakers. Then she propelled herself across the main room to the couch, barely pausing to turn on a light. How could she be this exhausted? She hadn't done anything. Apparently the more you slept the more tired you were. Good to know.

Phone in hand, she mentally ran through the now-imminent conversation about her future with the national team. There was really only one possible outcome. She tried telling herself she was okay with whatever happened, but that was a flat-out lie. Now that she knew the coaches had been planning to invite her on the road trip and, presumably, to Portugal, it was harder to accept the coming rejection than if she had never spoken with Ellie.

Stupid body. Three strikes and you're out, right? Fortunately, soccer didn't have a prescribed number of outs. Though it was possible Craig might feel differently.

She turned her phone back on and hit a button. Then she typed, "Do I have to do this? Can't I wait until tomorrow?"

"Do it," Emma typed back. "ESPN3 later, remember?"

"How could I forget? I mean, it's curling."

Emma sent her a kiss.

She touched the tiny red heart and sighed even though no one was there to appreciate her dramatics. "I'll call you soon."

Emma sent back a thumbs-up.

No more stalling. It was time to—huh, why did the only applicable clichés she could think of involve guns or toilets? Really, there should be… She forced her mind away from the tempting tangent, rubbed her palms against her Arsenal team sweats, and finally hit the call button.

Craig picked up on the second ring. "Maxwell. What's the

verdict?"

She gave him the news, forcing the words out of a throat that seemed determined to hold onto each syllable, and then tried not to bite a hole in her lip as Craig blabbed sort of generally about timing and fitness and the importance of building team chemistry before the Algarve.

Finally he worked himself up to the words she'd known were coming but that, even so, sucked the air out of her: "The thing is, this isn't the first time an injury has set you back."

He paused as if waiting for her to reply, but Jamie sat motionless, trying to ignore the impulse to hang up on him. She knew what he was going to say. She'd known before she called him. Why did she have to listen?

He spoke into the gap her silence left, his voice surprisingly gentle. "I'm sure you know you're a wonderful player, Jamie. It's been a real pleasure watching you play. The other coaches and I appreciate your work ethic and the effort you expend every time you get on the field, but we've talked and given this latest injury, we've decided to go in a different direction. It doesn't mean you're permanently out of contention. By all means, you should keep up your training and fitness not only for the NWSL but because you never know what can happen down the road."

Or at least, that was what she thought he said. Her mind sort of went blank when she heard the part about going in another direction. After that, she focused mostly on trying to make sure she didn't cry as she thanked him for the opportunity and wished him and the team luck. Then she sat silently again, waiting for him to hang up. Hitting the end button herself would feel too final, too much like saying a permanent goodbye even though he'd said the future wasn't set in stone. Right now she felt like she knew exactly what her future held: a short career in the States for as long as the NWSL stayed in business and then a few years bouncing around Europe eking out her playing years until finally it came time to retire and figure out what she was going to do with the rest of her life.

So many women she knew—and more she didn't—would have given anything for the chance to play on even the crappiest managed, least successful team in the NWSL. It was a privilege to serve both club and country, and she'd been lucky to ride the wave for as long and as far as she had. Now it appeared her luck had run out. She hadn't made the team, and from the genuine sympathy in Craig's voice, she had a feeling she wouldn't be getting another chance. Not on his watch, anyway.

He must have known she was waiting because with a final few words, he said goodbye and ended the call. She sat on the familiar couch in the living room of her childhood home and tried to accept that her childhood dream was over. Tried to accept that her stupid body had gotten her chucked from the stupid national team by a stupid bunch of coaches who surely would have put up with the groin and the ankle and the ACL if they only believed in her enough. They had to know that she had periods of perfect health that lasted MONTHS, for Christ's sake, and that no professional athlete could guarantee their body's functionality, especially not, as Emma had pointed out, when the career in question revolved around a contact fucking sport.

Emma. She almost wished now that she hadn't promised to call her. It wasn't that Emma had done anything wrong. If anything, it was the opposite. Somehow they had carried this dynamic over from teenage-hood, the one where Emma was older and more successful at nearly everything and Jamie was younger and still, somehow, floundering. She got that in the world she had chosen, in the profession she was lucky enough to claim as her own, she couldn't always win. No matter how hard she worked, there was always the possibility that she would come up short; the chance that she simply wouldn't be good enough to achieve the goal she had set for herself.

She knew all that, she really did. But still. Bottom line, she hadn't made the national team. And honestly? She would rather not have to admit that fact to Emma.

But Emma apparently had no intention of letting her sulk

in peace. As Jamie sat numbly watching the winter sky darken outside the living room window, her phone buzzed. Reluctantly she opened up the message, snorting a little at the picture of a laptop and a Seattle microbrew balanced on Emma's fancy corkwood lap board.

"Hello, I was promised a date," her message read.

"Right," Jamie replied, smiling slightly in spite of herself. "Give me a minute, okay?"

"Did you reach Craig?"

"Yeah." She sighed again. "I'll call you in a sec. Gotta get my laptop."

She was about to start up the stairs to her room when the doorbell rang. Great. Just what she didn't need. Her parents had lived in this house forever and seemed to know everyone within a ten-block radius, which meant neighbors were always randomly dropping by. She thought about not answering, but instead she limped to the door and pulled it open. Then she froze as the person on the front stoop spun around, eyes wide, fingers playing with the tip of her ponytail.

"Oh!" Emma said. "I thought you would take longer to answer."

Jamie stared at her, blinking rapidly. "But—but you're in Seattle."

"Turns out I'm not." She smiled, the expression teetering on the near side of maniacal as her eyebrows rose higher than Jamie would have thought possible. "Surprised?"

That was certainly one word for it.

Without stopping to think, Jamie limped forward and practically tackled Emma, her arms wrapping around her waist and squeezing almost spasmodically. Emma latched on in return, hands gripping at Jamie's back as she hummed what sounded like relief into her shoulder. Jamie's throat tightened. She was here. Emma was actually *here*.

"I can't believe you did this," she mumbled, inhaling the scent of Emma's hair.

"Well, someone has to look after you," Emma said, her voice suspiciously thick. "Might as well be me."

Damn it, why did she have to go and say that? Jamie sniffed, trying to hold back the tears that seemed determined to escape from her tightly closed eyes.

"It's a good surprise, right?" Emma's voice sounded less certain now.

She leaned back to peer into Emma's face. "Are you kidding? Like the best surprise ever."

"The best ever? Geez, James, I haven't even kissed you yet." Then she seemed to realize what she'd said and sucked in a quick breath.

Was it wrong that Jamie sort of loved seeing her flustered? She especially loved being the cause. "That's not exactly true," she pointed out. "It's been a while, though. We could probably use the practice."

"So smooth, Maxwell," Emma breathed out, gaze drifting down to her lips.

Jamie waited another beat, her heart racing so quickly it felt like her whole body was pulsing, and then she lowered her chin and pressed her lips against Emma's, hesitantly at first and then more firmly, bringing one hand up to cup her cheek. Emma leaned into the kiss, her hands shifting to settle against Jamie's ribcage where the heat of her touch radiated through Jamie's thin shirt. Eyes closed, Jamie gave in to the shiver working its way along her spine at the feel of Emma finally—*finally,* FINALLY—in her arms. In that moment it didn't matter that she might not play in the World Cup or that they would be rivals in the NWSL or even that they would be living three hours apart for the foreseeable future. All that mattered was the elation rising uncontrollably inside of her, happiness burning such a pure light against her eyelids that she couldn't imagine it would ever fully fade.

Admittedly, it was their first (second) kiss so it was bound to be imperfect as they moved their lips experimentally together, softness giving way slowly to a rising intensity. But Jamie easily got lost in the rhythm of Emma's kiss and the warmth of the skin at her waist where her fleece rode up—all on its own, *of course.* She was thinking of how to navigate gracefully to the couch without breaking the kiss because their lips probably shouldn't be apart anytime soon given how long they'd gone between kisses, and like, why was that anyway? How had she managed without this *feeling* in her life? And then Emma made an amazingly sexy sound against her mouth and pressed closer, her hands framing Jamie's hips. Which was lovely, really, except that their combined weight shifted directly onto her bad leg, and before she could stop herself she let out a—yelp. It was definitely a yelp.

Emma's hands tightened on her hips as she broke the kiss. "Oh my god, I'm so sorry! Are you okay?"

"I'm fine." Jamie smiled because it was physically impossible not to. "Of course that would happen."

Emma smiled too, eyes shining in the light from the living room. "Seems kind of fitting, doesn't it? But as a bonus, I promise not to run away this time."

"Well, that's a relief." All at once she realized they were still standing on the front porch, and while it was a better place to make out than, say, a club occupied by the entire national team, it was still a tad public. "Do you want to come in?"

"On one condition."

"What?"

"You change out of those sweats immediately."

Jamie glanced down at the Arsenal crest. "If I didn't know better, Miss Blakeley, I would say you were propositioning me." She held the door open wider as Emma's nose wrinkled adorably. "Come on. Last thing we need is a Blakewell sighting. I'd rather not piss Ellie off more than I already have."

"I don't think she's pissed at you." Emma pulled her carry-on in behind her, gazing around the interior of the house. "Geez. This place hasn't changed at all. Which is a good thing because I hate to say it, but I really have to pee."

Jamie lifted an eyebrow. "So smooth, Blake."

"Shut up. My flight got in early so I ended up having to kill time at Starbuck's."

Which explained why her lips tasted faintly of coffee and salted caramel. "You totally had a cake pop, didn't you?"

"Don't worry," Emma said over her shoulder as she headed for the hallway. "I brought you one too."

She was pretty awesome, that one.

Jamie checked her phone and settled on the couch, resting her injured leg on the coffee table. They had a couple of hours before her parents got home from work, which wasn't nearly enough time on their own. Maybe they should go away together, have a weekend in the city at a nice hotel. Then she remembered that she was living at home for a reason. Her savings wouldn't survive the hit of a stay in a fancy hotel, and she couldn't let Emma pay for everything. Or she could, but she didn't want to. They probably only had a few days together anyway before Emma would have to head home to get ready for the February road trip. The road trip Jamie would have been with her on if not for Taylor fucking O'Brien.

Oh god, that little shit had taken her spot on the roster, hadn't she?

As the reality of their situation sank in, she leaned her head back against the couch and shut her eyes. A moment later she heard Emma return, but she kept her eyes closed as she felt Emma settle next to her, movements slow and careful. She didn't even open them when Emma drifted closer and pressed a kiss to her temple.

"Are you okay?" Emma murmured.

"Yes." Jamie opened her eyes and glanced at her. "No. I have to tell you something."

"Okay," she said slowly, leaning away a little. "Is everything all right?"

"Not really. Though, I mean, it's not exactly a surprise." She looked down at her socks rather than meet Emma's concerned gaze. Great, there was a hole in her big toe. Nice. She was living with her parents and wearing socks that needed mending while Emma was… an actual American hero. Pushing the thought away, she took a breath and said, "Craig told me the coaches have decided to go in a different direction. As in, not with me. I'm out, Em, probably for good." It wasn't as hard to say out loud as she'd thought it would be. Probably she'd had enough time by now to get used to the idea.

"Oh, sweetie," Emma said, resting her chin on Jamie's shoulder.

Jamie tried not to focus on how the endearment made her feel all warm and safe and *loved*. "What I'm saying is that if knowing that changes anything," she made herself say, gesturing vaguely between them, "I would totally understand."

Emma was quiet for a minute. Then, her voice somewhere between irritated and hurt, she said, "Do you honestly think you not making the national team could change the way I feel about you?"

"No," she said quickly, trying to reel her doubts back into her brain where they clearly belonged. "That's not what I meant."

"Isn't it?" Emma cupped her cheek and turned her head so that they were staring into each other's eyes again. "Jamie, I want to be with you because you're you. You're kind and you're funny and you're sweet, and you talk about things like queer subtext and you love a capella music and you almost cried when you felt Tina's baby kick. I flew down here because of all of that, not because of soccer. How I feel about you has nothing to do with the national team or the pro league or any of those things. Soccer is my career. You're everything else. Do you understand?"

Jamie tried to keep her pathetic little heart from stuttering at Emma's words and the almost frightening intensity in her eyes, but it was a lost battle. She was a lost battle, and that was perfectly fine. "Yeah," she whispered, blinking back tears again. "But you forgot funny looking."

Emma pressed their foreheads together, her caramel-scented breath warm on Jamie's mouth. "See? That's why I'm here. Because you know my dad's old jokes and because honestly, I can't imagine being anywhere else."

As Emma leaned in to kiss her again, Jamie smiled against her lips. She couldn't help it. Emma wanted to be with her. Emma *loved* her, even if she hadn't said the words. Good thing, because the feeling was more than mutual.

"Dork," Emma said, still framing her face between her palms.

"Nerd," Jamie replied.

And she wanted to kiss her, she did, but even more she wanted to hold her and listen to her breathe in person instead of over the telephone. She wanted to *be* with Emma, in the moment, in this moment. So she turned slightly and slipped her arm across her shoulders, tugging at her until she settled down against her with a sigh.

"There wasn't a video chat with the charity people, was there?" Jamie asked after a little while.

"Nope."

"You really went all out. The photos were a good touch."

"Thanks," Emma said. "I like planning."

"I remember." She almost said it was one of the things she loved about her, but they weren't there yet. She had more hope now than ever before that they would get to that point someday, but for now she was content to say the words silently. She would know when the time was right, and for now that was enough.

They snuggled together on the couch, Jamie's hand playing with Emma's ponytail, Emma's fingers tracing the lines of her Sanskrit tattoo, and Jamie couldn't quite believe the swell of emotion rising in her chest, its lightness such a marked contrast to the hopelessness that had weighed her down only a little while earlier. It was a bit much to take—possibly losing her national team dream on the same day that Emma showed up on her doorstep and kissed her. Well, technically Jamie had kissed her. Either way, the two events didn't cancel each other out, and what was more, they didn't need to. The coaches' decision was obviously a serious setback, but it didn't mean she had to let go of her World Cup dream, not if she didn't want to. Look at her and Emma—she'd held onto that dream somewhere at the back of her mind for all these years, and now it appeared to be coming true.

The World Cup was still a year and a half away. That meant she had all summer to convince the coaches they couldn't afford to leave her off the team. She had a year even, if need be, to change their minds. And there, she realized, was the next goal to reach for, the one that would get her out of bed in her new city, that would keep her eating well and working out and going to bed early.

This was something she could do. She would make a plan, set an achievable short-term goal, and hope that something changed on the national team front. Because as much as loss was a guarantee in soccer, so was winning. Emma's words came back to her, accompanied by the wave of peace that she normally associated with meditation: "Everything will work out." Because one way or another, it always did.

Control the things you can and let go of the things you can't was all well and good when it came to the game of soccer. But Emma was right—soccer was a career; the people you loved were everything else.

And right now, Jamie didn't plan on letting go of the woman in her arms anytime soon.

Apparently Emma had other ideas, though. After a little while, she pushed up and away from Jamie, her lips curling slightly.

"Where are you going?" Jamie asked, her fingers lazily tracing the arc of Emma's collarbone because now that she had started touching her it was basically impossible to stop.

"Getting my laptop."

"But why?"

Emma hopped off the couch and looked at her in a way that could only be called askance. "You promised to watch curling with me."

"That's right. That's a thing, isn't it?"

Emma pulled her computer from her carry-on. "Don't think quoting *Pitch Perfect* at me will get you out of our date."

"It was worth a try. Aren't you forgetting something though?" As Emma paused, brow creased adorably, Jamie added, "I believe *I* was promised a cake pop."

"Oh! Right." Emma fished in a zippered pocket and came up with a Starbucks bag. "A sweet for my sweet," she said, presenting the paper bag with a flourish.

"So cheesy, Blake."

"You love it."

She did. She also loved cake pops, a fact that Emma had apparently remembered from the precisely one time she'd mentioned it in her presence.

While Emma fired up the laptop, Jamie devoured the sweet treat.

"Mm," she said dreamily when she finished. "That was yummy. Thanks, babe."

"You're welcome," Emma said, leaning in to taste the salted caramel that dusted her lips. "Mm, you're yummy…" A little while later she added, "You know what? Curling can wait."

As their lips met again, Jamie decided that truer words had never been spoken.

Thanks for reading! For a sneak peek at *Outside the Lines*, Book Three in the Girls of Summer series, please visit http://katechristie.wordpress.com/mailing-list and sign up for my mailing list.

Kate Christie
September 2016

ABOUT THE AUTHOR

Kate Christie lives with her family near Seattle. A graduate of Smith College and Western Washington University, she has played soccer most of her life and counts attending the 2015 World Cup finals game in Vancouver as one of her top five Favorite. Days. Ever.

To find out more about Kate, or to read excerpts from her other titles from Second Growth Books and Bella Books, please visit her author website at www.katejchristie.com. Or check out her blog, *Homodramatica* (katechristie.wordpress.com), where she occasionally finds time to wax unpoetically about lesbian life, fiction, and motherhood.

Made in the USA
Las Vegas, NV
26 November 2021

35322018R00164